PRAISE FOR STINA LINDENBLATT

This One Moment

"A thrill ride that kept me on the edge of my seat, *This One Moment* is hot, intense, and filled with emotion—contemporary romance at its finest. Nolan stole my heart from page one, and Hailey was a heroine with whom I could truly identify. I was in reader heaven!"—*New York Times* bestselling author Rachel Harris

"A well-written story that kept me entertained from start to finish."—*Harlequin Junkie*

"I loved this book; this is romance at its best, this is that perfect ending we all read romance for, this is an absolutely beautifully told love story."—*Guilty Pleasures Book Reviews*

"Very satisfying . . . Stina Lindenblatt is a new author to me and a very good one I may add. . . . I will sure keep an eye on her in the future. She is really worth it!"—*Collector of Book Boyfriends & Girl-friends*

"The story is amazing and the suspense is thrilling."—*Just One More Chapter*

My Song for You

"Romantic angst powers this fast-paced novel, and readers will return to the series to learn more about the enigmatic side characters whose own stories are waiting to be told."—*Publishers Weekly*

"The author has an amazing and deep connection with her characters. . . . I loved every single page."—*Extreme Damage Blog*

"From the first to the last page—greatness unfolded."—*Ellie Is Uhm . . . A Bookworm*

"Filled with romance, misunderstandings, lies and a whole lot of heat . . . [*My Song for You*] has everything to satisfy the romance itch in all of us."—*Twin Spin*

"Six stars—Stina Lindenblatt has a skill to write heroes with some depth like few can."—*Collectors of Book Boyfriends & Girlfriends*

"Oooh, a secret baby story with a twist . . . and I liked that twist. I also really liked that this was somewhat of a friends-to-lovers story. . . A really good, entertaining read and I enjoyed it a lot. I'd definitely recommend it."—*Smitten with Reading*

I Need You Tonight

"Ms. Lindenblatt has penned another remarkable read for this series. . . . Full of exquisite heat and passion, and the ending brought happy tears to my eyes. . . . I would highly recommend *I Need You Tonight*."—*Book Magic*

"*I Need You Tonight* is one of those books that you go into thinking one thing and end up getting your mind blown because you were not expecting the emotion that this made you feel. Honestly, this had to have been the best book of the series because of that."—*Life of a Crazy Mom*

"[Stina Lindenblatt's] writing shows superb talent and care for both the storyline and her characters. This is not a book you want to pass the chance at reading."—*Ellie Is Uhm . . . A Bookworm*

"There are so many, many things that I loved about this story. . . . I hadn't realized I'd been missing and I was craving the Pushing Limits boys until this one came along. And it came with a bang!"—*Collectors of Book Boyfriends & Girlfriends*

Tell Me When

TELL ME WHEN is a heartbreaking and emotional story. Be prepared to do nothing else but read once you start this book! —*Fresh Fiction*

"I felt that even though the subject matter is a little over used, Tell Me When did it in a way that was rawer, darker and more realistic and that made it feel fresh and unique."—*Bookish Treasures*

"If you're looking for an exciting read, filled with secrets, mystery, danger, and realism, this story is a perfect match! I give, Tell Me When, by Stina Lindenblatt, 4 Intense, Powerful, Healing, and 'Falling in Love' filled Stars!"—*A Bookish Escape*

"I. LOVED. THIS. BOOK!!!!"—*Seeking Book Boyfriends*

"If you are looking for well written story that will take you on a ride of highs and lows of our human emotional states and of the good and the bad of what life is willing to offer, then I highly suggest you read this fantastic story!"—*Biblio Belles Book Blog*

Let Me Know

"I love Stina's writing style. It's very emotive, and flows beautifully. I felt connected to the characters from very early on and cried several times at the pain these characters go through"—*Reading Realm Blog*

ALSO BY STINA LINDENBLATT

Contemporary Romances

Carson Brothers Series

One More Chance

One More Secret

Pushing Limits Series

This One Moment

My Song For You

I Need You Tonight

Lost in You Series

Tell Me When

Let Me Know

Romantic Comedy Novels

By The Bay Series

Decidedly Off Limits

Decidedly with Baby

Decidedly with Love

Decidedly with Mistletoe

Decidedly by Chance

Decidedly with Luck

Decidedly with Wishes

Visit stinalindenblattauthor.com for more books

ONE MORE CHANCE

A CARSON BROTHERS NOVEL

STINA LINDENBLATT

Cover design: Stina Lindenblatt
Cover and interior art: Deposit Photo
Editing: Lauren Clarke at Creating Ink
Copyediting: Flat Earth Editing (Hope)
Proofreading: Flat Earth Editing (Jessica) and Karen Hrdlicka

ISBN: 978-1-990177-28-6 (print)

ISBN: 978-1-7772625-8-7 (ebook)

To the littlest angels...

ONE MORE CHANCE

Letter # 83

Simone,

Thanks for the chocolate brownie cookies. They were great as always. I had to fight off the guys once they found out you'd sent them.

And that includes your brother.

By the way, he wasn't thrilled when he found out I got the cookies. I'm supposed to remind you that he's your favorite brother. Yeah, I know, he's your only brother. But as your favorite brother, he strongly believes he should have first dibs on the cookies.

Anyway, dumbass brother aside, please keep sending them. They're always a bright spot to my days here. Your letters are a bright spot to my days.

Not much for me to tell you about my time here in The Place That Shall Not Be Named. I miss playing hockey and I miss hanging out at the lake with you and our friends.

And most of all, I miss you, Simone. I miss kissing you and being inside you. I guess I shouldn't write that in case your brother rips this letter out of my hand so he can read it and give me a hard time. He won't be too impressed if he finds out how we've been involved off and on for all these years. He knows more ways than I care to elaborate on for torturing people—starting with stealing your cookies.

Can't wait to see you again on my next leave to the U.S.

Love,

Lucas

(Sent over ten years ago)

1

LUCAS

The familiar ache in my left deltoid twitches in sympathy.

Or maybe the sensation is just defiance as I glide the ultrasound transducer head over the gel on Carl's left shoulder.

I ignore the dull pain in *my* shoulder and focus on breaking up the scar tissue in Carl's muscles—scar tissue that was the result of shrapnel while he was deployed with the Navy SEALs. The smell of disinfectant and determination lingers in the air.

"So, how are things goin' with the outdoor program you and your brothers are planning?" Carl asks.

A smile as real as the local mountains stretches on my face. "Good. We put in an offer on Robert and Tuuli's plot of land that's for sale. Just waiting to see if they accept it." Or if they go with one of the other bids: a lodge that promises romantic mountain getaways, a logging company, and an environmental group.

"I hope they do. There aren't many outdoor rec programs like the one you're planning."

"I know that all too well from experience and from talking to other military vets," I say, moving the transducer head over his posterior deltoid. "I just want a place for vets of all different skill levels to enjoy what our mountains have to offer."

"Yeah. And one that doesn't give a damn if its visitors are dealin' with a disability or not."

He's right about that. It's one of the reasons my brothers and I decided to create the program. Besides, what's the point of living in the mountainous region of Oregon if you can't enjoy what nature has provided?

If my best friend, Aiden, were still alive, he would've loved the idea. He'd always thrived on the adventure of the great outdoors. We both had.

Or at least he'd thrived on the adventure before the crippling effects of PTSD destroyed him.

I turn off the thermal ultrasound equipment and wipe the gel from Carl's shoulder with a clean towel.

"Any idea when they're making the decision?"

"The last I heard, October fourth." In four months and three weeks.

"That's good. And as soon as the program's up and runnin', I'll be the first to sign up for it. Well, Sheldon and I will be the first to sign up for it."

"I get the impression Sheldon's excited about it. He went over to the Wakefields' the other day to make a case to them about selling the land to my brothers and me."

If Carl's grin is anything to go by, this isn't news to him.

His smile fades. "Heard you and your crew found those two missing hikers last weekend."

"That's right. They were lucky. One of them sprained their ankle, and they were both scratched up, but they'll survive."

"Damn city folk. They're always overestimating their abilities when it comes to our mountains." He shakes his head. His brother, Sheldon, is also a member of the Maple Ridge Search and Rescue group, so Carl has heard all kinds of stories about the trouble people get into.

"How's Sheldon doing?" I ask. "We were on different crews this weekend."

Carl's grin returns. "I'm gonna be an uncle. He and Sue announced the big news last weekend."

"Congrats, man."

"Thanks. I'm looking at doing some payback on my big brother. I'm gonna corrupt that little kid." He laughs, but I can tell he's excited about becoming an uncle. He's probably almost as excited about that as Sheldon is about being a father.

I finish up with Carl's shoulder and give him instructions for what to do until his next PT appointment with me.

After he leaves, I return to my office and tackle the two proposals waiting for me to finish them. One is due next week for a research grant. The other is for some new equipment for the clinic. The late afternoon sunlight streams through the slats in the blinds, casting diagonal shadows on my desk and the latest issue of *Physical Therapy*.

Beyond the windows, the lush mountain peaks, jagged against the pale May sky, beckon. But unlike the Sirens from Aiden's beloved Greek mythology, they won't be luring me to my death. I know how to deal with the hazards and unpredictability of the terrain. They're nothing compared to the hazards I faced in Afghanistan.

I open my inbox and read the reply to an email I sent to my old captain, Drew, two days ago:

Lucas,

Sorry to hear that your flashbacks have returned. Have you been using the coping techniques your counselor taught you?

I type back:

I have been. I just need to figure out what triggered them, then I'll be fine.

I send the reply and the proposals, change into my running clothes, and pack up for the day.

A handful of cars are in the dirt parking lot when I arrive at my favorite hiking trail, but the area is otherwise free of people.

I jump down from my SUV and breathe in the grounding scent of pine and soil and spring. The cool mountain breeze brushes my skin, bringing with it the tingling sensation of change. Thick clouds, bunched up on the horizon and dark with the promise of rain, advance toward the mountains.

I still have time, though, before I need to worry about them.

I jog to the start of the trail and stretch the tightness in my muscles. I concentrate on the movement, shutting everything else out for now.

Satisfied that I'm limber enough for what comes next, I begin running. Hard. Other than my panted breaths, the wind in the trees, the occasional call of a bird or the scurrying of a squirrel, and the muffled tread of my stride, the area is quiet.

The inner peace that comes from being surrounded by nature eases away any residual tension from my day. I keep running, thankful I have this place so close to home. Thankful I'm still alive to enjoy it.

I focus on the dirt path, littered with roots and stones. All thoughts are pushed aside to keep me from tripping and landing on my face or twisting my knee.

I run past several people hiking to their vehicles. No one I recognize.

Forty minutes later, clouds heavy with rain creep closer as the trail begins to loop back to the parking lot. Sweat drips down my body, soaks through my T-shirt.

My shoulder aches slightly, which is normal with the changing weather. It's been that way ever since the accident in Afghanistan that ended my military career.

The parking lot is empty by the time I approach it. The wind is stronger now, and I wouldn't be surprised if it's raining by the time I get home.

I take a moment to stretch out my muscles, paying extra attention to the injured shoulder.

By the time I steer onto my street, the clouds have surrendered all hope. I flip on my windshield wipers. Ahead of me, flashing red and blue lights streak through the pouring rain. Red and blue lights that are parked near my house.

But the lights aren't coming from one cop car.

Or two.

Three vehicles are lighting up the street as if it's opening night on Broadway.

It must be another boring night for Maple Ridge's finest, and they've all come to help Mrs. Johnson find the teapot she misplaced. Misplaced but misguidedly thought had been stolen. Again.

No, that can't be it. Even our police department doesn't get that bored.

A sinking feeling hits me, dragging my stomach with it.

Christ. Something must have happened to one of my neighbors.

Except, there's no hint of an ambulance. No sign of EMS.

It must have only recently happened.

I ease into my driveway. Before I can reach for the garage door opener, a police officer steps in front of my SUV from the path leading to my house. I press on the brake.

Four officers stand on my lawn, their faces as eager as a cougar before it rips the flesh off its victim. They don't even seem to notice it's raining.

What the fuck?

I park the SUV and climb out. My gaze flicks to Mrs. Johnson's living room window. Her wrinkled face presses against the glass, eyes straining for any delicious morsel, any savory crumb to report to the Maple Ridge gossip grapevine.

Roy's standing by my front door, so I rush through the rain to him. What's he doing here? And is he visiting as a friend or a cop?

I can feel the gazes of the other cops follow me, like the eyes on a creepy-ass painting in a B-grade horror movie.

There's a shift in the air, a bloodthirsty lust, a craving to whip out handcuffs and tasers and Miranda rights.

Something ignites inside me, kicking my heart rate up ten notches. The rush of my pulse echoes in my ears.

Breathe.

My eyebrows squeeze together in what I can only imagine is a grizzly-bear frown. Except I know not to snarl. "What's going on?"

Roy's expression is as readable as a newspaper left at the bottom of the lake for a week. "I'm sorry, Lucas, but we have a search warrant for your house."

"What the hell do you need a search warrant for?" I take it from him and begin reading. With each word I read, the more pinched my frown gets. "Controlled substances? I don't have drugs on my property. Not unless ibuprofen has become illegal since I last looked. This must be a mistake."

Breathe.

"We received a tip that there're drugs on your property."

"Well, there aren't. It must have been a prank call." I'm surprised it was enough to get a search warrant.

"Guess we'll find out soon enough." He asks me to unlock the front door. I do as requested. "Wait outside with Officer Reynolds."

"Christ, this is ridiculous," I mutter after Roy and the other officers step inside my house, leaving me with a cop who looks fresh out of high school. The unease from a moment ago flickers and flares. The same unease that crept in when something about a mission didn't feel right, seconds before everything went to hell.

Breathe.

Shit, shit, shit. Has to be some stupid fuckup. They went to the wrong house. There's no way in hell anyone would think I was stashing drugs in my home.

It's okay. They'll do what they have to do and realize they made a mistake.

The mayday blaring in my gut claims the opposite. And every nerve, muscle, cell, is screaming it won't be okay. And I always trust my gut. It's never been wrong.

Breathe.

Roy finally comes out of the house. Now his expression is shit-shocked.

My gut tightens. My heart slumps. My blood freezes. Freezes my body into the harsh, wintery deserts of Afghanistan. There's no sign of warmth in sight.

He grabs his handcuffs. "Lucas Carson, you're under arrest for the possession of narcotics with the intent to sell..."

Fuck. Fuck. Fuckity-goddamn-fuck.

2

SIMONE

The spicy aroma of the Tandoori-chicken flatbread almost has me purring as the waiter places my plate in front of me. He sets down Avery's order, asks if we need anything else, then leaves us to drool over our lunches.

The trendy Portland restaurant isn't busy yet. Avery and I managed to escape work early so we wouldn't have to wait for a seat. It might be only Thursday, but that doesn't stop the place from filling up with the eager lunch crowd.

"You know what the problem is?" Avery picks up a California roll and pops it into her mouth.

"Not a clue." I grin because I know she's going to tell me, and she'll be right. She's brilliant and rarely ever wrong about these things.

"Your subscription box idea is great, but you need to grow your online presence more. A lot of highly successful women have used social media to build their small business empires. But they're not just posting images of their products or services. They're including pictures of themselves with their loving spouses and adorable kids. This makes them more relatable to their customers."

The hostess approaches the table next to us, a group of five

8

women with her, their hands full with gift bags. Several of the women place their bags on the cushioned bench spanning the wall —the same bench I'm sitting on.

"I love your idea for the romance subscription boxes," Avery says, "but right now your Instagram feed looks impersonal."

"You're right. I've been thinking about that for a while now. But I don't have any romance in my life. No husband in my future."

I might not be the social media guru in the advertising and marketing boutique where we work, but even I recognize my feed isn't quite right. I've studied the popular Instagram influencer accounts, and they have something mine doesn't.

A personal theme.

A hint of their own brand.

Which is ironic since branding is my specialty.

But I work predominantly with large accounts, which tend to avoid the personal photos that appeal to a sizable proportion of women. The corporations use stock photos of people. Perfect-looking people. People who aren't related to or who aren't dating the other individuals in the image.

"There she is," one of the women at the table next to us declares, loud enough for those around her to hear.

My eyes inadvertently shift to the waddling woman approaching the next table—and my heart squeezes into a tiny fist.

It's only then that I pay closer attention to the gift bags beside me on the bench, and I barely bottle a groan. Of all the tables in the restaurant Avery and I could be seated next to, it had to be the one with a baby shower.

"Don't get me wrong," Avery says, not paying attention to the women. "The pictures are gorgeous. You've done a great job with your product shots, but you need to step up your game if you want to be more competitive."

The cheering from the women almost smothers Avery's words. She glances at their table, and this time she's the one who grimaces when she sees the mother-to-be.

Avery covers my hand with hers. "Are you okay?"

A smile stretches across my face, as natural as a bikini in a blizzard. "I'm fine. But it's not like I have a husband or boyfriend. And our apartment doesn't allow pets, so that option's out, too. But that's okay. Right now my number one priority is my job. And given that I'm in the running for the promotion, the position will mean less time for growing my business."

"Any idea when Irene plans to announce who she's giving the position to?"

"She hasn't said anything specifically about it yet, but I have a feeling it's this afternoon."

"Make sure you get plenty of sleep now," one of the women at the neighboring table says rather loudly. " 'Cause once the baby's born, you can say good-bye to sleep for the next eighteen years. And you'll look like a zombie for the first few months."

One of her friends pipes in, "I told James when Lydia was born that he has four options to choose from, but he only gets one each day: dinner, a clean house, a pretty wife, or a happy baby. And a happy baby makes for a happy wife."

Knowing laughs from several of her friends slice into me with scalpel precision.

Pretending I didn't hear them, I wipe the condensation on my glass with my thumb, eradicating a droplet sliding down the side. "And that's why we should celebrate tonight," I tell Avery. "I've done so much overtime lately, and Irene's been dropping hints about a big announcement today."

"I agree. You've worked hard for it. You deserve it."

"I know I do," I say, but a flicker of doubt shadows through me. "Although that's what we thought for the last promotion. But Irene gift-wrapped it for Matt."

"But this time, it's for the junior account manager position, and you've got it. No one has sacrificed as much for the company as you have. And you know it all, and everyone loves you."

Loud "awwws" rise from the table next to us. I glance at the pregnant woman who's holding an adorable toy bunny with floppy ears.

My insides tighten, crushing my uterus to dust.

Well, it would have if my uterus still existed after the car accident almost ten years ago.

The accident that stole my daughter, my unborn child.

My phone pings on my desk and I read the text. Around me, other like-minded creatives sit at their computers in the open area, working on their projects or talking business on the phone.

> Zara: Any word yet on the job promotion?

> Me: Not yet. But hopefully soon.

> Zara: Any word yet on when you're visiting Maple Ridge?

My phone rings, saving me from answering Zara's question. I miss my childhood best friend. But she knows why I'm not ready to go back to the small town I once called home.

Or rather, she knows going back to Maple Ridge is painful for me because my brother lost his battle with PTSD there.

She doesn't know the other reason.

Lucas. My brother's best friend.

The man I was secretly in love with in college. The man I had sex with a year after graduation, while he was on leave from the Marines. The father of the baby I lost. The baby he doesn't know about.

My gaze slides to the row of office doors, to the place where I imagine myself one day soon. Because as much as I love working with my teammates in what we've affectionately dubbed the "living room," I aspire to have my own office.

"Irene would like to see you in the conference room," Jenny, her assistant, says through the phone.

"Thanks," I tell her. "I'm on my way."

I walk down the hall and step into the conference room. Everyone who is vying for the position of junior account manager is here. A number of them I don't consider competition. They applied for the job just because they could.

It's Craig Philmore who has me the most concerned.

He's more competitive than an Instagram influencer hoping to land a TV reality show.

There's nothing he wouldn't do to gain what he believes he deserves.

I sit in the seat next to him, and he flashes me the grin that leaves me feeling as though I've been dropped into a pit of vipers, and they're slithering over me. I fight back a shudder.

"Good, you're all here." Irene glances around the room, taking inventory of us, and smiles. Unlike Craig's smile, hers is polite, friendly, warm. "First, I'd like to thank you all for applying for the position of junior account manager. It wasn't an easy decision to make."

Her apologetic gray eyes land on me for a rapid heartbeat, and a venomous fang yanks the breath from my lungs. "But in the end, it was the perfect decision for the agency. I would like everyone to congratulate...Craig Philmore."

I force a delighted smile on my face, the vipers now writhing in my stomach. Hopefully, the smile appears more heartfelt than it feels.

"Congratulations," I tell him.

The smile he directs at me is enough to make me want to scour my skin for an hour with steel wool. Because not only did he get the job—he's now the person I report to.

Avery walks into the conference room, chewing her lower lip. I've known her long enough to recognize her different tells.

There's the I'm-confused nibble. The *Crap-what-am-I-supposed-to-do-now?* nibble. And the I'm-screwed nibble.

This lip-chewing is none of those.

"Sorry to disturb you." Everyone turns to her. "Simone, the Maple Ridge police department is on the line. It's about your grandmother."

And just like that, my disappointment over Craig getting the promotion switches to ice-cold panic.

Oh, God. Not Grams. Please tell me nothing has happened to the most amazing and sweet woman alive. The woman who raised Aiden and me after our parents died.

The woman who I would do anything for.

3

LUCAS

The events after Roy tells me I'm under arrest...they're all a blur. The handcuffs. The Miranda rights. I'm rushed to the station. Prints are taken. Interviews conducted. I'm given one call, which I make to Troy.

I spend the night in the cold, hard cell, wondering: *Why, why, why? Why would someone frame me?*

When the bright light of morning filters through the windows, I'm arraigned in Eugene, plead not guilty. I'm released on bail.

I head home, unlock the front door to my house, and go inside. My blood burns beneath the surface.

Why, why, why? Why would someone frame me?

I crouch to untie my hiking boots, giving myself a moment to think.

When the hell did someone break into my house and plant the drugs?

Was it while I was at work? While I was running on the hiking trail?

Or did they break into my house while I was sleeping?

The *thud* of footsteps on the porch interrupts my thoughts. My brothers. I'd called Garrett and Kellan when I left the court building in Eugene and asked them to meet me here. Troy was the one who drove to Eugene this morning with a change of clothes and brought me back to Maple Ridge.

"Can you think of anyone who'd want to set you up?" Kellan walks through the open door. He doesn't bother to ask me how I'm doing. Not that I expect him to.

I stand. "I don't have a list of enemies, if that's what you're asking."

"Apparently, you do." Of my three younger brothers, Kellan is the only one who knows what it's like to do time. But in his case, he did commit the crime. Computer expert turned stupid hacker.

Garrett and Troy enter the house. Like Kellan, they have the same dark hair and tall, Marine-honed body as me. The only difference between us is Garrett, Troy, and I have our parents' brown eyes. Kellan's blue eyes belong to his biological parents. The parents who abandoned him at a young age.

I toe off my boots, put them in the hall closet, and head for the living room.

I'm not a neat freak, but my house is usually tidy. Organized. This—how the police left it—is not.

Couch cushions are on the floor, cupboard doors wide open, wicker boxes dumped out, and surveyor's maps for the Wakefields' land scattered everywhere.

Why would someone frame me?

Tension coils in my muscles, ready to snap like a resistance band stretched one too many times.

"Damn. It looks like someone threw a wild party in here." Troy walks over to the couch and picks a cushion off the floor.

"I've seen worse," Kellan says.

None of us ask him if he's referring to a mess from a party or the mess the police left at his house.

I stand there, not moving as my brothers straighten the room. It takes a minute for my legs to start working. I walk over to the bookshelf, to the picture frames lying facedown like a line of dominoes. The tension in my muscles tightens some more.

"Shit, who the hell framed you?" Troy grabs another cushion from the floor and tosses it on the couch. "Maybe it was someone you don't think could have a grudge against you but clearly does."

"What about the therapist you don't see eye to eye with?" Garrett gathers the maps and returns them to the coffee table.

"You mean Richard Diegel?" I pick up one of the photos on the bookshelf. It's a picture of Aiden and me right after our peewee hockey team won a playoff game. We were grinning at the camera, excited because we'd both scored goals.

But I'm not grinning now. Memories of that day plow through me like the blast of an explosion. Stealing my breath. Stalling my pulse.

Fuck, I miss him. I miss my best friend.

I wish he were here to talk through this shit show with me.

I inhale slowly like my therapist taught me to do back when I was struggling with PTSD—*One. Two. Three*—and put the picture upright on the shelf. I release a hard breath.

Troy puts his hand on my shoulder. "I'm sorry." He nods at the photos and drops his hand away. "I know how important they are to you."

"Thanks. I don't care about the rest of it." My gaze sweeps over the contents of the living room. "It's just stuff. Easily replaced."

"Unlike the photos. I know. It's never easy losing someone you love. Especially to PTSD."

Garrett starts pacing, like he tends to do when figuring out a plot point for whatever thriller he's working on. "At least you're out on bail. Thank Christ for Blake."

"For now, anyway. Who knows how long my freedom will last if we don't figure out how the hell the drugs got onto my property? And who framed me and why."

"I wish my connections with the FBI could help with the investigation," Garrett says. "But the local police have to invite the FBI into their jurisdiction before the agents can be involved."

Too bad Garrett's status as a *New York Times* and *USA Today* bestselling author isn't enough of an invite for the FBI. I seriously doubt Chief Wilson will be extending one himself.

The doorbell rings.

"Speaking of Blake." I take a step toward the hallway.

"I'll get it," Garrett says since he's closer to the door.

Blake and Garrett enter the living room. Blake, my lawyer and friend from our college days, is wearing a gray suit, a contrast to the jeans and T-shirts the four of us have on.

With the exception of Garrett, who's back to pacing, we sit. Kellan and I take the couch, Troy and Blake the armchairs.

"We're trying to figure out who the hell would want to frame Lucas," Troy tells Blake.

Blake pulls out a notepad and pen from his briefcase. "Is there any chance it was just someone who needed a safe place to stash their drugs and ended up in your house, Lucas?"

"Possibly. But I don't think it was that. Someone went to a lot of trouble to not only hide drugs here but to make sure I got caught with them."

"You're right. But for the sake of covering our bases, we should consider all possible scenarios. Any thoughts on who might want to see you behind bars?"

Garrett sits on the other end of the sectional. "So far we've got a therapist at the Veterans Center who doesn't see eye to eye with Lucas."

I fill in the blanks for Blake. "He means Richard Diegel. He wants to redirect funding from the PT department, as well as other departments, for his work with his PTSD clients." Which I know firsthand is important. "But I can't see him planting drugs in my house just to get the money. Not at the risk of his reputation."

"I've heard you two have butted heads on more than a few occasions," Kellan says.

I frown. "Just how common knowledge is that?"

He lifts his shoulders in a shrug. "I hear and see things. Chalk it up to being an ex-con."

"Yes, the PT department is less likely to get funding without me pushing for it, but someone else might be hired who will push equally hard to make sure it happens."

"Is there anyone else at the center who might hold a grudge against you?" Troy asks.

Garrett snorts. "Golden boy here? He's always trying to help people. Why would anyone have a grudge against him?"

"But not everyone appreciates that, do they?" Kellan's keen gaze is directed at me.

"Christ, are you a goddamn fly on the wall at the center?" He's not even the one who volunteers there. That would be Troy.

"Something like that."

"I'll admit that I've gotten into a few minor disagreements with some of the staff 'cause they don't care about the war vets or appreciate what they've been through."

"Just how many people are we talking about?" Garrett asks.

"I don't know. Maybe three." I jump to my feet and pace. I already dealt with the interrogations this morning at the station. I'm not in the mood for more.

"Great, so you possibly have four people there who wouldn't shed a tear if you left? Is that what you're saying?"

"I'm saying that I can't see any of them setting me up just to get rid of me."

Kellan leans back on the couch. "Keep an eye on them while you're at work. If any of them act suspicious, it could mean they're connected to what happened."

"Or not," Blake interjects, ever the defense lawyer.

"There's always the chance the break-in has something to do with the Wakefields' property and not Lucas's job," Troy points out.

I drop my ass onto the couch again and get Blake up to speed about the land we put a bid on and our reasons for wanting it.

"Any idea who else is interested in the land?" Blake asks.

"Kincaid Timber Corporation. Then there's a couple who wants to build a small lodge and turn it into some romantic mountain getaway."

Troy taps his knee with his index finger as if sending Morse code. Which he isn't. Too many typos. "There's also an environmental group pushing for the land to be left undeveloped."

Blake's phone pings. He checks the screen and sighs. "Sorry, guys. I have to get back to the city. The main thing I want you to focus on right now, Lucas, is keeping out of trouble. No fights, no arguments, no anything that can be used against you in court."

I snort a laugh, and my mouth curls to one side in a *Really?* smirk.

Blake raises his hands. "Right. Sorry. I just say that out of habit. I know I don't have to worry about you doing any of those things." He shoves his notepad into his case. "As soon as I hear about the trial date, I'll let you know."

"When do you think that will be?" I ask. "The trial."

"It's hard to know right now. It could be in five or six months."

So about the same time the Wakefields are looking to make the decision about their land.

Fuckity-goddamn-fuck. So I'm left dangling by my fingers from a bridge for the next five or more months, and there's nothing I can do about it.

Blake pushes himself off the couch, and I walk him to the front door. "Thanks for your help. I don't know what I would do without you in my corner."

He briefly glances back to the living room. "Are you going to be okay?" The volume of his voice drops, too low to be heard by my brothers, who are still talking in the other room.

"I'll be fine."

"Someone broke into your house, Lucas. It's okay not to be fine."

"I'll be fine." My tone has the emotion of a dud land mine.

His gaze searches my face, as if gauging how much of a lie made up my reply, and nods. It's the nod of a man who believes my answer as much as he believes in pixie dust but is willing to let it go for now. "Call me if you need anything."

"Will do."

He leaves, and I shut the door behind him.

I rest my forehead on the cool, frosted glass, and inhale several long, deep breaths. I spent six years in the Marines, fighting the enemy. Fighting for freedom. At least back then, I knew who the hell the bad guys were.

I knew exactly whom I was fighting.

Garrett is pacing again when I return to the living room. "Is there anyone else who might have a vendetta against you?"

I drop onto the couch, exhaustion from the lack of sleep catching up to me. I feel drained. Physically. Emotionally. I can't believe this is happening. "No one I can think of. At least not to the extent where they'd risk getting caught."

"Did the cops even dust for fingerprints?"

"According to Blake, they did. But unless the person's prints are in the system, they won't be much help. And that's assuming the cops found any. Mine obviously aren't on the drugs, but the police are claiming that's because I wore gloves."

"To hide drugs in your own house?"

"It makes sense," Kellan says. "That way if the drugs were ever found, Lucas could claim that he was set up. Or at least that will be the version of the truth the cops go with."

Garrett stops pacing. "The real question is, are the cops investigating how the drugs ended up here, or do they think they have enough evidence to prove Lucas is guilty?"

"So, we're saying we don't trust the cops to find out the truth?" Troy appears none too surprised by this.

"I never trust cops," is Kellan's honest reply.

"So maybe we need to do our own poking around and figure out who it could be," Garrett says. "Lucas, you'll be the best person for determining if it was someone at the center. If anyone seems nervous, let us know."

"Will do."

Garrett parks his ass in the armchair. "And while you're doing that, we should look into the other groups who also bid on the Wakefields' land."

"It's too bad you don't have security cameras on your property." Troy echoes what we're all thinking.

All of us except for Kellan, if his solemn expression is any indication. "Whoever did this knows what they're doing. I reckon they'd find their way past cameras, too. We're not looking at amateurs."

And that's exactly what I'm afraid of.

4

LUCAS

Friday morning, I'm walking to the PT clinic, coffee mug in hand, when my phone rings. I accept the call.

"Hi, Lucas. This is Maya, Chris McCutcheon's assistant. He's requested you come to his office now. He wishes to talk to you." Her tone is uncharacteristically crisp, professional.

Shit. Is it too much to hope that she's having a crappy morning, and everything's fine when it comes to me?

Chris, the center's director, isn't in his office when I arrive. Maya tells me to take a seat inside it. He'll be back in a minute. Her tone hasn't improved since she summoned me.

On the wall is a copy of Lee Teter's *Vietnam Reflections War Memorial* painting, framed and in a place of honor. My grandfather served in that war, and I always think about him when I see the print.

I salute the painting as if one of the reflections in the war memorial is him. "I miss you, old man."

Grandpa was the one who took my brothers and me fishing at least once a month. He taught us how to live off the land, to rock climb, to telemark and cross-country ski, to respect nature. He taught us everything we know about the mountains and how to survive on them.

The outdoor rec program for vets was his vision as much as it was mine. My grandfather willed my brothers and me the money to start the program. To fulfill his dream.

I sit in one of the chairs facing Chris's desk.

Chris strides into his office, the crisp linen of his Air Force uniform swishing as he swings his arms in a military walk. "Sorry for the wait. I had a meeting that unexpectedly popped up and went slightly over time."

He sits at his desk, brushes his hand over the graying hair at his temple. His expression is the same one Grandpa always had whenever I got into trouble as a kid. Not exactly pissed. More like disappointed. Yet, at the same time, Grandpa always managed to squeeze a smile onto his face. "How are you doing, Lucas? I can't imagine the past few days have been easy for you and your family."

"I'm doing as fine as would be expected, thanks."

He shuffles some papers on his organized desk. Not a single pen, paper clip, notepad dares be out of place. "I guess I should just get to the point. I'm sorry, Lucas, but in light of your arrest, the board has decided to terminate your employment."

It takes a nanosecond for his words to sink in. *Fuck. Fuck. Fuck.*

"That's bullshit." The words puncture the air like a round of bullets. "You know I'm innocent, right?"

"It doesn't matter what *I* believe. What matters is where the board sits on this. The best I can do is temporarily fill your position. If the court finds you not guilty, you can have your job back. But if you're found guilty..."

If I'm found guilty, I could be facing serious prison time.

"I understand," I say, hating that it has come down to this. Hating that everything I've worked hard for, sacrificed for, fought for, could be lost at the snap of someone's fingers.

Christ, this is bullshit.

Chris stands. "I'll walk with you to your office so you can pack up your stuff."

Shit, so much for me being able to investigate who framed me. "I'm a military vet. Does this mean I'm no longer allowed access to the center as a client?"

His answering sigh is that of a man who's shouldering the weight of the world several times over. "I think it's probably for the best, Lucas, if you avoid the place for the time being."

If I no longer have access to the center, at least my brothers still do. It won't be the same as me seeing what I can turn up, but it's better than nothing.

And right now, we're facing a big fat nothing when it comes to figuring out the truth.

Curious gazes follow me as Chris and I walk along the corridor leading to the clinic. I used to think the newly renovated building was warm, welcoming. Now, glacial stares creep over my body, condemning me for something I didn't do.

We enter the clinic and my first patient of the day is sitting in the waiting area, leafing through a magazine. Elsie's cane leans against the armrest of her chair.

The door shuts behind me with a click, and she looks up.

A smile appears on her face and accompanies her relieved sigh and the drop of her shoulders. "Thank God," Elsie says. "I heard you're no longer working here, and Rebecca will be covering for you until your replacement is hired. I'm glad to see she was wrong."

Rebecca heard about the firing squad before I did?

I shoot a permission-asking glance at Chris first and sit on the chair next to Elsie. "She's not wrong." The words feel like boulders on my chest.

"B-but you promised I'd be able to walk down the aisle at my wedding without needing my cane."

I fix my mouth into a reassuring grin, which feels as natural as walking through a grocery store while naked. "That hasn't changed,

Elsie. As long as you do what my replacement recommends, there's no reason you won't be walking down the aisle without the cane."

My reassurance does nothing to erase her dejected expression. "Why are you leaving? You're one of the best PTs around."

At least someone appreciates my hard work. "Thank you."

Chris shifts on his feet but doesn't say anything.

I walk to my office with him in tow.

Rebecca, the clinic director, steps out of her office, and tucks her chin-length blond hair behind her ear. "Lucas, I'm sorry about what happened. I let the board know that I disagreed with their decision. I still can't believe anyone could think for even a second that you're guilty—"

Chris coughs, a not-so-subtle reminder that he has places to go and this is taking too long.

Rebecca shakes her head in a *whatever* gesture, accompanied by a slight eye roll. "Remember, once your name is cleared, I want you back. No one fights for his patients as hard as you do."

I smile at my former boss. "Thank you. That's the plan."

Without a word, Chris watches me pack up my office and escorts me to the main entrance. It's only then that he decides to say anything. "I'm sure you'll be back before you know it. In the meantime, I'll keep pushing for the board to reinstate you. You've done great work here. I'm sure in time the board will realize their mistake in terminating your contract."

I can only nod and accept his condolence handshake.

Once inside my SUV, I send my brothers a group text.

> Me: I'm now unemployed. The center fired me because of the drug charges.

> Troy: Shit. I was hoping that wouldn't happen.

Another text comes through that has nothing to do with the group text.

Robert Wakefield: Lucas, could you come over when you have a chance? Tuuli and I need to talk to you.

Fuck, this day has just gone from bad to worse.

I SIT AT THE WAKEFIELDS' KITCHEN TABLE. THE TABLE HAS BEEN IN their family for the past three generations. The warm sunlight streaming through the window highlights the scratches and scars that mar the pine surface. The imperfections don't speak of neglect. They add character. They tell stories. Stories of births. Stories of deaths. Stories of accomplishments. Stories of failure.

I'm a failure.

The cuckoo clock on the wall next to me ticks loudly in the small space, lecturing me like a cross grandparent. Reprimanding me for a crime I didn't commit.

The last time I was here, the smell of fresh-baked cookies filled the air. This time, it's the burnt stench of the Wakefields' disappointment—the wince on Tuuli's face when she let me into the house—that weighs me down.

To the left of the clock, a large painting of maple trees and a bubbling stream hangs. The tree where Aiden carved the name of the girl he was crushing on in high school is beyond the maples captured on canvas. To this day, I have no idea if Tuuli or Robert ever stumbled across the rough letters.

Aiden and I spent our childhood on that land, camping and climbing and becoming men.

My gut clenches, tightening into a fist-sized boulder wrapped in regret and anger and shame and guilt. Whoever is responsible for the narcotics being in my house, for setting me up, had a reason. A vendetta. A desire to get me out of the way. A need to destroy me.

A way for me to let down those I care about.

Again.

Tuuli parks a coffee mug in front of me, and she and Robert take their seats on the other side of the table. She wraps her paint-stained fingers around her own mug, green and blue freckling her pale skin.

"Can you tell your mom that I'll be bringing my raspberry sponge cake to next week's book club meeting?" Tuuli asks, her Finnish accent faded from living in the U.S for the past forty years. She and Mom are the founding members of their book club, which has been going on since before I was born.

"Will do. I don't suppose you'll save me a slice?" I flash her the grin that used to always earn me a slice of cake when I came barreling into the house after school on book club meeting days. "Your text said you wanted to talk to me." I take a sip of coffee. My guess is they didn't call me here to discuss the dessert for Tuuli's book club meeting.

Robert shares an unreadable glance with his wife.

She smiles kindly at me, and removes the silk scarf that pulls her gray hair away from her face. "Before we get to that, we were wondering if you've heard anything new about Rose. I can't believe anyone would hit that sweet woman with their car and not even stick around to make sure she was all right."

My stomach bottoms out at Tuuli's news, and dread-filled shock hitches my voice. "Rose was involved in a hit-and-run? When? Is she okay?"

And how come no one has mentioned this to me until now? Not even Mom. Or my friend Samuel, who's an ER doc at Maple Ridge hospital.

Another emotion flashes hot inside me. Not because no one told me, but because someone hit Rose. Aiden's grandmother.

A woman who is like a grandmother to *me*.

"It happened yesterday morning. We only know that she didn't require surgery and doesn't have any broken bones. With rest, she'll make a full recovery."

Thank Christ for that.

"And rumor has it, Simone will be returning to take care of Rose. It will be wonderful to see her again. I can't remember the last time she was in Maple Ridge. I know her grandmother has missed her immensely."

An image of Simone flickers in my head, one I replayed plenty of times while deployed. She was wearing a pale-yellow sundress, like a ray of sunshine, her dark, reddish-brown hair tied in two loose braids. And she was standing ankle-deep in Tuuli and Robert's stream, like a water nymph, smiling shyly at me.

The memory is from right before I made love to her on the bank.

Something that Tuuli and Robert don't know about. And will never hear about from me.

"Maybe we should get to the real reason we asked you here." Robert throws his wife the same patient look he gives her whenever she goes off topic. "We heard you were arrested, Lucas."

"It's not what you're thinking." Hope coats my tone like maple syrup.

"We know things are not always what they seem," Tuuli says. "But we are concerned that you were arrested. It was one thing when we looked the other way when it came to Kellan's time in prison. He's worked hard to overcome the negative prejudices against him. And he has done a lot with the youth in town to make sure they don't follow his old path."

"You've decided not to sell the land to us?"

Shit, I'm on a roll when it comes to letting down people who are important to me. I screwed up when my best friend was struggling with PTSD. I wasn't there for him, and he committed suicide. I failed his sister because I hadn't kept her brother alive.

And now I've failed the vets who would've benefited from the outdoor program, and I've let down my brothers. The project was important to them, too.

"We haven't decided yet." Robert picks up his mug. "We greatly respected your grandfather, and we know the program that you're planning was important to him, too. But we also love Walter and Crystal's plans for the romantic getaway."

He smiles at his wife. His love for her is hard to miss in the curve of his lips. "Tuuli and I will have been married forty years this September, so you can imagine we're huge fans of romance. Romantic gestures are what have kept our marriage going strong all these years. And our anniversary is the reason we're waiting till October to sell the land. We want to have our wedding anniversary party there. Our Ruby anniversary."

Tuuli beams at her husband, the love in her expression matching his. "It's where Robert proposed to me." Tuuli flashes me an apologetic smile. "It would be different if you or one of your brothers were married. If you were settling down, starting your own family. But you're not."

Well, this is a first.

And here I thought they won't be selling the land to us because of the ridiculous drug charges. Instead, it's our single status that will be the demise of our dream.

Robert takes a quick sip of his coffee and sets the mug on the table. "We felt it's only fair to you and your brothers to let you know where we stand on things. And we wanted to make sure you understand it has nothing to do with the drug charges. We've known you, Lucas, since you were a little boy, and we know you're innocent."

"Thank you. And I appreciate the heads-up." I fight the urge to bang my forehead on the table.

Even if I wanted to get married, it's not like I can make a bride magically appear. And something tells me a mail-order bride won't cut it either.

So basically, my brothers and I are screwed.

Because even if Blake can prove my innocence, it won't affect whether I can buy the land that means everything to me.

5

SIMONE

Time has stood still in Maple Ridge since I was here last.

The clean streets lined with maple trees and middle-class homes. The squat high school with its green and white colors. The ice rink where my brother played hockey. The stores in chalet-style buildings, their shuttered second-story windows peering down at me.

Everything...everything has remained frozen in time.

The sidewalks are busy with tourists stopping briefly on their way to the mountains. I slow behind the truck ahead of me, and my gaze lands on the children's store. A jagged pain rises in my throat, and the flash of old grief tightens my chest.

I swallow and quickly look away.

Before my parents died, they used to take Aiden and me there whenever we visited Grams and Grandpa. It was like a wonderland, with unique toys that weren't available in the big-box stores.

One of my fondest memories of my parents used to be our visits to that store. Now, just glancing at the shop, with its antique cribs and cute dresses and stuffed bears, leaves my insides shredded.

Leaves me feeling the hollowness deep in my belly.

Beyond the town, mountain peaks slice into the cloudy sky,

taunting me with memories of hiking with a certain dark-haired, brown-eyed boy. Hopeful beams of sunlight squeeze past the narrow gaps in the clouds, ringing the gray pillows in a thin band of light. My car window is open, and the fresh, tangy scent of pine carries in the ghost of a kiss that was like no other.

I hastily shut the window and turn down a street toward another set of brick buildings that makes up downtown Maple Ridge.

Picnic & Treats is one of the few places that didn't exist while I was growing up. The two-story brick building was here, the contrasting white molding recently repainted. But the café's name and owner have since changed.

I find an empty parking spot on a side street and walk the short distance to the café. I pull open the door and step inside. A mix of delicious aromas greets me—spicy, yeasty, sweet—all hinting at the variety of dishes and treats the place offers.

Jazz music plays in the background. Other than the music, the place is silent, every gaze in the room directed my way.

In movies, the small-town folk stare suspiciously at the stranger who enters the bar as if expecting her to transform into a bat or something equally undesirable.

But I know that's not the case here.

Everyone recognizes me.

Everyone knows the reason I'm back.

Sorrow and shock line their familiar faces. Not shock that I'm here. Shock at the sequence of events that resulted in my return.

My rib cage tightens, squeezing air from my lungs. But there's also a warmth in my chest from their love and concern and unspoken prayers for my grandmother.

I turn to the front counter, and for the first time since hearing the upsetting news about Grams, my spirit climbs a few feet.

Zara is standing there, serving a customer. Her long caramel hair is tied up under a purple silk scarf, highlighting her beautiful copper skin and honey-brown eyes.

At the sudden tornado of whispered voices—everyone's shock now subsiding—she looks at me, and a huge smile spreads across her face. It's the grin of late-night sleepovers and secrets about boys we liked and dreams of the future. It's a knowing grin, a caring grin, an I've-got-your-back grin.

She says something to the other girl behind the counter. Then one minute I'm standing there, taking it all in, and the next I'm in Zara's embrace, and I know everything will be all right.

I'll survive this trip.

She steps back, eyes wide as if she can't believe I'm here. Like I'm an apparition. A figment of her imagination. A myth. "I'm so sorry about your grandmother. How's she doing?"

"Better now. I'm on my way to the hospital, but I wanted to pick up a treat for her."

"I happen to know her favorite is available. Do the cops have any idea what happened?"

"Not really. They figure it was a hit-and-run. The driver couldn't see her in the crosswalk because of the angle of the sun. They found the car, which had been reported stolen."

The main door to the café opens. Lucas walks in wearing worn-in jeans and a faded navy T-shirt that skims his Marine-cultivated chest and shoulders. And it's as if all the oxygen in the room has been sucked out, taking what little is in my lungs with it.

A craving stirs inside me to reach out and touch him, to have him hold me like he used to when I was afraid.

But that...none of that is possible.

Not anymore.

The last time I saw Lucas was at dinner over ten years ago with his parents, Grams, Aiden, and me. A series of memories from that night march through my head.

The stolen kiss between Lucas and me in the hallway outside the restroom. Making love to him that night—the last time we were together. The way he smelled like mountains and sunshine and hope.

He's not the same boy who was once my close friend. Nor is he the same man I sent letters to while he was in the Marines.

Sent letters to until everything crumbled into a pile of bent and twisted metal.

I draw in a long breath, reminding my body, my heart, my lungs, that I no longer feel anything for him. My eyes, though, take a moment to feast on the man he has become.

He's still tall and dark-haired with warm brown eyes, but there's a hardness to him that wasn't there the last time I saw him. A hardness I'd witnessed in my brother after he returned from Afghanistan, the playful boy I'd once loved long since dead and buried.

Why couldn't Lucas have waited another five minutes before entering the café?

I would've been gone by then. Seeing him, after all these years, hurts too much. Hurts because I lost Aiden. Hurts because I lost my baby—Lucas's and my baby.

Lucas is one more reminder, the biggest reminder, of all of that.

Fortunately, Troy is with him, and I relax a little. Troy is one more buffer between me and his brother.

Lucas sees me, and his eyes widen imperceptibly. "Simone. I didn't know you were here. I'm sorry about your grandmother. I just heard." Sadness seems to pull his lips into a smile.

And that smile, filled with sorrow and regret, squeezes the air from my lungs in a *whoosh*.

An image of what our daughter might have looked like sneaks in. Her warm brown hair and eyes and her love for everything to do with the mountains.

Like her father.

I shake the image from my thoughts. I can't go there. Not here. Not now.

Two of Grams's friends approach, their smiles wide. Delores hugs me. "Rose will be thrilled to see you, Simone." She steps back, and her eyes give me an appraising once-over. "You look amazing.

How's big city life treating you? I bet you have a special someone in your life?"

Samantha hugs me next. Her scent of lavender and eucalyptus and ginger reminds me of Grams, and I sink into her hug a little more, wishing she were Grams.

"If she did," Samantha says, "you can guarantee Rose would've already told us about him."

Delores lifts her chin, the familiar impish gleam in her eyes. "Maybe Simone has a secret boyfriend Rose doesn't know about."

Samantha chuckles, the sound of old paper softened with time. "If that's the case, do you really think she would tell us? You'd spill the beans faster than I can cable-knit a row in a sweater."

"I'm too busy with my career to worry about finding someone." I avoid looking at Lucas.

In reality, there's no point being in a relationship when no man wants to be with a car wreck like me—as my ex-boyfriend so kindly pointed out.

"How long are you in Maple Ridge for?" Lucas asks, and I don't have a choice but to look at him. He's smiling at me as if he can't believe I'm standing in front of him. Like I'm some sort of mirage.

And I can't help but smile back. "For as long as it takes Grams to recover. I quit my job."

"You did?" The only way I could have surprised Zara more would be if I'd told her I was moving to Iceland.

"I didn't get the job promotion. And what happened to Grams was a wake-up call. I've got money saved up"—the advantage of being a workaholic—"and I have a plan."

One of Zara's employees tells her she's needed in the kitchen. Zara replies that she'll be right there. Delores and Samantha return to their table.

"It's my turn to host game night tonight. So you can tell us all about your plans then. I'm dying to hear them." Zara tells the girl at the counter to give me two apple strudels, on the house, and rushes into the back.

And I'm left standing here with the man I'd rather not see and his brother.

Game night always included Lucas and his brothers and my brother. "Will you two be there tonight?" My palms grow clammy at that possibility.

"Wouldn't miss it," Lucas says.

Troy nods. "Yup. Kellan and Garrett will also be there."

Oh, good. About Kellan and Garrett. That means I won't be alone with Lucas.

I could skip out on game night, but I want to see my friends, and I can't avoid Lucas for the rest of my life—even if I was doing a great job of that until today.

"Soooo." Paragliding naked would've felt less awkward. "What are you to up to these days?" The question is for both men, but my gaze is focused solely on Troy.

"I own a construction company," Troy says, "that specializes in renovations and restorations."

"He also improves the accessibility for clients who have disabilities." Lucas smiles.

"That's great," I say to Troy and turn back to Lucas. "What about you?" The last I heard, he went on to do his physical therapy degree.

The smile on Lucas's face slips into a flat line. "Until this morning, I was a physical therapist at the Veterans Center. But I lost my job after someone planted narcotics in my house, and I was arrested for possession with the intent to sell."

Crap.

I stare at him for a second, positive I misheard him. The Lucas I knew would never have touched illegal drugs. And he certainly wouldn't have sold them. Why would the cops even think he's guilty?

Troy folds his arms, a frown on his brow. "Now he's working for me until we can clear his name."

"You mean while the cops clear his name."

Both men snort a derisive laugh, their expressions far from amused. A cold shiver skittles through me at the meaning behind the sound.

The hollowness where my uterus used to be, where our baby once grew, whispers for me to put as much distance as possible between Lucas and me. "I should go now. I'm going to the hospital to check on Grams."

I snatch up the box with the desserts and escape the café before anyone can ask me more questions.

6

LUCAS

The last time I saw Simone was over ten years ago. She was living in Portland but drove down to Maple Ridge that weekend to visit Aiden while he and I were on leave.

We'd joined their grandmother and my parents at a restaurant for dinner. Afterward, I'd sneaked into Simone's bedroom through her window, and we'd had sex.

Great sex.

The kind of sex that got me through the rest of my time with the Marines. The gunfire, explosions, destruction, the uncertainty, emptiness, fear. When things got rough, when I wasn't sure if I would return home in one piece, memories of that night and Simone's letters kept me going.

Or rather, the letters had kept me going until they abruptly stopped.

And she never replied to the ones I sent her.

I watch Simone walk out the door. And the shitstorm of emotions that surfaced when I first saw her—guilt, regret, joy, shame—eases slightly.

She's even more beautiful than I remembered. The reddish

gleam to her dark hair. Full lips. Hazel eyes rich with a trillion shades of green and gold.

The Simone I've thought about over the years is a pale comparison to the flesh-and-blood woman. They were flat, one-dimensional. The real Simone is light refracting through a prism, a rainbow of colors.

"She's looking better than the last time I saw her," Troy says.

"Aiden's funeral?"

He nods, and a tsunami of guilt drags me down. Suffocates me.

I wasn't there for Simone during the most painful period of her life. At the time, I claimed I couldn't get a leave of absence from my PT practicum. That was a pile of shit.

"She looked like a ghost." Troy murmurs the words as if saying them louder will turn them into shrapnel.

"How come no one told me about Rose?" I ask, needing to change the topic. "I had to find out about the hit-and-run from Robert and Tuuli this morning."

"You spoke to them this morning?" The wince in Troy's tone manages to stay off his face. He can tell it's not good news.

"I'll tell you about it after we get our food. So any word about what happened to Rose?"

"It was a hit-and-run. She was in the wrong place at the wrong time, and the asshole didn't bother to stick around to make sure she was okay." So pretty much what Tuuli told me. "We didn't tell you because you were dealing with enough crap with your arrest. We didn't want to dump that news on you, too. That, and I thought Mom would tell you."

"Guess you were wrong about that. I take it the cops have no idea who hit Rose?"

"No more than they have any clue about how the narcotics got into your house. Their level of incompetence is really comforting."

We walk to the counter, place our orders, and find an empty table next to the window.

The condemning stares and the murmur of voices scrape

against me like barnacle-covered debris. Under different circumstance, I wouldn't give a damn what other people think of me. But this time, too much is at stake.

Troy bites into his sandwich.

"The Wakefields contacted me this morning. They're reconsidering our offer." I get him up to speed on my conversation with them.

A groan vibrates through Troy's chest as if he's been punchkicked in the gut. "Great, because none of us are interested in getting married, we're looking at potentially losing the land?"

"I don't think it was an issue before. But they're big fans of romance, which puts the lodge a step ahead of us."

"I thought they were supportive of our reasons for wanting the land."

"They are. But in their books, love trumps all." I mean, Robert did propose to Tuuli there. I don't think my telling him and Tuuli that Simone and I had sex by their stream will cut it for the Most Romantic Gesture of the Year Award.

Even if it had felt special to me.

"Just don't tell Kellan that," Troy says. "I can't imagine he'd agree that love trumps all after the love of his life betrayed him and he ended up in prison."

"I don't suppose there's anyone in your life you're interested in marrying? You know, to help out the cause."

Troy barks out a laugh. "You mean to take one for the team?" His tone holds a nice-try smirk and a not-happening snort.

"Pretty much."

"Nope. What about you and Simone?"

"Simone?"

"I'm not an idiot. I know you and Simone used to hook up behind everyone's backs. Plus, you and she used to be close."

I keep my ass firmly glued to my seat, avoiding any telling signs that I'm about to lie. "I don't know what you're talking about with the first point. And as for the second one, we haven't spoken to each other in almost a decade." After she quit responding to my letters and never sent any more of her own.

"You do realize I know when you're lying? So you can cut that crap about not hooking up with her. I saw her more than once in college sneaking out of your apartment. And it didn't look like either of you had stayed up studying for an exam—if you know what I mean."

"Fine. Who else knows?"

"I didn't discuss it with anyone, if that's what you're asking. And I have no idea if Kellan and Garrett knew about it. Kellan was too deep in his own shit and gaming to have noticed. And who knows with Garrett, but I wouldn't be surprised if he did. I'm certain Aiden was clueless since you're still alive." He winces, and his gaze averts to the sandwich in his hands.

"There's nothing going on between Simone and me now. We're not friends. Hell, we don't even live in the same city, and I have no interest in moving to Portland."

"As I see it, she's now unemployed, single, and has no reason to move back to Portland."

I shake my head, my decision firm. "She's not the solution to our problem, Troy, so forget it. What happened between Simone and me was a long time ago. She's not into me anymore."

7

SIMONE

The dim fluorescent lighting reveals the pale, frail form with the puff of white hair asleep on the hospital bed.

My chest tightens, struggling under the weight of the elephant in the room. The sharp disinfectant odor assaults me with memories of the last time I was in a hospital. An IV dripping meds into my arm. The ache where my uterus used to be.

The void where my daughter once grew.

It's going to be okay. Everything will be fine.

I walk cautiously to the bed, carrying the box from Picnic & Treats and taking care my heels don't click against the floor. Large floral arrangements brighten the otherwise drab room.

Grams's withered hand rests on her stomach, IV fluid emptying drop by drop into a vein on the back of it. The same hand used to stroke my cheek when I woke from a nightmare. The same tender fingers wiped away my childhood tears.

"I hope that box contains what I think is in it." Her voice might be weak but the smile to her tone isn't. "I also hope that's you, Gumdrop, and not a figment of my imagination."

Despite the grim reason for my being here, I can't help but grin at the nickname she gave me as a kid because I loved the candy.

41

"No, I'm definitely here." I bend down and kiss her soft, wrinkled cheek. She's paler than I remember her being when she visited me in Portland at Christmas.

"The nurse told me it was okay to give you this." I lift the lid and show her the two thick apple strudel slices.

The toothy smile from my childhood curves onto her face. "Thank God for that. I forgot how bad hospital food tastes. Are they afraid if the food actually tastes good, patients will never want to leave?" She shakes her head.

"How are you feeling?"

"A little sore."

When I was a kid, I was positive she was made of steel, like Super Grams. But even steel can be dented. Weakened. "The nurse told me you'll be here for at least a week."

Grams snorts with more sass than you'd expect for someone her age. "I'll be running around the track before you know it."

A soft laugh rumbles in my chest. "I don't doubt it."

"And jumping hurdles." She flashes me an impish grin that adds a glow to her wrinkled face. Then her smile fades. "You didn't need to come here, Gumdrop. I know you're not a fan of the town."

"Yes, I did. It shouldn't have taken me this long to visit you. But I'm here now." She knows how returning to Maple Ridge pains me. She just doesn't know the full reason for it. No one does, other than Avery.

"How long are you here for?"

"Until you're better and walking again."

"But what about your job?"

"I was up for a promotion, but they gave it to someone else. And that wasn't the first time they'd passed me over for a promotion. I decided it was time for me to move on and re-establish my priorities. I've been working on something for the past few months that can easily be done in Maple Ridge while I'm here." And now that I'm no longer working at the ad agency, I have more time to focus on my subscription box business. "And I figured this is the perfect time to spend it with you and catch up with my friends." Whom I haven't visited in forever.

"You won't get any complaints from me, Gumdrop. I've missed having you around."

The smile that spreads across my face feels brighter than the midafternoon sun. "I've missed you, too, Grams."

"THESE ARE GORGEOUS." I POINT AT THE HALF-DOZEN FRAMED PHOTOS on Zara's living room wall. "This has to be my favorite."

Each photo looks as though it came straight from an issue of *National Geographic.* Or *Vogue.*

Zara's wearing a black string bikini in a couple of the photos. Her long braids cascade over her bare shoulders. But the bikini and braids are not what make the images breathtaking. The majority of her hair, face, and body have been painted with streaks of shimmering gold. The lake in the background is dark, the images either taken early morning or late in the day, further emphasizing the smears of paint on her copper-brown skin. "Did Kim shoot these?"

Zara nods. "That one has won numerous prestigious awards. And she's also won awards for several of her other pieces, including one from *National Geographic.* Most of the photos are from around here, but she and Jerome visited her grandparents and extended family in South Korea last summer, and she shot a number of photos there."

"Wow." I knew some of this, but a twisting in my gut reminds me of just how much I didn't know about Kim's photos. Once Lucas moved back here after completing his physical therapy degree, I'd avoided Maple Ridge. The pain of seeing him was too much.

"I'm not surprised she's done so well. Kim was super talented in high school. And that was before she studied photojournalism." I turn away from the pictures.

Zara's apartment looks the same as it did the last time I was here: neutral tones livened up with the scattering of bright-colored pillows. The only difference is, she has a few more carved wooden elephants and gazelles in the living room compared to the last time I was here.

"Is Samuel joining us?" I ask, referring to the oldest of her two brothers.

"No, he's on call at the hospital."

As Zara pours me a glass of Cabernet Sauvignon, the buzzer to her building alerts her of the new arrivals.

The apartment door opens a few minutes later, and a flash from my past strolls into the living room. I place my glass on the coffee table and jump to my feet.

Kim is as beautiful as she was in high school, with the same slim, athletic build that won her numerous track and field trophies. Her long black hair accentuates her high cheekbones. "I was beginning to think we'd never see you again." She hugs me like she hasn't seen me in twenty years and has to make up for every missed hug.

I hug her back equally enthusiastically. "I was beginning to think that, too."

I hug Jerome, her husband. His black hair is shaved short, and he has the same golden copper skin as his sister, Zara. He releases me and settles his hand protectively on the curve of Kim's spine.

Before I can say anything, Emily bounces over to me and flings her arms around me. "I can't believe you're finally back." The petite, curvy blonde squeezes me as if she never plans to let me go. If I had any doubts about joining them tonight, the doubts have since left the building.

"I've missed you." I release her and look at the three women who were my best friends all through school, when Aiden and I moved in with Grams. "I'm sorry I've been a crappy friend and haven't kept in touch like I should have."

"Well, you're back now, so you're more than forgiven." Zara lifts her wineglass as if to toast me.

The apartment door opens a heartbeat later, and the four Carson brothers stroll in. And my insides warm at seeing the men who were like brothers to me. Well, all except for Lucas.

"Hey, Golden Girl." Garrett hugs Zara, making her laugh. He releases her and steps toward me.

"Golden Girl?" I ask as he wraps me in a huge big-brother bear hug. He swings me around, and I laugh. Nope, he hasn't changed much—other than growing into a more muscular version of his younger self.

He puts me down.

"That's what he's been calling me ever since Kim took the photos of me with gold paint on my body," Zara says.

"I love those pictures," I tell Kim. "They're gorgeous."

A slight blush rises on her beige skin. "Thanks. I'm always looking for models if you're interested in having paint poured on you."

The idea of anyone seeing me in a bikini sends a shiver of *That's so not happening* down my spine. It's not the idea of a bikini that's off-putting as much as the four-inch scar on my belly that will lead to questions I don't want to deal with. "I'll have to get back to you on that."

I flash her a smile that feels a little wonky and quickly shift my focus to the four Carson brothers.

Troy and Kellan hug me like a little sister, minus the swinging me around. God, I've missed these guys.

Lucas approaches.

Knowing I'll never survive if he hugs me, I grab my wine from the coffee table, using it as a shield for my heart.

Confusion and hurt flicker in his eyes before his expression settles for unreadable.

We sit at the long dining room table. Somehow Lucas ends up next to me. My body stiffens like a plank of wood, easily broken with the right pressure.

What happened almost ten years ago wasn't his fault. He wasn't the driver who hit me. He didn't cause me to spiral into depression because of the loss of our baby and my uterus. But that doesn't mean parts of me don't bleed when I look at him.

If only…if only he didn't smell like the man I used to be in love with. The man linked to too many memories—the good and the bad and the painful.

Zara shuffles the cards and deals them.

"Now that I don't have to worry about any more customer interruptions," she says after we've been playing poker for several minutes, "are you going to tell us about your mysterious plans now that you're no longer working at your old job?" Her gaze is on me, and the rest of the group peers at me expectantly.

"I started a subscription box business a few months ago. Each month's box contains high-quality items based on the theme of love and romance." Just because I'm not looking at either one in my future, it doesn't mean I'm against the idea. I haven't become a cynic. I enjoy the idea of doing whatever I can to help others appreciate love. To help nurture it.

Because God knows there's not enough love in the world.

"No one knows what's in that month's box until they receive it." Or until the unboxing videos and photos show up on social media. "And the items aren't just about romantic love. It's about loving yourself as well as loving other people."

"That's a great idea," Emily says. "How's it going?"

"So far, not too bad. I'm currently growing my customer base. Now that I've left my old job, I'll have plenty of time to do that and search for products to include in each month's box. But I also need to revamp my branding. Some of the successful female entrepreneurs and Instagram influencers post photos of themselves with their boyfriends or husbands. It's intentional, branded, not your standard selfie."

The three women nod. They've seen those images just like Avery and I have. They know what I'm talking about.

"I don't suppose any of you know where I can rent a husband?" I laugh, not meaning it.

"Is that really a thing?" Jerome frowns in that way men do when they're confused about something a woman has told them and they're trying to puzzle it out.

The other four men's expressions mirror his.

Emily, Zara, Kim, and I crack up laughing. Kim lovingly pats her husband's hand.

"Even if it were a thing," I say, "I wouldn't rent a husband. Marketing works best when you're being authentic. Especially if you're running a small business. If you claim to be someone you're not, it will come back and bite you in the ass."

Zara looks at Kim to see what she wants to do with her cards.

Kim fans them and places them on the table. "Full house." The men and Emily groan and toss their cards down. "If you're looking for a photographer to take pictures of you for your social media, I would love to help you out. At least while you're in Maple Ridge. Maybe we could get photos of you and your grandmother. And what about photos on the Wakefields' land? The place is beautiful and romantic, especially by the stream. You could talk about how special the place is to you."

I stare at Kim for a fraction of a second. *She's not talking about what Lucas and I did there. She has no idea. None of them know…other than Lucas.* "I would love that. Thank you." I place my cards on the table. Four of a kind. Queens.

"Didn't you have your first kiss there?" Emily asks. "What was that boy's name?"

Zara lowers her cards. Four of a kind, but with only twos.

"I didn't kiss Eddie there. And I hardly think that kiss counts. We were in fourth grade." I squirm at the memory of how Lucas and I did kiss by the stream. Many, *many* times. And then I squirm some more at what else he and I did there.

My elbow accidentally knocks into his arm, and I turn to apologize. My gaze lands on the light in Lucas's eyes, and I can tell he's also remembering those times. The apology stalls on my lips.

I quickly turn away from him and grab my wineglass.

We play another hand, which Troy wins.

"So, what's next, Lucas? Are you actually waiting to see if the cops figure out how the drugs ended up in your house?" Emily's questioning eyes shift to each of the brothers and settle on her boss: Kellan.

"That's probably not a good idea," Zara says. "As far as they're concerned, they've arrested the guilty party. So unless they know their case isn't rock solid against Lucas, they won't be pushing hard, if at all, to figure out who hid the drugs in his house. We should—"

"*You* aren't doing anything," Garrett practically growls as Jerome says, "Forget it, sis."

"This isn't a fucking Nancy Drew novel," Garrett continues as if her brother hadn't said anything. "This is real life. So you leave this to the men."

Zara, Emily, Kim, and I exchange grinning glances and burst out laughing.

"I hope you left your caveman bat at the door when you came into the apartment." Zara crosses her arms and raises an eyebrow at Garrett.

He doesn't bother to take a moment to look sheepish. He just keeps scowling at her until she rolls her eyes and shakes her head. "Fine, what are you cavemen planning to do to prove Lucas is innocent?"

"We're looking into the people who have a reason to want Lucas locked away for a long time."

"And how's that going?"

"It would be simpler if I hadn't been fired from the Veterans Center," Lucas grumbles, pain and frustration in his tone.

But it's not just because he lost his job due to the drug bust. I sense there's more to it.

"But since I'm now unemployed," he says, "I have all the time in the world to figure out who set me up and why."

I take a sip of my wine. "That's going to be a little hard, isn't it? Whoever did this won't be thrilled with you nosing in their business. They'll be expecting you to try to figure out who framed you."

I mean, the jerks seriously didn't expect him to take this lying down and wait for the cops to figure things out, did they?

And if they did, they underestimated Lucas—because that doesn't describe the man I used to know. Nor does it describe his brothers.

"So if I happen to overhear something at the café that might provide a lead," Zara says, a stubborn gleam in her eyes, "you don't want me to mention it to you?"

Garrett pinches the bridge of his nose. I wouldn't be surprised if he was counting to ten so he doesn't tell her what he thinks of that idea. "No, you can pass on that information to us."

"But that's all," Troy adds. "Whoever is responsible for this means business. As much as you four women like to believe you're badasses, Lucas, Garrett, Kellan, and I are the ones who served in the Marine Corps. We know all about being badasses."

"And asses, too, it would seem," Zara mutters. Kim snorts a laugh.

"Yeah, that, too." Garrett's smug expression is met by a look from Zara that makes me think she's going to give him a good ass-kicking later. Kim, Emily, and I snicker.

With that settled, as far as the men are concerned, we play another game of poker. I deal this time, and Emily wins.

Tonight feels like I've stepped back in time. It's painfully familiar, but it's also the most fun I've had in a while.

Lucas laughs at something Garrett said, and a gnawing emptiness stretches and twists inside me. The emptiness that took root following the accident that claimed my unborn child. The same emptiness that grows like a patch of deforestation, consuming but never given time to heal.

The loss of my brother only compounded it.

I excuse myself and step onto the balcony, sliding the door shut behind me.

The cool night air kisses my cheeks, and the soothing scent of rosemary, thyme, and mint lingers in the air from the plant pots on a wooden shelving unit. I breathe in deeply, filling my lungs with the calming scent.

"That's better," I murmur to myself and sit down on a lounger.

Millions of stars wink at me from the velvety sky. Memories of stargazing with Aiden leak in unrestrained. Of hanging out in Grams's backyard with him, both of us snuggled under a pile of blankets. He'd been telling me the story of Apollo or Athena or Demeter. I can't remember which one.

The stories didn't matter to me. I just loved spending this time with my brother, and I loved watching him come alive with each mythological tale he told.

The balcony door slides open behind me, and for a brief moment, the chatting and laughter from inside spills out.

I peer over my shoulder to see who's joining me and try not to groan out loud.

Lucas.

8

————

SIMONE

I tear my gaze from Lucas and go back to staring at the stars. "I miss him."

"Me, too." Lucas lowers himself onto the other lounger, not needing me to clarify who I'm talking about.

We're quiet for a few minutes, just staring at the stars. The cool mountain air ruffles my skirt and brushes my bare skin, yet I feel...I feel warm with him sitting so close.

That much between us hasn't changed.

"I miss camping with him on the Wakefields' property, near the stream, and watching the stars at night," Lucas says. "He always told the best stories with Greek demigods living among us and battling creatures that mere mortals couldn't see."

I smile at the memory of Aiden telling me the same stories, but I'm not sure how much of the smile shows on my lips. The heartbreak at losing my brother weighs down the corners of my mouth. "Did he do that when you were in the Marines?"

"Sometimes, but not as much as when we were growing up. At that point, our priorities were different. It was more about staying alive."

A familiar, blissful silence surrounds us, even though my heart

51

thump-thump-thumps loudly at how close Lucas is. If he can hear my heartbeat, he doesn't give any indication.

I shove aside all thoughts of what happened almost ten years ago. Of the poor judgment one man made when he got behind the steering wheel intoxicated. The single action that triggered a sequence of events. The loss of my daughter. The hysterectomy.

Instead, I'm the girl who listened to her twelve-year-old brother's stories, the girl who admired Lucas, loved him, but hadn't developed romantic feelings for him yet.

"What made you decide to be a physical therapist?" Not once while Lucas was studying kinesiology had he shown an interest in being a PT. I always figured since he was playing hockey at the time, he would go on to do something with that.

"I was shot in the shoulder during my last deployment and spent countless hours in PT before my shoulder was fully healed. During that time, I witnessed how my therapist and his hard-ass attitude refused to give up on any wounded vet. Even those who had given up on being ambulatory again. There were times when many of us wanted to throttle him." Lucas laughs, the sound rich with affection. "But in the end, our grumpy asses had to agree he was right, even when we wanted him to be wrong. I realized I wanted to be just like him. Maybe not at first. Not while I was dealing with my battle with PTSD. But later, he and I talked a lot about his job and his training. I knew then that I was meant to be a physical therapist. Someone who makes a difference in a patient's life."

"You love doing it, don't you? Being a PT?"

Lucas smiles. "Very much. What about you? I take it you still love living in Portland?"

I don't look at him. I keep watching the stars. "I do."

"You don't miss Maple Ridge?"

I don't answer right away. I could lie and tell him I hate being back, but Lucas knows me better than that. Growing up, I was never the girl who counted down the days until she could escape her small town.

"I miss Grams and I miss my friends." *I miss you and I miss Aiden.* "And yes, there's a part of me that misses living here."

"Have you given any thought to moving back here?"

"Not really."

"Your subscription box business. Do you have to be in Portland to do it?"

Even with my gaze locked on the stars, I catch him swinging his feet onto the ground and sitting up. "No, I can do it anywhere. As long as I have Wi-Fi and a post office nearby. But I would need to go to the city from time to time to buy items for the boxes. The rest of it I order online."

"Any particular reason you want to return to Portland and not remain here?"

"I like it in Portland. The city has so many things to offer its residents."

"You used to love it here, too."

My heart aches at what else I used to love in Maple Ridge. The feel of Lucas's arms around me. The press of his mouth against mine. The way my body responded to him. The way he made me feel like I was the most important thing in his life. Only I didn't realize any of these things until it was too late to tell him I loved him.

And then...and then none of that mattered anymore.

"True," I say. "But things change. People change. Why are you asking me all these questions about Portland?"

"I have an idea that will help you with your business."

"What's that?"

"My brothers and I want to start an outdoor rec program for military vets." He explains their idea to me, and how it would benefit veterans of all abilities.

"That all sounds great," I tell him once he's finished telling me about the program. I mean it. What they want to do does sound amazing. "This doesn't mean you're giving up being a PT, does it?" Because that wouldn't make sense. From what I've heard over the past two years, he's amazing at his job. "Or will that be part of the program?"

"I have no intention of giving up on being a PT. The recreational program is seasonal and will start out as a weekend thing. At this point, we have no plans to add PT services. Not yet, anyway. I took an adaptive physical education course during my kinesiology degree. Our initial plans are more related to that. And depending on how things go, we plan to add staff as the program grows."

"So you would still be a PT?"

"That's the plan. My PT hours at the Veterans Center are flexible. Or they were until I was fired."

"Could you add the PT services to the recreational program if you don't get your job back? Have it in the same building?"

"I could, but it will require more capital for the equipment than we have. So it's not in the books right now. But down the line. That's my ultimate goal once the outdoor rec program has grown to the point where I can run my own clinic in conjunction with it."

"It all sounds great, Lucas. But what does your program have to do with my subscription box business?" We're not exactly talking about the same target market.

"We found the perfect spot for our program's building and guest cabins. Robert and Tuuli are looking at selling some of their land. It's the same location where Aiden and I used to hang out. Where you and I..."

His unspoken words flap in the breeze and bring a flush to my face.

"But we aren't the only ones interested in the land. Things were looking good when it came to our bid..."

This time I fill in the missing words. "But then you were arrested?"

He nods, the pain all this is causing him visible in the movement. "Our bid is still under consideration. Robert and Tuuli respected our grandfather, and they like what we want to use the land for. But there's another couple who wants to build a lodge on the land and market it for romantic getaways."

"And the Wakefields are leaning more toward the lodge because they're romantics at heart?" I ask.

Romantics, that's the Tuuli and Robert I remember when I was growing up. One day, she and I were making cookies for the book club she and Lucas's mom had started. Robert came into the kitchen, grabbed Tuuli's hand, and twirled her around to the song on the radio.

Then he kissed her.

It was the sweetest thing ever.

Lucas shifts on the lounger and scrubs his hand against the scruff on his jaw. This conversation is clearly making him squeamish. "They've been married for almost forty years, so yeah. They're more likely to sell the land to the couple because my brothers and I aren't married, and none of us are in a serious relationship."

"So what's your idea? I send them one of my subscription boxes to sweeten the deal?" I can definitely do that.

"Not exactly, but that wouldn't hurt. If I got married, it would increase the chance of them accepting our bid."

A smile cracks on my face at the ridiculousness of the idea. "Do you really believe that?"

"No, but it will reduce the chance of them eliminating us without further consideration."

Good point.

Possibly.

"Okay, so what does this have to do with me and my subscription boxes?"

He glances at the mountains for a fraction of a second before returning his gaze to me. "You said that having a husband would benefit your business."

When I was nine years old, Aiden and I went canoeing on

Windermere Lake. At one point I thought I saw a large fish swimming just beneath the surface, its scales gleaming in the sun. I'd foolishly thought it was a mermaid. I leaned over the edge of the boat to get a better look...and caused it to tip over.

And damn, the water was cold.

The initial shock I felt when I landed in the water is nothing compared to now. At what Lucas is suggesting.

I stagger to my feet. The man has seriously lost his mind. "Sorry, not happening."

9

———

LUCAS

Laughter spills from inside Zara's apartment through the closed balcony door. The amused sound is a contrast to Simone's disbelieving expression.

Can't say I blame her. What I'm asking of her is off the Richter scale when it comes to harebrained ideas. Besides, what happened between us occurred a long time ago, even though I still think about it. We aren't the same people now as we were back then.

But that's how desperate I am.

"Even if it means helping with your business?" I ask. "You said in Picnic and Treats that you've been too busy to date, which means you're single."

"So you think that's a good enough reason for me to marry you? Because it *might* reduce the chance of the Wakefields writing off your bid? Have you thought that maybe there's more to marriage than it being convenient for your goals?"

I'm guessing sex isn't the answer she's looking for here. Although from the way she's glaring at me, I'm assuming that option would be off the table if she did agree to help me.

"You're talking about love, right?"

She rolls her eyes, indignation flaring strong in them. "Of

57

course I'm talking about love." She turns away from me and rests her folded arms on the balcony railing. A slow breath escapes her, but it does nothing to ease the tension knotted in her shoulders. "How long are we talking about?"

"How long for what?"

"How long would we be married?"

I push myself up from the lounger and walk over to the railing to join her. "Till death do us part."

Surprise widens her eyes. "You mean you expect us to stay married forever? This isn't a temporary thing that ends once you and your brothers sign on the dotted lines, or the Wakefields sell the land to someone else?"

"My parents have been married for over thirty years. My grandparents were married for forty-five. Marriage is about a partnership with someone you respect and admire. It doesn't have to be about love. So yes, if I'm getting married, I plan to endure it for the long haul."

She makes a sound that's a mix between a choked laugh and a snort. "You always did have a way with words, Lucas. You might want to avoid putting it that way to Tuuli and Robert."

"My grandfather told me marriage is hard, and you have to work equally hard to make it work."

"Did your grandfather also tell you to marry so you can buy the land you want?"

I chuckle. "I must admit that conversation never came up." But neither had the possibility of me being framed.

I mirror her stance, folded arms on the wooden railing. "I don't expect you to stay married to me if my lawyer's unable to prove I'm innocent. Not when I could be facing a lifetime in jail. That wouldn't be fair to you."

Her expression softens, and she nods. "God, this is so fucked up."

"Tell me about it."

Our back-and-forth debate falls silent. No more rebuttals. No closing arguments. There's nothing more I can say to convince her.

The decision—my future, our future—is in her hands.

If she says no, I have no backup plan. No countermove. If I have to get married, there's only one woman I envision as my wife. And she's standing next to me.

Simone might not know all my secrets, but I don't know hers either.

And that's fine with me.

"Why the Wakefields' property?" she asks. "I'm sure they aren't the only people selling land. Eventually you'll find something else equally great or better."

"Aiden and I created a lot of memories on that land." I glance up at the stars, unable to look at her for the next part. "I still feel connected to him when I'm there. My brothers and I want to honor his memory by having the program where he and I practically grew up."

"But what if they don't sell the land to you even after you marry?"

"Then we can divorce if that's what you want. Or we stay married to help your business. I won't end our marriage just because the Wakefields sell to someone else. I won't leave you high and dry like that."

Simone's gaze turns skyward, and she worries her lower lip. "I'll do it," she says after a moment. "I'll marry you, but on one condition. Well, four, really."

"What conditions?" Why do I get a feeling she won't be going easy on me?

"I want a cat. But not just any cat," she quickly amends. "It has to be a British shorthair kitten."

"Why a British shorthair kitten?"

"Because they're adorable as both kittens and adult cats. And— and I've always loved the breed, but my apartment doesn't allow pets."

"Okay, I'll get—"

"And I want a puppy. A golden labradoodle puppy. That's my second condition."

"I'm almost afraid to ask what the other two conditions are." The first two were specific enough.

"The third one is a horse." The corner of her mouth twitches. Not enough to be called a smug smile. But enough to betray the hint of one.

"What, no specific breed?"

"Er, one I can ride? So not one of those huge horses like a Clydesdale."

In the game of negotiation, the golden rule to winning is always aim higher than you're willing to settle for. That way the other side feels like they're the winner when you agree to their terms when in reality you got exactly what you want.

And I have no doubt that's what she's doing.

"What's the final condition?"

"If I'm offered a great job in Portland, I get to move back there, and we'll just have to manage a long-distance marriage. Portland isn't too far away, so it's doable."

"What if the job offer is for somewhere else? Somewhere much farther away?"

"On the rare chance that happens, we'll get a divorce. But other than the few résumés I sent out last night, I'm not actively looking for a job. I want to focus on my subscription box business and work at making it a success." She turns to me. "I've been away from Grams for too long. The hit-and-run was a wake-up call. I want to spend more time with her while I can. So what's it gonna be? Do you agree with my conditions?"

"No horse. Only the puppy and kitten. And I agree to the fourth condition. I don't want to hold you back on what you've worked hard for." It wouldn't be fair of me to expect otherwise.

"Great. I guess I'll start shopping for pet supplies."

"Any idea where we get these animals from?" I'm assuming it's not as easy as walking into a store and purchasing them.

"I know a labradoodle breeder. I'll need to do research for a British-shorthair breeder." Her eyes light up at the mention of the animals.

"Are you positive you want to do this?" I don't want Simone to regret her decision down the line. "What will people think if they find out the man in your social media photos is facing felony charges? That won't do much for your image." Simone's image has always been important to her. Even in high school.

"That's true. But this is different. I believe in you, Lucas. I believe you're innocent. And I'm doing this in memory of my brother. That's the most important reason of all."

I nod. "Okay. So does that mean you'll marry me?"

The emotion of a dozen thoughts flicker on her face. She holds her hand out to me. "Yes. You have yourself a deal."

The tightness in my muscles loosens. My lungs inflate. I can finally breathe, can finally scale the mountain of hope.

I shake her hand, even though I'd rather kiss her to seal the deal. Something tells me we're not quite there. There's a reserve to her that wasn't there ten years ago.

There is one thing I do need to know before we figure out how we're going to announce our engagement to everyone. "Can we get married first? Or do we have to wait until after we've adopted the animals?"

"After we're married is fine. I'm guessing you want to get married sooner rather than later." She turns back to the view, the mountain barely more than a looming shadow cutting into the night sky. "So what are we telling everyone? I haven't lived in Maple Ridge for over ten years. Everyone knows we weren't having a long-distance relationship. Won't Tuuli and Robert be suspicious when you're suddenly engaged shortly after they tell you they're leaning toward selling the land to the couple who wants to build a lodge for romantic getaways?"

"You and I aren't strangers. We've known each other for a long time. So us wanting to get married won't sound so farfetched. The best thing we can do is keep as close to the truth as possible."

"You mean that you asked me to marry you for business purposes?" A one-sided smile lifts her lips, and damn if she doesn't look as sexy as sin.

Focus.

"No—that we were involved in college." Since Aiden can no longer kill me for having sex with his sister, it's okay to admit that truth. He can haunt me, perhaps.

But definitely not kill me.

Her brows raise, dark against her pale skin glowing softly in the light spilling from the living room. I don't dare to turn to see if anyone in the apartment is watching us.

"You actually want us to admit to that?"

"Sure, why not? We're in our thirties now. We're adults."

She nods, understanding the message beneath the words. "Do you think people will believe that? I didn't tell anyone—not even Zara, Kim, or Emily—that we were sneaking around."

I kind of figured that at the time. The three of them weren't very subtle back then. It would've been obvious if she had told them. "They will if they see how we are together."

She frowns. It's a good thing her expression isn't visible to everyone in the living room. "How we are?"

"We have to show them we're in love and have been for years, but your job in Portland kept us from making things official."

"Wow, you've really thought this out, haven't you?"

"I have." Ever since Troy suggested this afternoon that I marry her, I've been thinking about how she and I could make this work. Because sure, the idea was farfetched, a little ridiculous, perhaps, but I couldn't let it go. *Just like I haven't been able to let her go.* Troy has no clue that I had considered asking Simone after I told him she wasn't the solution to our problem. Even Garrett and Kellan have no idea what I'm doing on the balcony. They only know about the conversation I had with the Wakefields this afternoon.

"But we should start with telling my brothers and our friends in there first." I nod at the apartment. "If we can convince them we're getting married because we're in love, we can convince everyone. Because the fewer people who know the truth, the less likely things will go wrong with the plan."

"How are we going to convince your brothers and our friends?"

I shift my body slightly, gazing into those beautiful hazel eyes of hers, and lower my mouth. It's just the brushing of lips. Nothing X-rated. But my body responds like it always did when I kissed her. My skin zings. My breath quickens. My heart trips over itself. I've kissed many women over the years. None have left my body feeling this way. This exhilarated.

Simone releases a small gasp, but she doesn't pull away or slap me.

Always a good sign.

I step back in time to see her expression shift from surprised to satisfied. Not just the satisfaction that comes from a great kiss. She also believes we can pull this off.

I smile at her like a man who's utterly in love—for the benefit of everyone in the living room. "Are you ready to tell our friends that we're engaged, or do you want to back out while you still can?"

"You think they'll buy it?"

"I have no idea. They might be skeptical at first. Troy knew back in college that you and I were sneaking around. He won't require much convincing. But you were joking about renting a husband. And my brothers know that one of us being married would sweeten the deal with the Wakefields. I guess we'll find out soon enough."

"You do realize Tuuli and Robert are the most romantic people I know? It won't be easy to fool them into believing we're in love. They'll be able to sniff out our lie faster than a bloodhound sniffing out a dead bird."

I grin. "You really know how to talk dirty, don't you? Speak like that around them, and we'll have them convinced in no time."

She laughs. Christ, how I've missed her laugh. It always made me feel better when I was having a crappy day. Even when I was being the grumpiest of grouches.

"We'll wait until I've given you a ring before we announce our engagement to everyone else," I tell her. "But our friends and my brothers won't care if you don't have a ring yet."

"Okay."

"You ready to do this?"

She nods, the movement uncertainly determined. "As ready as I'll ever be."

10

SIMONE

Lucas and I step inside Zara's apartment.

The spicy scent of chilies, ground beef, and coriander greets me, and my stomach does a loop-the-loop at the memory of her samosas.

God, I'd missed them while I was living in Portland. Sure, they have samosas there. Great tasting samosas. But Zara's the queen of them all.

They're the perfect comfort food. Which is what I'm going to need after Lucas and I tell his brothers and our friends our big announcement. After we convince them that we know what we're doing.

After we convince them we're in love and want to get married.

I have no idea how long our friends have been watching us, but it's clear they all know about the kiss. They're staring at us, a kaleidoscope of emotions on their shocked faces.

They're waiting for an explanation. An explanation Lucas and I don't exactly have.

Oh, crap.

"Sooooo," he begins, and I have to hiccup back a laugh at how

65

smoothly this is going. "I guess it's time for Simone and me to come clean about something that happened years ago."

The awkwardness of his words spreads through the room.

"We never mentioned it before 'cause Aiden was my best friend..." His voice catches on the name. The pain in his voice and my brother's name are the fishhooks that tug on my heart. I grab Lucas's hand, a move not missed by his brothers and my friends, and give it a light squeeze.

Despite everything that has happened over the past ten years, holding Lucas's hand feels right. Natural. Like the piece of a puzzle slipping into place.

Because of Aiden.

And how the three of us will always be intricately linked together.

"Simone was his little sister," Lucas says, his voice recovered and more determined than before. "So we hid our feelings for each other from everyone. But we've decided to make things official."

"So you're dating now?" Zara purses her lips, but I can't tell what she's thinking.

"We're—we're engaged," I blurt, the words stumbling over each other.

The room goes clock-ticking quiet. Zara, Kim, and Emily stare at us as if we've turned into prancing unicorns. Troy, Garrett, and Kellan have their lips pressed together, silencing what could be laughter. Or not.

Jerome's expression is a cross between them all.

Did Lucas's brothers know he was going to ask me to marry him? Did Lucas pull the short straw when it came to who would be tying the knot, and I happened to be convenient due to our shared history?

"Is that why you guys were so awkward when you saw each other earlier at Treats?" Zara asks. "Was that because you were trying not to jump each other's bones?"

"Yes, it was exactly that," I say in a rush. That excuse works for both Treats and when Lucas showed up here. *Thanks, Zara, for saving our asses.*

"This isn't because of what I said this afternoon, is it?" Troy's winter-harsh tone makes it clear what he thinks of our announcement. "For Christ's sake, I was joking."

Appearing more confused than before, Emily turns to him. "What are you talking about?" Her gaze cuts to Lucas. "What's he talking about?"

"Robert and Tuuli Wakefield are starting to have second thoughts about selling the land to us," Troy says, not giving Lucas a chance to answer. "Not because of the drug charges. But because none of us are married or dating."

Kellan nods as if he's analyzing our news from all possible angles. "It might work."

"Might work?" Troy exclaims. "It's an idiot idea."

Lucas snorts a laugh, the sound more irritated than amused. "Thanks for the vote of confidence."

Troy's glare homes in on Garrett, who doesn't so much as flinch. "And what do you think about this?"

"It might work. Or it might explode in our faces." Garrett's voice is deep and even, not giving away what he's really thinking.

"We're marrying because we're in love." My words sound a little sturdier on their feet than when I blurted Lucas and I are engaged.

The clock-ticking silence returns for an encore. So I bandage up old wounds and fasten a smile on my face. I can do this. Aiden would've loved the brothers' plan for the outdoor program for vets. It fits right up there with his college degree.

After our parents died, Aiden was there for me. When I woke from nightmares during stormy nights, he would sneak into my bedroom and hold me until I fell asleep. Grams had done everything she could to make things easier for us during those early years, but Aiden was my lifeline.

My reason to keep living.

I owe this to him.

Lucas's arm circles my waist, and he pulls me to him. He's more muscular than he was the last time I was with him, but otherwise, there's a familiarity about him that hasn't changed.

"Simone's right. We're marrying because we're in love." He kisses me on the temple, and I swear I hear dreamy sighs from my girls.

Emily grins like the mother of the bride and walks over to us. "Well, in that case, congratulations, you two." She throws her arms around us, and I laugh at her exuberance. "I always suspected something was going on between you two back in college." She steps away from us and holds out her hand to Zara and Kim. "Okay, you two, pay up."

Zara shakes her head. "We made that bet during our freshman year of college. It doesn't count anymore."

"You bet that Lucas and I were involved?" How did I not know this?

Emily laughs. "This is a small town, what else did you expect us to do?"

Except, we were in Eugene at the time. And Eugene is a city.

"How come you never mentioned this before? You never asked me if we were sneaking around." And here I thought I'd done a great job of hiding Lucas's and my secret. And if they'd figured that out, what else have they figured out?

Kim lifts a shoulder, eyes gleaming with barely suppressed laughter. "Because it was a forbidden fling, so we didn't expect either of you to own up to it."

Emily nods, all kinds of emotions on her face, but mostly eager. Maybe a little too eager. "Plus, we thought it was romantic."

Kim and Zara each hand Emily a single dollar bill.

"That's all you bet?" Talk about making me feel cheap.

"What did you expect? We were nineteen at the time." Zara gives Lucas and me an enthusiastic hug, which is followed by Kim hugging us with the same level of enthusiasm.

At least they're all for our marriage.

Troy studies Lucas and me for a beat. I have no idea what he sees in our expressions. I suspect there's a heavy layer of guilt on mine. I don't like lying to my friends, but that doesn't mean I haven't done it before.

"I guess there's nothing left to say on the topic other than welcome to the family, sis." Troy hugs me. Maybe not with the same level of enthusiasm as my girls, but the sincerity is there. "I hope you know what you're doing," he whispers in my ear.

That's the thing. I don't know what I'm doing. Lucas and I don't know what we're doing. Being in love isn't new to me. Faking it is.

Garrett is next to hug me, squeezing me like he had when he showed up at the apartment. "I've always wanted a little sister to boss around."

Lucas smacks him on the arm. "You don't get to boss my future wife."

Kellan is the last Carson brother to hug me. "Are you sure you want to be part of this family?" He nods at his three brothers.

I smile, mostly out of relief. Everyone is buying that Lucas and I are supposedly in love. "Of course."

The truth is, growing up, I'd always felt like I was part of their family. Both Aiden and I had. After our parents died, their mom and dad treated us like we were their own. Joanna was the person I went to when I felt awkward talking to Grams about certain things. Like boys.

Lucas sits in an armchair. I make a move for the couch. He grabs me by the waist and pulls me onto his lap. And like everything else, the familiarity of the move washes over me in a warm embrace.

"When's the big day?" Emily is practically glowing. If there were a prize for Most Excited at our news, Em would win it.

Lucas's thumb caresses the skin on the back of my hand. "We haven't discussed it yet. But we'll let you know as soon as we figure it out. And we'd appreciate it if you don't mention it to anyone yet.

We want to wait until Rose is home and we've told her first before we announce it to everyone else."

There's a fluttering in my chest at how he's thinking of Grams. The news of our engagement will be coming out of nowhere. She'll be a little shocked when we tell her. But Lucas is right. She needs to hear it from us first.

His touch is a soothing balm. I lean into him, absorbing his heat and strength. His arm tightens around me, and I lock away the pain that has plagued me for so long.

Now that everyone has accepted our news, the topic switches to things that don't involve our surprise engagement, what happened to my grandmother, or the drug charges.

Once everyone calls it a night, Lucas walks me to my car at the far end of the visitor parking lot. "How are you doing?"

He could be referring to so many things, but I go with the simplest answer. "I'm fine. Just getting used to the idea of being back here—especially now that it's no longer just for an extended visit."

The pine-scented breeze flutters a strand of hair in my face. Lucas tucks it in place, his calloused thumb brushing my skin. At his touch, I feel the thump of my heart, hear the thrum of my pulse.

He leans down, his velvety lips against mine an invitation to the fiery pits of hell. *It's all for show*, I remind my body. *Like the earlier kiss on the balcony.*

After everything crumbled between us following the accident he doesn't know about, I swore I'd never be able to be near Lucas again. But here we are, with me getting ready to spend the rest of my life with him.

With me too afraid to tell him the truth about the condom that failed, the accident that killed our unborn daughter, the hysterectomy.

Too afraid...too afraid to ask him what happened in Afghanistan. What happened that left Lucas and my brother so broken when they came home.

11

SIMONE

The next morning, after my daily run, I enter Zara's café to pick up a treat for Grams and to have lunch before heading to the hospital. Kim and Emily are waiting for me at a table next to the window.

A group of women in their fifties sitting at a nearby table all turn to look at me. I don't recognize any of them, but I get the feeling they know who I am. Because I'm Rose's granddaughter? Or because I'm linked to Lucas?

Ignoring the women, I wave to Kim and Emily and walk to the counter to put in my order. The yeasty scent of fresh-baked bread mingles in the air with an assortment of spices, leaving me drooling and my stomach rumbling.

Zara flashes me a grin that somehow says she still can't believe I'm engaged. "Did Em tell you why she wants to meet us for lunch?"

"Nope. Not even a tiny hint."

"Do you think it has anything to do with yours and Lucas's big news?" The volume of Zara's voice drops. Any lower, it'll be sweeping the floor.

"I can't imagine what she could want to talk to us about that has to do with that." I keep the volume of my voice level with Zara's.

I tell her my order and pay for it. One of Zara's employees takes her place at the counter, and Zara and I walk over to join Emily and Kim at their table.

The whisper of voices from the group of fiftysomething-year-old women follows me there. I survey the other customers while embracing my 007.

A few individuals glance at me, but I don't get any vibes that scream they're capable of planting drugs in a house. Or even breaking into a house and hiding drugs for whatever reason.

But what do I know?

"Wow, your slave driver of a boss lets you leave this early for lunch?" I say to Emily, referring to Kellan.

"It's the weekend. And besides, I have Kellan wrapped around my little finger."

"When are you finally telling your boss that you're in love with him?" Zara's you-know-I'm-right grin is directed at Emily.

"*Shh*, people will hear you." Emily's voice is quieter than a baby field mouse. "Anyway, we're not here to talk about my unrequited love life. We're here to talk about Simone's W-E-D-D-I-N-G."

Kim and Zara laugh.

I check over my shoulder to make sure Lucas's and my secret is still safe. No one seems to be currently interested in our conversation or me. I turn back to my friends. "You think people won't understand what you're spelling?"

Em shrugs halfheartedly. "So, I wanted to talk to you last night about something, but I don't want Kellan to know about it. Not yet, anyway. I want to create a wedding consulting company that specializes in mountain weddings. Specifically, our mountains. Zara, you've been thinking of expanding your business to include catering. And Simone, I thought maybe you would like to put together special bridal subscription boxes for it. Kim, have you ever thought of doing wedding photography?"

Kim picks up her glass of iced green tea. "Not really. The

thought of dealing with bridezillas gives me a bad case of hives in places that you never want to experience hives."

We all cringe at the image.

One of Zara's employees brings Zara and me our food.

Zara cuts a piece of her *KuKu Paka*. "I wonder if there's a way to figure out if a bride-to-be is going to turn into a bridezilla before you agree to work with them."

I pick up my overstuffed veggie delight ciabatta sandwich, taking care the fillings don't fall out. "Maybe there's a questionnaire you can get them to fill out." I'm joking. Kinda.

"I like that idea." Kim lowers her glass to the table. "Then I'd be more interested in doing the occasional wedding photography. But only if the bride and groom share my artistic vision. I want to have fun shooting the photos."

"I was hoping you'd say that," Em says. "I'll keep looking for someone to take regular wedding photos if the bride and groom lack the imagination to go beyond the typical. But if we have some photos of your vision to show prospective clients, they'll know ahead of time what they can expect with you as the award-winning photographer."

Emily turns to me. "I was hoping to be *your* wedding consultant. It would be great exposure. So what do you think?"

"I have to talk to Lucas first, but I can't see him having any issues with that, Em. He's a guy. What does he know about weddings?" That makes two of us. It's not as if for the past decade I've been creating Pinterest boards for my dream wedding.

"Perfect. This would also be a great opportunity to promote your subscription boxes. Maybe you could come up with special wedding-day and honeymoon boxes."

"Oh, I love that idea. I could even come up with a series of boxes leading up to the big day." I mentally jot down a few ideas for them. That would certainly help grow my business.

"If I get to shoot your wedding photos," Kim says to me, "and it's all right with you and Lucas, we can use some of the images for our individual businesses. I would also shoot some photos of the reception setup, so we can showcase the food."

"I was hoping you three would be my bridesmaids. How will you do that if you're also catering, organizing, and shooting the wedding?"

Zara pats my hand. "Don't worry. We're talented multitaskers. We'll figure something out. We have no intention of missing out on your big day."

Emily removes a thick, well-used agenda from her oversized purse and starts writing down notes.

A woman in her early twenties approaches our table. She's pretty and perky. Like an overzealous cheerleader hyped on caffeine. "Is it true?"

"Is what true?" Zara asks even though the question wasn't directed to any of us in particular.

"That Lucas Carson is selling moon rocks?" The girl almost whispers the question.

"No, he's not a drug dealer. Never has been one. Never will be one." Zara's voice has a *shoo-shoo* command as if she's trying to get rid of a pesky raccoon rummaging through the dumpster.

I bite into a piece of fermented cabbage, holding back what I want to say to the girl. Is this what it will always be like? Because the cops found drugs in Lucas's house? "God, this *kimchi* is incredible." I level a *scram* glare at her.

The girl gets the hint and scurries from our table.

Zara watches her leave the café, then waves her fork at Kim. "Thanks. Kim's mom taught me how to make it. She taught me how to make all of the South Korean foods I rotate on the menu."

Kim laughs, the sound bright and carefree. "Yes, she hasn't let me forget that you make a better *kimchi* than I do."

Zara grins like a girl who just got straight A's on her report card.

"For your business social media photos, what are you thinking of doing?" Kim asks. I explain my vision for them. I've had time to do some research over the past few days and narrow things down.

"If you want, I can regularly take photos of you and Lucas together to post on the sites. Assuming he's okay with that."

"Thank you. I'm sure he will be." I assume he understands that would be part of our business arrangement of being husband and wife.

"Does the wedding consulting business mean you're quitting your job with Kellan?" Zara digs her fork into her rice.

Shaking her head, Em picks up her glass of water. "No. Not right now, anyway. It'll take time to develop a clientele base to the point where it will be worth it for me to leave my job, which I still love doing."

"What exactly do you do for Kellan? I thought you were teaching elementary school in Maple Ridge." I take a bite of my sandwich.

"I was until two years ago, thanks to budgetary cutbacks. Since then, I've been doing this and that for Kellan."

Zara releases a deep-throated laugh. "Don't even try to get more than that from her. She likes to keep an air of mystery about what she really does with the big guy."

A blush spreads up Emily's neck and pinkens her cheeks. "You make it sound dirty."

"No, it's only you who has dirty thoughts when it comes to your boss," Zara says.

A weird sensation prickles the back of my neck, and I glance over at the table with the fiftysomething women. None of them are paying attention to me. No one in the café is looking my way.

But knowing that still doesn't smother the feeling that someone is watching me.

12

LUCAS

"You want to explain why we're going to Eugene?" Troy asks from the driver's seat of his truck. He pulls onto the quiet street from my driveway. A few doors down, a neighbor is mowing his lawn, and the two young kids across the street are chasing each other around their mom's rock garden.

If I had my way, I'd be in the driver's seat. But the agreement was, if he came to the city with me, he was driving. "I need to get an engagement ring for Simone, and I need your help."

"Not sure where to start with any of that. How about with you needing my help. Why the hell would I know anything about engagement rings?"

"I dunno. I figured between you, Garrett, and Kellan, you're most likely to have a clue."

"They shot you down, didn't they?"

"Yeah. That, too."

Troy laughs, shaking his head.

An ache twitches in my injured shoulder, and I attempt to knead it out. I don't even have to look to know storm clouds are gathering in the west.

"Why are you really marrying Simone?" Troy asks after we've

been driving for about twenty minutes. A mix of farmland and woods stretches in all directions along the highway, the vegetation swaying in the wind. "And don't give me that crap about you two reconnecting after sneaking around together all those years."

"Hey, weren't you the one who suggested only yesterday that I marry her to keep our bid for the land alive?"

"I told you I was joking. I didn't think you would actually ask her. Especially after you told me she wasn't the solution to our problem."

"What can I say? Simone and I talked on the balcony and came to a mutual decision that would benefit both of us. Our marriage will help her with her subscription box business as much as it will help us secure the property."

"Christ, with romantic sentiments like that, it's a wonder you were still single until last night."

"Hey, at least one of us is romantic," I say, knowing damn well what he's implying. "Otherwise, we'd have no chance in hell to buy that land."

He turns his head a fraction to flash me a raised eyebrow. "That's your idea of romantic?" He grunts a laugh and returns his attention to the highway. "You think it'll make a difference? With the Wakefields?"

"I have no idea, but I don't have a choice. Someone wanted to take me down for whatever reason, so it makes sense I'm the one who gets married and tries to fix the damage."

"We're not talking about fixing a stalled engine. We're talking about marrying Simone."

"There's nothing wrong with Simone."

"Never said there was. But you've never been interested in marrying, so are you sure this is the right thing to do? Doesn't Simone deserve better than that?"

"Of course she does. But you're forgetting, she gets something out of this, too."

"Right, a husband for hire." His tone is sharp enough to slice and dice. "Do you think this is what Aiden would've wanted?"

Guilt surges through me like a tidal wave, threatening to drown all in its path. *Shit. Shit. Shitcrap. Shit.* Why did he have to mention her brother? My best friend?

It was a low blow. And Troy knows it.

"No, but Aiden is dead." My tone is harsh, wintery. "This is what Simone wants. For her business."

The inside of the truck falls silent, with the exception of country music playing at a low volume. *Crap.* I'm not doing this. Not with Troy. He's the one who always has my back. He's not being the asshole.

That honor goes to me.

Dammit.

"Do you love her?" His question comes out of nowhere, his tone once again calm and even.

At the turnoff ahead of us, a car waits for the chance to steer onto the highway. Turn right and it heads toward Eugene. Left, the Three Sisters mountain range and Maple Ridge. Cross the highway and it heads south.

Or the car can turn around and head back to where it started.

The driver's choices are simple.

"Does it matter if I love her?" I ask. "We've already agreed to get married. There's no turning back now."

"You can always turn back. If this is really what you and Simone want, then fine. I'll support your decision. But Simone is like a sister to me. I don't want to see her get hurt. I don't want to see either of you get hurt."

"I know. She's like a...well, she's not like a sister to me. But you're overthinking this. You know how much she loved her brother. She's doing this for him as much as she's doing it for herself and for us."

"What happens if the prosecutor proves without a doubt you're guilty? You could be facing a lifetime in jail. Then what happens with you and Simone?"

"Simone and I have a plan in place in case that happens. She still wants to marry me, despite the risks," I tell Troy, my own doubts lingering at the edge. What if this blows up in our faces? Simone will be the one hurting the most.

And what if it doesn't?

A half smile jerks onto Troy's face. "Then I guess she deserves the best engagement ring you can find for putting up with your dumb ass."

"Do you have any idea what style you're interested in?" A long glass counter filled with several rows of diamond rings stretches between the saleswoman and me.

At my clueless expression, she lists words like "princess" and "straight trillion" and "radiant." They make as much sense to me as "balls to the wall" and "lifer" and "ditty bag" probably do to her.

"Something that looks good." I scan the rings in the display case. The woman hovers like a magpie searching for something big and sparkly. And she's homing in on my wallet.

"Aren't you supposed to spend two times your monthly salary on the ring?" Troy asks, peering into the glass case. The question is asked so casually, innocently, but I know better. "Now that you're unemployed, that's not a lot of money."

Any other time, I'd glare at him for the reminder about my job. But he's not doing it to be a jerk.

The woman makes a tiny sound that borders on a choked huff. "Well, I'll let you keep looking." She flashes me a smile that has been stuck together with superglue, but the pieces don't fit perfectly together. Then she walks away, writing me off.

"I owe you one," I say under my breath.

Troy knows that hovering salespeople irritate the hell out of me. "Not to sound like her pet parrot, but do you have any idea what you're looking for? We're not talking about selecting a burger at a restaurant."

"I'm well aware of that. I just figure I'll know what I'm looking for when I see it."

"Maybe you should've asked Jerome to help you. He's married. He knows how to pick out an engagement ring."

"He and Kim went away for the night."

"And you couldn't have waited till he got back?"

"Simone and I don't have time for that." I continue studying the rings. "Rose should be home later next week if nothing changes with her condition. And I plan to propose to Simone in front of her."

"Didn't you propose to her on Zara's balcony?" He points to a silver ring with a square diamond. "How 'bout that one?"

"I did, but I want to make it official. And nothing says official like proposing in front of the woman's grandmother. I like that one better." I point at the square diamond with the corners cut off.

"Didn't Jerome give you any hints?"

"He told me to pick something that Simone will like and fits her personality."

"You haven't seen her in what? Nine or ten years? How are you supposed to know which ring fits her personality?"

"I doubt she's changed that much since I last saw her." I wave to the woman, indicating I've found the perfect ring.

13

SIMONE

A week after Lucas and I decided to marry for business reasons, I push Grams's wheelchair up the ramp Troy installed to her house. Fluffy white clouds float overhead like welcome-home balloons.

Even though she won't need the wheelchair permanently, Grams will be in it for the next few weeks, so Troy made some modifications to her home.

"You know, Troy is single," Grams says as I unlock the front door.

"I know."

"He's a nice boy. Nice to look at, too." She winks at me with the sass of someone her age minus six decades. "But then, all the Carson boys are nice to look at."

I can't stop the laughter that bubbles up.

"Bigger muscles, too." She pretends to flex her muscles—frail arms hidden beneath the sleeves of her emerald-green blouse. Her body is still bruised, but the worst of the marks have faded.

I chuckle, the sound throaty and rough at the memory of those bruises. "Yep, definitely bigger muscles." Some very nice ones from what I can tell.

81

I ease the wheelchair into the house, and we enter the living room.

Grams gasps, surprise and delight widening her eyes as she takes in the dozen floral arrangements scattered around the space. "Did my house turn into a florist shop while I was away?"

"A lot of people in Maple Ridge love you, and they wanted to make sure you know that." I park her wheelchair next to the couch and pick up a giant card from the dining room table.

On the front is a painting of a smiling tree and a smiling sun. The flowers standing on the grass are also smiling. "One of the second-grade classrooms painted the picture," I tell her. "And everyone at the school signed the card."

I open it up to reveal several pages filled with scrawled kids' names, as well as the neat signatures from the school staff. Grams used to help with the school's reading program. She began volunteering there when I was seven years old and kept on volunteering until a few years ago, when age deteriorated her eyesight.

I pass her the card. The tremor in her hands becomes more noticeable.

She scans the names. Her eyes glisten, damp with longing and delight and frustration. "I wish I could remember what happened." She closes the card and places it on her lap.

"I know." I sit on the couch and cover her hand with mine. She remembers nothing from the hit-and-run—not even leaving her house to go for the walk.

"At least then the police would have more leads." Her voice isn't strong and determined like it was when I was growing up. Now softened with age, her voice is a whisper of what it used to be. But there's still an edge to it, blunted slightly with time, that hasn't changed.

"I don't know if it would have made a difference. There were witnesses, and none of them could identify the driver. I'm not sure if you could have either." I stand and kiss her forehead like she did whenever I scraped my knee as a kid. "The physician said your memory of what happened might return. Your main goal right now is to recuperate. Let the cops figure out the rest."

Hopefully they do a better job than they are with identifying the culprit who set Lucas up.

"How's Lucas doing? Penny Whithouser visited me in the hospital, claiming he was the one who hit me." Grams's tone is one I recognize from when I was a kid and tattled on Aiden.

"Considering everything, he's doing okay. He's not guilty of what the police are accusing him of. Someone set him up."

"I know. Penny's a troublemaking busybody who has nothing better to do with her time. Lucas is a good boy who's not capable of anything he's been accused of." She squeezes my hand. "I don't suppose you can make me some tea?"

"One tea coming up. Did you want me to put the TV on for you?"

"Yes, please." She requests her favorite mystery show, with a sleuth in her seventies. "Let's see if I do a better job solving the crime on this episode than the police are doing figuring out who hit me and left the scene."

My mouth twitches into a barely-there smile. "I'm sure if you do, the chief of police will be more than happy to hire you to help with their caseload."

I assist her onto the couch, then walk to the kitchen. I fill the kettle and place it on the stove. "If you'd like, I can take you to the store next week to pick out some annuals. I'll do the garden, and you can tell me what to do and entertain me with some of your childhood tales." I never get tired of hearing them.

"I would like that." Her eyes remain glued to the TV screen.

The doorbell rings.

"Are you expecting anyone?" I ask.

"This is Maple Ridge. We don't book appointments to see friends. We just show up."

I walk down the hallway and open the front door, expecting to find one of Grams's friends on the stoop.

I'm wrong. It's my future husband.

It's really happening.

It's really happening.

It's really happening.

We're about to tell Grams that we're engaged.

"Hi?" My voice squeaks like a hinge thirsty for WD-40.

The Lucas I know lives in worn jeans and plain T-shirts. This version is wearing a white dress shirt and black slacks. The top two buttons of his shirt are undone.

And damn, he's hot. Hotter than hot.

I've worked in a world where business attire is the norm. The concept of men in suits isn't new to me. But this is the first time seeing a man dressed this way has caused warm fluttery sensations in my stomach.

"Are those for Grams?" I point to the bouquet of dahlias in his hand, trying to ignore the impact he's having on my body.

"No, they're for you." He hands me the assortment of pastel flowers. My favorites. "Do you still love dahlias?"

My breath hitches and I feel my eyes widen. "You remember that?"

He nods, relief filling his eyes, his smile.

"They're really for me?" There's a breathlessness to my voice.

"You sound like no one has ever given you flowers."

"Um...well, they haven't." My ex-boyfriend didn't believe in giving flowers to the women in his life. He wasn't even allergic to them. He just figured, what was the point? It isn't like they last long. By the time they hit the store, they're flawed, imperfect. Much like me. "They're beautiful. Thank you."

I kiss Lucas on the cheek, lingering as I inhale the scent that's all mountains and sunshine and man. "You ready for this?"

"Definitely. You?"

"Absolutely." Well, almost ready. More so than I was yesterday. And the day before that...

God, what's Grams going to say? She loves Lucas like a grandson. Even when he was getting into trouble as a kid and acting like his nickname, a loose cannon.

But marriage?

And so soon?

Lucas takes off his shoes and follows me into the kitchen. I'm holding the dahlias like a bridal bouquet. And the smile on my face feels three sizes too big—but more natural than any I've worn in a while.

I grab an old-fashioned milk jug from under the sink and fill it with water. Lucas goes over to visit with Grams on the couch. He leans down and hugs her and kisses her cheek like a dutiful grandson. Or in this case, a soon-to-be dutiful grandson-in-law.

Grandson-in-law. This isn't how I imagined my life. I thought I would fall in love. The man would declare his love for me. He would propose. We'd get married. Have a family.

The traditional way.

Lucas sits next to Grams. She pauses her show and grins at him like he's her favorite TV sleuth come to life. And he has just asked her to help him solve a crime.

"How are you doing?" He asks as if he genuinely cares. Because he does.

"Better now that Gumdrop is back to stay for a bit." The smile Grams directs my way is even brighter than the one she gave Lucas. "As much as I love visiting you in Portland, it's wonderful to have you home. Even if it's just for a short time while I recover."

"How would you feel if she stayed longer?" Lucas grins at her. It's a sexy, boyish grin. And my stomach goes warm and fluttery once more.

I place the bouquet on the coffee table—the only place left that doesn't have any get-well-soon floral arrangements. I sit in an armchair.

My fingers play with the hem of my tank top, twirling it around my index finger.

Twirling. Twirling. Twirling.

To the point that the fabric is almost cutting off my finger's circulation. I untwist and start again.

Grams's eyes sparkle like the sun on the lake. "Any time she can give me is a gift."

The kettle whistles on the stove. I race over to it and turn off the burner. They talk while I make her a cup of tea, filling it only halfway.

I bring the tea to her. She takes the cup and saucer from me, her hands jerky. China rattles against china. I steady her hands with mine. I'm not used to seeing her quite this shaky, but it doesn't seem to bother her.

She manages to take a sip. "Oh, that's just what I needed. So what's this nonsense about you being a criminal, Lucas?"

Grinning, I sit in the armchair near where Lucas is sitting on the couch.

"It's nothing you have to worry about. My lawyer will prove I'm innocent."

Hopefully Lucas is right about that. He's got to be right.

"Any idea who set you up?" Grams has the same expression her favorite sleuth gets when she's hot on a lead.

"Grams, you're not getting involved." My tone isn't sharp, but hopefully it's still enough to get my point across. It's a good thing she has to get around in a wheelchair for another few weeks. Otherwise, as soon as I turn my back, she'll interview everyone in Maple Ridge, dig for their biggest secrets, snoop into their lives. Put herself in danger. I almost lost her once already. I won't lose her to whoever is trying to ruin Lucas's life.

"Simone's right." Lucas's warm but firm gaze is steady on Gram's.

She doesn't flinch. She just gives him the same innocent expression twelve-year-old Aiden used on her whenever he planned to get into trouble.

"Rose, whoever set me up isn't playing games. Let the cops deal with it."

Her frail shoulders lift, but a fire flickers and flares in her eyes. "All right. For now."

"Good. Now there is a reason I'm here, besides missing your sparkling personality." Lucas winks at Grams. She giggles like a girl crushing on the high school quarterback.

Here we go.

I open my mouth to explain that Lucas and I are engaged. The words don't come out. They're stuck—stuck in my mouth with superglue.

Lucas stands in front of me and takes something from his pocket. He drops to one knee, and the movement jump-starts my heart, hot-wires my tear ducts. I gulp in a lungful of air.

OhmyGod...he's...Lucas is...

When I discovered I was pregnant with his baby over ten years ago, I fantasized about this moment. Fantasized about Lucas being excited that he was going to be a father. The father of our child. That he would tell me how much he loved me and would ask me to marry him.

But then fantasy and reality crashed head on. Left nothing but crunched and dented dreams.

"Simone, I've been in love with you for as long as I can remember. And now that you're back in my life, I'm hoping you'll be my wife." He lifts his hand, revealing the ring box, and flips the lid open. The air in my lungs rushes out in a *whoosh*. "Will you marry me?"

Stupid tears fog my vision. Tears mourning how none of this is real. We're not marrying because we're in love and can't live without each other.

A whirlwind of emotions stirs up inside me, sweeping me up in stunned shock, heartbreak, awe, regret, joy, guilt, sorrow. Tears stream down my cheeks.

I open my mouth to tell him yes. But instead, laughter erupts from my lungs, loud and uncontrollable.

I slap my hands over my mouth. But it's not enough. I can't stop giggling—and that's making the tears come harder.

I don't even know why I'm giggling. It's as if my emotions have no idea what I'm supposed to be feeling and short-circuited my brain.

Since I can't say the words, I nod, my hands still over my mouth. Lucas smiles, seemingly not at all confused by my reaction to his news. Or maybe he just thinks I'm that good an actress.

Grams is grinning so hard; her cheeks will be sore for the next few days. "I always knew you two had a thing for each other. I just didn't realize you've been dating all this time."

"We've been keeping it a secret," Lucas says. "We wanted things to progress at their own pace without feeling any pressure from family and friends."

Great answer.

He removes the silver ring from the box and slides it on my finger.

"It's beautiful," I manage to say between giggles. It's the type of diamond I would have chosen. The radiant-cut gemstone is big, but it doesn't scream, *Look at me.* It says it's confident in our commitment.

Confident it will fool even the disbelievers.

"Kiss the groom-to-be!" Grams's high-pitched tone rings like a wineglass being tapped.

My gaze lands on a framed photo on the mantel of Aiden, Lucas, and me. It was taken the summer before they left for the Marines. We were happy. Smiling.

No, that's not entirely true. There's something about Lucas in the picture. Something brighter. Like the spotlight on a lighthouse, guiding ships to safety. The beacon in the storm.

His arm is around my shoulders in the photo. Strong and reliable. The person I could always rely on.

My uncontrollable giggling dies away.

"Yes, Simone, kiss your future husband." Lucas's words are said with such tenderness, they tug at something inside me.

It's really happening. We're officially engaged.

Lucas presses his lips to mine. A chaste kiss. Something to appease my grandmother. Nothing more. His hands rest lightly on my hips. My skin under his palms tingles at his touch.

More. I need more.

Grams huffs, the sound slightly whiny and comical. "God, if that's your idea of a kiss, I definitely shouldn't expect great-grand-children."

My muscles tighten and my smile strains and shame knots deep in my belly. I should tell her I can't give her great-grandchildren. But admitting the truth also means telling her things I've kept locked away from her for so long.

That I've kept locked away from Lucas.

Lucas laughs the deep-throated rumble that shoots straight to my core and pushes aside my thoughts. His thumbs caress my hips. "We should give her what she wants."

"Make it passionate." Grams's movie-director tone comes complete with clapperboard. "I've just been freed from a boring hospital stay and need something to get my blood pumping."

How I don't burst into another round of giggling after her comment is beyond me.

"You heard the lady." The grin on Lucas's face should be registered as a lethal weapon. A weapon that leaves a girl defenseless.

He leans down and goes in for take two. Our lips move lightly together, teasing, remembering. I half expect Grams to yell "Cut!" and tell us to try again. To save her the effort, I open my mouth and let him in.

The moment I do, I know I'm in trouble.

Lucas's tongue brushes mine, and the memory of all those times we kissed in the past come flooding back. Waking my body up to all that I missed. With Lucas.

My arms loop around his neck, pulling him closer. His arms wrap around my waist, accomplishing the same.

Flames flare inside me, their heat licking me thoroughly. I can't remember the last time kissing a man felt this delicious.

This dangerous.

This real.

14

LUCAS

"All right, you two," Rose says. "Details. So how long have you been dating?"

Simone returns to her armchair, face damp with tears. Simone's acting is better than I realized. She even had me convinced for a second that she was excited I asked her to marry me.

I sit on the chair next to her and take her hand with the engagement ring. Judging by Rose's expression, she approves of the move. Her gaze volleys between us, waiting for one of us to speak first. She's grinning and buzzing with energy. I don't remember the last time I saw her like this.

"We started dating Simone's freshman year in college," I tell her.

"You did?" Rose's smile is bright and eager, and I'm glad what I told her isn't a lie. Well, mostly not a lie. If you ignore how the statement implies we never ended things.

Simone nods but doesn't speak. If anything, she looks slightly freaked out. Like she did when Rose mentioned great-grandchildren. I trace the back of her hand with my thumb, letting her know

91

everything will be all right. Us getting married isn't the worst thing that could happen.

I should know. Watching friends die in battle. Struggling with PTSD. Losing your best friend. Those are way worse.

Rose glances between us, her excited energy dialed up a few notches. "How come this is the first I'm hearing about it?"

"Because Aiden was my best friend, and Simone was his little sister. We knew he wouldn't approve."

Confusion tugs Rose's eyebrows together. "Why would he have been against it?"

"It's a generally accepted rule that you don't date your best friend's sister. Especially his little sister." Because things get royally screwed if the relationship blows up in your face.

"Ooh, so a forbidden romance. Even better." Rose rubs her hands together and nods for me to continue.

"Our relationship ended once I left for the Marines. It didn't feel right to have a girlfriend waiting for me in case I never returned home." Sticking close to the truth always works best in situations like this. Then it's harder to be tripped up on the lie.

Pain flickers and flares on her wrinkled face, her smile temporarily hidden behind a cloud. Aiden didn't come home the same man he'd left as.

Neither of us did.

"But once you returned home, things reignited between you and Simone?" Rose lifts her teacup to her mouth.

"No, I was injured and dealing with other issues." PTSD. "It wasn't until I visited Portland after I graduated the PT program at Washington State that I bumped into Simone. And the moment I saw her..." I smile at Simone, letting Rose fill in the rest.

"But you still kept things a secret?"

"That's right. We wanted things between us to progress at their own pace. I knew if Mom even suspected something was going on, she would've immediately been planning our wedding." I don't have to exaggerate this. I can only imagine what it will be like once we announce our engagement.

A dreamy sigh tumbles from Rose. An equally dreamy smile spreads on her lips, lightens her eyes. "That's so romantic. We should celebrate. How about we order in some Chinese food for dinner? Maybe you should invite your parents over, Lucas. And you can tell them the big news. Or did you tell them you were proposing?"

"No, Mom and Dad don't know yet."

"Are you sure you should be eating Chinese food while recovering from your injuries?" Simone asks. "You should probably have something healthier."

"No, I'm pretty certain after being stuck in the hospital I get to eat Chinese food." Rose lifts her chin.

A laugh jolts from my lungs. Simone levels a you're-so-not-helping expression at me. I try to flatline my lips, but the corners of my mouth won't have it.

Simone heaves out a breath. "All right, we can have Chinese food tonight. But then you're back to a healthy diet."

Rose grins. "As long as it's not hospital food, you have yourself a deal." She has the tone of someone who has won the first round and plans to win many more.

"How about we go for a walk, then I'll call my parents?" I tell Simone. "There are a few items you and I should discuss first." Before I break the news to them and things get out of control.

Rose picks up the TV remote from her lap. "That sounds like a great idea. And while you do that, I'll go back to watching my show."

Simone removes the cup and saucer from Rose's lap. She makes sure her grandmother is comfortable, and we head out.

"After hearing about your reaction in there when I proposed"—I jerk my head toward Rose's house—"people will have a harder time believing our engagement isn't real." And I know they *will* hear about it once the gossip grapevine catches wind of it.

Simone smiles and her cheeks turn pink. "Who knew an A minus in high school drama would pay off? Too bad Grams didn't record it on her phone. Then everyone could see it."

Yeah, too bad about that.

We walk down the sidewalk, past houses that were built before the Second World War and past infill homes that are fancy, shiny, and new. Past gardens bursting with color. Past yards sadly lacking and blue. And it quickly becomes clear that the woman I proposed to has disappeared into herself.

I reach for Simone's hand. She startles and snatches it away. She's not the same woman who sent me letters while I was deployed. I shouldn't be surprised that she's changed. It's been over ten years since we last saw each other. And we've both lost someone important to us.

The someone I promised Simone I would keep safe.

"I'm sorry," I say for so many reasons. "I figured if we're announcing our engagement soon, people should see us holding hands whenever we're together."

"Good idea." She threads her fingers with mine.

"Blake called me this morning. About the trial date. It's set for Monday, October twelfth."

Simone pauses, and I can tell she's doing the math.

"In four months and twenty days. Robert and Tuuli will be announcing their decision about the land on October fourth."

She nods, the pain in her eyes stealing my breath. Their wedding anniversary is late September, a few days before the third anniversary of Aiden's death.

Silence settles over us as we walk through the neighborhood. The buzz of a lawnmower, the bark of a dog, the chirp of a bird are the only sounds that cut through the silence like cracks in a pane of glass. But it's not enough to shatter the shield Simone has erected since she returned to Maple Ridge. That silence goes deeper than the absence of any sound.

"Troy built that house," I say after we've been walking a few minutes, and I point to the narrow, two-story building. It's modern, but it still holds the charm of the neighborhood. It belongs here without trying to be something it isn't.

Wonder widens Simone's eyes, and a smile as beautiful as a sunrise brightens her face. "He's really talented. I can't believe he went into the Marines after college instead of doing this right away."

"I think it was because at the time he was still looking for adventure." We all were—Aiden, Garrett, Kellan, Troy, and me.

"He joined the military because he thought it would be a great source of adventure? You know, there are other ways to be adventurous. Like traveling the world, exploring new cultures. All without risking your life."

"There was more to it than that. My brothers, Aiden, and I were all searching for a chance to make a difference. For Troy and me, that wasn't such a bad thing. It shaped us into who we are today."

"How so?"

"My injury didn't just make me realize I wanted to be a PT. I wanted to be a PT for military vets. I can relate to what they're going through. I understand the challenges they face, and I don't just mean the injury I'm helping them deal with."

"What about Troy?"

"A lot of his projects involve modifying homes for vets or anyone who can no longer live in their home because of a disability or medical condition. He adapts their home to meet their new needs so they don't have to move if they don't want to. If it hadn't been for his time in the Marines, he probably wouldn't have ended up doing that."

"That's incredible." She looks around. "I can't believe how much this area has changed since I was a kid. But at the same time, a lot of it hasn't changed at all."

"I think they call that progress."

Simone laughs. "Very astute...Cannon." She grins at me with the same impish gleam she had when she first gave me that nickname. After Mom grumbled I was like a loose cannon. I can't remember what I was doing at the time to earn that title.

I pull Simone to me and kiss her forehead. Then rest my brow against hers. If someone witnesses our tender moment, all the better. "So, Trouble, we should probably figure out our wedding date before my parents come over."

Simone pulls away with a soft smile and starts walking again, tugging me along. Our fingers remain threaded together. "Emily has offered to help us plan the wedding. She wants to be a wedding consultant for couples who want a destination wedding in the mountains. We'll be her practice clients."

"Does Kellan know about this?" Given that she is his employee.

"No, not yet. And you can't tell him about it. It's not like she's planning to quit her job. Not yet, anyway. But she's hoping we'll be her first clients."

"You do realize my mom will want to take over the planning?"

"She will?"

A black car drives past us, its speed barely more than a crawl. I can't see the driver to figure out if they're looking for a specific house or if there's another reason for the car's slow speed.

"You've met my mother, right?" I say, continuing to watch the car. I don't recognize it. "She's been in wedding-planning mode since the day we could walk. With the way my brothers aren't rushing to settle down, I'm sure she'll think I'm her only chance for planning a wedding."

"I guess it will be good experience for Em when it comes to working with the bride and her family."

The car slowly turns the corner. It's probably a lost tourist who took a wrong turn on Main Street.

"When do you want to tie the knot then?" I ask.

"We probably don't want to wait too long. But we also don't want to rush things. We don't want the Wakefields to think we're getting married just so your bid isn't eliminated from consideration. We want them to believe we're marrying for love."

"Knowing the people in this town, they'll probably assume I knocked you up if we get married too soon."

Simone glances over to the other side of the street, where a dog is barking at a squirrel that ran up a tree. "Yes, that, too. But I don't want to wait just to prove them wrong."

"How long will Em need to plan the wedding?"

"Dunno. I've never planned a wedding before. But Zara is looking to cater weddings, and Em convinced Kim to do wedding photography for certain clients. Both want to be involved with our wedding—if that's okay with you—so that will save us time looking for those two things."

Simone stops walking and types on her phone. "We should arrange for the local newspaper to post our engagement announcement." She continues typing. "Given the gossip chain in Maple Ridge, news about the announcement will quickly reach Tuuli and Robert. But I'm sure they will have already heard the news by then from your mom. The announcement in the newspaper will make things more official." She shrugs. "Or I'm assuming it will."

Her phone pings, and she checks the screen. Types something else. Another ping. "Em said she ideally needs about four weeks. She wanted to know what's the rush, so I told her we've waited long enough to be together as husband and wife. Given that she wants to get her business up and running, she's more than okay with us having a short engagement. So, we could have the wedding next month. Or if you want to wait longer, that's fine, too. I'm good with whatever works for you. As long as we get photos of us together for my social media accounts in the meantime."

We continue walking and holding hands.

"If we're aiming for a normal marriage," I say, "I get that will involve holding hands in public. But what will it entail when it's just the two of us alone? I want to make sure we're on the same page."

"Are you asking me if sex is on the table, Cannon?"

"Table. Bed. Shower." I know that's not what she meant, but she must know she was setting herself up for that answer.

She snorts a laugh. "Cute." Then she releases the long sigh I recognize to mean she's thinking things through. "I don't want to have sex just because we agreed to marry for business reasons. I have to care about the guy enough to want to have sex with him." She shakes her head. "That probably sounds silly to you because you're a guy. Guys don't need to be emotionally involved for sex to be great. And well, we have had sex before. You and me. Together. Lots of times."

Her cheeks redden, and now she's the one who is damn adorable.

"So you want to wait?" There's no judgment or disappointment in my tone. Just straight honesty and understanding.

She nods, pulling her bottom lip between her teeth. "That's probably not what you want to hear…"

Given how that move with her lip is making me hard, she's right about that. But I do respect her wishes. Always have. "No, that's fine. If you want to wait, we can wait until when and if you're ready."

Simone looks over my shoulder. "Uh, oh. Is Beatrice Lewis still head of Maple Ridge's Gossip Grapevine?"

"As far as I know…" It's not something I keep track of. "Why?"

"She's standing on her porch, watching us. Maybe we should kiss. That will help our engagement appear more believable."

"Good idea, Trouble." I pull Simone to me, moving our bodies so Beatrice gets a better view. I cup the back of Simone's head.

Then our lips meet in a kiss worthy of the gossip grapevine.

"I KNEW IT!" MOM SAYS, NEXT TO DAD ON THE COUCH. SIMONE AND I have just announced our engagement.

"Knew what?" I ask, linking my hand with Simone's and resting them on the arm of her chair.

"That you two were in love in college. Anyone with two eyes could see it. Can I see the ring?" Mom's eyes are as shiny as the diamond in Simone's ring.

Simone leans across the coffee table to show it to her. Mom inspects the ring. "This is gorgeous." She smiles. "I used to think of you like my daughter, Simone. But now you really will be." Mom releases Simone's hand, letting my fiancée sit back in her chair.

Fiancée. That's one word I never thought would be part of my vocabulary. It feels odd. Foreign. It's also a word I won't have to think about for long. Soon, it will be "wife" I'll need to wrap my brain around.

"Have you picked a date yet?" Mom asks.

"We were thinking next month," I reply.

"Next month? So soon?"

"When you realize you want to spend the rest of your life with someone, you want the rest of your life to start as soon as possible." Simone sounds like she's reciting a passage from a book she needs to know for a test.

Mom sits up straighter, grinning. "Oh. *When Harry Met Sally*. I love that movie."

I glance at Dad to see if he knows what the hell Mom's talking about. He just lifts his shoulders in a shrug.

SIMONE

On Sunday afternoon, I place a glass of pink lemonade in front of John McTyre, one of Grams's neighbors. "I'm just going for a short bike ride," I tell Grams and her friends, who look up at me from behind hands full of cards. "Is there anything else you need before I go?"

"Are you meeting up with that handsome fiancé of yours?" Grams's tone is all smiles and sunshine. It's been that way ever since Lucas proposed to me in front of her two days ago.

"No, it's just me." I owe Avery a phone call, and I'd rather talk to her where no one else can overhear me. "Good luck with bridge." I wave good-bye to them and head to the garage to retrieve my old bike.

I inflate the tires, then pedal toward the lake. The late May sun is warm, but the mountain air is a cool kiss against my bare arms.

I'm getting married.

I've repeated that to myself numerous times during the past nine days, when Lucas first suggested we get married. The idea of it still doesn't feel real.

Maybe it'll feel more real once I ask Avery to be my maid of honor.

The main beach isn't as busy as it will be in another month, but it's busy enough for me to keep pedaling past it. I stop at the rocky inlet farther along the path, at a spot where Aiden and Lucas used to fish when we were kids. I remove my shoes, sit on a boulder, and dangle my bare feet in the cold water.

The only sounds surrounding me are the occasional rustle of leaves and the caw of a crow. I pull up Avery's contact information. It's hard to believe that ten days ago I was waiting to find out if I got the promotion Irene ended up giving to Craig.

Ten days ago when I quit my job and decided to come back to Maple Ridge while Grams recovered from the hit-and-run—and then found myself engaged.

Avery answers her phone on the third ring. "Hey, I was just thinking about you. How's your grandmother doing?"

I get her up to date on the latest when it comes to Grams. This isn't the first time I've spoken or texted Avery since arriving in Maple Ridge. But I always skip over one major detail.

"Remember how you told me a lot of women who have successful small businesses post pictures of themselves with their loving spouse and adorable kids?"

"Yes?" Her reply is drawn out and a faint question mark lingers at the end. "I said your Instagram feed is impersonal. But you don't have a husband or a boyfriend."

"That's right. I didn't."

There's a momentary pause. Then a gasp from Avery's end. "Are you telling me you have a boyfriend? Already? You've only been in Maple Ridge for, what, ten days? And you already have a boyfriend? Wow." She truly does sound stunned. And impressed. "Wow. I never thought this day would—"

"I don't have a boyfriend. I'm engaged."

A clock-ticking silence reaches out from the other end of the phone line.

Followed by, "What the freaking Fudgsicle? Is this some kind of joke?" She laughs. "Phew, you had me worried for a second, Si.

Because we both know having a fake fiancé or a fake husband is not how you grow a loyal subscriber fanbase."

"You're right. It isn't. But Lucas isn't my fake fiancé. He's my real fiancé. And he'll be my real husband."

"Lucas? As in the father of...your..." The voice on the other end of the line sounds like it came from someone who just sat down hard on her couch.

"Yes, as in Lily's father."

"Does he know?"

I shake my head even though she can't see me. Saying the words out loud hurts too much.

"I'll take your silence to mean no, you haven't told him about her. What about the hysterectomy? Does he know about that?"

"No." The word comes out softer than the breeze.

"Doesn't he deserve to know about that and about Lily?" Avery's tone is free of judgment and full of the compassion I know her for.

I close my eyes against the pain of hearing my daughter's name. "It might not make a difference. The hysterectomy, I mean." I tell her everything that has happened in the last ten days. About the arrest. About the Wakefields' land and what Lucas and his brothers want to use it for.

"I'm hoping you'll be my maid of honor." I need her by my side, to be there for me. She's the only person who knows about the pregnancy and the accident and the hysterectomy. She's the only person who knows that I was once in love with Lucas. She was there for me during my darkest days. She was the light that got me through it.

And now I need her to be my light again.

"You can't marry him, Simone. You deserve true love and not a marriage of convenience. Any man would be lucky to have you. Don't settle for anything less."

I snort at the lucky part. My ex didn't share Avery's sentiments. Why should I believe it won't be the same for the next man I fall in love with? "I'm not settling for less. What Lucas and his brothers want to do is something my brother would have loved. I'm doing it for his memory. This is important to me, A."

The new silence that stretches through the phone line feels like a gaping hole in my heart.

"Are you positive you've thought this through?" she asks.

No. "Yes."

"Are you still in love with Lucas?"

"No. I haven't been in love with him in a long, long time. And he's not in love with me. Never has been. So this arrangement will be perfect. No one will get hurt, and people will only benefit from it." Hopefully. Assuming that Tuuli and Robert sell their land to Lucas and his brothers.

Avery releases a long breath that, on the phone, sounds like a heavy wind traveling through a tunnel. "I don't like that you're settling for less than you deserve, but I will definitely be there for you, Si. So yes, I would love to be your maid of honor."

16

SIMONE

Four days after Lucas officially proposed to me, I rummage through my closet. Grams never bothered to clear it out after I moved away to college and then to Portland.

She kept everything in case I wanted it at some point in the future.

I remove the wicker box from the top shelf and brush the dust from the lid with my hand. Do I open the box? Or shove it back in the closet and pretend it never existed?

Do I read the letters Lucas sent me while he was deployed? Or throw them into the firepit?

The last time I read them was the weekend of Aiden's funeral. The weekend Lucas never made it to Maple Ridge.

My breath releases in a slow exhalation, and I return the box to the shelf. I should toss the letters, but even after all these years, I'm not ready to go there yet.

I shift my attention to the large plastic container next to the wicker box. A thick layer of dust also covers its lid.

I tug an old top off a hanger, wipe the lid clean, and carry the box over to my bed. I sit down, snap open the lid, and peer inside.

Everything looks the same as it did when I left for college. I remove the pendant I wore the last time I made love to Lucas. Time has tarnished the thin metal disc, but the words stamped in it are still visible: *dreams come true*

A small dandelion, turned to fluff, is stamped to the left of the words, with a few seeds floating above them. I had looped a fine silver chain through the hoop and added a garnet Swarovski crystal. My birthstone.

I take the pendant to the bathroom, search through the drawer that contains my stuff, and remove the container of silver cleaner. It doesn't take long before the pendant looks new again, the tarnish dissolved.

I unfasten the clasp, place the chain around my neck, and let the cool disc rest against my skin, visible above the V-neck of my T-shirt.

I examine the pendant's reflection in the mirror. The last time I hammered a stamp into metal was fourteen years ago. Fourteen years since I felt that creative power hum through my fingertips.

I return to my room and take inventory of my supplies. Satisfied I have what I need, I carry the box outside. Grams is having a nap, and I don't want to wake her with my banging.

The midday sun shines approvingly on me as I set everything up on the table in the backyard. And for the next fifteen or so minutes, I work away on my project. It feels freeing to pound the stamps, create designs in the metal, form words with the letters.

By the time I'm finished, the new disc resembles the pendant I'm wearing, only this time the message reads "*you came true.*"

I study the disc, worrying my lower lip. Is this good enough for my subscription boxes? I would love to include some items that I've made, but what if they aren't good enough?

"What are you up to?" Lucas asks behind me, and I let out a startled gasp.

I glance over my shoulder, shaking my head at being so easily spooked. "God, no wonder you were such a good Marine. You probably scared the shit out of the enemy with all your sneaking around."

He gives a noncommittal shrug and sits next to me on the bench. "So, what is all this?" He's referring to the contents of the plastic container that are spread out on the table.

"I found my old metal-stamping supplies and decided to see if I remember how to use them."

He picks up the pendant I'd just made and inspects it. "I remember you making these. You gave my mom a bracelet one Christmas. She still wears it."

This makes me smile. "I thought I could start doing it again and include the products in some of my subscription boxes. I have the time now. But—but I'm not sure if this is good enough."

"I don't know what you're talking about. This looks great." He hands the pendant to me. "Mom still gets tons of compliments on the bracelet you made. I think you should definitely include your products. You're super talented."

I don't need a man to give me confidence, but Lucas's support means everything to me.

My smile this time is even brighter. "Thank you. I'll do that, then." I put the pendant on the piece of wood that I hammer on.

"Aren't you gonna kiss your fiancé?" Lucas's face is free of even a hint of a teasing smile. And his eyes...his eyes are all heat.

My breath hitches, and it takes a nanosecond for me to pull myself together. "I guess we could use some practice before the big day next month." My lips tug into a grin. "And I saw John McTyre pottering in his garden earlier." I teasingly trace my thumb along Lucas's lower lip. "Maybe we should give him a show."

The heat in Lucas's eyes dials up another notch. "Trouble, if there's one thing I'm pretty sure you and I have down pat, it's how to kiss. But if you want to practice, I'm not standing in your way." He leans in and captures my mouth with his.

We haven't kissed since the day he proposed in front of my grandmother. We've seen each other over the past few days, but we haven't kissed. Not like this. Just the thought of kissing him has my heart rate beating in triple time. My lips part, and I welcome him in.

I thought the kisses we shared in college were the best ever. I was wrong. Like with wine, his kisses have become infinitely better with time.

Our mouths move together, our tongues tangle and tease. His warm palm cups my face, and my body goes tingly. Why? Why the hell did we wait so long to kiss again? I'd forgotten just how much I loved making out with Lucas. All sense of time used to vanish whenever his lips were on mine.

Before the kiss can get too heated, I pull away and start packing up my supplies. "Grams should be getting up from her nap soon."

"Good. I'm actually here to see her. I'm volunteering to work with her between sessions with her physical therapist."

"To make sure she does it?"

He nods. "Her condition will improve quicker if she follows the schedule her therapist laid out. And I can make sure she's doing the exercises properly."

"That's great. Thanks." I smile at him, the gentle curve of my lips softening the blow of my next words. "I know we're getting married next month, but I was wondering if maybe we should wait a bit for our honeymoon. I mean, not that I'm expecting to go on an actual honeymoon. Our wedding isn't your typical wedding with the bride and groom rushing off to some romantic destination for a week of alone time and lots of sex." Heat rushes my face. God, I sound like a babbling idiot.

He sits next to me on the bench. "Won't people think it's a little odd if we don't go on a honeymoon?"

"People will believe what they want to believe. And as long as you're facing prison time, you'll be in the spotlight. It's one of the joys of living in a small town." Unfortunately.

I've heard enough gossip during the past few days to remind me how bad it gets. The heads of those same gossips would explode if they ever learned about the events from ten years ago.

"Besides it's not as if the terms of your bail allow you to fly off to Hawaii or somewhere like that." I place the small Ziploc bag with the metal discs into the plastic container and click the lid shut.

"Is that where you want to go? To Hawaii?"

"To be honest, it's not something I've given much thought to." Truth. The lack of a wedding-themed Pinterest board wasn't the only consequence of my ex-boyfriend's callous comments.

That's not to say I don't have a travel bucket list.

I just don't have a honeymoon-themed bucket list or Pinterest board.

"We can still go on a honeymoon, Trouble. If you want. But you're right about the terms of my bail. It does limit where I can go for now. Or we can wait until after I'm found innocent of the charges."

A slight smile plays on my lips, and I pray Lucas is right. That his lawyer will prove Lucas wasn't responsible for the drugs being in his house. "I think that's a good idea. And who cares what other people think about us delaying our honeymoon? It doesn't mean our marriage isn't real. Plenty of newlyweds delay their honeymoons."

"You're right. No matter what we do, people will be quick to judge us and our actions. Have been quick to judge. We just have to show them they're wrong. Like we've been doing."

I grin because that's the part I've been enjoying the most. "Exactly."

I just hope it's enough to convince everyone that we're marrying for love.

Enough to convince the Wakefields. Enough to benefit my business.

17

SIMONE

Grams is on the couch, watching her favorite mystery show, when I walk into the living room. Her wheelchair sits next to the couch, empty but not forgotten.

I hand her a smoothie I made especially for her. I started making the drinks a few years ago after I began seeing a naturopath. I still have both ovaries, but the fear of developing early onset menopause was real. The smoothies were a precaution. Just in case.

"How about I take you for a walk once your show's finished?" I ask.

"That sounds great, dear." Her gaze remains on the screen.

I walk down the hallway to my bedroom, but then change my mind and continue to Aiden's childhood room.

I pause at the closed door, and a gentle tugging in my gut tells me it's time that I go into his room. My palms grow clammy. I wipe them on my shorts. *Just do it. At some point you'll need to face your ghosts.* Some of them, anyway.

I take a deep breath...and for the first time since returning to Maple Ridge, I open the door and step inside Aiden's old room.

The room hasn't changed much from before he left for college.

109

The same faded navy and white quilt. Photos on the corkboard above his desk. Pictures of him in his hockey uniforms. Pictures of his friends. Pictures of Grams and me.

One of my favorites is from the last time all our friends stayed at Granddad's hunting cabin, a week before Aiden and Lucas left for basic training. We'd been sitting around the fire, drinking beer and making s'mores. I was seated in the middle of the log, Aiden and Lucas flanking me. We were laughing at something Zara had said.

We looked happy, carefree. Unaware that a few years later everything would change, and Lucas and I would be left with an empty hole where my brother used to be.

A familiar numbness creeps under my skin, bringing with it a flood of memories.

Memories of Aiden helping me with my math homework. Of the nights I'd woken in tears from a nightmare. He'd let me climb into bed with him and tell me stories about Mom and Dad.

I unpin the photo of the three of us from the corkboard. After he left the Marines, Aiden lived with Grams for a few months before moving into an apartment. She said it was because he was a grown man who needed his privacy. Now I have to wonder if it was due to something else.

If it was because of the demons he was dealing with.

Demons he didn't want us to know about.

I open his desk drawer and search through it. It's pretty much empty, other than some scraps of blank paper, pens, and paper clips. I remove them, shut the drawer, and return to my room. I place them in the box on my bed containing the stuff I'll eventually take to Lucas's home. My new home.

I slide open my desk drawer to see if there's anything useful there. I haven't looked inside it since coming back to town. If memory serves me correctly, it's mostly just junk that teenage-me thought was valuable.

Turns out I'm right.

I remove the glittery stickers, multicolored gel pens, hair elastics, and dump them into the box. Once I've cleared out the stuff I want and tossed the rest into the trash can, I push the drawer shut.

A scrap of paper, folded several times, lies on the floor near my feet. A scrap of paper I'm positive wasn't there before I opened the desk drawer. It must've gotten caught on something and fallen out when I removed whatever the paper was attached to.

I pick the paper up and unfold it, revealing a single word on the page.

CATFISH

I don't know what it means, but I recognize Aiden's handwriting.

I flip the paper over, but there's nothing on the back.

When we were younger, we loved to play spy games. We even created a code based on something our World War II history buff of a father had taught Aiden. But nothing about the word hints that this was a message Aiden had left me. And what does it matter even if it was a message? Aiden is dead.

I crunch the paper into a tight ball and drop it into the trash can.

18

LUCAS

Tuesday afternoon, I leave the worksite two hours early and drive to Heart Valley, a town located in the foothills north of Maple Ridge. I've got four months to prove I'm innocent of the drug charges. Four months to find evidence proving I was set up. Four months to figure out who broke into my house and planted the drugs there.

Because someone will be spending a good portion of their life in the slammer for those drugs, and I have no intention of it being me.

I drive down the road that sees little local traffic. There aren't any houses on the outskirts of the small town of thirteen thousand people. Mostly, it's just industrial buildings here and there that are trying to blend in with the tranquil mountains and endless forests.

Kincaid Timber Corporation is no different.

The company is nothing more than a large concrete building. Functional in structure but that's about it. A crane stands among sky-high piles of logs, loading them onto one of the logging trucks. And the sound from the sawmill is a steady buzz that drowns out the quiet sounds of nature.

The owner of Kincaid Timber told Robert and Tuuli that he

isn't planning to turn their land into another industrial site. He wants to build a head office in Maple Ridge. The town is centrally located in relation to his other properties.

I glance around the large yard. Half of it is an empty parking lot—there's plenty of room for Kincaid Timber to build their head office here. Why is the owner so determined to buy the Wakefields' property?

I approach three men wearing hard hats and standing beside the crane, consulting a clipboard together. One man has on a business suit that looks out of place here. My guess is he's in his late fifties. The other two men talking to him are wearing jeans, T-shirts, work boots, and reflective vests.

"This is private property," the taller of the two men in T-shirts tells me.

He spits at the ground in front of my feet, then wipes his hand across the two-inch scar running diagonally down one cheek. I've been shot at by the enemy and I've been through hell while serving with the Marines. His form of intimidation is nothing more than a joke.

"I was hoping to talk to the owner." I address the comment to all three of them, but my gaze lands on the man in the suit. None of them are wearing IDs or badges identifying them as visitors, so I can't tell if he's the owner or just someone doing business with Kincaid Timber.

"And who would you be?" Again, the man with the scar addresses me. He's about my age and not the owner. That much I do know.

"Lucas Carson." The name doesn't come from me. It's from the man in the suit, who looks vaguely familiar. "He's one of the parties interested in the Maple Ridge property."

I raise an eyebrow. He knows more about me than I know about him.

He antes up my raised eyebrow with a smug smile. "I did my homework."

"You must be Jason L. Kincaid." I also did my homework. The man needs to update his photo on the company website. It's about two decades out of date.

"What is it you want to talk to me about? And just so it's clear, I have no intention of dropping my bid on the Wakefield property. So if that's why you're here, you might as well turn around."

"Why do you want that land? There must be plenty of other properties for sale that fit your needs."

"I have my reasons. They might not be sentimental like yours, but they are important, nonetheless. My company has a solid business goal and financial backing. It isn't run by a bunch of hotheads wanting to relive their glory days on the battlefield."

Relive our glory days? *Asshole.* "I take it you've never served in the military."

"Let's just say, while you were playing with toy soldiers, I had bigger plans for my life. I worked hard and sacrificed to get there."

Fuck, the man wouldn't know sacrifice even if it ripped a chunk out of his ass.

"Now, as you've already been told, this is private property. So either leave willingly or I can have my security escort you off it. Or if you would prefer, I can call the local sheriff's office and file a report with them. But given your current criminal charges, you'll want to skip on that option." Kincaid rocks back on his heels.

"So, you know about that," I say, not ready to leave. Not yet, anyway.

"Anyone capable of reading a newspaper knows about the charges. And like I said, I did my homework. I also know about Kellan's criminal record." The smug smile returns to his face. "Your parents must be so proud of their sons."

The other two men chuckle. Scar-face takes a step toward me. I ignore him.

"What else do you know about my criminal charges?" My tone is deceptively smooth. It's the unexpected undertow that I hope will knock him off his feet, trick him into saying something about the case he shouldn't know.

"Nothing more than what is public knowledge. And let me be clear, we don't like your sort on our property."

"What sort is that? The sort who isn't planning to go down for someone else's illegal activities?"

"The sort who doesn't know when he's overstayed his welcome." He nods at the man without the scar on his face.

The man removes his phone from his jeans and taps on the screen.

I raise my hands. "Okay, I'm going." He's right; I can't afford any more scrutiny when it comes to the law. I return to my SUV and climb inside.

I do a quick reconnaissance of the area, noting the security cameras. There's no way I can enter the property without setting off alarms. Not without the equipment and the backup I don't have. And I refuse to drag my brothers into this mess any more than they are right now.

Refuse to be the cause for them to end up on trial—like me.

SIMONE

The month after Lucas proposed to me goes by in a blur of wedding planning, dress fittings, photos for my social media account, creating pendants for an upcoming subscription box, taking care of Grams.

And talking all things wedding-related with Tuuli and Lucas's mom.

Three days before the big day, I sit on Grams's couch and log into my Instagram account. I'm greeted with a thousand new followers since I logged in yesterday morning. The photo of my pendant that I posted two days ago went viral.

But it's not just that picture that has a ton of likes and comments. The romantic photos Kim took of Lucas and me have seen an uptick of social interactions.

And since my wedding countdown began a week ago, I've been getting a flood of comments wishing me and Lucas all the happiness on our wedding day. I've also seen an upswing in subscriptions for my boxes.

Everything is going perfectly.

So why do I have an uneasy feeling something's about to go wrong?

LUCAS

"The place looks incredible." Mom surveys Rose's lush backyard, the colors golden in the early evening sunlight.

In the middle of the lawn, white chairs have been set in rows with tulle bows and burgundy flowers decorating the aisle seats. Dozens of small jars dangle from the lower branches of the oak tree, their tiny lights flickering like fireflies.

Six-year-old Simone would have once believed the lights were fairies. Her love for fairy tales was as great as her brother's love of mythology.

Shit, what would Aiden say if he were alive?

I doubt he would have approved of us getting married. If he were Zeus, he would impale me with one of his lightning bolts.

"You did a great job with it," I tell Mom.

"It was all Emily. That girl has an eye for details and aesthetics."

I grin, unable to keep what I'm thinking off my face. "Don't tell Kellan that."

"Don't tell me what?" my youngest brother asks, approaching us. Like Troy, Garrett, and myself, he's wearing a royal-blue suit, a burgundy tie, and a small ivory rose fastened to the lapel.

Mom smiles at him. "That Emily did an incredible job organizing Lucas and Simone's wedding. Especially since she only had a month to do it. She could go into business as a wedding coordinator."

I cough back a laugh, smothering it with my hand. From what Simone told me, Emily hasn't announced her plans yet.

A confused frown pinches Kellan's eyebrows. "A wedding coordinator?"

"You know, the person who helps the bride and groom organize their big day," Mom helpfully explains.

The frown deepens. "But Em has a job."

"I'm just thinking of other options she might like to explore. I'm sure she loves working for you, Kellan." Mom pats him on the shoulder. "But maybe she doesn't want to be your personal assistant for the rest of her life. She used to be a teacher. If another teaching job becomes available, she might even want to return to doing that."

Kellan appears no happier with that revelation than he did at Mom's suggestion about Emily being a wedding coordinator. His gaze goes to the house, where the woman in question is somewhere inside with Simone, Kim, Zara, and Avery, getting ready to walk down the aisle.

Tuuli and Robert see me and come over to join us.

Tuuli hugs me. "The place looks incredible, Lucas. I can see why you and Simone wanted to have the wedding here."

She and Robert had offered to have the wedding on the land they're selling because it means so much to Simone and me. But it was too difficult for some of our elderly guests to negotiate the terrain with their walkers and wheelchairs.

"Thank you. And thank you both for coming." I give Robert a man hug.

"We wouldn't have missed it for anything," he says. "I must admit when we talked to you about you and your brothers' single statuses, we had no idea it would result in this." He gestures to the wedding setup with the wave of his hand, then grins. "But I can't say I'm too surprised."

Before I can ask him what he means, Delores approaches us with her husband, Fred. Both are beaming at me brighter than a bogey caught in the sunlight.

"Are you ready for your big day?" Her warm voice is soft and crackles with age.

"Yes, ma'am."

"When Fred and I first met, it wasn't uncommon for couples to meet, fall in love, and marry a few weeks later. Now when you do that, folks believe the man knocked up the bride, and it's a shotgun wedding." She and her husband peer at me through questioning eyes. And I know what she's really fishing for.

"Simone isn't pregnant."

"Oh, well. I'm sure that will be coming soon enough. You look like a virile young man." She winks. Fred chuckles.

The truth is, Simone and I haven't discussed having kids. I figure that option is on the table once we're ready. Assuming I'm not in prison. She has always loved kids, and I have no issues with having them. Just...not yet.

I smile politely at Delores. I don't have an answer for her or my mother or Tuuli, all who are listening in. Hope glows on Mom's face like a beacon in a storm. All four of her sons are in their thirties. All of us are capable of giving her grandkids, as far as we know.

But until a month ago, all of us were supposedly single.

Troy comes to my rescue. "Em just let me know that everyone is ready to start."

"That's our cue to take our seats," Fred tells his wife.

Grateful to escape Mom's hopeful expression, I walk over to Jerome, our wedding officiant. He's busy chatting with the two teenage girls who will be playing the music for the ceremony. One holds a violin, the other a cello.

"We're ready," I tell them.

Mom positions Rose's wheelchair at the end of the row and sits next to her. The rest of the twenty or so guests also take their seats.

The music begins.

Kim walks down the aisle in a short burgundy dress and is carrying a bouquet of roses. She stops where my brothers and I are standing under the glowing lanterns. Kim passes her bouquet to Rose. Kellan hands Kim her camera, and she gets into position to shoot the rest of the wedding.

Emily is next, followed by Zara. Zara's mouth curves wide when her gaze lands on me, the smile genuine.

Which is more than I can say about Avery when it's her turn to walk down the aisle. She arrived in Maple Ridge two days ago, and I get the impression she's not a fan of mine. I have no idea why she doesn't like me.

The music switches, and everyone who can stand does.

Simone appears at the far end of the aisle. And for a moment, I'm positive I'm hallucinating. That the woman I've known for most of my life isn't walking toward me in a short white dress with my father next to her.

I close my eyes for a fraction of a second. When I reopen them, she's still walking toward me. She didn't change her mind. She didn't flee town.

And fuck...and fuck, she's gorgeous.

Simone is wearing a knee-length, sleeveless dress covered in floral lace, her hair is pulled up on one side, and she's carrying a bouquet of white roses. But it's her smile that is the most breath-taking part of her, shyly confident and bright. It's her smile that catapults my heart rate into high gear.

For a moment, I allow myself to believe we're not doing this to help our businesses. We're doing it for love. The way it's supposed to be.

The way it should have been.

With her brother as my best man.

Simone hands her flowers to Avery and turns back to me. The

shyness has vanished and she's all soft smiles. I take her hands in mine and give her fingers a light squeeze.

When Jerome asks if anyone finds a reason we shouldn't get married, I half expect Avery to yell, "Hell, yeah."

She keeps quiet. And I release the breath I've been holding.

Troy hands me Simone's wedding band. I place it at the end of her ring finger, and repeat after Jerome, "I take you, Simone Angela Hensley, to be my lawfully wedded wife. To love and to honor you in sickness and in health till death do us part." My voice comes out loud and strong and without a flicker of hesitation.

I slide the ring onto her finger.

Avery passes Simone my ring, but not without tossing her a look first, questioning Simone if she's sure she wants to go through with the wedding. A look hopefully only noticed by Simone and me.

Simone responds to the unspoken question with a nod and slips the ring onto my finger. "I take you, Lucas Cameron Carson, to be my lawfully wedded husband. To love and to honor in sickness and in health till death do us part." She pushes the ring over my knuckle.

"With the power vested in me by the state of Oregon," Jerome says, "I pronounce you husband and wife. You may now kiss the bride."

I lean into Simone and brush her lips with mine. But once I can steal her away for a few minutes? I have every intention of kissing her out of her loving mind.

My arms circle Simone's waist from behind. "How about a real kiss?" The volume of my voice drops, the words gravelly against the curve of her ear.

She glances around Rose's backyard, at the people socializing, drinks in hand. "I thought the kiss when we said our I-do's was a real kiss."

"You know what I mean. We just got married. People are expecting us to be unable to keep our hands off each other. And that includes sneaking in kisses whenever possible." I don't have to look to know we're the center of attention. I can feel the weight of everyone's stares.

She chuckles. "Good point, Cannon. Okay, we need to give them a kiss they won't forget anytime soon. But it has to be somewhat PG friendly."

"Deal." I stand still, memorizing her lips, reliving in my head the first time I kissed her. I'd fantasized about it for months. When the moment finally came, it was better than anything I'd imagined. I trace my thumb along her lower lip. Her breath hitches, her eyes darken, and I can't resist any longer. I cup the back of her head, and my mouth meets hers.

I keep kissing her until she's trembling in my arms. Until my body feels as though it's about to evaporate. I'm vaguely aware of music and talking and laughter coming from the reception, but none of it matters. The only thing I care about is this woman in my arms. That, and making sure she's thinking about me tonight while alone in the guest room.

My mouth moves to her jaw, the shell of her ear, her throat. Her fingers dive into my hair, keeping me close. Tiny moans fall from her lips. Encouraging me. Reminding me how good we are together.

If I had my way, we'd skip the party and go to our house.

If I had my way, Simone would change her mind about staying in the guest bedroom.

I rest my forehead against hers. "Tonight, when you're in bed, I want you to remember how it felt when I used to eat you out. How it felt when I touched you." I brush my thumb along the side of her breast. "How it felt when I was inside you. How wet you were."

She releases a whimper.

I smile, knowing I've got her exactly where I want her.

"That wasn't quite the PG-rated kiss I was talking about," Simone says, sounding a little dazed.

A rumble of laughter builds in my chest and powers its way to my throat. "You're probably right."

A few hours later, as we make our way to the dance floor, Delores steps between our target and Simone and me. "What a handsome bride and groom you two make."

Simone and I both thank her.

"And I'm sure it won't be too much longer before we hear the pitter-patter of little feet."

Simone's muscles tense against my body. Gone is the soft woman in my arms, replaced by a block of wood. And I have no idea what to make of that.

I arrange my face into what feels like a polite smile. "We're not in a big rush for that quite yet. We want to enjoy married life first, just the two of us."

That, and I want to be in my child's life. To watch them grow up. To be everything to them that my father was for my brothers and me. I can't do that from a prison cell.

I don't plan to spend my life in prison for a crime I didn't commit, but I also wouldn't be the first man a jury finds guilty when he's innocent. The trial isn't for another sixteen weeks and two days. Simone and I have to wait that long before we know what future I'm facing.

Not wanting to say this to Delores, I make an excuse that Simone and I are heading for the dance floor, and we make our hasty escape.

I sway Simone in my arms. "Sorry about Delores. I guess that means she believes I'm innocent."

Simone watches me with round eyes that glisten in the glow of the lights strung above our heads. "Is that what you want? Children?"

"Sure. I love kids. But not yet. You believe I'm innocent, but that doesn't mean the courts will." I flinch, remembering exactly what I'm up against.

Pain flutters on her face. She nods, closes her eyes, rests her head on my shoulder.

Guilt and anger detonate inside me. Guilt that I'm responsible for the pain. Anger at the person who caused me to hurt her. Simone has never done anything to hurt anyone, and yet she'll be punished if I'm found guilty.

I tighten my hold on her as if that's enough to make everything better.

I wish it were that simple.

21

LUCAS

The weekend after Simone and I are married, we drive to the dog breeder where we're adopting our nine-week-old golden labradoodle puppy.

I expected Simone to be excited that we're finally getting our dog. It's the first step in making our marriage real, beyond the exchanging of wedding vows. The first step to creating our family.

But instead of being happy, Simone seems distant. Distracted.

"Are you okay?" I briefly take my eyes off the sunny stretch of road ahead of us. Fields lie on either side of the highway, green crops bowing in the wind.

"Huh?" Simone turns to look at me. "Sorry. Yeah, I'm fine. I was just thinking about how Aiden wanted a dog when we were growing up. He used to beg my parents to get him one. After they died, he begged Grams to get us a dog. But we still didn't get one, as you know."

She reaches over and links her fingers with mine. "I was just thinking that maybe if he had gotten a dog, especially a PTSD-service dog, after the Marines, he might still be alive. But instead of Aiden getting a dog that could've saved his life, I'm getting one because people love seeing adorable dog photos on Instagram. How messed up is that?"

"That's not messed up. You both have always loved dogs. And yes, it's always easy to look back and wonder what would have happened if we had done things differently. But you'll only drive yourself crazy if you dwell on the what-ifs." God knows I've wondered too many times what I could have done differently to prevent Aiden from committing suicide. Wondered why I'd thought he was getting help to deal with his ghosts the way I had. "You're not getting a puppy because you're hoping it will help grow your subscriber fanbase. You're getting a puppy because you have so much love to share, and this is the right time in your life—in our life—to get one."

She smiles, the tilt of her lips small. "You're right. I know it's been almost three years since he died and I should move on. But it's those little things, like getting a dog, that remind me of how much I miss him."

"I know. Me too. I doubt that will ever change. It might hurt a little less over time, but I don't think we'll ever stop missing him."

"I keep telling myself that it will start hurting less. Maybe one day I'll actually believe it." She goes back to looking out the side window.

"How's the subscription box business doing?" I ask, mostly because I want to focus on something that will make Simone smile again.

"Great so far. It was scary quitting my job and taking a risk on the boxes. And maybe I wouldn't have quit if Grams hadn't been involved in the hit-and-run. But now that I've been spending more time on planning each month's box and growing the business, it's really starting to take off. The photos of us on social media are also helping. People love seeing those small moments between us."

"So no one suspects they're staged?"

I turn to her long enough to see her cringe. "I'm sure everyone has figured out the photos are staged. Most Instagram influencers do the same thing. It's a good thing I'm not promoting a course on having a successful marriage. I have no idea what I'm doing there." She chuckles, the sound sheepish more than amused. "But candles and handmade lavender-scented soap? That's a different matter."

"So you don't regret marrying me?" My tone is casual, but on the inside, I'm hoping the answer is no. I failed her brother. I don't want to steal her life from her, too—metaphorically speaking—because of the bullshit drug charges. If I'm found guilty...

Her responding laugh to my question isn't the one I think about late at night. The rich, warm sound that sneaks into my dreams. This laugh, soft and silky, is a shot of adrenaline straight to my heart. "Do I regret that we're on the way to pick up our puppy? Not at all. I only regret the reason you were forced to marry, Lucas. I can't wait for you to follow through on your dream and make a difference for all those vets."

"That makes two of us."

I eventually pull into the driveway of a sprawling ranch house. The distracted Simone at the beginning of the trip has transformed into the grinning woman next to me. We walk up the path to the front door.

"You ready, Trouble, to get our puppy?"

"Absolutely, Cannon." She directs her grin at me, and it's the best feeling.

Simone rings the bell. The crisp sound fades, replaced by the rapid fire of little barks from the other side of the door that grow louder.

The front door clicks open and several little noses poke out through the narrow gap.

"Hi, Simone," the woman says, still keeping the door mostly shut. "And you must be Lucas."

"That's right. And you're Tina?" I reply.

Simone is too busy smiling at the yapping golden furballs to pay attention to us.

"That would be me. Hold on a second." Tina shuts the door.

When she reopens it a moment later, the puppies are chasing after a ball that is rolling in the opposite direction. "Come on in."

We step into the house. A few of the puppies decide we're more interesting than the ball and come tumbling toward us.

"They're so adorable!" Simone crouches and holds out her hand for them to sniff. They lick her fingers, and her expression almost does me in.

I'd get her a dozen puppies if it kept that smile on her face.

Tina kneels and pets one of the dogs. "This would be the one you fell in love with when you saw the videos. Why don't we go into the backyard so you guys can get to know the puppies better before you make a final decision."

We follow her into the fenced off garden, the puppies bounding after us. They're small now, but they'll end up bigger than Troy's Cavapoo.

We spend the next hour playing with them.

Simone tosses the ball. A few of the puppies are now snoozing in a sunny spot. Others have gone off to explore a different distraction. One little guy goes chasing after the ball and pounces on it. Simone laughs, threads her fingers with mine, and takes me over to where he's playing.

She releases my hand, crouches, and fusses over the pup. He yaps and wrestles with her fingers. He's a cute and rambunctious little squirt who already has Simone wrapped around his paw.

I crouch next to her, but instead of watching the puppy, who is now tugging on my sneaker shoelace, I smile at the way Simone is all lit up as *she* watches him.

"What do you think?" she asks me, her eyes bright. "Who's your favorite?"

My smile widens into a grin. "The same one who has stolen your heart." I pat his head and gently disengage him from his target.

SIMONE

My husband of eleven days is standing on the scaffolding, fastening the window trim to the house Troy and his crew are renovating. Lucas's shirtless muscles flex and bulge as he works, and the hot midday sun is turning his tanned body into a glistening tease.

I lick my lower lip, imagining what it would feel like to trace my tongue over the finely crafted ridges and valleys of his body.

Tasting him.

Exploring him.

The air releases from my lungs with an audible sigh. Or whimper.

This...this Lucas is not the one from my college days. This Lucas is all man. All mouthwatering, leaves-my-body-tingling-at-his-touch man. And I want him. Badly.

"Hey, Simone," Troy calls out.

The shrill pitch of the electric screwdriver stops. Lucas looks down at me, and I silently curse Troy in a million enlightening ways for halting my entertainment.

Not once while I was single did I imagine getting married and never having sex with my new husband. But that's exactly what has happened.

Regular sex isn't the only important factor for a successful marriage. Communication is also important.

And currently, I'm zero out of two on both points.

Lucas told me on our wedding day he sees us eventually having kids. The pain of his words still vibrates through me. I should just dive into the deep end and tell him the truth. But I can't form the words. Can't spill my secrets.

What if he changes his mind about us being married? I've already lost my parents, my brother, my baby. I don't want to lose Lucas, too.

Except, that's exactly what might happen—and it could have nothing to do with my inability to have kids.

Justice. I don't know if it's blind or not, but it's the one thing that could destroy our marriage.

I shake the thought from my head and remember why I'm here. I lift the two bags from Picnic & Treats. "I brought you lunch."

Troy walks over to me, an easygoing grin on his face. "No wonder you're my favorite sister-in-law."

A chuckle bursts from my chest. "Sorry. I didn't bring *you* lunch. Does that mean I'm demoted to your least favorite sister-in-law?"

Lucas drops down from the scaffolding and walks toward us.

Troy rubs the top of my head, messing up my hair. I duck away from his dusty hand and crouch to stroke Butterscotch, his adorable Cavapoo. The dog's happily snoozing in a sunny spot.

Lucas gifts me with one of his smiles that make my insides swoon. "Hey, wasn't expecting to see you here."

"I figured since it's nice out and you need to eat, I'd visit you for lunch."

As it is, we haven't spent a lot of time together since the wedding. Lucas has been busy between helping Troy, being called on search-and-rescue missions when tourists get lost in the mountains, and looking into possible leads as to who set him up.

So far, the latter hasn't amounted to much.

"I think women call this a romantic gesture," Troy says. "All right, you two lovebirds, you get an hour lunch." His voice hits hard on *lovebirds* as if they're magical creatures he's having a tough time believing in.

Lucas grabs his T-shirt from a scaffolding rail and pulls it on over his head. His ab muscles flex—and tease me some more.

We walk to his SUV. "You wanna have lunch at the lake?" he asks.

"Sounds good."

He drives to a spot where few people visit. We walk down to the water's edge and sit on the grassy bank. Several ducks are swimming a short distance from us. Their quacks and the soft rustle of the willow canopy swaying in the breeze are the only sounds around us.

I remove the chicken-and-bacon club sandwiches from the bags and pass him one. "How's the job going?"

"It's hard work, so that's good."

What he's really saying is it's enough to momentarily distract him from thinking about the job he's great at but can't do because of the drug charges. I've seen him work with Grams. It's clear how much he loves his job and how great he is at it.

"What are you up to today?" Lucas takes an impressive bite from his sandwich.

"Not much. I worked on a new design for a bracelet and went to the post office. And I'm going over to see Grams after lunch to spend time with her. So lots of excitement." Somehow, I keep the underwhelmed sigh from my voice.

"This isn't how I imagined married life," Lucas says as if reading my mind. "Somehow I thought I'd get to kiss my wife first thing in the morning and before going to sleep."

He could if I were sleeping in the same bed as him. Because I wasn't ready to go there yet after we got married, I've been sleeping in the guest room.

An unexpected bubble of laughter escapes me at his comment. "You probably also expected to have sex with her several times a day."

We haven't kissed since the wedding, if you don't count the kisses when we're in public. But that's all for show.

What isn't for show is how they're also the match to the slow-burning fuse that leaves me sexually frustrated all day and all night. Frustration fueled by Lucas's words when he told me during the reception he wanted me to remember how it felt when he was inside me.

"That's true, too," he says.

We finish our food in silence, a tension charging the air between us. I squirm on the spot and watch a duck poke his head under the water, his butt sticking up in the air.

"Why did you stop writing me letters while I was in Afghanistan?" Lucas's question is one I hadn't expected to hear. Not now. Not anytime.

I squirm again. "I guess I became too busy with work. I lost track of time. And then the next thing I knew, you were no longer with the Marines." It's a lame excuse, but it's the best I can do without opening Pandora's Box.

"I wrote to you several times after you stopped writing, but you never wrote back."

The truth to his words kicks my heart, feeds my guilt. "I didn't realize. I never received them." More like I never opened them.

I feel his gaze on me. Mine is still on the ducks, afraid if I look at him, he'll see the truth in my eyes.

"I meant it, Simone, when I said I want to make this marriage work. I know we got married for the wrong reasons, but that doesn't mean I don't want a normal marriage."

This time I do look at him. "I want that, too. I want a normal marriage." Or as normal as it can be given we're not in love.

"That means kissing whenever we want." Lucas rests his hand on my thigh and leans in, caressing my lips with his. "And I want to be able to kiss you in whatever way I crave." He deepens the kiss, and I eagerly welcome him in.

His other hand cradles the back of my head, and the world beyond the willow branches disappears.

His calloused fingertips trace up the inside of my thigh, the sensation rough and teasing. I don't try to stop him. I stay perfectly still, wordlessly pleading for them to keep traveling north.

His fingers reach the seam of my shorts. A moan slips from my mouth, and I slowly roll back, vertebra by vertebra, onto the grass. Our tongues continue to stroke and explore, remind, and remember.

God...oh God, I can't remember the last time it felt this way... this way with another man.

Lucas nudges my legs apart a little more, and his fingers press against my mound, hidden under the cotton of my shorts and panties. "Do you want me to stop?" His question is a warm breath fanning my lips.

"No." The word tumbles out on a shameless gasp.

"Good." He resumes the gentle pressure as his fingers draw tight circles.

The tension between my legs grows tauter and tauter until I can't take it anymore. An orgasm, more intense than anything I've felt in a while, explodes through my body, pulling me off the grass like a tightly drawn bow. *Oh. God.*

Lucas's lips curve into a smug smile, and he kisses me one more time.

"Thank you," I get out between panted breaths. "It's been a while."

"Define a while."

I do the mental math and give up. Math was never my best subject. "Well, it depends if we're talking about a man or me doing the pleasuring."

Lucas's head flops forward, resting on my shoulder. "Christ, the image of that last part is killing me." He lifts his head. "I don't wanna know about specific men, but if we're talking hypotheticals, then yes, how long has it been since a man gave you an orgasm?"

"A few years, I guess." At his raised eyebrows, I add, "I was busy with work, trying to get ahead. Dating wasn't a priority."

"You don't have to date to have sex."

"You're right, you don't. But I wasn't into one-night stands either, so that left me with being celibate." I laugh at the confusion lining his face. "Contrary to what most guys think, no one has ever died from not having regular sex."

Lucas pushes himself to sit. "I know that. Believe me, I know that more than anyone."

He checks his phone and sighs. "I have to head back to work now. The last thing I need is to piss off my boss, even if he is my brother. I'll see you later when I come over to help Rose with her exercises." He flashes me my favorite panty-soaking grin. "Be prepared for a make-out session when I get there to rival any we did in college."

"HOW'S MY GREAT-GRANDBABY DOING?" GRAMS ASKS. THE midafternoon sun is a warm kiss on my upper back as I push her wheelchair along the sidewalk.

I know she's referring to Jasper, but that doesn't stop the hollowness that stretches and writhes in the empty space where my uterus used to be. Claws at my vital organs. Echoes my old grief. Fortunately, she can't see the pain on my face.

"He's doing great. Once he's had all his vaccinations, I can bring him with me when I visit you."

"I'm looking forward to that. Then I can take him for a spin on my set of fancy wheels." Grams pats the arm of her wheelchair. The wheelchair she can't wait to be rid of.

We walk to the nearby park, and I position her wheelchair next to the bench where Delores and Samantha are sitting.

"So, where are you and Lucas going on your honeymoon?" Delores asks.

I sit next to her. "We haven't decided yet. We're waiting until after his trial"—in three months and eleven days—"before we go anywhere."

"There are plenty of romantic locations even in Oregon. Especially along the coast. You can stay at a bed-and-breakfast. That's what Fred and I did when we got married."

"Or maybe they can find a romantic lodge like what Crystal and Walter want to build."

Samantha's words get my attention.

"What lodge is that?" I already know the answer. I just didn't know Crystal and Walter were the couple who wanted to build it.

"They recently came into some money and figured that running a small lodge would be a great idea. It was their son who suggested it. He'll be helping them run the place."

Samantha scrunches up her nose. "I can't believe he even suggested it. Since when did that lazy man ever raise a finger to help them? They'll be the ones doing all the work. But I wouldn't be surprised if he's the one who will profit."

Her reaction stokes my curiosity, adds more tinder to my need to help Lucas. "You don't believe they really want to build the lodge?"

"No, I think they do. But if it weren't for their son, they certainly wouldn't have thought about building or running it."

I catalog everything she tells me to pass on to Lucas when he comes over to see Grams after work. "Are they the couple interested in purchasing the Wakefields' land that's for sale?"

"That's right."

"And if they don't get it?"

"I don't know. I haven't discussed it with them." Samantha looks at Delores, who responds with a shrug.

They might not have discussed it with Crystal and Walter, but what's stopping me from asking Crystal a few questions?

Maybe their bid has nothing to do with the drugs found in Lucas's house. Or maybe there's more to Sebastian wanting the land than Lucas and his brothers realize.

23

———

LUCAS

I fasten the bead molding to the window with the electric screwdriver. Even though my lunch date with Simone was incredible, it can't make this job feel any less like work for me. I miss being back in the PT clinic and helping my patients. But until I clear my name, that's just not going to happen.

I pull the small white plug from my tool belt and push it into the hole in the PVC. A vehicle door bangs shut behind me. The neighbor's front door squeaks open. Once I'm done here, I'll check to see if Mrs. Jenkins would like me to oil her hinges.

I glance in the direction of her house. She's eyeing me like I'm a rabid raccoon she's not sure how to exterminate.

Okay. Maybe that's a no to the hinges being oiled.

I return to screwing in the trim.

"Lucas," Troy calls out while I'm pushing another plug into a hole.

I swivel to see what he wants.

A cop is standing next to him, gaze locked on me, expression as readable as a dog tag blown to dust.

"The officer wants to talk to you," Troy says, frowning.

I put the power screwdriver on the working platform, climb

137

down the ladder at the end of the scaffolding, and walk over to the cop. "What do you need to talk to me about?"

He's shorter than me by a couple of inches. He lifts his chin as if that will make a difference. "A witness reported that you were selling drugs to a group of teens this afternoon. I need you to come in to the station for some questions."

"I wasn't selling drugs this afternoon or this morning or any other time. Whoever told you that I was is lying."

Troy's frown deepens, his gaze focused on the cop. "When and where exactly is he accused of doing this?"

"The witness reported that you were seen talking to two teens in front of this house at around one-oh-nine p.m."

Christ, this is bullshit. "Talking to teens isn't illegal. Even if it were, I haven't talked to any today." My voice is granite cold, the temperature dropping with each word. "I've been on the scaffolding for most of the day. Your witness lied."

"I can vouch that he hasn't spoken to any teens today," Troy says.

"Look, we can do this the easy way or the hard way." The officer's tone cuts the air, electric blade to metal.

"Can you tell me what teens I supposedly sold the fictitious drugs to?"

"Are you going to cooperate or not?"

Mrs. Jenkins walks down her porch steps and positions herself so that she has a better view of what's going on.

Troy gives me a barely perceptible nod, and I relent. Not because I don't think this is fucked up. I don't want to hurt Troy's company. The longer I'm out here disagreeing with the cop, the greater the chance more people will witness what's happening, and it could turn nasty for my brother.

Shit. Shit. Shit. This is so goddamn ridiculous.

I step toward the cruiser, shame and anger, dread and regret handcuffed to me.

Mrs. Lewis, my high school chemistry teacher, shuffles across the street to where we're standing. She's been sitting on her porch since I arrived this morning, knitting. "What's going on?"

"Nothing you need to worry about, ma'am." The cop barely acknowledges her with a glance.

Troy walks up to her. She was also his teacher. "The officer believes that Lucas was selling drugs to some teens on the front lawn because someone claimed they saw him doing that this afternoon."

The cop tasers us with his glare. "I didn't say it was on the front lawn."

"Well, if he did sell drugs to the teens, it would have to be at the front of this house because that's where he's been since he returned from lunch just over an hour ago. And that's where he was working this morning."

Mrs. Lewis's gaze volleys between us. "Teens? There haven't been any teens on this street this afternoon. And I should know. I've been sitting outside all day—other than when Lucas left for an hour around eleven thirty with his wife."

"Maybe you just didn't see them," the cop says. "Or you happened to be turned away when they were talking to Lucas."

Mrs. Lewis's wrinkled cheeks turn pink. "Right. Have you seen him?" She waves her hand at my shirtless body. "Trust me, a woman wouldn't look away from this fine specimen if she can help it. I've been sitting on my front porch watching him work. So, whoever told you they saw him selling drugs to teens was lying or needs to get their eyes checked."

"If you want, you can search my SUV," I tell the cop. "You won't find any drugs."

He does exactly that while Mrs. Lewis, Troy, and I watch. He unsurprisingly finds nothing.

"God, that was fucking bullshit," I mutter under my breath as he climbs into his vehicle. Then cringe. "Sorry." I smile at Mrs. Lewis. The smile starts out apologetic, then switches to grateful. "Thank you for telling the cops what you saw."

"You're welcome. I'm sorry you had to go through that, Lucas. Maybe I should invite my bridge club over tomorrow so we can make sure no one else tries to accuse you of something you didn't do. We can be your own personal bodyguards." She winks at me, and I chuckle. "Well, I'll let you gentlemen get back to making my day a little brighter." She shuffles across the street and returns to her porch.

The rest of the day continues without incident, but the shitload of emotions at what happened earlier sets up camp in my gut. By the time I head to Rose's house to help her with her PT exercises, I'm drained. Fed up. Ready to punch something. Go for a hard run. Yell.

I ring the doorbell. Simone answers the door. Before she can say anything, I pull her into my arms and kiss her.

The kiss is far from gentle. It's greedy. Fueled by anger and determination and lust and desire. I need Simone. I need to keep kissing her until the anger burns up in an out-of-control blaze.

I get lost in the kiss. Get lost in Simone's floral scent.

She meets me stroke for stroke, not once slowing down. My hands grip her waist, pinning her to me.

I continue kissing her until Rose asks who's at the door. As much as I would love to keep kissing Simone, I stop and rest my forehead against hers. "Thank you. I needed that."

"Bad day?"

The TV is on in the living room, loud enough that I don't think Rose can hear me. But even so, I keep my voice low. "Someone at the job site told the cops that they saw me dealing drugs to some teens."

Simone inhales sharply, and her eyes widen. "They arrested you?"

"No, another neighbor told them none of that was true. I swear half the town believes I'm innocent of drug possession, and the other half has found me guilty."

"Is that you, Lucas?" Rose's voice travels down the hallway to us.

"I'll be right there, Rose," I call out. "I'm just kissing your gorgeous granddaughter."

"Kiss her all you want," Rose calls back, a grin in her voice. "I'm not going anywhere."

"We'll just be outside for a moment, Grams." Simone's eyes warn me she has something to tell me she doesn't want Rose to overhear. The underlying message is downplayed by the singsong quality of Simone's voice.

We step onto the front stoop. Simone shuts the door and sits on the top step. I join her.

"How much do you know about why Crystal and Walter want to build the lodge on the Wakefields' property?" she asks.

"All I know is that it's going to be a romantic getaway type thing, which is why Robert and Tuuli were leaning toward selling them the land."

Until Simone and I got married. Now, who Tuuli and Robert will sell to is anyone's guess. We won't know for another three months and three days.

"Do you know anything about Sebastian, Crystal and Walter's son?" Simone tells me about a conversation she had with Rose's friends this afternoon.

"Can't say I've ever met him. As far as I know, he doesn't live in Maple Ridge."

"It sounds like he's moving back if they go ahead with their plans. Which means, if what Samantha was saying is true, he has more than enough reason to not want you and your brothers to win the bid."

"Looks like my brothers and I need to do a little digging into Sebastian."

"I can talk to Crystal and see what I can discover about him."

"I don't think that's a good idea, Simone."

"Sure it is. It can't hurt to try. She won't even know the real reason I'm visiting her. I'll just see if I can casually bring up his name in conversation. We need to start somewhere, and this is our best bet."

I mentally analyze the pros and the dangers of involving her. Whoever framed me isn't playing games. They don't care who gets hurt—as long as they don't get caught.

I can bask in the river of denial all I want, but that won't change anything. The day Simone and I exchanged vows, she became involved in my fucked-up life. And this is Simone we're talking about, the stubborn girl I grew up with.

She believes I'm innocent and will do whatever she can to prove it—even if I tell her to leave it alone.

Dammit. Dammit. Dammit.

But as much as I hate the idea of involving Simone, I don't have a choice. Besides, we're not talking about her visiting drug lords or someone equally dangerous. We're talking about her visiting an older couple who are well respected in the community. "All right. Maybe you'll be able to find out something that will help me."

Hopefully, her visit won't open a crate of explosives.

24

SIMONE

I remove the bouquet of flowers from the passenger seat of my car and walk up the path to the small, two-story house. I don't know Crystal and Walter very well, but they did send Lucas and me a vintage frame as a wedding gift. The frame sits on a bookshelf in Lucas's living room—my living room—with one of the wedding photos Kim took of us.

The perfect excuse for why I'm here on a Wednesday afternoon while Lucas works with Grams on her PT exercises.

I rub my palm against the cotton of my dress, pretending to smooth it. For the past six weeks, Lucas and his brothers have tried to clear his name. I've been sitting on the sidelines, working on my subscription boxes. Enough is enough.

It's my turn to see what I can dig up.

The Drysons' house reminds me of a fairy-tale cottage. Colorful blossom-filled flower boxes sit under shuttered windows.

I ring the door chimes.

The door opens a minute later. Crystal smiles at me. "Hello, Simone. I was just thinking about you the other day." She opens the door wide and waves me inside.

"These are for you." I hand her the bouquet. "Thank you for the wedding gift. Lucas and I love it."

"You're welcome. Would you like something to drink? Tea, perhaps?"

"Tea would be great, thank you."

"Why don't you go into the living room, and I'll bring it out once it's ready."

She points to the sunny room overlooking the front yard and disappears down the hallway. The furniture in the room and soft ivory walls fits perfectly with my image of a fairy-tale cottage. And the place has the same rusty Scandinavian feel that Tuuli loves.

Which is not great news for Lucas and his brothers if this is a taste of what the lodge will look like.

I study the framed photos on the nearby bookshelf. Crystal and Walter are in most of them in various locations I don't recognize. A dark-haired boy and a girl are in some of the photos. In three of them, only Crystal and Walter and a sullen teenage boy are visible. The girl is missing.

Crystal walks back into the room, places the tray on the coffee table, and picks up a photo with both kids in it. "Not a day goes by when I don't look at those. This is my son, Sebastian. And his twin sister, Bethany. She died of kidney failure when she was twelve years old. You never really get over the loss of a child."

A dull ache clutches my belly, tiny fingers tightening like a vise. A phantom pain that drags grief and guilt along for the ride.

She's right—you never get over the loss of your child. But it does get easier with time. For the most part.

I swallow the urge to spread my hand where Lily once lived and give away my secret. "I'm sorry for your loss."

"Thank you."

"I don't remember Sebastian from when I grew up in Maple Ridge. Does he still live here?"

"No. Not yet, anyway."

"He's planning to move back?"

Crystal returns the frame to the shelf. "I'm sure you know Walter and I are hoping to build a lodge on Tuuli and Robert's land that's for sale. Sebastian will help us manage it. It was his idea to build it. It will be our legacy. A way for people to remember us."

She walks to the couch and sits. I join her. "Where is Sebastian now?"

"I'm not sure. He travels a lot."

"For his job?"

"No, he's—he's in between jobs right now. He was in Eugene for a week or so back in May. Now he's out on the Northeast Coast, checking out various lodges and getting ideas."

"I must have just missed him when I moved here in mid-May."

"Unfortunately, he didn't have time to visit. He was busy getting quotes from construction companies. Walter and I told him we wanted to hire Troy's company to build the lodge. But Sebastian didn't think it was a good idea due to conflict of interest." A blush hijacks her cheeks, and she glances at the contents of her cup.

"You mean because Troy and his brothers have also bid on the land?"

She nods.

I pick up my cup from the coffee table and take a sip of the berry tea. "Are you looking at any other locations? Assuming there are other properties for sale in the area like the Wakefields'."

"Not right now. Sebastian saw the land and said it was perfect for what we need. We've talked to him about the possibility of building elsewhere if Robert and Tuuli decide to sell to someone else, but he said it has to be that land. Nothing else is comparable."

"But what if they don't sell it to you? Does that mean you won't build the lodge or will you keep looking?"

"I don't know. To be honest. We're still counting on getting that land. It's perfect. I couldn't imagine a more romantic location for the lodge." Crystal smiles, and it's clear the love she feels for the land is real. But even so, the land doesn't hold the same meaning for her as it does for Lucas and me. "Can I ask you the same? Do you know if your husband plans to keep looking if Robert and Tuuli sell the land to someone else?"

"Do you know what Lucas and his brothers want the land for?" I say instead of answering her question directly.

"To build a paintball park."

Okay. Wasn't expecting that.

"Not exactly." I explain the purpose of the program, how it will benefit military veterans, and how eventually Lucas wants to have his own PT practice there. The latter which won't be possible if Lucas is sentenced to life in prison. I skip mentioning that detail. "In addition to being the ideal location for their goals, the land means a lot to Lucas. I don't know if you are aware of it, but Lucas and my brother were best friends. They practically grew up on the Wakefields' land.

"Tuuli and Robert let them camp there as kids, and they had all kinds of adventures there. For Lucas, Aiden's memory is heavily tied to that land. It's part of his soul. The program will benefit military vets and it will honor my brother's memory. Both of those are extremely important to Lucas. And to me."

Crystal's lips tug into a three-quarter smile, more understanding than before, but also a little guarded. "I'm glad you told me that. I guess I didn't understand why Lucas is so determined to build on that land...nor did I fully understand the purpose of the program he wants to start."

"Do you think the logging company and environment group are still in the running when it comes to their offer?" Maybe she and Walter have some insight into those bids that Lucas and his brothers don't have.

"I have no idea. I would like to believe it's just down to our bid and your husband's at this point, but there must be more to the other bids that we don't know about, or else Tuuli and Robert would have already eliminated them."

"I don't suppose you have any idea what that could be?"

"None at all. But I have heard the logging company is desperate to get their hands on the land. They've increased their bid."

They have?

And just how desperate are they to have the winning bid? Desperate enough to want Lucas locked away in prison?

If that's the case, what does that mean for Crystal and Walter? Are they at risk of something happening to them? Something like what happened to Lucas?

Or something worse?

25

SIMONE

I sit on Lucas's guest bed, the bed I've been sleeping on for the past eleven nights. The conversation I had with Crystal an hour ago repeats in my head.

Not the conversation about Sebastian. The one about his sister, Bethany. Now that I'm alone, I spread my hand over the spot where Lily once grew, like I wanted to do when Crystal told me you never really get over the loss of a child.

Downstairs, Lucas is cooking dinner. He's oblivious to the pain I went through ten years ago, the pain that still flares in me on a regular basis, just not as intense as during those first few years.

I told Lucas when I got home that Kincaid Timber has increased their bid. He doesn't need to know about the conversation Crystal and I had about losing a child.

I shift to crouch beside the bed and pull the wicker box out from under it. The wicker box containing the letters Lucas sent me while he was in the military. I have no idea why I brought them here when I moved in. I still haven't read them since returning to Maple Ridge.

My hand rests on the lid, my fingers trembling with the

memory of waking up in the hospital with Avery sitting next to my bed, looking devastated. For me. Tears prick my eyes.

It's too soon. I push the box under the bed. Once I've pulled myself together, I go downstairs.

I enter the kitchen. "Wow, what smells so good?"

"Garlic butter chicken." Lucas removes two wineglasses from the cabinet and places them on the granite counter. He then fills them with red wine and hands me one. "It's a Cabernet Sauvignon."

My favorite.

I take a sip and lean back on the counter next to the sink. "So are you and your brothers planning to increase your bid on Tuuli and Robert's land?"

"No. They aren't your usual landowners who are looking at selling to the highest bidder. Kincaid Timber doesn't understand that. Or maybe they understand it too well. My brothers and I and the Drysons have history with Robert and Tuuli. That's more important to them than anything else. We've already put in a fair bid on the land, and all the interested parties know it."

None of what Lucas said surprises me. But does Kincaid Timber realize any of this? They're an outside corporation with no roots in the community.

"Is there any recent news from Blake about your case?"

"Nothing. So far, the police haven't turned up any new leads."

"*They* haven't, but what about you and your brothers? There must be something you've overlooked. Some clue or possible witness. The trial starts in fourteen weeks and five days."

"You're beginning to sound like Rose." Lucas lifts the lid from one of the saucepans on the stove and stirs the contents.

I huff out a breath. "I'm serious."

"I'm sorry. I know you are. But it's a good thing you're living with me now. I wouldn't want you getting any ideas. As it is, I'm glad John McTyre is keeping Rose busy so she doesn't start questioning people in an attempt to drum up leads."

"What's her boyfriend doing? Tying her to the bed and making love to her so she's too preoccupied to snoop?"

Lucas opens his mouth to answer, amusement dancing in his eyes.

I lift my hand before he can say anything. "Don't even go there. The last thing I want to discuss is Grams's sex life." Or lack of it, given her age.

"I was just going to say—"

I press a warning finger to his lips. His mouth turns up at the corners. "Don't. Say. It."

He steps away, laughing, the sound a sexy rumble in his chest, and takes a sip of his wine.

I lower my hand. "Maybe we should try what the cops do, where they stick photos of their suspects and details about the crime scene and the victim on a huge board."

Outside the window, thick clouds hunker in front of the sun, the world suddenly dimmer with the promise of an early evening thunderstorm.

"Are you saying you want to turn my living room wall into a giant corkboard?"

"Not exactly, but maybe then we can keep track of everything, and the answer will become more obvious."

Lucas's eyebrows pull into a dark ominous line. "We? There's no we about this. You're my wife, not my crime-solving partner."

"And you're a PT, not a PI. And yet you're trying to figure out who framed you."

Lucas sets his glass on the counter and folds his arms across his chest. His frown deepens. "That's different."

"Really? And how's that?"

"Because you're my responsibility. And I'm a Marine."

"You're seriously planning to throw that caveman crap at me? I'm your wife, not your responsibility. They're two different things."

His eyes darken—and I get a glimpse of what the enemy once saw. Only I'm not too worried about it. "Like fuck they are. Your brother's dead, so someone has to make sure you don't get into trouble." His words drop like a nuclear bomb, leveling everything in a fifty-mile radius.

I can't...I can't...I can't believe he said that. The comeback I might have hurled at him fizzles in the air. Limp. Deflated. I can only stare at Lucas.

Jasper bounds over to us and sits his butt on the hardwood floor. He watches us expectantly as if waiting to see who's next to volley angry words.

Lucas shoves one hand through his hair, forcing the short strands into messy spikes.

"I don't need a babysitter. And in case you haven't noticed, I'm not the one who's facing a felony conviction. As for my brother..." My voice spills out rougher than sandpaper, the words sharp against my raw throat. "Neither of us can determine what he'd want because he's not here to tell us."

"If he were here, we wouldn't be married." Lucas turns away from me. His hands fist on the island counter, and his head sags forward.

Part of me wants to say we don't know that, but it would be a lie.

I squeeze his shoulder. I'm not the only one who's hurting, hurting because Aiden gave up on life. His death scarred us both. It changed us from who we once were, but it doesn't need to be the thing that adds another scab to our fragile relationship.

Lucas turns back to me. Desire and fear and resignation flare in his eyes. I feel naked, exposed, unable to register what any of them mean to him. To me. To us.

I cup his cheek with my hand. "I'm so scared," I whisper. "I'm scared I'm going to lose you because of..."

I let what I don't say hang with the weight of a million unspoken meanings.

His gaze absorbs everything my eyes are telling him. He nods. Then his mouth is on mine. Our tongues glide together, and I slip my hands around his neck. My thumb strokes the smooth skin at his nape. Lucas dips down, sliding his hands behind my thighs, and in an easy move, hoists me up onto the counter.

God...God, I want this man.

My legs circle his hips, bringing him closer. Letting him know just how much I want him.

26

LUCAS

I have no idea how Simone and I went from standing in my kitchen, cooking and discussing Rose's antics one moment, to Simone on the counter, her legs circling my hips, and I'm kissing her.

All I know is that I was angry she was willing to put her life at risk to help me; then I was lost in her beautiful hazel eyes. Lost and alive and calm. Calm like the lake on a windless day. But when she told me she was scared of losing me, everything I'd been feeling—fear, frustration, want—collided.

The perfect storm.

I lean into her, my length hardening in my shorts. My hands roam along her body, worshiping the feel of her under my palms.

Christ, I want her now, on this counter, stripped bare.

But as much as I crave her this way, it's not going to happen.

A high-pitched squeak reminds me of one reason why not. Jasper. He drops a squeaky chew toy next to my foot, and I swear the little cockblocker grins up at us.

Simone laughs, the sound soft and husky as if she's equally affected by what just happened between us. She unwraps her legs from around my hips and leans forward to see the puppy better.

153

"You want me to play with you while Lucas makes dinner?" She looks up at me. "Unless you need help."

"Go ahead. I'm almost finished here. It should be ready in about twenty minutes."

They head outside, and I watch them through the living room window. Simone tosses Jasper's squeaky toy a short distance. He goes tearing after it and brings it back to her.

I pick up the remote from the kitchen table and click on the local news. A video pops on the screen showing a building somewhere in the Middle East. One second the building is there.

The next it implodes into a pile of rubble.

Everything blurs in front of me. My mind takes over, sending me to a different time and place.

AIDEN RUFFLES THE SEVEN-YEAR-OLD BOY'S HAIR AND TELLS HIM HE'S LIKE a superhero. Brave and smart. Of course the boy doesn't understand him. We've often seen him when we patrol the area. Despite the crappy situation he's been dealt with, he always has a smile for us.

Aiden and I walk away, ever vigilant of the dangers around us. The hot sun bears down on us, the heat made worse by the heavy equipment we're carrying and the uniform we wear.

The wind stirs up the dry dirt, creating a dust storm. It's not as bad as on some days, but it's still annoying. I squint and keep moving forward, the metallic taste of unease lingering on my lips.

A series of gunshots explodes behind us. Adrenaline surges through my body. Aiden and I dive for cover, our training taking over for us.

We survey the area, try to determine who's doing the shooting: our side or theirs. The rotting smell of fear and regret battles in the air. I fight to fill my lungs with the memories of back home, of the clean mountain air. Of the taste of freedom and of hope.

The dust settles, the wind retreating a step. But the boy is no longer standing where we left him. He's slouched on the ground, bleeding out.

Aiden yells something and staggers to his feet. I'm right behind him.

And that's when everything goes to hell.

MY LEGS COLLAPSE UNDER ME AS I RETURN TO THE PRESENT. I LAND on my knees, struggling to pull air into my chest.

Breathe. It's not that hard to do. Breathe in and breathe out. I repeat the mantra in my head again and again, but it's not working. I'm trapped in a *haboob*, the Afghan dust rushing into my lungs, squeezing out the last drop of oxygen. My pulse thrums loud and fast in my ears.

Simone calls my name. Her voice sounds far away. Faint and unclear. A spicy aroma hints I'm no longer in Afghanistan. That what I experienced isn't real. Or what I think I experienced. The last few moments are becoming foggy.

A steadying hand rests on my lower back. Tenderly draws circles. I focus on that. Focus on the way it feels.

Heat sinks into my icy body, thawing me from the inside.

"You're okay, Lucas. You're safe. Listen to me. You're safe." With each word, Simone's voice grows stronger, clearer. With each word, it becomes easier to breathe.

She repeats them until I can finally nod, letting her know I'm okay now.

I take a deep breath and stand.

Simone's hands remain on me, ensuring I don't collapse into a pile of debris. My body trembles and sweat soaks my T-shirt. Disgust rockets through me at her seeing me like this. Chipped. Cracked.

"What happened?" she asks.

I can feel her eyes trying to catch mine, but I can't bear to look at her. Can't bear to have her see the slashes on my soul. I shake my head, unable to answer.

"I'm gonna take a shower," I say after a moment. My voice is gruff, short-fused; I barely recognize it.

In the bathroom, I strip out of my clothes and step into the hot shower. My body's still trembling, and I have to fold my arms on the cold tiles to steady myself.

I rest my brow on my forearms and let the water sluice over me. During the lowest of low months of struggling with PTSD, I'd locked the memories of that day in a metal box to be sunk in the deepest ocean. In time, my therapist had me face them. In time, the flashbacks' control over me lessened.

Until one day they didn't come as frequently.

But there are times when I can't escape them. When they come out of nowhere. Thank Christ those times have faded to far and few between.

I remain leaning against the shower wall until the tremors finally subside, until the water shifts from hot to warm and threatens to turn cold.

I turn the shower off and walk ass-naked into my bedroom to change into clean clothes.

When I return to the kitchen, Simone is stirring the food in the saucepan. I walk to the pantry, pull out the bottle of whiskey I've stashed there for moments like this, and pour myself a glass, neat.

Simone doesn't say anything, but I can tell she has questions. The need to know what happened is in her eyes, is on her face.

I toss back the drink and give it a second to heat my veins from within.

When I first returned to the U.S. after I was wounded, I sunk into a world of alcohol to drown out my horror-filled memories.

But it had only been a temporary fix. A fix that pulled me farther into hell. With each bad memory I blocked out, the good ones were also locked away. My friends. My family. Simone.

Eventually, it became impossible to hide how much I was struggling. My parents helped me reach out to the Veterans Center, who in turn assisted me in straightening my life out and quitting my addiction. I've been lucky. Alcohol doesn't control me. I can drink it without being dragged down that hole again.

I place the empty glass in the sink.

Jasper drops his squeaky toy by my feet. I crouch and pet his silky fur.

He looks up at me with sweet, trusting eyes, and I lower my ass onto the cool tiles.

Jasper parks his front paws onto my thighs and licks my hand. His tongue is soft and ticklish, and I can't help the small smile that tugs at my mouth.

Simone's toned legs walk over from the stove, but I can't find the will to look up at her. She sinks next to me, weaves her fingers with mine, and rests her head on my shoulder.

We stay like this, silently fussing over Jasper, letting him distract us from what just happened.

Eventually, sitting on the hard floor grows old, and I help Simone up. We finish making dinner, exchanging a few words, all related to the food. The silence could be uncomfortable, but it isn't. It feels as natural as hiking in the mountains. And the way we work together, each anticipating the other's move, is oddly soothing.

Once the food is ready, I pull Simone into my arms and kiss her temple. "Thank you." My voice is still cheese-grater rough, but less so than before.

"You're welcome," she whispers, warm breath fanning my throat.

We spend dinner making small talk. Simone has never seen me like this. I don't know how I feel about it.

Simone finishes her glass of wine. I switch to water. I refuse to revisit the path once traveled. Refuse to let Simone see the man who relied on alcohol to numb his pain.

We clear away the dishes and Simone suggests watching a

movie. "You know what we should watch?" An impish smile lights her face, and I know I'm in trouble. "A romantic comedy."

"You're kidding me, right?"

"Nope. If we had done things properly, we would've been dating long before we got engaged. And part of the dating rite of passage involves watching rom-coms with your girlfriend, whether you want to or not."

I know what she's doing and I appreciate it. Even if it means watching something I've managed to avoid my entire life.

While Simone takes Jasper out to relieve himself, I refill her wineglass and grab another glass of water. We make ourselves comfortable on the couch. She flips through Netflix and settles on *Isn't It Romantic?*

I can't help the groan that slips out.

Simone's impish grin returns to her face. "Don't worry, you'll love it. It makes fun of romantic comedies."

"That sounds like my kind of movie."

Turns out both of us were wrong. It's definitely not my kind of movie, but I'll admit it is funny. I settle my arm around Simone's shoulders, and she curls into me. It feels good, like I remember from college.

And just like that, I stop paying attention to the movie. I watch Simone. Notice things I'd forgotten about her. The way she laughs at the funny parts. The way she smells like a mountain breeze. Clean. Fresh. Freeing. The way she feels soft and warm against me.

She turns her face to me, a dangerously tempting smile on her lips. Her gaze lands on my mouth—and her breath and my heart rate hitch. All I can think about is tasting her. Exploring her inside and out.

She doesn't return to watching the movie. She just drinks me in for a long, dizzying moment. My heart rate kicks up, playing a loud upbeat rhythm in my chest. I could stay like this forever and be content.

Well, almost content.

I lower my mouth to hers and lick her bottom lip. Taste the drop of wine that lingers there.

Our mouths move together in perfect harmony, talking without words.

Jasper's soft snores come from his dog bed and the movie plays undisturbed in the background. Neither of us stops kissing. Kissing Simone is an addiction. A healthy addiction. One I never want to end.

I'm also not in a rush to move from the couch. When we were younger, the span of time between when we started making out and when I was buried deep inside her was a small blip. Barely noticeable. Now I just want to savor her a little longer before we get to dessert.

But in time, my need to only kiss Simone and my libido part ways, and I trace my fingertips along her ribs to her breasts. My thumb draws tight circles around her nipple while my mouth enjoys her wine-tinged kisses. I'm in heaven, and it will only get better.

Simone's back arches, pressing her firm breast into my palm. She moans.

"Should we stop now?" I somehow manage to say and pull away, my voice husky and aching with hunger. Aching with the need to do the right thing.

Confusion and disappointment flicker on Simone's face. "You want to stop?"

Hell, no.

"I just want to make sure this is what you want." I know we're married, but we didn't get married under normal circumstances. I don't want us to do something she'll later regret.

"I'm positive this is what I want." She runs her thumb along my bottom lip, her eyes confirming that I'm what she wants, what she craves.

"We might want to continue this upstairs." I nod at the snoozing puppy. "I'll put him in his crate afterward."

"Your room or mine?"

"Definitely mine." For one, I have the queen-sized bed.

We head upstairs, and I close my bedroom door behind us. Then I'm kissing her again. Gently. Reverently. She could have turned her back on me when she witnessed me having a flashback.

She could have told me to get a grip.

She did neither.

I show her with my lips and my hands my gratitude for everything she did downstairs. My fingers explore her soft, sweet-smelling skin and slowly peel her clothes off her. She helps quickly rid me of mine.

She scoots onto my bed, and we lie down, my lips and fingers not once pausing their seduction. I caress her tits and the hard nipples with my hands, and then with my tongue.

Her hands travel over the terrain of my stomach and chest.

My gaze takes in the smooth stretch of her stomach and lands on a four-inch scar on her lower belly. The horizontal scar isn't jagged like the ones on my shoulder. It's straight and silvery in the dim light of the room. It's not the only thing on her stomach that wasn't there the last time I made love to her. A small flower, like a lily, lies near her right hip. But instead of a leaf, a single wing grows from the stem.

The design is beautiful like the woman whose skin it's on.

I lean down and kiss the ink. Simone's breath is a gasp, so small I almost miss it. I glance up. Her eyes are wide and shiny as she watches me.

"Any particular reason you got a tattoo of a flower with a wing?"

She worries her lower lip between her teeth. Then she slowly shakes her head. "I saw the picture on Pinterest and liked it."

I press my lips on the tattoo once more. "It suits you." My mouth travels to the faint scar, and I kiss that as well. "What's this from?" My gaze flicks up to hers.

A tear slides from the corner of her eye and merges with her hairline. And I instantly wish I hadn't gone there. Seeing Simone cry always leaves my insides knotted.

"It's nothing. I was involved in an accident years ago. But it's no big deal." Her voice cracks with unspoken pain.

"What happened?"

"Honestly, it was nothing, Lucas. I was just in the wrong place at the wrong time. Like I said, it happened a long time ago. It's not important." She sits up, and her fingers brush the scars on my left shoulder. "What happened here?"

"It's the reason I was discharged from the military."

"This is from when you were shot? How did it happen?" Now it's Simone who's kissing old scars, and I close my eyes against the memory of how I got the one on my shoulder.

"Doesn't matter how I got it. It's the past."

She nods, and we come to a silent understanding. Our past wounds aren't up for discussion. We only want to focus on the future. Our future. She kisses the tattoo on my right bicep of a cloud and a thunderbolt. "What's this for?"

"It symbolizes Zeus and Thor." Two of Aiden's favorite gods.

"I bet he would have loved it," she says, understanding my reason for the tattoo. She kisses it once more, and I resume my careful exploration of her body.

By the time my fingers brush the silken heat between her legs, I'm intimately reacquainted with every part of her.

And *Christ*, I've missed her body.

27

SIMONE

I've missed sex. God, how I've missed sex.

I just didn't realize how much until Lucas's fingers pressed inside me and found a part of me that's been hibernating. His thumb caresses my clit, and my body lights up, every synapse working overtime. *Oh God, oh God, oh God-o-licious, high-and-mighty God.*

I don't...I don't remember...it being quite this good. With Lucas. With any man.

With each pass of Lucas's thumb, the tension inside me tightens. My body is an elastic coil close to its limits. One more circle, one more tease, and I'll unravel. I moan against Lucas's mouth.

His calloused pad circles my riled-up nerves for another pass, and I can't take any more. An all-consuming release implodes inside me, and I cry out Lucas's name.

Praying he'll catch me if I fall.

I drift down to his bed like a feather floating on a breeze, the crinkle of a foil package barely penetrating my brain. Lucas rolls the protection onto his length, positions himself, and with a level of control I didn't know he possessed, slowly pushes inside me.

At the feel of him, thick and ready, I gasp.

He rocks into me, and I hold on tight to the sheets. Our panted groans are the only noise in the room.

Lucas's thrusts are slow and deliberate, as if he's got all the time in the world to make me come once more, to shatter me in the best possible way.

It's not until I'm closer to the edge of no return, to spinning among the stars, that he shifts the pace. Moving harder. Faster.

One more thrust and I come apart around him, crying out his name again. My body hugs him, never wanting to let go, and I tumble into the abyss, white-hot heat filling and surrounding me.

Lucas lasts for several more thrusts and grunts out his release, the sound sweet music to my ears.

His body weight presses down on me. Makes me feel safe. We stay that way for a few moments, waiting to regain our breaths.

Lucas shifts off me. "Don't go anywhere."

I don't think I could move even if I tried. My body is a limp rag. A very satisfied limp rag.

He pulls on his briefs and his shorts and leaves the room to dispose of the condom that he doesn't need to use. Or doesn't need to use when it comes to birth control.

I curl into his pillow and inhale his spicy scent. It soothes my rambling thoughts, lulls me. But it's not enough to quiet the voice pointing out I could have told Lucas the truth about the accident, but I didn't say anything. I came close to explaining what the scar means. The impact it has on his plans for us to one day start a family.

But then I remembered my ex-boyfriend's face when he found out about my hysterectomy. Disgust. Annoyance. Indifference.

Indifference toward me.

Shame sharpens its claws inside me. I'm not ready to tell Lucas the truth. Soon, but not yet.

Mine. Lucas is mine.

An easy smile slips onto my lips. We're married now in every sense of the word. We can have sex together whenever we want—an additional perk to our business relationship.

Business relationship? Nothing about what is happening between us feels like a business arrangement—not when we're striving for a real marriage. Other than the part where I'm sleeping in the guest room.

Lucas returns, strips out of his clothes, and climbs under the covers. "Jasper's in his crate now."

"I bet he wasn't too thrilled about that. He looked content asleep on his bed in the living room."

"He might have been asleep when we left, but..." Lucas's words trail off, and a sexy smirk graces the lips I kissed not long ago. "I'm now down one cushion."

I wince in sympathy for what I assume are the remains of a chewed cushion.

Lucas kisses me on the forehead. It's unexpected and tender and sends a thrill trembling through me. "Stay with me tonight, Trouble."

I pretend to consider his request. The truth is, I don't have the energy to move. "Since your bed is comfier than the guest bed, that can be arranged."

The responding smile on Lucas's face is enough to heat my blood during the coldest winter nights.

I HAVE NO IDEA WHAT STIRS ME FROM MY SLEEP. EXHAUSTION CLINGS to me thanks to the two additional rounds of sex during the night, but I manage to pry my eyes open. The early moments of dawn stretch through the slits in the blinds.

There's a muffled grunt behind me. The mattress moves beneath me like a series of small aftershocks.

I flip over to find Lucas twisting and squirming on the bed. It's nothing like what happened last night before dinner. Then, he seemed to be frozen in place, struggling to breathe and trembling.

This time it's as if he's fighting an invisible enemy. Invisible to me. My heart splinters at seeing Lucas this way. And I feel so helpless. Helpless not knowing how to save him.

"Lucas," I say softly so as not to freak him out.

He keeps squirming, oblivious to my presence. The bedding tangles around his legs like a deadly serpent working its way up for the kill.

I lightly grab his shoulder. "Lucas. It's okay. You're safe."

He groans, the sound pained. My heart breaks some more.

I try again.

His eyes snap open, but even in the dim light I can tell they aren't focused. Terror stares back at me. He's not seeing me. He's not seeing anything in his bedroom. A sheen of sweat covers his naked body.

His arms flail, catching me off guard. A fist lands in my face. A sharp pain cuts into my cheek. A surprised yelp escapes me.

I press my hand against the stinging.

"Simone?" The terror on Lucas's faces switches to horror. "Shit, did I hit you?"

He sits up and reaches for my face, his hand shaky. I flinch away from him. He curses under his breath.

Wetness trickles down my cheek. I wipe it with the back of my hand, and wince at the sharp sting, at the blood smeared on my skin. "Were you having a nightmare?"

He rests his forearms on bent knees, his head drooping forward, and nods.

I kneel next to him. "Do you often have them?"

"Not really. Not until about two months ago. I've had a few since then. The same with the flashbacks. I was a mess when I returned from Afghanistan. It took time, but with therapy the nightmares and flashbacks became less frequent. To the point where they almost went away."

"What are they about?"

He shakes his head once more, only this time harder. More adamant.

He won't tell me, no matter how much I want him to. It's the same stubbornness I recognize from growing up with him. All I can do is be here for Lucas.

"Okay," I whisper. If he doesn't want to tell me, he must have his reasons. I'm not a therapist. I can't expect him to open up as if I am one.

His gaze studies my face, the guilt and shame in his eyes piercing my heart. "Shit. I can't believe I hit you."

"It's okay," I say, doing my best to soothe him.

"It's not okay." His tone is sharp, and the bite of his words punctures through to my bones. "I fucking hit you, Simone."

"You didn't mean to. It was an accident."

He scoffs. "Said every abused wife."

"You're not an abusive husband. I've known you most of my life, Lucas. That's not you. We just have to figure out what triggered the episodes and make sure they don't happen again."

His breath comes out in a hard, defeated sigh. "I need a shower and I need to patch up the cut on your face."

We both climb off the bed, and he directs me to the bathroom. I sit on the toilet seat, and he examines my cheek. Guilt stares back at me from his pain-filled eyes.

I cup his face with one hand. "It's going to be okay, Lucas. We'll figure it out."

He's been under a tremendous amount of stress because of the drug charges and the approaching trial. The cop showing up at the worksite yesterday, after someone claimed they saw him selling drugs, didn't help his situation any.

Most people would crumble under the strain he's been forced to endure.

He cleans the small cut, which has stopped bleeding. Then

without a word, he climbs into the bathtub. He's hurting, and it's killing me to see him like this. I just want to take his pain away.

I slide the curtain to the side and join him.

His hand leans on the tiles, his head hangs forward. Water sluices over his head and down his back. I can't tell if he realizes I've climbed into the tub with him.

I pour some body wash into my cupped hand and tenderly lather up his back and arms. His muscles are rigid under my touch, the tension in them practically vibrating.

With each stroke, the knots in his muscles begin to loosen. Lucas turns to face me, gratitude in his eyes.

And then we're kissing.

The kisses are tender. Sweet. Love and desire and hope soak each stroke of the tongue, each brush of the lips.

He pulls me closer. My arms go around his neck. His hardening length presses against my stomach, but he makes no move to take things further.

The tension in his body shifts, his muscles no longer as tight as they were. We keep kissing, in no rush to leave the shower. The only place I want to be is here, helping him get through whatever he's dealing with. In this moment.

Our kissing changes direction, interspersed with lathering each other's bodies. Our touches linger and caress. But that's as far as we take it. Sex isn't what Lucas needs to chase away his demons, to heal his past hurts.

The water gradually switches from hot to lukewarm. Not one for cold showers, I step out of the bathtub and dry myself. Lucas remains standing under the water as I return to my room to retrieve clothes.

I quickly change. Jasper's awake. I can hear his little barks alerting me that he's ready to get out of his crate.

As I enter the hallway, Lucas walks out of the bathroom, naked except for the green towel wrapped around his waist.

I smile at him while my gaze takes in the few remaining water droplets sliding down his body. *Lucky droplets.* "I'll take Jasper into the backyard. We won't be long."

The mountain air is chilly as the puppy and I head outside, but the sky is cloudless, hinting at another beautiful day.

Lucas is in the kitchen, making breakfast, when we return. "I might as well get an early start at the worksite," he says.

"Will you be okay?"

He doesn't look okay. Dark circles I hadn't noticed before now form crescents under his eyes.

"I'm fine."

A concerned frown wrinkles my brow. "Did you get much sleep last night?"

"I got enough."

I remove my supplies for my morning smoothie from the fridge. "I should probably sleep in the guest room until we figure out what's causing your flashbacks and nightmares."

He nods, but I sense he's refortifying the wall around him brick by thick brick. It's stronger this time. Impenetrable. But it somehow…somehow it pokes holes in *my* wall. Makes me bleed for what he's going through.

I want to take away his pain, but I don't know how. "Is there someone you can talk to at the Veterans Center about what's going on?"

He shrugs and takes a mouthful of cereal. The sugary kind he loved as a kid.

"What about Richard Diegel? Isn't he supposed to be renowned for his work with PTSD?" I'd read an article about him the other day. His research sounds promising.

"I'm fine, Simone. I don't need to talk to him." The bite in Lucas's tone makes a great white's teeth seem dull. God, was my brother this stubborn when it came to admitting he had a problem?

If Aiden had acknowledged he was struggling, if he had stopped hiding the truth from me, would he be alive?

If I had come back from Portland and not hid like a coward, could I have saved him?

We finish breakfast in silence, and Lucas appears as deep in thought as I am. He leaves the house first, mumbling that he'll be back late.

My morning is spent sitting at the patio table, creating the necklaces that will be part of an upcoming subscription box. Jasper snoozes in the sunny spot on the cobblestones near my feet.

Around eleven, I pack up my supplies and head to Treats. Emily, Kim, Zara, and I are meeting for lunch.

Grinning, Kim dips a yam fry in Emily's container of hot sauce. None of my friends have commented on the small cut on my cheek, hidden under my makeup.

"So, I have some big news. Jerome and I are pregnant." Kim's words come out so fast, I almost miss them. But as the words begin to register in my head, they feel less like good news and more like ash raining down on me, filling my lungs, making it hard to breathe.

Emily and Zara shriek their congratulations.

A memory of the day I finally accepted I was pregnant leaks in. When I knew that not only was I going to be a mother, but I was excited about it.

I was fourteen weeks pregnant when I finally clued in I was going to have a baby. Sixteen weeks when I got over the shock and fell in love with my child. At twenty weeks, I had the ultrasound, found out I was having a little girl. At twenty-one weeks, I wrote a letter to Lucas, telling him the news. I wanted to tell him first that he was going to be a father, and then tell Grams.

I never had a chance to send the letter. And I refused to break Grams's heart and tell her that her great-granddaughter had died. I also couldn't find the strength in me to tell her about the accident and the hysterectomy.

I let her believe everything was okay.

That I was fine.

I blink away the forming tears, and my ex-boyfriend's words replay in my head. I'm defective. Broken. I'll never get to experience the joy again that has Kim glowing.

Guilt and grief threaten to suffocate me. I don't let them. This is Kim's moment. And I couldn't be happier for her.

I jump out of my seat and hug her, squeezing her tight.

But I can't deny her news is another reminder of what I'll never have. The babies. The happy marriage. A partnership where two people are completely open—instead of one where we're both hiding things.

Emily, Zara, and Kim talk all things pregnancy. I just smile and nod at everything they say. No one notices the crateful of emotions battling inside me.

Not all the emotions are due to Kim's news. The worst of them are linked to Lucas's flashback and nightmare. The brief fear on his face. The way he looked ready to run and never turn back.

If only chasing away his demons was as simple as checking under his bed, kissing him on the forehead, and telling him the monsters are gone.

If only...if only I knew how to help him.

28

SIMONE

"The gang's over there." Grams points a knobby finger at the deck chairs on the lawn behind the town hall. Every Fourth of July, Maple Ridge celebrates with a barbecue and festivities. They've been doing this since before I was born. The sky is clear blue, no hint of clouds on the horizon that could impact tonight's fireworks over Windermere Lake.

I wheel Grams to the picnic table where Delores, Samantha, and John are sitting, and say hello to them. A folk band is playing a lively tune on the stage, and little kids are bouncing to the fast-playing fiddle. They aren't the only ones dancing. Several older couples are also making the most of the music.

After checking that Grams has everything she needs, I walk to where Lucas is standing with his brothers, Jerome, and Zara near the hayride. Emily volunteered to help out and is collecting tickets from the group of people wanting to climb on. Kim has her camera strap looped behind her neck, shooting photos that will end up in the local newspaper.

Lucas's worn jeans and soft gray T-shirt hug his muscles in the best possible way. I'm not the only woman who's shamelessly checking him out. But as his wife, it's my duty to ogle him.

171

And to give him a quick kiss.

Lucas's mouth tilts in a sinful smirk. "That's the best you can do, sweetheart?" He places extra emphasis on the last word so it comes out as a drawl. "People won't believe we're married with that kiss." Lucas's hand goes to the curve of my spine, and his thumb caresses the skin under my sundress. Electricity strums beneath his touch, and my heart rate soars. Soars high up where birds sing, the fast cadence of their tune matching my heart rate, beat for beat.

And just like that, a needy whimper escapes me.

I pull away, and my lips morph into a smile that asks, *Your place or mine?* "Now there's no doubt in everyone's mind we married for the right reasons." It certainly convinced my body.

"You might be right about that." His voice is low, gravelly, yet smooth like hot lava. The sound of it pours over me, caresses me. My skin tingles and my lady bits sigh.

I scan the faces turned our way, pretending I'm looking for someone, gauging people's reaction to our show of affection.

One face in particular is scowling at us. Not the reaction I was expecting. Or more accurately, if looks really could kill, Lucas and I would be incinerated to a smoking crisp.

Shaved short dark hair. Scraggly beard. Antarctica-chilled demeanor. The man is a stranger to me.

"Why is that man glaring at us?" I nod in his direction.

Lucas turns, but the man in the grayish-blue camo pants and navy T-shirt has already stalked away, blending in with the families enjoying the festivities. "What man?"

"I don't know who he was. I've never seen him before."

"What did he look like?"

I describe him.

"Doesn't sound familiar."

"Is something wrong?" Kellan asks us.

"A man was glaring at Lucas and me, but I didn't recognize him."

A frown creases Zara's brow. "Glaring at you because you two were kissing?"

"I have no idea. Maybe he has a thing for Lucas and wasn't thrilled I was the one kissing my husband." The joke was meant to calm the uncertainty uncoiling in my belly. It falls flat.

"You were sniffing around Kincaid Timber a few weeks ago," Garrett says to Lucas. "It's possible you pissed someone off."

I hug myself, uncomfortable with where this conversation is headed. "Did you find out anything?"

"They weren't exactly forthcoming."

I sense there's something Lucas isn't telling me that his brothers already know about. None of them question him about what he found out. Because this isn't news to them.

"Well, whoever the man was, he seems to have a problem with you or me or us both. But I doubt it has anything to do with the conversation I had with Crystal on Wednesday."

I give Zara the highlights of what little I learned from Crystal. "But the man I saw wasn't Sebastian. That much I know. Crystal said he's out east right now, checking out lodges and inns for inspiration."

Lucas's hand returns to my lower back. The protective move eases the tangle of nerves knotted in my gut. "We don't know that for sure. You said he was allegedly in Eugene around the time I was arrested. Unless there are witnesses who can place him there the entire time, we can't discount the possibility he drove to Maple Ridge."

"The pictures I saw of Sebastian were of him when he was a teen and younger. So anything is possible. I have no idea what he looks like now."

"Why don't you and I check out the sights," Lucas says, "and see if you can spot him. I am curious what his problem is."

"We'll wait here for you," Kellan tells us. "Em's shift will be over soon."

Lucas threads his fingers with mine, and we wander the

grounds, pretending to check everything out while I keep my eyes open for the man. The smell of beer from the nearby tent mixes with the odor from the busy petting zoo as we walk past. I don't see the man who was glaring at me in either place.

"Let's try over there." I point toward the area where the artisans are set up and lead Lucas up and down the rows, inspecting the jewelry, candles, soaps, and other items that might be good for my subscription boxes. I buy a few things and collect business cards from other booths. The entire time I keep my eyes open for the man.

I sniff a handmade bar of lavender soap. "What do you think of this?" I hold it up for Lucas to smell.

He chuckles, his hand on the lower curve of my spine. "In my non-expert opinion, it smells good."

"Hey, Lucas." A woman with chin-length blond hair joins us. She smiles at me. "You must be Simone, Lucas's wife. Congratulations, you two."

"Simone, this is Rebecca," Lucas says. "She's the department head for the PT clinic where I used to work."

Rebecca nods. "And where you'll hopefully be working again soon. All your patients have been asking when you are returning. A few of them have been giving Jodi, your replacement, a hard time because they want you back."

"How is she?"

"She's good. But she's not you. And she doesn't have your military background. Which is a sticking point for some of the veterans."

"I can imagine. Hopefully they'll let her do her job to help them. I'd hate to see their progress regress by the time I return because they're being stubborn."

"When's your trial?" Rebecca asks.

"October twelfth."

"Well, I'll be keeping my fingers crossed it's over quickly and I have you back in the clinic just as quick."

A little girl appears at Rebecca's side and tugs on her hand. "Mommy. Can we see the baby goats now?"

Rebecca smiles at her. "Of course. One petting zoo coming up." The pair leaves, and I pick up a different soap.

I sniff it. "Are the temporary PTs in the clinic hired like you were? Or do they come from another source that hires them out as needed?"

"The latter." Lucas sniffs the proffered soap. "I only know that because the clinic had a temporary PT last year when one of the staff was on maternity leave. The Eugene Extended Care Center is responsible for filling temporary staff at the Veterans Center."

After I fail to spot the man who was glaring at us earlier, we return to the hayride. Zara has already left for the culinary competitions.

"I was beginning to think you two got lost," Kellan says, sounding slightly out of sorts.

Emily pats him on the arm. "Ignore him. He's hungry. He's always grumpy when he's hungry."

"I'm not grumpy when I'm hungry," Mr. Grumpy proclaims.

Emily raises her eyebrows in a gesture that leaves Kim and me laughing.

"Any sign of the man?" Jerome asks us.

I shake my head. "Whoever it was is either gone, or I just didn't see him."

The horse and wagon move forward, revealing the man in question talking to a man wearing a baseball cap, jeans, and a checkered shirt.

Neither is looking in our direction.

The man in the baseball cap appears to be counting out a large wad of money.

"There he is." I point, and all four Carson brothers and Jerome turn toward them. "He's the one without the baseball cap."

"Stay here." Kellan glances at Emily, Kim, and me, making it clear whom the order is for.

29

LUCAS

The man in the baseball cap hands the wad of cash to the guy who was glaring at Simone and me earlier. The guy stuffs the money into his wallet and shoves that into his camo-pants pocket. Behind us, one of the horses from the hayride neighs.

My brothers and I converge on the duo, not a single word exchanged. Jerome follows our lead.

Camo Pants doesn't seem familiar, but Baseball Cap certainly does. He's one of the men I spoke to when I went to the Kincaid Timber sawmill last month. The man with the thin, two-inch scar that cuts diagonally down one cheek. The man who spat on the ground near my feet.

Which means he's damn well difficult to forget.

"Great day for a celebration, isn't it?" My voice is the low rumble of an approaching storm.

Recognition flickers on Baseball Cap's face. It's replaced with an expression that's as readable as a blank piece of paper. "Little hot for my taste. But, yeah, sure…"

He gives the other man a look I can't decipher.

176

"You work for Kincaid Timber, don't you?" I ask, to see if he remembers me, though I doubt he has forgotten my visit.

"And what if I do?" His friendly, get-out-of-my-face attitude hasn't changed since last month.

"No reason in particular. Just curious why you'd be at this event. It isn't exactly in your neighborhood."

"Not for now, anyway. What can I say? Me and the wife found a nice house we might like to buy."

"You can't go wrong living here," I tell him. "It's a nice community. Great schools."

"So I've heard."

Camo Pants shifts on his feet as if he's holding a grenade that's about to explode, and he doesn't want to be the one left with it. Garrett and Troy casually break position, cornering him. Camo Pants's expression still doesn't give anything away.

I tilt my head, trying to get a better read on him. "If you're already house hunting, guess you're hoping Kincaid Timber will open up shop here."

The closest of their holdings isn't anywhere near Maple Ridge, so it's a little premature to be looking for homes here. Unless he likes super long commutes.

"Wouldn't complain. There're definitely pros and cons to this town."

I turn to Camo Pants. "So, you wanna explain why you were glaring at my wife and me earlier?"

"No idea what you're talking about." He crosses his arms as if trying to intimidate, but it's not working. His stance, legs apart, suggests a military background. Or maybe he's watched too many movies.

I believe him as much as I believe Jesus is my cousin once removed. But I can't exactly beat the man up for making Simone nervous. As tempting as it might be.

Troy steps closer to Baseball Cap like a cougar targeting its prey. "So what's up with the exchange of money we just witnessed? Is it something Maple Ridge's finest would be interested in?" The muscle in his jaw twitches at "finest," an imperceptible tell to those who know him.

"It's nothing you need to be concerned about. But if you really want to know what the money was about—" Baseball Cap nods at Camo Pants, who picks up the black case next to his feet.

Smirking, Camo Pants clicks the case open and shows us the contents. A clarinet?

A massive grin spreads on Baseball Cap's face, and he chuckles. "Not quite what you were expecting, huh? My daughter plays the clarinet. My wife and I decided to get her one for her birthday. But they're super expensive new." He nods at Camo Pants. "He knows someone who was looking at selling theirs because they bought a professional-level instrument."

Yeah, didn't see that coming. "I guess that's what you meant by pros and cons about living here. Maple Ridge isn't known for having an abundance of music teachers."

"Yup, that's one of the cons. But we'll make it work. Do you have kids?" Baseball Cap's gaze travels over my brothers, Jerome, and me.

"Not yet," I say, answering for all of us. He doesn't need to know about Jerome's fatherhood status.

"Well, once you do, you'll know what I mean. You'll do anything for them."

Troy, Garrett, Kellan, Jerome, and I return to the women, feeling a little stupid for thinking the two men were up to no good. But at the same time relieved we don't have to worry about the man who was glaring at Simone.

"What was that all about?" Emily asks.

"The guy was buying a clarinet for his daughter. No idea why the other man was glaring at Simone and me. He claims he wasn't." I can only shrug because I have no idea what to think. I believe Simone when she says she saw him glaring at the two of us. But maybe he was glaring at something else and it just seemed like his anger was directed at us. "I don't know about you, but I'm getting hungry. Let's check out the barbecue."

We walk to where the food tents are located. A sensation I know only too well from two deployments prickles the nape of my neck. Adrenaline floods my veins, taking my heart rate for a rapid spin around the block.

Someone is watching me.

My training kicks in, an old friend who never goes away, who always has my back. I scan the area, searching for a sniper. Searching for signs the calm is about to end.

My mouth feels as dry as the Afghan desert during the summer heat. Find the threat. Immobilize it. Protect the civilians.

Protect my girl.

My gaze shifts from one potential hiding place to the next. I can't locate anything out of sorts. Nothing that sets off sirens. But knowing that doesn't chase away the unsettled feeling in my gut.

30

SIMONE

I sit on the couch and study Jodi's Instagram feed. So far, her social media accounts haven't given me much intel about Lucas's replacement in the PT clinic.

Correction. The sites have provided me with lots of info about the woman, her cat, her general interests and day-to-day activities, and her boyfriend, Rick. What they haven't done is answer my questions on how she ended up with the temporary position. Was it random? She happened to be available at the right time? Or did she put in a request to be sent to Maple Ridge if a position opened up?

So far, she seems to love her new job and hopes it will become permanent. Jodi normally lives in Eugene. Her boyfriend lives in Maple Ridge.

It's been almost a month since Rebecca mentioned Jodi to Lucas while we were at the July Fourth festival. I hadn't planned to look Jodi up. I stumbled across her account after she commented on one of Zara's posts for Picnic & Treats.

I grab my purse, load Jasper and his crate into my car, and head to the worksite where Troy is working. He's placing tools into a toolbox when I pull up. I attach Jasper's leash to his collar so he can visit with his new friend, Butterscotch, and we walk over to the duo.

The dogs sniff each other. Jasper lies down, then jumps up and plays with Butterscotch.

"You almost finished for the day?" I ask Troy.

"Yup, just cleaning up now. You come to pick me up early for our date at Barside Brewery?" He gives me the signature Carson Brothers' flirty eyes that he's so good at.

I laugh. "You wish. No, it's something even better. You and I are going to Eugene. You're the muscle in this escapade. But don't worry, we'll be back before we're supposed to meet everyone at Barside."

He picks up the toolbox on the ground near Butterscotch. "Can I assume at some point you're gonna stop talking in code and tell me what's going on?"

"Where's the fun in that?"

"You're not dragging me clothes shopping, are you?" Troy glances at me like a shopping-phobic boyfriend, and I laugh.

"Since when have I ever dragged you clothes shopping?"

"Hey, I'm just eliminating the possible reasons for you wanting me to join you. Experience has taught me that when it comes to women, needing muscles usually involves some sort of shopping trip."

"Don't worry. I'm not dragging you clothes shopping. But I do need your help. Lucas isn't around to help me out, and I need to pick up some supplies for my subscription boxes. My order is ready, but something came up and the small business owner has to fly out tonight to go to Texas. Plus, there's somewhere else I need to go while I'm in Eugene. And that's where I need your help."

"All right. But I'm driving."

"I need to drop Jasper off at Grams's first." Lucas went hiking, which means I have no idea when he'll be back. "Meet me at her house in say, thirty minutes?"

Troy pulls up in front of Grams's house shortly before he said he'd be there, and I climb into his truck.

"If Tuuli and Robert sell the land to you guys," I ask at one point during the drive to Eugene, "what will happen if Blake can't prove Lucas is innocent? *We* know he wasn't responsible for the narcotics in his house, but his trial is in ten weeks and three days, and there's still no proof he was framed. If Lucas is found guilty, are you still going ahead with the plans for the outdoor program?"

It's a question I've wondered for a while now. But it's not one I can ask Lucas. His response might not match what his brothers are thinking.

"To be honest, I have no idea. But it is something Garrett, Kellan, and I have discussed." Troy looks at me, and I nod at the unspoken message in his expression. What he's about to tell me is not something he wants me to share with Lucas. For now, anyway. "Our grandfather had the idea for the program years ago when Lucas was doing his kinesiology degree. It didn't fit with what Garrett, Kellan, and I were studying in college, but it was perfect for Lucas. I just figured the idea died with our grandfather when Lucas went on to get his PT degree. It wasn't until a few months ago that he brought up the idea again. He'd heard the Wakefields were planning to sell their land. It was the only place he could imagine having the program. But I think you know why that is."

"I do. It was because of Aiden."

"That's right. Garrett, Kellan, and I were all for the idea, but when it comes down to it, Lucas is the most qualified of the three of us to run the program. Who better to understand the challenges some of the vets will be facing than someone with a PT degree and a background in adaptive sports? Each of us will be using our own talents to help the program succeed, but Lucas is still the mortar to our bricks. Without him, I'm not sure where the program stands."

"So even if the Wakefields sell you the land, the program might not happen if Lucas is found guilty?"

"It's not about the land at this point, even though Lucas would say otherwise. It's whether he will be a free man. And Robert and Tuuli know that. I wouldn't be surprised if the sale of the land does go through that there's a provision in the contract that will make it void if Lucas is found guilty. They know he's the force behind the program."

So everything really does come down to the trial. Lucas's freedom. His long-term goals. Our marriage. Our ability to grow old together. All of it is dependent on the jury's decision.

Knowing this feels like a kick to the solar plexus. And I just want to...want to...knee someone where it will hurt. What the hell did Lucas do to deserve this?

We drive to the woman's house where I'm picking up my order of handcrafted picture frames. After that, we go to the mall so I can pick up a few other items I need for the subscription boxes.

"There's just one more place I want to visit before we leave." The real reason I wanted Troy with me. I direct him to the extended care center near the hospital. "Lucas told me that the Veterans Center hires temporary staff through this place. Have you or your brothers looked into his replacement, Jodi, yet?"

"I've met her once there, but I'm guessing that's not what you mean."

"You're right. I'm just curious why she was picked to replace him. Her boyfriend lives in Maple Ridge, so that's her motive for wanting the job."

"Who's her boyfriend?"

I open the truck door and jump down. "I have no idea. Some guy named Rick."

Troy flashes me an amused glance. "That doesn't exactly narrow things down, even for a small town."

"I know, but it's the best I've got."

We walk up the path to the glass doors and enter the building. Inside, a light disinfectant odor lingers in the air, and I wrinkle my nose. This isn't a hospital, but it has the smell and feel of one. Death and pain and forgotten memories haunt the sterile hallways.

Troy and I walk to the front desk, and I smile at the receptionist, a blond girl who could be in her mid-twenties. "Hi, I was wondering if you can help me. Do you know if the extended care center places physical therapists in rural locations, like, for example, Maple Ridge?" I know the answer to this, but I want to see how much she knows about the inner workings of the place.

"Er, I have no idea. I can direct you to the rehabilitation unit. They might be able to help you."

She tells us how to get there, and we head down the brightly lit hallway toward another reception desk. My heels click lightly on the polished floor.

"I need you to flirt with the next receptionist," I say to Troy.

"Flirt?"

"You know, that thing you and your brothers do that turn women all starry-eyed. Especially that sexy smile the four of you've perfected."

A wry smile flickers on his face, one part charm, two parts patting me on the head like I'm his little sister. "I know what flirting is. But why do I need to flirt with the receptionist?"

"You'll see."

This time when I ask the next receptionist the question, Troy smiles at her. She stares at him, momentarily dazed—which is what I'd counted on.

Troy, Lucas, Kellan, and Garrett are all hot. A smile from one of them is like truth serum. Women are willing to divulge all their secrets. It's been this way for as long as I can remember. Even when they were kids, one of those smiles could easily get them out of all kinds of trouble. It had been the same for Aiden, too. Grannies were the most susceptible to their smiles back then.

Now that the four brothers are adults, Troy's smile seems to be the most potent. Which is what I was counting on when I invited him on this mission.

I clear my throat. That's enough to snap her out of whatever spell she's under.

"Yes," she says, her attention still on Troy. "We aren't responsible for all the centers, but we do have contracts with some of them."

"If one of them needs a temporary replacement because of an extended leave of absence, you can assist them with that?" I ask.

"That's right."

"Is the Maple Ridge Veterans Center part of that list?" Troy's voice is deep and rumbly, and I wouldn't be surprised if she just came in her panties.

Perfect.

"Yes, it is."

I smile. It's not flirty or designed to knock the panties off anyone, but it does hold its own. "Are replacements randomly selected or can individuals put in a request to work in certain locations?"

"It depends. In the case of the Maple Ridge Veterans Center, someone there requested a specific physical therapist. And she was more than happy to accept the placement."

"It must have been Chris McCutcheon," Troy tells me. "He's the center's director."

The woman types on her keyboard. "No, it was Richard Diegel."

Troy and I exchange confused glances. Her response doesn't make sense. "Since when does the head of counseling get any say in whom the rehab department hires?"

Troy's brow pinches into an almost-there frown. "Good question."

The woman leans closer, a gleam in her eyes. "He's her boyfriend."

And that information is the mallet hammering the silver disc into shape.

We thank the receptionist for her help and return to Troy's truck.

"Diegel really does benefit from Lucas losing his job at the center," I say as Troy pulls out of the parking lot. "It might mean Diegel's department will get more money because Lucas won't be around to argue on behalf of the PT department. And his girlfriend can live in the same town as him."

"Which means Diegel probably won't be too disappointed if Chris, for some reason, decides not to rehire Lucas."

"Do you think that could happen? If Lucas is found innocent, he might not be rehired after all?"

"Anything's possible," Troy says. "But I can't imagine that happening. Lucas is well respected at the center. As it is, there's been some grumbling over him being fired. People have wondered what happened to innocent until proven guilty. But there are others who have already convicted him without the benefit of a trial."

So no different from what it's been like in town.

"Does Chris or the board know anything about your plans for the Wakefields' land?"

"I'm sure they do. But they also know that Lucas has no plans of leaving the center for a few more years—if at all. He's not throwing his lot into our project without some sort of safety net. He loves his job at the center. He's not ready to give it up just yet."

That sounds like the Lucas I've always known. When he takes risks, they're always calculated risks. He doesn't jump into the deep end unless it's absolutely necessary.

I gaze out the side window for a few minutes, letting everything go by in a blur of green fields and blue sky. It's so peaceful on the stretch of highway between Eugene and Maple Ridge. Nothing like where Aiden, Lucas, and his brothers were deployed with the Marines. "When you left the military, did you struggle with PTSD?"

"No. I was lucky. But I know many people who were messed up with it." Troy cringes, his own pain and guilt and regret staring back at me. "Sorry. I didn't mean it like that."

"You're right. It did mess up my brother. If it hadn't, he would still be alive."

"I had a friend who recently died because of PTSD," Troy says after a beat. "He was my best friend. He hadn't been with the military, but he was a paramedic and witnessed the results of a horrific accident on the highway." He nods to the stretch of open road in front of us. "I completely missed the signs he was struggling with PTSD. If I could go back in time and help him, I would."

"I'm sorry about your friend." I swallow down my own pain of how I failed to protect my brother from his own demons.

"Lucas told me what happened a few weeks ago. With the flashback while he was watching the news and then the nightmare he had while..." Troy leaves the sentence hanging.

"While he was in bed with me?"

"Yeah, that. Has he had any more since then?"

"I don't know. I haven't witnessed any more flashbacks. But I also haven't slept with him since that one time, so I don't know if he's had any more nightmares. If he has, he hasn't told me about them." Lucas is so paranoid that he will have another nightmare and accidentally hit me again—or worse—he still insists that I sleep in the guest room. "Has he ever told you what happened that led to them?"

"No. As far as I know, the only person he's ever discussed it with was the therapist he was seeing in Seattle. It could be he hasn't had any since the last ones he mentioned to me. He hasn't had any issues on the job sites. Let me know if he has any more of them. With everything he's going through, he might need to talk to someone so the situation doesn't get worse."

"I will. Thanks."

Because the last thing I want is for Lucas to return to that dark time of his life again.

Which is what might happen if he's found guilty.

LUCAS

I push my legs hard as I run up the trail, paying attention to the roots poking out of the dirt as if they're land mines. My wet T-shirt clings to my sweaty body, and my lungs are ready to explode from the exertion.

I've yet to see any hikers. It's late, and most of them have gone home. It's just me and the forest and the demons chasing after me. Past colliding with present.

I leap over an exposed root. My lungs burn and my legs want to collapse from the punishing pace.

This won't solve anything.

This won't help me figure out who framed me and why.

I pause to catch my breath.

A powerful need to thrust my fist into a tree trunk surges in me. I shove the urge aside and resume running, only this time the pace isn't as grueling.

I arrive at my SUV an hour later, my frustration less than when I got here. I drive home. The sun is low on the horizon by the time I pull into the driveway. Simone's car isn't here. I go into the house, expecting to hear Jasper tell me he's bored of the crate. Nothing.

Simone must have taken him for a walk.

Upstairs, I grab my clothes and head to the bathroom. I'm in the shower, hot water sluicing off me, when the door clicks open.

"Lucas?" Simone's voice calls out through the steam.

I smirk, even though she can't see me through the shower curtain. "I hope so. Otherwise, a burglar is taking a shower in my bathroom."

She doesn't say anything more, and I continue scrubbing the sweat from my body.

A moment later, the plastic curtain slides partly open, revealing Simone. She's naked, and my cock greatly appreciates the view.

Without looking at me, she steps into the bathtub, and her gaze meets mine. "I hope you don't mind if I join you."

Her beautiful hazel eyes, rich with various shades of green and gold, darken with hope—and *fuck*, I want to be buried inside of her in so many ways.

There are plenty of things I could say—should say—but all I can do is pull her into my arms and kiss her.

Christ, I've missed her.

Her arms go around my neck, and we continue kissing.

Unspent need doesn't fill the kisses, but they consume me all the same. I focus on the feel of her warm body against me. Focus on the light floral scent of her hair.

Deep down a voice questions if this is a good idea. I bottle the question away for now. When it comes to Simone, I've never done the smart thing. I usually do what feels right at the time.

She looks up at me. There's an emotion in her eyes—gentle, nonjudgmental—that I can't fully read, but it makes me smile all the same. "I want us to try sleeping together tonight."

"I don't kn—"

Her finger presses against my lips, silencing the rest of the sentence. "I do. We need to find out if the nightmare was a one-time thing. Have you had any more since then?" She lowers her hand.

I shake my head. "No flashbacks either."

"Good. Have you had dinner yet?"

"No. I just got back from my hike."

"All right. You finish off here, and I'll whip something up. Troy and I went to Eugene this afternoon, and I have some stuff to tell you."

"You did? Why?"

"I had to pick up an order there for my subscription boxes. The artisan had a family emergency and had to fly out tonight. I dragged Troy along to help me. But while we were in Eugene, we went to talk to someone about your replacement, Jodi, at the Veterans Center. I'll explain once you're finished here."

Before I can stop her, she pulls the shower curtain aside and steps out of the bathtub.

And I'm left mentally cursing that I didn't take advantage of shower sex while she was in here.

I go into the kitchen to find Simone stirring something spicy in the wok. Her hair is tucked behind her ears, the ends damp. Her tank top and denim shorts reveal acres of smooth, lightly tanned skin.

Seeing her like this takes me back to high school. Back to when I first noticed her as more than Aiden's little sister. She'd been wearing a similar outfit and had resembled every teenage boy's fantasy times two. Every heterosexual guy at school wanted her—but they weren't dumb enough to admit it in front of her brother.

Now, she looks like every man's fantasy, the fantasy only I get to act on.

Her lips curve into a hint of a smile. "I'm making chicken stir-fry. Hope that's okay."

I pick up a thin slice of carrot from the cutting board and pop it into my mouth. "That's more than okay. So you wanna tell me what you found out about my replacement?"

"Jodi's boyfriend lives in Maple Ridge, so she obviously wants to be here because of that. Turns out Richard Diegel put in a request for her. He's her boyfriend."

"That would explain why he wanted her in Maple Ridge. But the PT clinic director would be the one deciding who replaces me, not Diegel. Do I think his girlfriend was motive enough for wanting me to lose my job? No. I think Diegel just took advantage of the situation."

Simone turns off the stove. "That's what Troy and I thought, too. What about funding for his clinic? Do you think that would be enough of a reason to want you fired?"

"Yes. But I honestly don't believe he'd try to get someone fired to increase the chance of him getting more funding. If someone royally fucked up and put his patients at risk, then yeah, he would push to have them removed. But Diegel likes to win because he outsmarted the competition. He loves the challenge. Planting drugs in someone's house is beneath him."

I remove the plates from the cupboard. Simone scoops the stir-fry onto them. By the time we've finished dinner and cleared the dishes, it's time to head out to Barside Brewery, where we're meeting my brothers and our friends.

We arrive at the bar to find Garrett, Jerome, Kim, Troy, and Emily at one of the pool tables in the back. Jerome is surveying the balls on the table, pool stick in hand.

A hey-there smile stretches on Emily's face. "Zara's on her way. She got held up at the café. And I have some news." Her smile brightens. "I landed my first client! The bride and groom are getting married in December. They hired me to be their wedding coordinator."

This is all directed at Simone. So while Simone and Kim get excited over Emily's news, I join my brothers and Jerome at the pool table.

I slap Garret on the arm. "I see you dragged yourself away from your latest thriller long enough to join us."

He throws me a dark look I recognize.

"Plot issues, huh? Maybe you should've joined me on my hike this afternoon. Then you wouldn't be stuck."

"If I'd known you were hiking, dumbass, I would've been racing you up the goddamn mountain."

"And we both know I would have won."

"Not so sure about that. But at least I would have solved my problem. What about you?"

There's no fooling my brother. He knows why I run up the tough inclines that most people prefer to hike. Well, he might not know the exact reason this time, but he gets it.

"Anything you want to discuss?" he asks.

I shake my head. He also knows me enough not to push it.

For now, anyway.

"The usual?" My question is directed at Simone, who's busy talking to Em and Kim.

"Yes, please."

I walk over to the bar and wait for Evie to finish with the customers at the other end of the counter.

"I swear they'll sell the property to my parents," a man beside me says to the guy next him. His back is to me, but his friend's face doesn't look familiar. "They'd be fools not to."

"I'll be sure to relay that to my boss." The other man's voice is low and prickly. I can barely hear him over the country music in the background. "He's none too happy with the delay as it is."

"Look, it will happen. I just need more time."

"He don't care about that. He only cares about you fulfilling your end of the deal."

Evie turns to me and begins wiping down the counter. "What can I get you, Lucas?" She has the same long black hair as her sister, but unlike Kim, Evie's hair has purple streaks in it.

"Cabernet Sauvignon and the house special on tap, please."

She flashes me a dimpled grin. "So, the usual?" She turns and grabs a bottle of wine from the bar behind her.

"I hear you're going to be an aunt," I say as she pours Simone's glass of wine. "Congratulations."

She grabs a glass and fills it with beer from the tap. "Thanks.

That should take the pressure off me for a while when it comes to getting married and giving Mom grandkids. Taylor and I aren't in any rush to tie the knot or adopt. The microbrewery and bar keep us busy enough."

A patron at the other end of the bar waves for her attention. I pay Evie and return to where Simone is setting up the balls on one of the available pool tables. I place her drink on the table where our friends are sitting.

"Was that Sebastian Dryson next to you at the bar?" she asks.

I swivel in the direction she was referring to, but the two men I overheard talking are no longer there.

"I've never met the man. You really think that could be him?"

She gives a small shrug. "He kinda resembled the guy in some of the photos I saw at Crystal and Walter's house earlier this month. His hair's a bit longer now. But otherwise, it looked like him."

I scan the bar, but I can't spot either man.

"Is something wrong?"

"No, everything's fine. You ready to play?" I nod at the pool table, and my mouth tugs into a reasonable replica of a smile. The men's conversation replays in my head. He must have been talking about the Wakefields' property. But who wasn't happy with the delay? What delay? Robert and Tuuli plan to announce the winning bid on October fourth. That date hasn't changed.

Simone lightly drags her index finger down my chest. "Yep. I'm ready. How about we make a bet?" Whereas my smile is fake, hers is one hundred percent I-want-to-jump-your-bones genuine—and I shove the overheard conversation to the side, to be analyzed later.

"What do you have in mind?"

Simone leans into me. Her light floral scent teases me over the strong smell of spilled beer, burgers, and fries. "Winner picks position tonight."

I don't need a translator to understand what she's getting at, and I grin. "You've got yourself a deal."

"Hey, you guys finally made it," Emily says as I take my shot.

I glance up to see Zara and Kellan approach our group.

"I got a flat on the way," Zara tells us matter-of-factly, as if this happens all the time. "Luckily for me, Kellan was in the neighborhood and fixed it."

At the other pool table, Garrett straightens from the shot he was about to make. "Hey, I could have changed your tire if you had called me."

"I know. But there was no need to call you. Your brother helped me out." Not giving Garrett a chance to say anything else, Zara weaves through the crowd toward the bar.

Simone sizes up her next shot and gets into position. The hem of her sundress rides up, exposing the backs of her thighs. I walk behind her and brush the tantalizing skin with my stick—as she's taking her shot.

The touch is enough to distract her, and her stick skims over the top of the ball, setting it in motion.

It barely rolls two inches.

Simone spins around and glares at me. "Cheat."

I match her glare with a grin. "I would never do that."

She prods me in the chest with her index finger. "Keep your stick to yourself, Mister." *Poke. Poke.*

My grin widens. Fuck, she's adorable, even when she's pissed at me. *Especially* when she's pissed at me. "Okay, for now. But I'm definitely up for sharing my stick with you later."

She opens her mouth in rebuttal. A crash behind us halts her words. We jerk around to see what's going on, but there are too many people blocking the entrance to the pool tables to get a good view.

"Stay here," I tell Simone and weave through the crowd. I make it to the front in time to catch the man I saw talking to Sebastian take a swing at him. The stranger's face is red, expression contorted into a snarl. He launches himself at Sebastian.

The stranger has an extra sixty pounds of muscle on him

compared to his target, but what Sebastian lacks in muscle, he makes up in agility. He ducks out of the way.

The music stops abruptly, and the volume in the bar drops to near silence. Everyone's attention is on the fight in the center of the room. Usually you'll get several morons cheering and chanting on a fight. Not this time.

The two men circle each other. Patrick, the bouncer, approaches the pair. Size-wise, he matches the stranger. He places his body between them and exchanges words with the man.

The stranger grunts several obscenities at Patrick and Sebastian, then turns to leave. Patrick walks behind him, escorting him out.

Sebastian snatches up a nearby stool and swings it back.

I don't care about the stranger. There's something about him I don't trust. It's Patrick I'm worried about.

I step in front of Sebastian, ready to jerk the stool out of his grasp if it comes to that. "I'd leave if I were you, Sebastian." My tone is that of a black bear protecting his territory, or in this case, protecting a friend's territory. Evie and Taylor don't need anyone damaging their business. The business they've poured their hearts and money into.

"I don't have to leave if I don't wanna. You don't own this place."

"He might not," Evie says, having stepped out from behind the bar. "But I do." She nods at me. She might be barely five foot five on a good day, but her scowl is all badass.

I'm more than happy to escort Sebastian Dryson from the bar. I'm also more than happy to ask him some questions about the conversation I overheard.

Sebastian sways on his feet. Great. The idiot's drunk. Drunk and stubborn, because he still doesn't bother to move.

"We can do this the easy way, and you leave of your own accord. Or she calls the cops." I nod at Evie so he knows who I'm talking about. "Your choice."

A redheaded woman pushes between the onlookers and tugs

on Sebastian's arm. When it's clear he's not planning to move, she says something in his ear. That seems to be enough to get him to leave the bar. I follow them.

Patrick and the other man aren't outside when I exit the building, and the parking lot is empty of people. Dusk is settling over the town like a blanket, the long, dim shadows swallowing up the area.

"Do you know who I am?" I ask Sebastian.

"Do I look like I give a fuck who you are?"

Given that he's partly responsible for my brothers and I being in limbo when it comes to the Wakefields' land, I try not to take his slight too personally.

"Does the name Lucas Carson ring a bell?"

He eyes me with the intensity of a mosquito that wants to suck my blood. Guess that answers that.

"So what is it you really want the Wakefields' property for?" I ration a small amount of patience into my tone.

Something heavy and hard hits me on the side of the head. Whatever Sebastian's answer is, I don't get to hear it.

Everything goes black.

SIMONE

"Did you see what happened?" I ask Zara. Kim and Jerome left during the altercation to check on Evie. Lucas is nowhere to be seen in the dimly lit bar, thick with people standing around like pine trees in a dense forest. Even his brothers have vanished.

Zara shakes her head.

When the fight broke out, the brothers switched into Marine mode. Lucas told me to stay put and disappeared into the crowd.

Troy approaches us, frowning. This isn't his annoyed or confused frown. It's a frown that sends my heart into palpitations, that leaves horrifying scenarios flashing in my head.

"There's been an accident." The comment is directed at me and does nothing to calm my adrenaline tsunami.

"What do you mean an accident?"

"Your grandmother has been in an accident."

The Maple Ridge police officer's words pound in my head, and a wave of dizziness crests inside me. *Please, please, please not again.*

"Come with me." Troy walks away from us. I follow him, weaving through the bar patrons to the front entrance. We exit the bar.

The night air is a cold kiss on my bare arms. Goose bumps prickle my skin.

Lucas is sitting on the curb a short distance from us. The dark-green T-shirt Kellan was wearing when he arrived at the bar is pressed against Lucas's temple. Patrick and Garrett are also with them.

The breath I'd been holding rushes out in a *whoosh*, and I hurry over to the four men.

I crouch in front of Lucas. In the glow of the nearby streetlight, I make out dark stains in the green fabric. Stains that weren't on Kellan's T-shirt when he showed up at the bar. Lucas's faded blue T-shirt is also smeared with blood.

My pulse throbs loudly in my ears, drowning out the noise of the passing vehicles. I touch Lucas's cheek so I have something to do with my hands. "What happened?"

His eyes look slightly dazed, but from what I can tell, his pupils are evenly dilated.

"I was asking Sebastian what he really wanted the Wakefields' land for. And the next thing I know, someone hit me on the side of the head."

Patrick crouches next to me. "I found him unconscious."

I brush my hand against the one holding the cloth to Lucas's temple. "We need to get you to the hospital."

"Police and ambulance are on the way," Garrett says.

I glance from Patrick to the three men standing. "Any idea who did this?" From what Lucas said, it doesn't sound like Sebastian was the guilty party.

"No idea. It wasn't the man Sebastian got into the fight with," Patrick tells me. "I was escorting him off the property when it happened."

"Whoever it was, Sebastian can identify him." Lucas makes a move to stand.

I rest my hand on his thigh, telling him without words that he's going nowhere for now. The whirring of sirens calls out, growing closer with each second.

"Nice of him to stick around to identify the person," Kellan grumbles. "Or provide medical assistance."

"He conned his parents in to buying the Wakefields' land for his own self-interest. I doubt doing the right thing is high on his to-do list." Disgust radiates through Lucas's tone, bleeding into each word.

"Which means he can't be trusted." A slight tremble takes over my voice. "We've been digging into things we probably shouldn't. We've pissed someone off. We have to stop...we have to stop before one of you is killed."

Lucas turns to me and gently touches my jaw. "Hey, it's okay, Trouble." His tone is as tender as his touch. "Nothing's gonna happen to us."

"You don't know that. You might get killed."

"And I might end up in the slammer for the next twenty-five years. I can't sit around waiting for the cops to figure things out. At the rate they're going, that might never happen."

I know he's right, but that doesn't make my fears any less painful.

I sniff. He brushes his thumb against my cheek. "If we're going to have a chance—you and I...I need to do this."

"Even if it means you could be killed?"

"Even if it means I could be killed. But I'll do everything in my power to keep that from happening. We all will."

The EMS and police arrive, preventing any further discussion. But it doesn't matter. I know these guys. The brothers won't stop searching for the truth just because I'm scared. They won't stop until justice has been set straight.

While Patrick and Lucas's brothers explain to the cops what happened in the bar, the EMS checks Lucas over.

"You need stitches, and you likely have a concussion," the woman tells him once she's finished examining him.

I sense Lucas wants to argue and skip going to the hospital, but he just nods. He probably doesn't want to risk another outburst from me. Hey, whatever it takes.

Garrett tells them he can drive his brother to the hospital. *Now.* His expression doesn't allow Lucas room for argument.

"I'll meet you there," I tell the two men and watch while Garrett escorts Lucas to his car.

I walk over to Troy and Kellan, who are talking with the cops. Zara and Emily are with them. Patrick has returned to the bar.

"Did you see anything, ma'am?" the officer asks me.

"I was in the bar when it happened. And I only heard the fight inside. I didn't see it." I want to ask him if he thinks the attack has anything to do with the drugs found in Lucas's house, but the cops still believe the narcotics belonged to Lucas. I doubt he's going to give me the answer I'm looking for.

Lucas is right. So far, the cops have done little to figure out who's setting him up for the fall.

Troy drives me in Lucas's SUV to the hospital. We climb out of the vehicle, but I can't make my legs move toward the ER entrance. I stare at the red brick building where Grams was a patient over two months ago.

The fear I'd experienced then is no different to now. Lucas was fine when he left Barside. But what if his condition quickly deteriorated after that?

"He's going to be okay, Simone. He's got a hard head. I'm sure Mom dropped him on it a few times as a baby."

Troy might be saying that to put me at ease, but his concerned tone suggests the opposite. He's as worried as I am.

We enter the ER. Weary eyes peer up at us from the waiting room chairs. I recognize a couple of faces, but the rest are a blur. Lucas and Garrett aren't here.

A Code Red is announced through the loudspeakers in the ceiling. The tension in my muscles tightens at the urgent voice.

It's not Lucas. It's not Lucas. It's not Lucas.

Repeating that in my head on an endless loop, I will my legs to keep moving and join the end of the line for admitting.

The heavy disinfectant smell mocks me, dredges up memories of the last time I was in an ER. Medical staff rushing in and out of my room. The beeping of the heart rate monitor. The crippling pain. The bitter taste of loss.

The emptiness.

I hug myself, a blockage against further memories. My lungs are shrinking, shrinking, shrinking, and drawing air into them is a challenge.

I'm vaguely aware of a warm hand on the curve of my lower spine. "Breathe, Simone. He'll be okay." Troy.

I nod, the movement mechanical, and close my eyes.

"I'm sorry. There was nothing we could do."

A salty wetness touches my lips. I wipe my cheek with the back of my hand.

"Simone, honey." Zara's voice sounds distant, faint. "Why don't we go outside so you can get some air? Troy will track us down once he has an update on Lucas."

I nod again, the movement belonging to a rusty robot. Zara and Emily escort me outside.

We step into the pine-scented night, and the air can finally ease in and out of my lungs. We walk along the sidewalk and around the corner to a small flowering rock garden. Artisan lampposts light up the three empty benches there. We sit on the closest one.

I pull my feet onto the seat and hug my knees. "I'm sorry." My voice is low and scratchy as if it hasn't been used since the night of the accident. "I was in a bad car accident ten years ago. I'm not a fan of ERs."

Emily puts her hand on my shoulder. "How come we didn't know about that?"

"No one does. Other than Avery and my coworkers at the agency where I was working. Grams doesn't know about it. And I'd prefer to keep it just between the three of us." I feel bad not including Kim. But if I had my way, Em and Zara would also be in the dark about what happened.

"Why doesn't your grandmother know about it?"

"It's not something I like to talk about." My voice is soft, the message clear. Both women nod.

"So your reaction has nothing to do with Lucas?" Zara asks.

"It has a little to do with him. I'll be a lot happier once I know he's okay."

Emily texts Kellan to tell him where Troy can find us once he has news about Lucas's condition.

It's Kellan who eventually comes to find us. "He's going to be okay. Samuel stitched him up and he has a mild concussion, so you'll need to keep an eye on him. But other than that, he's free to go home."

"Thank you." I rise to my feet.

"Is he still in the ER?" Zara lightly rubs my arm, but her question is directed at Kellan. "Or have they released him?"

"He's filling out the paperwork now," Kellan says. "He should be done in a few minutes."

Zara continues to rub my arm. "We can wait for him at the front doors, Simone. Then you don't have to go back inside."

I nod, hoping Kellan doesn't ask me questions about what's going on with me. He's usually good at not prying into people's lives, something he's avoided doing since he was a kid, but who knows if this will be one of those rare times when he crosses the line.

We walk to the entrance. Kellan disappears inside the sliding doors. We remain outside. He returns with his brothers. Troy pushes Lucas in a wheelchair. Sterile gauze is taped over Lucas's left temple, and he's wearing a perturbed expression.

A giggle stumbles from me. I bite my lower lip to keep back its friend. "I take it you're not thrilled with being in the wheelchair."

He grunts his opinion. "I can walk to my SUV." Lucas makes an attempt to stand.

I put my hand on his shoulder. "Humor me for a moment and stay in the wheelchair till we get to your vehicle." I kiss him gently on the lips and gaze into his warm brown eyes. "Pleeeease."

He releases a forced-out breath, but his expression doesn't soften. "All right."

His brothers help him into his SUV, and he tells them to meet us at our house.

I climb into the driver's side. "Shouldn't you be resting once we get home? I don't think Samuel meant for you to have a party after he released you."

"I'll be fine. And it's not a party. I just want to talk to my brothers about what happened at Barside."

"Can't it wait until tomorrow, when you're feeling better?"

"No. Not if what happened tonight could be linked to the drugs found in my house."

I don't say anything else. There's no point. Lucas has made up his mind.

Just be happy no one told him what happened in the waiting area.

33

SIMONE

At home, Lucas changes into clean clothes, and I help him get comfortable on the couch. "I'm taking Jasper out back. I'll only be a few minutes."

He grabs hold of my wrist. "I'd rather you don't go out there without someone keeping an eye on you."

"I'm going into the backyard. Nothing will happen to me." I bend forward and give him a quick peck on the lips. "You were the one who was attacked at the bar. It had nothing to do with me. Besides, Jasper is an amazing guard dog. Isn't that right, boy?"

Jasper barks his non-scary puppy yap and sits next to the couch.

I crouch to his level and scratch him behind the ear. "That's right. You're a big scary beast. No one would dare mess with you." I grin at his adorable cocked-head expression.

"I still don't like the idea of you going out there on your own."

"You can see me through the window. I'll be fine. We won't be gone long. Nothing's going to happen to us."

I take Jasper into the backyard to do his business. I don't, however, brush off Lucas's concern about my being out here with only a puppy to protect me. The outside light is on, and I'm alert to my surroundings, every sound a potential threat.

The doorbell rings as Jasper and I step back into the house. I go to answer it.

Lucas's brothers and Jerome are waiting on the porch when I open the front door. Behind them, Emily, Zara, and Kim are discussing something.

We go into the living room and take a seat. I sit next to Lucas. He threads his fingers with mine. The move is natural and surprisingly soothing after everything that happened tonight.

"Before Sebastian got into the fight with the other man," he says, "I overheard them talking at the bar. At the time I didn't know it was Sebastian. His back was to me. It wasn't until Simone pointed him out that everything clicked."

Garrett leans forward in his chair, elbows on knees. "What were they talking about?"

"I think the Wakefields' property. Sebastian was telling him he was positive the Wakefields are going to sell the land to his parents. The man Patrick kicked out of the bar told Sebastian he would relay the information to his boss, but his boss already wasn't happy with the delay. There was something about Sebastian paying, but I missed that part of the conversation."

Emily's fair eyebrows leapfrog up her forehead. "Do you usually listen into other people's private conversations?"

"They were sitting at the bar, so I would hardly call it private. If they didn't want anyone to overhear them, they should have sat somewhere else. There was something about the man that gave me an uneasy vibe."

"What did the cops say when you told them this?" Zara asks.

"I didn't. With the way they're not doing enough to figure out how the drugs ended up in this house, they're hardly gonna care about info they can't easily link to the case."

"I wonder who the boss is the man was talking about," I say. "All we know is that Crystal and Walter Dryson are hoping to build the lodge because their son has been angling for them to do that."

"It doesn't sound like he's planning for it to be the romantic getaway they believe it will be." Lucas's mouth flattens into a thin line.

"You think the romantic-getaway part might be a cover? To make people less suspicious about the lodge's real purpose?"

Kellan shrugs. "This is all speculation. We have no proof that either man is up to no good. We need to keep an eye on Sebastian. But unless the other man plans to stick around town, there's not much we can do about him."

"It would help if we knew who hit you on the head," Garrett says to Lucas. "You really have no idea?"

"None. One second, I was asking Sebastian about the conversation I overheard. The next, Patrick was shaking my shoulders to see if I was conscious."

"Could Sebastian be the one who knocked you out cold?"

"No, it wasn't him. But I'm sure the cops will be asking him questions."

I tighten my hold on Lucas's hand. "You think he might be indirectly involved with what happened? And that's why he didn't stick around to talk to the cops?"

"Possibly. But why not stay? It's not like he'd be arrested because someone hit me on the head."

"Maybe he got scared off," Emily suggests. "He was afraid whoever hit Lucas would go after him next. You said the boss wasn't happy about the delay. It's possible what happened to Lucas was a warning to Sebastian. A 'Get your act together or else you're dead' warning. Why would he want to hang around for that?"

Cold dread fills the pit of my stomach. "If that's true, Tuuli and Robert could be in danger."

"She's right," Troy says. "Maybe you should talk to the cops again and make sure they understand the seriousness of the situation. If the cops don't believe you, that's on them. But this is Robert and Tuuli we're talking about. I suggest having Blake with you. That way if they fuck up, you have a witness who heard what you told them. They'll be accountable for their mistakes, not you."

Lucas agrees to contact Blake in the morning.

By the time everyone leaves, I'm ready to sleep for a hundred years.

Except, I won't have that luxury.

I shut the front door behind Kellan, lock it, and lace my fingers with Lucas's. "All right, time for bed, Cannon. I'm sleeping with you, and I'll wake you up every few hours."

"That's not a good idea, Trouble." His frown says he's going to stick to his guns on this. My expression replies, *Fat chance.*

"It'll be okay. If you have a nightmare while I'm with you, we'll also deal with that. I'm not leaving you alone until you're fully recovered from the concussion."

He doesn't say anything, but it's clear I haven't erased his fears. The frown stays in place.

We get ready for bed and slide under the covers. Lucas pulls me against him. I'm on my back. He's on his good side, arm draped over me.

His thumb strokes my bare arm, his touch raising tingly goose bumps over my skin. "Troy told me you had a panic attack in the ER."

So much for hoping no one mentioned it.

"I was worried about you."

"It's more than that. You saw me at Barside. You weren't a wife who just learned her husband was horrifically injured. Why the panic attack, Simone?" Lucas's deep voice is a soothing caress.

Deciding it's better to tell him the truth—a portion of it, anyway—I gather the strength I need to get past the next part. I know he's still curious about the scar. Maybe this will help erase his lingering questions.

"I freaked out because of the accident I told you about. When I was twenty-three, a drunk driver lost control, and my car got tangled in the pileup he caused. Being in the ER tonight reminded me of how alone and helpless I felt." Avery had been there for me, but it was Lucas who I'd wanted. Unfortunately, he had been thousands of miles away.

"What do you mean alone?"

My vision clouds with tears, but I'm too afraid to close my eyes to blink them away, too afraid to relive the memory of the accident. I shift the arm that Lucas isn't stroking and rest my fingers where our baby used to be—thankful Lucas won't understand the meaning behind the movement.

"No one knew about it. Other than Avery and my colleagues at the ad agency where I worked. Grams didn't know. No one in Maple Ridge knew."

He quietly curses under his breath. "Why not?"

"Because I wanted it that way." Because I didn't want anyone to know I'd been pregnant and then lost the baby. It would've been too difficult, and the news would've ended up hurting too many people.

Lucas shifts his body so he's gazing down at me. And I pray the moonlight isn't strong enough to illuminate my tears. Pray he doesn't see the pain on my face.

His mouth presses softly against mine, and I breathe in his scent of mountains and sunshine and hope. I'd be more than happy to spend the rest of our days growing old together this way. This content.

We don't talk. We just tenderly kiss. And my heart melts. Melts with the realization that I'm not falling in love with Lucas again.

I've never stopped loving him.

I just didn't realize it until now.

34

LUCAS

Monday morning, I head to the police station. The brick building isn't the same one as from my youth. This one is bigger, newer, with large windows spanning the front.

Inside, the dark-blue plastic chairs are empty except for a bald man in gray overalls. Engrossed in a magazine, he doesn't bother to pull his attention from it when I enter. The American flag stands in the corner, the only thing in the place that isn't strictly blue or white. Even the rectangular floor tiles are a checkerboard of the two colors.

I used to like blue. But after my last experience here, I've developed an adverse reaction to it. My skin feels tight and itchy—a reaction even a shot of Benadryl won't cure.

Blake steps into the building and waves to me. I unfold from the chair and join him. Like me, he's dressed in a suit, but I can guarantee he spent more on his than I did on mine.

We step to the side, out of range of the man leafing through the magazine.

"We'll tell the officer what you've told me. If they give a damn about doing their job properly, they'll look into it." Blake jots something on his phone.

We head toward the reception desk. Three officers are having a discussion on the other side of the glass partition. The officer manning the desk glances up from whatever he was doing.

"Hello," Blake says, showing the man his ID. "Is Officer Mitchell here?"

The man swivels to his colleagues and repeats the question to them. One of them replies, and the officer turns back to us. "Can I ask what this is regarding?"

"Someone attacked my client, Lucas Carson, Friday evening at Barside Brewery. Officer Mitchell responded to the nine-one-one call. We have some additional information for him."

The man nods, and a minute later, the officer from Friday steps out of a door farther down the corridor and approaches us. "How are you doing?"

"I'm doing better. Thanks. I just wanted to check what's being done to protect Robert and Tuuli Wakefield. Like I mentioned before, it's possible they might inadvertently be linked to what happened to me on Friday night. I want to make sure I told you everything that happened. I was dealing with a concussion at the time, and it's possible I might have missed telling you something important."

"And you would be...?" His question is directed at Blake.

"Blake Wright. Mr. Carson's lawyer."

Mitchell leads us to a room that contains nothing more than a table, a couple of wooden chairs, and a mirror. It's the same room I was in when I was arrested. This chair is the same one I sat on, my body sweaty from my run. From what I've heard, they also have a comfortable interview area that resembles a small living room. Clearly, he doesn't think this call warrants that.

He has us sit. His expression fails to reveal what he's thinking, how he feels about talking to us. Is he interested? Distrustful?

Bored? Or is he mentally reciting the list of groceries to be picked up after his shift? "Okay, let's go over your statement again."

I fill him in on the sequence of events on Friday night, the conversation I overheard between Sebastian and the other man. I also tell him about the property my brothers and I want to buy from the Wakefields and how Sebastian's parents are also interested in purchasing the same land.

"I don't know if the two are connected, but if they are, I'm worried what it could mean to his parents and the Wakefields." I get the feeling that Sebastian is playing with fire, but his parents or the Wakefields will be the ones getting burned.

Mitchell writes down the information. "Most of this you had already told me when I spoke to you on Friday. But I appreciate the additional information you provided this time."

I push my fingers through my hair, taking care not to touch my stitches. "Does this mean you'll keep an eye on the Wakefields? Make sure nothing happens to them?"

"I'll talk to them and apprise them of the situation." He stands. Conversation over.

Outside, Blake walks me to my SUV. He stops, turns to face me. "I told you to stay out of trouble, Lucas. How can following Sebastian outside the bar, after what happened, not be considered getting into trouble?" He levels an exasperated glare at me.

"In my defense, I didn't know someone was going to hit me on the head while I was talking to Sebastian. At the time, I was only concerned about one other person, and Patrick, the bouncer, was escorting him off the premises."

Blake shakes his head. "Okay, well, I'll have one of my private investigators look into everything you told them in there. But can you promise me something?"

"What's that?"

"Try not to let anyone else attack you. I won't do you much good if you're dead for your trial date. I mean it, Lucas."

I release a snorted laugh. "Thanks for the advice. I'll keep that in mind for next time."

My phone rings and I check the screen. Drew. "I've gotta get this," I tell Blake.

"I'll talk to you soon." Blake walks away, leaving me standing by my SUV. A mother and her two kids are walking on the sidewalk near me. The little blond girl is about six years old, her brother three. Both are eating chocolate ice cream, which is melting on their faces and dripping onto their T-shirts.

My heart squeezes at the sight of the little girl, so happy and carefree. Even her brother doesn't seem to have a worry in the world, other than eating his treat. But I've long since learned outside appearances can be deceptive.

I accept the call from my old captain as I continue to watch the trio. "Hey, what's up?" I can't help the concern that leaks into my tone.

"Hi, Uncle Lucas." Not Drew. It's his daughter, Ashley.

"Hey, Sweet Pea. How're you doing?"

"I'm doing good. Momma and Daddy took me to Portland on Friday and we went to the zoo. I got to see the cougars and polar bears and otters." Her words tumble out in an excited rush.

I smile. "That sounds like fun. Did you have a good time?" Carl and his brother Sheldon are walking on the other side of the street. They spot me and wave. I wave back in greeting.

"Yep. Are you still coming to see me on Thursday?" Ashley's sweet voice asks me.

"Absolutely. I wouldn't miss it for anything."

"Okay, see you then."

She ends the call before I can ask to talk to her father.

<h1 style="text-align:center">35</h1>

<h1 style="text-align:center">SIMONE</h1>

"I can't believe what an ass Craig is being," Avery grumps on the other end of the phone. Jasper is at war with one of his chew toys. The occasional sound of surrender squeaks in the living room. The living room that is currently a neat chaos as I work on assembling the subscription boxes due to go out this month.

"What did he do this time?" I can only imagine. He was the main reason I quit my job once he got the promotion.

"He made Danielle cry. Who the blippity-hell would want to make that sweet woman cry?"

Good question. For the past year, Danielle has been bringing cupcakes to the office every Friday. *Cupcake Friday.* Delicious cupcakes that she bakes and decorates.

"Don't worry, there's a special place in hell for men like Craig," I tell Avery.

"I hope you're right. But in the meantime, that doesn't solve a problem like Craig."

I laugh under my breath. "You've been watching *The Sound of Music* again, haven't you?" I can always tell. I'm sure even the nuns in the movie wouldn't know how to solve a problem like Craig.

213

"I might have watched it last night. But in my defense, I really needed to see it after I interviewed someone who I thought would be a great fit as a roommate."

"I take it things didn't go so well." A bolt of guilt shoots through me that I left her without a roommate. But when I originally returned to Maple Ridge, I hadn't expected to move back here permanently. I still need to retrieve what's left of my stuff from the apartment. I've just been putting it off.

Putting it off until I know for sure what Lucas's fate will be.

And so far, it hasn't been necessary for me to drive to Portland to get my things. I've been saving that trip for when I go there to buy supplies that I can't get in Eugene for my subscription boxes.

But soon...soon I will need to go there. Will need to return the city linked to so much heartbreak. Will need to visit my daughter's grave.

"I think I prefer not having a roommate," Avery says. "If I can't find another roommate as amazing as you were, I'd rather live on my own. I should probably start looking for a one-bedroom apartment since this lease expires soon. And start looking for a new job."

"I thought you loved your job."

"I do. Or I did. But your business is doing so well, and it made me realize I'm ready for a change."

"Craig's ego really has grown to massive proportions, hasn't it?"

"Godzilla massive. And yes, maybe he's part of the reason I feel like it's time to move on to something better. And as soon as I figure out what that is, I'll be sure to let you know." Avery sighs, and I can hear the inflated frustration in it. "Oh, well. Break's over. I guess it's time to return to that insufferable ass. Love you, Si."

"Love you, too, A." I end the call and go back to working on my subscription boxes. My phone pings with a text.

Emily: Clementine Hollis just posted about your subscription boxes on Instagram!!!! She posted a video of her unboxing the one you recently sent out. The comments are going crazy! People love it!

I stare at Em's text for what could be thirty seconds, shock rendering me incapable of replying. Clementine Hollis is a huge Instagram influencer. She must have...*wow*. She must have subscribed to my boxes under a different name.

Me: I had no idea. Wow. Wow. Wow.

Emily: I hope that results in more subscribers for you!!!

I check my Instagram feed. In the short time since Clementine posted the video, I have two hundred new followers.

I log into my website and discover that I have another fifty subscribers for the boxes.

I spend the rest of the afternoon still in shock and filling the subscription boxes I had planned to put together today. I carry them upstairs to the guest room, which has become my temporary storage site.

Lucas doesn't have a choice now about me staying in his room. My boxes have taken over the guest room.

And thanks to Clementine, it's going to be even more crowded in here by the time I've finished with this month's boxes.

I've been staying in Lucas's bedroom for the past three nights, and he hasn't had any nightmares. Or if he's had nightmares, I've been oblivious to them.

I tidy up the living room and return the rest of my supplies to the guest room. Dinner is simmering in the slow cooker Lucas and I got as a wedding gift. Lucas is due home soon.

"You ready to go outside and play?" I ask Jasper. He replies with an enthusiastic puppy bark.

I take him into the backyard and stand barefooted on the lush lawn. The sweet scent of freshly mowed grass perfumes the air. Jasper brings me his favorite ball, and we spend the next twenty minutes playing catch. I grin at the puppy's endless energy.

I throw the ball again. But he doesn't drop it at my feet after he retrieves the ball, he bounds past me to the house. I swivel to see what has him so excited. Lucas is standing in the doorway, his hair damp from a shower, and he's smiling like I'm the sun to his galaxy.

He walks toward me, but as he draws closer, I notice he seems exhausted. Emotionally drained. The toll of the past twelve weeks is wearing him down. And it won't get any better. His trial is in ten weeks. Ten weeks today.

The black stitches on his temple ignite a firestorm of anger and frustration and sorrow inside me. I still can't believe someone hit him. Hit him because he was asking questions they didn't like.

"Are you okay?"

Lucas doesn't answer. At least not with words. His mouth is on mine, and he's kissing me like there's nowhere in the world he would rather be.

I loop my arms behind his neck. My tongue meets his, stroke for slow stroke. We continue kissing, temporarily pushing aside all our problems. Kissing until Jasper grows bored of waiting for us to pay attention to him. He jumps his paws onto our legs.

I drop to his level. Only to be rewarded by his enthusiastic puppy kisses. I fall back on my butt and laugh. Lucas helps me to my feet.

"I take it things didn't go well today?" I ask as we walk to the house.

"It's been a long day. Let's just leave it at that."

"Is there anything I can do that might help?"

He stops walking and turns to me. His mouth tilts into my favorite panty-melting smile, and he rests his hands on my hips. "I can think of one thing."

"What's that?"

He kisses me once more, a tornado of emotions filling each kiss as his mouth moves against mine. His hands skim down to the backs of my thighs, and he hoists me up. I wrap my legs around his hips.

We go into the house with Jasper bounding alongside us, releasing little puppy yaps. Lucas puts me down long enough to get Jasper into his crate. Then he's carrying me upstairs.

We walk into our bedroom, still kissing, and Lucas lays me on the bed. My fingers find the hem of his T-shirt and slide it up his body. Lucas tugs it over his head while I wiggle out of my sundress. He quickly strips out of his shorts, then his warm strong hands are caressing my bare skin.

My fingers do their own exploring, savoring the strength of his muscles flexing beneath my fingertips. Our movements aren't rushed. They're slow and exquisite.

Lucas unhooks my bra and drops it on the floor. We shimmy out of our underwear.

And then it's just him and me and nothing between us.

Well, nothing except for protection.

Even though we're married, we use condoms. Lucas, because he thinks we need the birth control. Me, because I haven't found the will to tell him the truth.

His fingers find the most sensitive part of me. My fingers embrace his length. And our breaths weave together as we create music, a symphony of moans and groans and whimpers.

"I need you, Cannon. Inside me. Now." My voice gets lost in another moan.

A low chuckle brushes my neck. "Glad to hear that, Trouble. That's exactly where I plan to be." Lucas adjusts his position and slides inside me. With each thrust of his hips, I'm propelled closer to the edge. Closer to shattering. *Closer, closer, closer.*

His movements are slow, deliberate. There's no rush to the finish line, no race for completion. Something has shifted between us. Shifted. Collided. Sparked. Lava boils inside me, sweeping me up in the tide, creating something new and shiny.

A shard of colorful glass.

Lucas switches his pace, pumping harder, faster. My soft inner muscles clench his thick length, and I splinter into a million sparkling fragments.

I cry out my release.

Lucas comes apart soon after, his mouth at the nook of my neck.

He lowers himself onto me, his body a welcome weight. His head rests where my heart beats strong and rapid. His fingers trace along the faint scar across my stomach. He hasn't asked any more questions about it. I'm grateful he doesn't bring it up now.

We lie on the bed, not saying anything, catching our breath. Lucas's fingertips lightly explore my body. His touch is soothing against the memories from ten years ago.

Soothing against my fears about what the future might bring.

36

SIMONE

Thursday afternoon, I drive to Ash Falls to meet with my second artisan of the day.

"These are gorgeous." I inspect the palm-sized, wrought-iron candleholder with intricate swirls and hearts. Katie handcrafted it. Even the candles are handmade by her, with various petals captured in the pastel-colored wax. "They're perfect for my premium subscription boxes."

I tell her how many subscribers I currently have for that level. Her eyes grow as round as a tea candle.

"How long will it take you to make that many?" I ask.

"I have several other orders I need to do first. Due to the elaborate design of these"—she picks up the design I love—"I would say three months."

We agree on a date and a payment plan.

By the time I leave her house, my body feels like it's been filled with hydrogen, and I can't hold back my grin. My premium box subscribers will love Katie's beautiful work.

I walk along the sidewalk toward where I parked my car. Roses, lavender, daylilies, peonies are in full bloom in the gardens lining the path, reminding me I should start thinking about what flowers I want to plant in Lucas's garden for next year. No. Not Lucas's. *Our* garden.

The sound of giggles behind me tugs hard at my heart. The girl's laughter is full of life. I close my eyes, letting the sound wrap around me. Letting myself imagine for the briefest moment the laugh belongs to Lily.

At one time those little girl giggles would have left me in tears. Would have seen my soul ripped into shreds.

I breathe in deeply. Let the mountain air soothe me.

The girl giggles again. I open my eyes and turn to see what made her laugh.

She's across the street, and looks to be about nine or ten years old. Lily's age. Or what she would be if she were still with me. The girl is petite with long, light-blond hair that glows in the sunlight. Like a fairy. A fairy wearing shorts and a pale-pink T-shirt.

She spins around, and it's only then that I notice her hopscotch partner. Lucas?

Lucas grins at the girl as if she's his entire universe wrapped up in a glittery pink bow. He crouches in front of her, hugs her. Still holding on to her, he stands and swings her in a circle.

She giggles some more.

My hand goes to my stomach where his daughter once grew, and I try to breathe through the pain.

During those rare times in the beginning when I wasn't struggling with grief, I wondered what Lucas would be like as a father. And now I know.

Even though my insides feel like someone has dented them with my stamping hammer, I can't help but smile at the goofy man pretending to lose his balance so the little girl wins the game. There's nothing wrong with Lucas's balance. The man is a brick wall in a strong wind.

The love in his eyes...oh, God, the love in his eyes as he looks at her.

An image of him cuddling a tiny baby in a pink blanket flickers in my mind, robs me of my breath.

Who is she? The little girl.

Oblivious to me standing here, staring at them, the duo hops along the sidewalk like bunnies. Then he lifts her onto his shoulders and they walk away.

I don't follow.

I just stand on the spot as though Medusa had strolled through the neighborhood and turned me into a statue.

But while my body might have turned to stone, my mind is buzzing like a swarm of bees. I have no idea who the little girl is. It doesn't matter who she is. What matters is the pure joy on Lucas's face while he was playing with her.

He looked at her as though she were his daughter.

The daughter I can never give him.

I should just get in my car and drive home. But my legs have other plans, and I walk along the sidewalk until I end up at a small park.

I sit on a bench and watch the young kids running and giggling, but not close enough for anyone to see me struggling because of the daughter I failed.

The gentle fingers of the midafternoon sun caress my face like an angel absorbing my grief. It helps a little, but it's not enough. I'm not sure anything will ever be enough.

Several mothers are sitting together on a bench near the playground equipment, keeping an eye on the kids. The women's smiles are echoed on their children's glowing faces.

This is the life I'd once dreamed of, the life I'll never have.

Deep down I know it shouldn't matter. My business is flourishing. I'm more in control of my career than I've ever been. And I'm married to a man I love. He might not love me in return, but maybe eventually that will change.

But even though it shouldn't matter that I can't have children, a gnawing pain chews me up from the inside. I rest my hand on my lower belly and stroke my thumb where Lily used to be.

A tear drops.

So does another.

Things won't get any easier over the next few weeks as I approach the anniversary of her death, followed two weeks later by the anniversary of Aiden ending his life. My grief will consume me. A grief for what I once had but lost in a heartbeat. Lost when someone got behind the wheel when he shouldn't have.

That much never changes.

"Hi!" A little girl is standing in front of where I'm sitting. Her hair's tied in two auburn braids, and she's wearing a T-shirt with little duckies on it. "Hi! HiHiHiHiHiHi!"

"Hi," I reply, smiling at her. It's hard not to. I sniff and dry my face with my fingertips.

"HiHiHiHiHiHi!" She lifts her stuffed floppy chick for me to see. Clearly, she has a thing for birds.

"That's a cute birdie. Does she have a name?"

"HiHiHiHiHiHi!"

"Hazel," a woman says, approaching us. I assume she's referring to the girl, not the toy.

"HiHiHiHiHiHiHi!" Hazel holds her arms up to the woman who I'm guessing is her mother. They have the same hair color.

The woman picks up her daughter and studies me for a second. "Haven't seen you here before." Her voice holds a silent warning. A mother-bear warning. And I flinch at what she must be thinking.

"I live in Maple Ridge. I was just driving through and thought I'd stop to get some air."

I stand. This was a mistake. I shouldn't be here.

The woman and her daughter head back to the playground equipment, and I return to my car. I unlock the door.

"Trouble?" Lucas's voice comes from behind me, and I spin around. There's no sign of the blond girl with him.

"I didn't realize you were going to be in Ash Falls, Cannon." I keep my tone breezy, not wanting to give away that I'm dying on the inside.

"Ditto. What are you doing here?"

"I was meeting with two artisans in the area. I had just finished meeting with the second one when I saw you playing hopscotch with the little girl. Who is she?" Who is the girl who has stolen your heart?

"Ashley. She's the daughter of one of my Marine brothers. He saved my life in Afghanistan. I haven't told you about him because I didn't want to cause you more pain due to what happened with Aiden. Drew was our captain. And..." Pain flickers and burns so bright in Lucas's eyes; I almost have to turn away. "Ashley was diagnosed three years ago with leukemia. She fought it and went into remission. But the cancer is back."

The pain and despair on his face jolts the air from my lungs, and my veins turn to ice. "Oh, God."

He pulls me to him, and I hug him, resting my head on his shoulder, letting him know that I'm here for him. He loves Ashley even though she isn't his daughter. That much is obvious.

He pulls away after a moment. "Now that you know about Ashley and Drew, I'd love to introduce you to them. If that's okay with you."

I know what he's asking. "I'll be fine, Lucas. He's your friend and he was an important part of Aiden's life at one point."

Lucas takes my hand, and we walk to the bungalow he was playing in front of a short while ago. A ramp of paving stones curves from the driveway to the front door. We walk up it, and Lucas rings the doorbell.

A young girl's voice calls out that she'll get it. The door opens.

Ashley sees Lucas, and her face glows like he's the moon and the stars and an ice-cream sundae. "Hi, Uncle Lucas." She turns and yells, "It's Uncle Lucas and a pretty woman."

"This pretty woman is my wife, Simone." He rubs the top of the girl's head, making a mess of her hair. "And this is Ashley."

"Are you planning to let them in or make them wait outside?" A man's voice, stamped with amusement, comes from inside the house.

Ashley opens the door wider, and we step into the foyer. A good-looking man with sandy-brown hair wheels down the hallway toward us. His navy T-shirt stretches across a well-toned chest, and his biceps bulge as his arms push the hand rims of his wheelchair.

He grins at us. Father and daughter share the same bright blue eyes and mischievous smile. "So, this is the gorgeous woman you've been keeping to yourself." He winks at me, and I grin back.

"Simone, this is Drew Tanner," Lucas says. "My old captain."

Drew and I shake hands. "I'm sorry about your brother. Aiden was a great man. Not to mention quite the prankster."

I flash him a politely gracious smile, the same one I paint on every time someone talks about my brother. "Thank you. He was."

"I'm sorry we couldn't make it to your wedding." His smile shifts into something sadder. "Ashley had a medical appointment in Portland we couldn't change. But congratulations. You couldn't have picked a better man."

I smile at Lucas—all the love and admiration I feel for him poured into the smile. "I know."

The grin Drew directs at his daughter is brighter than the one I just witnessed. "Why don't you tell your momma we've got guests?"

"Okay, Daddy." Ashley skips down the hallway, and Drew leads us out onto a patio filled with planters crowded with colorful flowers.

Lucas and I sit at the table. Drew navigates his chair into place. "I didn't have a chance to tell you earlier, but Ashley's oncologist called while you two were playing."

My heart clenches at oncologist. I glance at Lucas in time to catch the pain flicker back on his face before it extinguishes.

"Her doctors think she might be a good candidate for a new drug they want to try."

Ashley runs out of the house, giggling, before Lucas and I can respond. She tears around the backyard, blowing bubbles and chasing them and popping them.

Lucas and Drew are talking. About what? I don't know. All I can think about is the memory of Lucas playing with Ashley and how great a father he would be. The topic of kids is one I always avoid whenever it's brought up.

But it's also a topic I'll eventually have to face.

I just...I just need to get through the next few weeks first.

I just need to survive the anniversary of Lily's death.

37

LUCAS

A week after I introduced Simone to Drew and his family, I leave the florist with a bouquet of dahlias.

I head for my SUV, parked in front of the store. A truck pulls up alongside it, and Sebastian climbs out. He pauses and checks his phone.

Perfect timing.

I stride up to him. "Sebastian." My tone is brisk, and he looks up. If his expression is any indication, I'm the last person he wants to see. "You were there when someone attacked me outside of Barside Brewery. Who was it?"

His gaze darts down the sidewalk, then shifts back to me. "I already talked to the cops about what happened."

"Great. Now you can tell me."

"Like I told them, it was too dark and I didn't see who it was. I didn't want to be next on the attacker's list of victims, so I ran. Figured you'd be fine." Sebastian shrugs. "We were right outside the bar. I knew someone would find you. Like that bouncer."

"So you have no clue who attacked me?"

"Nope."

I don't believe him. And I also don't know if he's telling the truth about why he bailed. Was he really afraid that he would be attacked? Or did he not want to be caught in the presence of the attacker for another reason?

"Now, if you don't mind," Sebastian says. "I want to get my mother some flowers before the florist closes." He walks past me.

I turn around, not interested in leaving things where they are. "You might want to mention to whoever you were talking to that night that I told the cops what I overheard in the bar. They're keeping an eye on the Wakefields." And if my brothers and I get even a whiff of suspicion that Robert and Tuuli are in danger, we'll be out there stalking their property, making sure whoever is threatening them ends up in jail.

Sebastian doesn't respond and enters the store.

I drive home. Simone and Jasper are in the backyard when I arrive. Simone is playing chase with him and laughing. Her hair glows softly in the sun, the beams of sunlight kissing her bare arms and legs. Fuck, she's gorgeous.

Gorgeous and she's mine.

She looks toward me and grins. "Hi, Cannon."

I walk over to her and gather her in my arms, careful not to crush the flowers I bought for her. Then I kiss her—because I can.

38

LUCAS

lmost two weeks after I confronted Sebastian, I walk into the dim kitchen to find Simone sitting at the table, looking the same way she has for the past week.

Like a zombie.

Rain hammers the window, but even two days ago when it was hot and sunny, Simone wasn't the same woman she was a week ago.

The change in her has taken root over the past several days, like a vine creeping up a wall. Slowly. Imperceptibly. I didn't notice it at first. Now the leaves are starting to show, and I can't ignore something's not right.

She lifts her spoon to her mouth as if the effort is too much to bear. I'm not sure she even registers that I'm in the room. Her eyes are vacant, staring at something other than the wall I'm seeing.

Even though she works from home, she usually dresses as though she's going out. She puts effort into her appearance. Hair, clothes, makeup always perfect.

Now, she's wearing black yoga pants and one of my T-shirts. Her hair's pulled up in a messy ponytail, and she doesn't have any makeup on. She's damn sexy as hell—even more so because she's in my old San Jose Sharks T-shirt. But this isn't the woman I'm falling in love with.

This is a shell.

I lean down and kiss her cheek. "Any big plans today?"

She startles. The tension in her body doesn't lessen when she realizes it's just me. It slopes her shoulders another fraction of an inch.

She shakes her head, and her gaze shifts to the window. "Are you working in that?" She nods at the rain.

"No, Troy has some jobs on the interior that need to be completed." *Thank Christ for that.* As a PT, I never had to worry about the weather. I could just focus on helping my patients recover, get stronger. *Shit.* I miss my old job.

"That's good." Her voice lacks all hint of emotion, and she goes back to chewing her cereal as if it were Styrofoam.

I grab a bowl from the cupboard and sit next to her. "You okay?"

"I'm fine."

She's anything but fine. It doesn't take a genius to figure out why.

We're approaching the anniversary of Aiden's death.

The guilt over what happened always cranks up for me at this time of year. That's bad enough. I can't imagine what Simone is going through.

When I was ten years old, I discovered an injured bird in a neighbor's garden. I had no idea how to help it, but that didn't stop me from digging up worms for it. I'd felt helpless trying to get the bird to eat them. Telling it the worms would make the bird big and strong.

How I felt then is nothing compared to now with Simone.

"Has Kim ever been depressed?" I ask Jerome.

He and I are sitting on Barside Brewery's patio. The crappy weather from this morning ended around noon, and the puddles left in its wake are drying up in the heat of the sun.

I called him earlier at the law firm he works for, hoping he can help me. Of all my friends, he's the only married man of the bunch. What I need is advice from someone who knows what the hell he's talking about.

I also trust that he won't share our conversation with anyone—including his wife.

"Are you talking clinical depression?"

"I don't know. Simone's been emotionally pulling away from me for the past week. The anniversary of Aiden's death is next month, so it's probably related to that."

His lips roll into a contemplative line. "Kim has her emotional ups and downs—maybe even more so now that she's pregnant—but I don't think she's ever struggled with depression."

"Any ideas what I can do?" I ask, sounding a bit too hopeful that he has the Holy Grail of answers for me.

"I'm not an expert on the topic, but the best thing you can do is be there for Simone. If things get worse, maybe contact her physician and see what he suggests. Does she usually struggle with the anniversary?"

Hell if I know. I don't know Simone as well as I once did. As well as I should considering everyone believes we've been secretly a couple, on and off, for over a decade.

I sip my beer, deciding how many of my cards to lay out. Around us, the patio is busy with after-work patrons.

I lean forward in my chair, ensuring no one overhears what I'm about to reveal to Jerome. "I have no idea. Before Simone showed up in Maple Ridge three months ago, I hadn't seen her in more than ten years. Some of what we told everyone is true. We were involved in college, but it wasn't quite the romantic affair we made it out to be. The romance is there now." I think I love her—even though I sense she's keeping something from me like I'm keeping things from her.

Jerome's dark eyebrows rise. I couldn't have shocked him more than if I told him Simone was a deadly sniper. "So you really have no clue if her current emotional state is typical for her at this time of year?"

"Exactly. I still struggle with the anniversary of Aiden's death, and she misses him more than she admits to her friends."

Jerome considers my words for a moment. "Talk to her. Let her know you're there for her. I've seen what the anniversary of his death does to you, Lucas. You shut yourself away from the world for a few days. But this time neither of you has to face it alone. You have each other."

"Thanks, I'll do that."

Simone is in the backyard playing with Jasper when I arrive home an hour later. I watch her for a few minutes as she runs barefooted on the grass. She has changed since I saw her earlier, now wearing a white floral sundress. In the low angle of the sun, her hair glows like a flame.

She resembles a nymph from one of Aiden's mythology books.

She laughs. It's not one of her rich laughs that I love. The type of laugh that makes everyone's day brighter. Fuller. This laugh is streaked with sadness. And I'm at a loss as to what to say to her. What to do.

A cascade of emotions churns inside me.

Love and guilt and frustration.

Helplessness.

I'm back on enemy soil, taking care not to step on a land mine. While I might not lose a limb if I say or do the wrong thing, the aftermath might be just as devastating.

"How was your day?" I ask.

"It was good. Yours?" Sadness clouds her eyes, hiding the life usually there.

"Not bad."

"Except you miss your patients, don't you?" She cups my face with her hand, her thumb caressing my cheek.

I lean into her soothing touch, needing this as much as I need to help her wade her way through to the other side of her depression. "Yes," I murmur. "At least I have a job. I can't complain."

A job that keeps me mentally and physically busy so I don't have time to think about everything I've lost—everything I can still lose.

Jasper barks, not wanting to be forgotten, and sits next to us.

Simone drops her hand from my face and picks up the ball Jasper dropped by our feet. She throws it, and he chases after the ball.

He mouths it and jogs back to us. This game continues with Simone and I taking turns with throwing the ball.

"So when are we getting Jasper his kitten sibling?" I ask.

"We should probably wait until he's no longer a puppy. Right now, an energetic puppy and kitten might be too much. We have enough problems with Jasper chewing on everything."

She has a point. Jasper is a force of destruction on his own. I'm not sure if we're ready to add a kitten to the mix. Can't imagine what it will be like once we have kids. At least they won't be chewing on everything.

Jasper releases the ball next to my foot. I pick the ball up and toss it farther than before.

While he retrieves it, I deliberate what to say to Simone. I know I should bring up the conversation about the upcoming anniversary of Aiden's death. I should...but I can't form the words. I spent years learning to bury my emotions for my country because emotions can get you killed. Talking about mine or anyone else's is as comfortable as sitting on a grenade after the pin has been pulled.

There are times when I'm brave, invincible. This isn't one of them.

So I choose the coward's way out and ignore the problem.

Hope it gets better.
And if it doesn't?
I'll fight that battalion when I come to it.

39

LUCAS

The following afternoon, I step out of Blake's office building and walk the short distance to the parking lot. The clouds have thickened since I arrived in Eugene to discuss with Blake what his investigator has learned so far.

I approach my SUV. A light blue piece of paper is caught under my windshield wiper and is flapping in the wind. It looks like one of those flyers that local businesses send out. I lift the blade and remove the paper.

It's blank. I flip it over. Someone has scrawled a message on the other side in black Sharpie:

I know who was responsible for the drugs. Meet me at the back of Picnic & Treats Café at 5:03 pm. Come alone.

There's nothing to indicate where it came from. No other message. No names. No local business info. Nothing.

I glance around the parking lot. But other than a mother loading her two young kids into a red van, no one else is here.

I take in the squat brick buildings surrounding the area. If anyone's watching, they aren't visible from where I'm standing.

It's 3:40 p.m. If I leave now, I'll just make it to the meeting place in time. I climb into my SUV. It's possible the note is nothing more than a prank. But I can't risk that it isn't.

I arrive in Maple Ridge without any delays, park my vehicle on a side street, and jog to Picnic & Treats. Simone is exiting the café as I approach.

"Hi, didn't expect to see you here." The sadness clouding her eyes from yesterday is still there. And her smile—it's as if her lips have forgotten how to form the shape.

A screech of tires slices the air. My head jerks up in time to catch a pickup truck jump the curb, hurtling toward us.

I yank Simone into the alley next to the building. The momentum causes us to lose our footing and we go down. My body lands first, hip and shoulder taking the brunt of the impact. Simone falls on top of me, her knee narrowly missing my junk.

The truck speeds past. *Fuck.* The driver didn't even stop to make sure we're okay.

Simone doesn't say anything. She's trembling, and her breathing sounds like she sprinted the block. I help her to her feet and check for injuries. Physically she appears to be okay.

"Is your shoulder hurt?" Her voice trembles, the dry sound barely more than a whisper. She rubs her arms.

"It'll be fine," I say even though that's a goddamn lie. I landed on my wounded shoulder, and it's not too impressed.

But right now, my major concern is Simone. That, and how the hell am I supposed to meet the person who left the note on my windshield?

Leaving Simone alone isn't an option—not after an incident like that. Nor is bringing her with me. I intertwine our fingers and lead her into Picnic & Treats. "Let's get you a hot chocolate to calm you."

Zara is working the front counter when we enter. She glances toward the door, spots Simone's pale face and our dirty clothes, and rushes over to us, abandoning the customer she was serving. "What happened?"

"Can you take her to your staff room while I check something out? I'll be right back."

Zara nods, and I'm out the door before Simone can say anything.

I sprint around the corner to the alley and scan the area. No one is here.

Dammit.

They might have slipped away while I was taking Simone into Treats. Or worse yet. What are the odds the note was a setup? That the truck intentionally tried to hit us?

Or specifically, me.

I search the dingy alley. No one is hiding behind the dumpster. I kick the metal container with my hiking shoe. "Is anyone in here?"

No one answers.

I pull out my phone, dial 9-1-1, tell the dispatcher what happened, and return to Picnic & Treats. Simone is sitting on the couch when I enter the staff room. A brightly colored blanket covers her shoulders. Zara is on one of the armchairs.

"I'm sending out an officer now," the dispatcher informs me. I end the call and sit next to Simone, slipping my fingers between hers. She's still trembling and her hands are cold.

"The cops are on their way," I tell her and Zara. "How are you doing?" I direct the question to Simone.

"Where did you go?" she asks.

"I needed to check on something. Are you okay?"

"I'm fine. You're the one who hit your injured shoulder."

I wrap my good arm around her shoulders. She wasn't fine before, and she definitely isn't now.

The door opens, and Tracy comes in carrying two ceramic mugs on a tray. She hands one to Simone and the other to me.

"Hazelnut hot chocolate with whipped cream," Zara explains. "I figured after what you two just went through, you need something. Unfortunately, that's the hardest-hitting stuff I can offer."

Simone takes a sip of her drink.

"I can't believe someone lost control of their vehicle and couldn't be bothered to stop to make sure you two were okay," Zara says.

"I don't think it was an accident." My gaze flicks to Simone to gauge how she's taking the news. She's still pale, but the trembling has lessened. "Someone left a note on my windshield while I was meeting with Blake." I tell them what it said and how no one was waiting for me when I checked the alley.

"Do you think it was a setup?" Simone asks.

I shrug, then flinch at the ache in my shoulder. "Could be. Or whoever was going to meet me was scared off. For all I know, they witnessed what happened and disappeared before I showed up."

Simone's face pales, and I mentally curse myself. She's scared enough by what happened, she doesn't need me telling her anything else that might send her over the edge.

"You should get your shoulder checked out." Her soft tone pleads with so much concern, if I didn't know better, I would think I was bleeding out.

I kiss her temple. For her benefit and mine. After what happened, I need to touch her, to make sure she's still alive. "My shoulder will be fine. But if you want to massage it tonight, I won't complain." I flash her a teasing smile, mostly to distract her from what happened with the truck.

Zara groans.

"How did your meeting with Blake go?" Simone asks.

"His investigator hasn't discovered much that we don't already know. Other than Sebastian has been involved in some shady dealings in the past. But nothing that would link him to the narcotics found in my house. And nothing that puts him on the law enforcement's radar."

Simone exhales a long hard breath that does little to deflate the tension in her muscles. "I wouldn't mind getting some good news for once."

"Me too," Zara says. "Garrett hasn't gotten anywhere with his FBI connections either."

The staff room door opens again. This time a cop enters. Zara excuses herself, and we're left to deal with the man.

Simone and I tell him everything that happened this afternoon when it came to the note and the near miss outside the café.

He bags the note for evidence. "Why do you think it was intentional?"

"Unlike when the driver hit Simone's grandmother and left the scene, the angle of the sun wasn't an issue. So unless the driver had a medical episode or was on their phone, there was nothing to cause them to end up on the sidewalk. And my gut says it was neither of those." My tone is steady, untrusting. This guy is fresh from the academy. Unlike most new cops who want to make a mark early in their career, he looks ready to go off shift. Not because he's had a hard day. Just the opposite.

He's bored. Our near hit-and-run isn't exciting enough for him.

Sorry to disappoint. Maybe next time you would prefer to be the one in front of the speeding vehicle.

40

SIMONE

Monday morning, Lucas's phone rings on the nightstand. If it had rung five minutes ago, it would have interrupted us doing more than just lying in bed, catching our breath.

Lucas answers it, and I tug the bedding over my chest, even though the person on the other end of the call can't see me. Sunlight spills through the window onto the bed, casting faintly striped shadows.

"Where was he last spotted?" Lucas rips the covers off him and swings his feet onto the floor. "All right, I'm leaving now. My ETA is about an hour."

He ends the call and gives me a quick kiss. "Sorry, I have to leave. An eleven-year-old boy went missing while hiking with his family in the mountains." He steps into the walk-in closet and reemerges in his Maple Ridge Search and Rescue gear. "Troy and Garrett have also been called up. If you need anything, Kellan is still around."

"Any idea how long you'll be gone?"

"If we're lucky, only a few hours." The last time he was called in for a search and rescue, he was gone for several days.

239

He leaves, and I get up to begin my morning.

I take Jasper out to do his business, and we go for a walk. But it's not enough to soothe the restlessness that's been building over the past week. I need to get out of town.

I need to visit the one person who understands why the next several days will be the toughest. Avery has been there for me for each anniversary. Not just for the death of my baby but also for Aiden's.

While I'm in Portland, I might as well stock up on supplies for my subscription boxes and pack up what's left of my stuff in Avery's apartment—my old apartment.

I call Grams to see if she's okay if I drop off Jasper with her. She loves it whenever he visits, and Avery's apartment doesn't allow pets. Then I call Zara to cancel out on girls' night since I won't be back in time.

"You're bailing on us?" she says on the other end of the line.

"Sorry, something came up."

She snort-laughs. "If I didn't know better, I'd say that's a euphemism for Lucas is screwing your brains out. But since Lucas, Troy, and Garrett are searching for a missing boy, I know that's not the case."

A sighed laugh slips from me. "I wish it were a euphemism."

There's a pause on her end of the line. And for a fraction of a second, I wonder if she's dropped the phone or vanished from the planet. "So, you're okay?" Doubt cuts her voice like a serrated knife, and not for the first time, I question just how much Zara has figured out about what's been going on with me.

About Lily.

About so many things.

"I'm fine. It's not the first time those guys have been called to help rescue someone, and it won't be the last."

"That's not what I'm talking about, and you know it. Something's going on with you—and Kim, Em, and I are worried."

That's the thing about being friends with people you grew up with. Even if you leave town for a decade and rarely contact them, they can still shovel through your bullshit.

I close my eyes and heave out a quiet breath. "I promise you I'm fine."

"Okay. But remember we're here if you need to talk."

"Thanks." The word comes out as a choked whisper, knowing I can't tell my three closest friends the truth. It wouldn't be right to confide in them and not tell Lucas.

We end the call.

I text Avery to let her know that I'm coming and that I will see her later. She's at work.

> Avery: I have a late meeting at work. Did you want to meet up for drinks or just hang out at the apartment?

> Me: Drinks. I'm going to visit Lily's grave first.

> Avery: Did you want me to come with you?

> Me: No, I think this time I need to go by myself. But thank you.

> Avery: Do you still have the apartment key?

> Me: Yes. :)

We make arrangements for the time and place we're going to meet up.

I go into the bedroom closet and retrieve Lucas's empty suitcase. I don't think he ever uses it. It's larger than most men need when they go on trips, but it's the perfect size for packing some of my clothes while in Portland.

I wheel the suitcase out of the closet, set it on the bed, and unzip it. I lift the top and peer inside. Other than a shoebox that's big enough to fit hiking boots, the suitcase is empty. I open the box. Inside is a thick stack of envelopes.

I pick up the top one, and then the next envelope, and the one after that. Recognition taunts me. Each envelope has Lucas's name on it. Each name written by my hand.

I open the first envelope and remove the letter I wrote to him while he was in the Marines. I sit on the bed and read the letter. I do the same for all the other letters I wrote him.

I can't believe it. He kept them.

He kept every single one I wrote to him while he was away.

All except for one.

I push myself off the bed and go into the guest room. I kneel on the floor and pull out the wicker basket from under the bed. The wicker basket that contains the letters he sent me while he was in the Marines. As far as I know, he hasn't found them.

I leaf through the letters, but the one I'm looking for is where I left it—at the bottom of the pile.

This isn't the final letter he sent me. But it is the last one I wrote him. Only I never sent it.

I remove the letter and Lily's ultrasound image from the envelope. My vision blurs at the sight of my once-perfect daughter. I trace my finger over her body and her features. Tears drop onto the picture, and I choke back a sob.

I put the ultrasound in the wicker box, blink to clear my vision, and read the letter.

Letter # 103

Dear Lucas,

I miss you so much. There isn't a day that goes by when I don't think about you. You're the last person I think about when I go to bed at night. I reread your letters and pretend you're here telling me about your day.

The last time we were together, I wanted to tell you that I'm in love with you. But I didn't. I fell asleep, and then you had to leave. But there you have it. It's not how I wanted to tell you, but it's important that you know. If I were there with you, I would tell you I love you to your face.

I hope you feel the same way about me. Actually, I'm sure you feel the same way. I've been replaying our last night together since you left, and I'm positive you love me, too. Your actions and the way you look at me tell me there's a strong possibility I'm right.

Oh, God, I hope I'm right because there's something I need to tell you. Something I recently discovered. I haven't told anyone yet. I want you to be the first to find out. I'm pregnant, Lucas. With your baby. I realize telling you the news by way of a letter is probably not the best idea, especially since you're somewhere fighting a war. But I'm pregnant and I wanted you to hear it from me. I didn't want you to get the wrong idea if you heard the news from someone else.

I know there's a chance I have things wrong and you don't love me. And I know there's a chance you won't be excited like I am about the baby growing inside of me. I'll admit I was shocked at first. We used a condom. I hadn't planned or expected to be pregnant. And because of that, it took me forever to realize I'm pregnant. I was scared when I learned the truth and didn't know how I felt. I imagine you feel the same way reading this letter. That's understandable.

I'm rambling. I'm sorry. I just wanted to say that I'm having your baby and that I love you. I won't say anything about it to anyone in Maple Ridge until you and I have a chance to talk. I've enclosed our daughter's ultrasound so that you can see our beautiful baby.

I love you. Stay safe!

Simone

I fold the page and return it to the envelope.

I never had a chance to mail the letter. I never had a chance to tell Lucas or Grams or my Maple Ridge friends. That was the day a stranger got behind the steering wheel after consuming too much alcohol.

And afterward, I was drowning in too much grief to even read the letters that Lucas sent me while he was deployed. But instead of ripping the letter I wrote into a million pieces and tossing them into the trash, I hid it in my old bedroom with the letters Lucas sent me. I never sent any more letters to him after that. He sent a few to me, but I never opened them. Reading them would have hurt too much. So I threw them away unread. Eventually...eventually the letters stopped coming.

And that hurt more than I had cared to admit.

I pack up Jasper's supplies to take to Grams's house and drive there. The energetic puppy is happy to see her. He jumps his paws high on her thighs, almost knocking her over.

It's not until she's fussed over him enough that he settles.

"Are you okay with looking after him while I go to Portland?" I ask.

"Of course. I love having the company. Plus, I enjoy showing him off to my friends."

I kiss her on the cheek. "If my trip to Portland takes longer than expected, is it okay if Jasper spends the night with you?"

"Absolutely, Gumdrop. I know you're dying to see Avery again."

The drive to Portland isn't bad. It doesn't rain and traffic doesn't slow me down. I take my regular detour so I can avoid the site of the accident where I lost my daughter.

I stop at several stores on the way to Avery's apartment and purchase items for my subscription boxes. Afterward, I pick up food from my favorite deli and head to my old building.

I step into Avery's apartment, flattened packing boxes under my arm. I put the boxes on the floor and walk to the window over-looking the street. I slide the window open, greedily inviting in the fresh air. The air doesn't have Maple Ridge's clean mountain fresh-ness. A light metallic odor lingers on the breeze.

I go through the bookshelf in the living room and organize my books in three piles: the books I'll keep, the ones I'll drop off for donations, and the books to be tossed. Avery can decide which books from the latter two piles she wants to keep before I get rid of them.

I'm halfway through the second shelf when I pull out a hard-back copy of a Greek mythology encyclopedia Aiden had sent me a few weeks prior to his death.

I open the book and read the inscription on the title page:

Simone,

Never give up fighting for your dreams.

Love,

Aiden

"Sure, you tell me to never give up fighting for my dreams, but isn't that *exactly* what you did? You fought for your country and for the right to freedom, but you couldn't fight for your dreams or your life?"

I sniff, blink back the tears threatening to blur my vision, and flip through the pages.

I'd started reading the book when I received it but didn't get very far. Aiden died and the pages no longer brought me comfort. Just the opposite.

But I'm stronger now. The book doesn't bring me pain. It brings memories of the little boy who discovered Greek and Roman mythology.

The little boy who thought he was invincible like Hercules.

I turn the page to Themis. Next to the illustration, Aiden had written "CATFISH."

Why does that seem familiar? It takes a moment for the memory to take shape. It's the same word he wrote on the scrap piece of paper I found in my old bedroom at Grams's. The piece of paper that had fallen from my desk drawer when I opened it to pack the contents.

I sit on the couch and read the description for the Greek Titaness. Themis was the personification of divine order, fairness, and law. She was the symbol of justice.

But there's nothing in the entry that explains why Aiden wrote "CATFISH" next to the illustration.

I shrug it off and place the book in a moving box.

Once I've finished packing all my things, I drive to the cemetery where Lily rests in peace. On the way, I stop to pick up a small bouquet of pink lilies and baby's breath.

I walk along the path leading to where she's buried. The sun is warm on my bare arms and legs as it attempts to heat me up. As it lends me its support.

After all these years, visiting Lily's grave hasn't gotten any easier. And this time, the pain digs deeper. The last time I visited, I wasn't married to her father. The last time I visited, I hadn't seen Lucas since the night our daughter was conceived.

I locate her tiny plot and place the bouquet of flowers on the ground in front of the small stone. I trace my finger over the etched lily and along the letters of my daughter's name and the date she died. Avery had arranged a fundraiser at the ad agency so I could bury my unborn child here.

I don't know how I would have survived without Avery. She was the one holding my hand when I woke up from surgery. She was the one who stayed by my side while grief sat on my chest, making it difficult to breathe.

"You're not going to believe this," I say to the stone, tears distorting my words. I swallow the tears and close my eyes for a second, trying to regain a thread of composure. "Your father and I are now married. It's a long story." I don't recount it to her. I just tell Lily about the things I've been doing since the last time I visited her and about Maple Ridge.

No one is around to hear my confessions. No one is around to witness my heartbroken tears. Tears for the loss of my daughter. Tears from my fears that I could be losing Lucas soon. His trial is in six weeks.

"I love you, Lily. I will always love you. And I plan to tell your father all about you. One day very soon. Because I know he would have loved you as much as I do, had you been allowed to be in our arms and not just our hearts."

41

SIMONE

Four hours later, Avery and I meet up at our favorite lounge for drinks. The rich honey-brown walls remind me of Lucas's eyes when he makes love to me. I haven't heard from him since he left the house this morning. I have no idea how the rescue mission is going.

I have no idea how Lucas is doing.

"How's married life so far?" Avery all but snorts.

She's the only friend who knows the real reason Lucas and I got married. But that was before I realized I'd never stopped loving him. Before our marriage started to feel real.

"It's good."

Avery laughs. "What you mean is the sex is good."

Heat rushes to my face, which only makes her laugh harder.

"Have you told him yet?"

"Told him what?"

Avery takes a long sip of her martini as if giving me a moment to figure it out myself.

I have, but she's not the only one skirting the issue. I suspect, though, she's about to make a direct hit. Whereas, I'm happy to skip right past reality and live in the land of denial and forgotten truths.

Or I would be if the truth let me.

"I'll interpret that to mean you haven't told him about the baby."

She doesn't say it unkindly, but I still flinch.

"The anniversary is next week," she tells me, even though she knows I don't need the reminder. "Simone, you need to tell Lucas. I don't want you to be alone that day. You need to be with someone who can help you get through it. And if it isn't Lucas, maybe you two shouldn't be married."

I open my mouth to remind her why he and I got married but don't get that far.

"Yes." The word comes out on a worried sigh. "I know you didn't marry for the reason most couples do, but he does love you. I saw it the day you two got married, the way he looked at you. He might not realize he's in love with you, but he is. And you're in love with him. Don't even try to deny it." Her lips tilt into a grin.

"I do, but that doesn't mean I'm ready to tell him about Lily. The worst part is, I've seen how wonderful Lucas is with kids. He would make a great father, but it's something he'll never get to experience."

She studies me over the rim of her drink before taking another sip. "Has he said he wants children?"

I nod.

"Is that why you haven't told him the truth yet?"

Again I nod, the movement barely noticeable, and I finish my martini.

"You do realize you two can adopt, right? Or is he one of those men who only wants children if they're biologically his?"

"His youngest brother was adopted, and as far as Lucas is concerned, they're blood brothers. So no, he isn't against adoption. It's just..." I look down at my drink, unable to voice the next words.

"You feel like you're less of a woman because of the hysterectomy and because you can't have babies the old-fashioned way. The way that doesn't require a surrogate. That's complete bullshit, by the way. You're no less a female than I am. It doesn't matter if you have a uterus or not or whether you're able to have babies, you're still a woman. None of those things determine if you are one. You're a woman because that's just who you are. Lucas won't think less of you because you had a hysterectomy. And if he does, that's his problem, not yours. Divorce him if that's the case."

"Deep down I know you're right. But it's one thing to understand that and another to accept it. I thought I had accepted it for the most part until he told me he wants kids one day—depending on what happens with the felony charges."

"Maybe it's time you start seeing a therapist. Other than the few times you spoke with someone after the accident about the loss of your baby, you've never really addressed the issue. You've never really addressed that and the hysterectomy. You just buried yourself in your work and chased after job promotions that never happened."

"I know—"

"You have a man who clearly loves you, so why not tell him the truth?"

"All of this is a moot point if Lucas's attorney can't prove his innocence. It won't matter if I end up working in Portland or that I can't have babies or that I had a hysterectomy. If he's found guilty, we won't be together other than for permitted prison visits."

"If he isn't found innocent, what are you planning to do?"

"Be there for him." I don't even hesitate before saying it. "I believe in Lucas. I know he had nothing to do with the narcotics. And I plan to wait for him to be released if it comes to that."

I refuse to walk away from the man I love because the justice system let him down.

The waiter pauses at our table, and we order another round of martinis.

"Is that what he wants?" Avery asks after the waiter leaves. "Does Lucas want you to wait around if he's found guilty?"

"We haven't really discussed it. Not lately, anyway. The original agreement was I could divorce him if it came to that."

"But you have no intention of divorcing him."

It's not a question, but I respond as if it were. "That's right."

A smile flickers on her face. Then it vanishes. "Does he even know about the accident?"

"I've told him pieces about it, but I haven't told him everything."

"I get that you don't want to tell him all the details, but you should mention that you can't have babies. Then you can look into other options if you two decide to adopt."

"I will. But I want to wait a little longer. I'll tell him next week." After the anniversary.

"Promise me you'll talk to him and tell him the full story about the accident. I'm no therapist, but I suspect it will go a long way in helping you move on."

"I will."

She nods, satisfied I'm telling the truth, but concern still lingers on her face, in her eyes. "Perhaps you should stay here until he returns from the rescue mission. And then you won't be alone."

"I'll be fine. Maybe the grief won't be as bad this year." Even as the words slip out, I know it's wishful thinking. Things haven't been fine for the past week. Just the opposite. Even visiting Lily's grave before coming here wasn't enough to lessen what I know is coming.

If Avery's expression is any indication, she doesn't believe me any more than I do.

"Okay, but if you need someone to talk to, call me and I'll do what I can to talk you through it. It won't be the same as me being there, but it will hopefully be better than nothing. But promise me you'll talk to Lucas once he returns from being a badass superhero."

I grin. "I'm glad you're finally warming up to him."

The waiter stops by our table to deliver our next martinis.

Avery waves me off. "I'll warm up to any sexy superhero in

uniform." She picks up her martini and raises her glass in a toast. "To sexy superheroes in uniform."

I laugh and raise my glass.

42

LUCAS

I sit on the dirt and lean back against the rough bark of the tree. A crow caws from a branch above my head. I don't have the energy to glance up and check its exact location.

Clouds the color of a fresh bruise converge and glower in the near distance. The search party has an hour—two tops—before we'll be facing a deluge.

The endless forest terrain surrounds my team and me, bringing with it the sounds and smells that typically ground me. Usually, I view the mountain as my best friend. Now, it feels more like the enemy.

"Where the fuck could he have gone?" I gulp down some black coffee from my thermos. I've consumed enough coffee over the past four days that caffeine is now the only thing pumping through my blood vessels.

My team is on a break after we spent the morning combing our assigned territory. There hasn't been a single sighting or clue of the boy's whereabouts since he was reported missing.

Each passing hour we don't find him takes us a step closer to the mission becoming a recovery instead of a rescue.

"You're a Marine," Sheldon says a few feet from me, his eyelids closed. "Would've thought you can sniff him out."

"You must be confusing me with a bloodhound."

The other five guys on the crew bark a laugh, the sound weary at best.

"Heard you got yourself married a few months ago." Ben, a hulky man in his late forties, scratches his jaw and the lumberjack beard growing from it.

"That's right."

"How's it going?"

"How do you think it's going?" Sheldon asks. "The man is in his early thirties and he has a beautiful wife. I'm sure things are going great." He pries his eyes open and gives me a lecherous smile.

The other men chuckle.

"Didn't realize you were seeing anyone, let alone engaged," Ben says.

"Long story."

They all peer at me like little boys waiting for the teacher to read them a book.

Sheldon unscrews the lid of his travel mug and swallows down some of the contents. A frown etches onto his brow. "My wife saw Simone in the grocery store the other day. Sue said your wife looked distracted. Sad, even."

"It's almost the anniversary of her brother's death," I explain. "They were close."

Ben stands and stretches his arms above his head. "How did he die?"

"Suicide. He was struggling with PTSD and it got to be too much. His body was found at the bottom of a cliff near his cabin in the mountains." I pick up a rock next to my knee and hurl it to the side. It hits a bush, rustling the leaves.

"Shit," Ben mutters. "Has she ever talked to anyone about it?"

"I don't know."

"She should talk to someone. It couldn't hurt."

Ben's right. If she's struggling now, how bad will things be on the anniversary of Aiden's death in a few weeks?

Sheldon looks at his phone and groans. "All right, men. Break time's over."

We get to our feet. A crackly voice on his walkie-talkie alerts us that Command is on the line. Sheldon tells them our location. The person on the other end responds. Sheldon's face pales, defeat and disappointment slumping his shoulders. And we all know. We all know we won't like his next words.

Fuuuuuck.

I DOUBLE-CHECK THAT MY CLIMBING HARNESS AND LOCKING carabiner are secure, then Sheldon and I rappel down the side of the cliff to the ledge about twenty feet below us.

I'm the first to place my feet on the ground, and I race to the crumbled body of the missing boy. His eyes are closed, his clothing dirty and torn. "Dustin?"

He doesn't respond. I feel for his carotid pulse but find nothing. His skin is cold to the touch. Even though I know better, I start to administer CPR. "C'mon." My whispered words are yanked away in the wind.

Sheldon stands at the side of the ledge and waits for the team to lower the stretcher. I continue performing CPR. *C'mon, dammit. Breathe—fucking breathe.*

Sheldon strides the short distance and lowers the stretcher alongside the boy. He checks for a pulse. "*Fuck.* He's dead, Lucas. You can do all the CPR you want, it's not gonna bring him back."

I don't listen to Sheldon. The boy on the ledge is no longer the missing kid we've been searching for. He's the boy from Afghanistan.

The boy Aiden and I tried to save.

Someone grabs my uninjured arm. "He's dead, Lucas. There's nothing we can do. We've gotta get out of here."

I yank my arm away. Pain screams in the opposite shoulder. I bury the burning ache deep beneath the surface, to be dealt with after I save the boy. "He can't be dead. He was alive a minute ago."

But as much as I don't want to believe the kid's dead, I know the Marine's words are true. The boy who Aiden and I have been sneaking candy to, the boy who always has a smile for us, is dead.

I stand and scream out a stream of curses. Then back away from his body, my own body numb.

And the ground disappears from under me.

"Lucas!" A voice yells, the sound barely heard over the rush of the wind.

My body slams into the rocky surface of the cliff, jarring me out of the flashback. That's the only explanation I have for why I'm dangling over the side of a cliff when a moment ago I was checking the missing boy's pulse.

I grab at a protruding piece of rock. My feet scramble to find purchase. If it weren't for the safety harness and top rope belay, I would be a broken mess at the base of the fifty-foot cliff.

Sheldon yells my name again. I look up to where his voice is coming from. He's lying on his stomach, leaning over the edge, and reaching toward me. "You've gotta help me here, Lucas. Grab my hand."

I glance at the rock surface. He's right. There are no other handholds near me beyond the one I'm gripping. He's my only hope of getting out of this situation with as few injuries as possible. I'm in too awkward a position for the team to pull me up.

Using the footholds as leverage, I reach up. My fingertips brush his, but it's not enough for him to grab my hand.

Sheldon wiggles forward another inch, and I try again. The wind is growing stronger, as though it wants to push me to the side, away from Sheldon. The muscles of my arm gripping the handhold of the rock are quickly fatiguing.

I try again. My feet slide on the rock as I push myself up. Just. A. Little. Farther.

Sheldon's hand wraps around mine and he pulls me up and onto the ledge.

I climb up and collapse onto the ground, breathing hard. Sheldon has rolled onto his back, and for a moment, all we're capable of doing is staring up at the stormy sky.

"Thank you," I say once I've got enough air in my lungs to speak again.

"You're welcome. But please promise me something, Lucas."

I turn my head to him. "What's that?"

"You never do that to me again. I think I just lost ten years off my life."

"That makes two of us. Sorry, I had a flashback."

"You okay?"

I sit up. "Will be once we get him out of here."

We get to our feet and face the heart-wrenching task of retrieving the boy's body for his family.

SIMONE

I scrub the kitchen cabinet like I've been doing for the past five minutes. Four minutes longer than I needed to, but I don't care. I'll scrub at it for another hour if it promises to distract me.

In the background, a steamy romance audiobook plays through the speaker on the counter. Jasper is snoozing in a sunny spot on the living room floor, his snores faint over the male narrator's voice.

The doorbell rings.

Groaning at the interruption, I peel off my rubber gloves and wash my hands.

I pause the audiobook and walk to the front door. My legs feel as though they're walking through a dense swamp. Every step I take seems slower than the last one, gravity sucking me down.

I'm empty and I'm numb.

But not numb enough to block out the grief. To block out the loneliness and despair.

To...to block out what today means to me.

My hair is sloppily pulled into a ponytail, and I haven't even bothered with makeup. For once, I don't have the energy to give a damn how I look.

The polished hardwood floor is cool against my bare feet as I walk toward the front door.

I'm not the only one making the trek. Jasper's jogged footfalls follow me. The puppy is always eager to make new friends.

I open the door, praying I can quickly get rid of whoever interrupted my scrubbing and steamy romance.

Emily is on the porch, arms filled with canvas shopping bags. Her bright smile is honey poured on an open wound.

"I had to go to Eugene today and bought something I'm dying to show you," she says.

By some small miracle, my mouth tugs into a smile. A tiny smile that takes all my energy to maintain. I open the door wider and let her in. "Sure. I'm just cleaning the kitchen."

She does the obligatory fussing of Jasper. He won't let anyone into the house until they've done that. If a burglar ever breaks into the place, the only threat they have to worry about is an attention-seeking puppy jumping on them.

Em follows me into the kitchen. "Holy shit, Simone. I don't think I've ever seen this room look so sparkly. Heck. I don't think my own kitchen has ever been this clean."

"I figured since Lucas is away, I would clean the place." The lie slips easily from my lips.

Emily gives me a double take. Lucas isn't known for being a slob. His house is always clean. Tidy. But not in an OCD kind of way.

"So what did you want to show me?" I ask.

Her smile slides back into place, her excitement reflected in her eyes. She places her bags on the freshly polished granite counter. "I bought Kim's baby shower gifts while I was in Eugene."

An unexpected chill seizes my body. Of all...of all the days she could have picked to show me what she bought Kim, it would be on the anniversary of my daughter's death.

But how would she know that?

How would Emily know how much this day hurts? How I'm

struggling to just keep breathing? I haven't told her or any of our friends about Lily. And I'm not planning to begin now. Lucas...he deserves to hear the truth from me first. I'll tell him as soon as he returns from the mountains.

I use my waning energy to refasten the smile onto my face. It's a little dimmer than usual, but I'm hoping Emily doesn't notice. "The baby isn't due for another four months. I know you're organized, Em. But wow," I finally say, hoping I don't sound too shocked.

Her smile brightens. "I couldn't resist it. Plus, it's never too early to start planning the surprise baby shower."

The soft laugh that erupts past my lips is genuine. "I take it you've already started organizing it."

"Well, given the man of my dreams hasn't exactly fallen in love with me, I have to live vicariously through other people. Like you and Kim. At the rate I'm going, this is the closest I'll ever come to having a baby shower." She busies herself searching through the bags, deluding herself if she thinks I can't see the disappointment and frustration on her face.

I cover her hand with mine, as if that's enough to solve her problem when it comes to her heart. "Give it time, Em. He'll eventually open his eyes and realize what's in front of him. Kellan's your typical guy with sawdust for a brain when it comes to his heart."

"Kellan?" She glances up, an incredulous expression rounding her mouth into an O. "I'm not talking about Kellan. I haven't found the man of my dreams yet."

Her words would be more convincing if I hadn't witnessed the way she looks at him when she believes no one—including Kellan —notices. Her words would also hold more conviction if she wasn't doing everything to avoid eye contact with me. As much as she wants to deny it, my friend has it bad for the youngest Carson brother.

"Besides, he's my boss," she adds. "Dating your boss is a no. Everyone knows that. And one wedding does not a flourishing bridal business make. Anyway, I found this and thought it was adorable." She opens one of the bags and pulls out a cute floppy bunny. The kind of toy you would give a baby.

The same stuffed beige bunny I bought Lily as soon as I embraced my pregnancy.

A wave of dizziness hits me. I place my hand on the cool granite counter to steady myself.

Don't let Emily know how much you're hurting.

She passes me the rabbit. Shaky fingers accept it, and my heart breaks all over again.

"I got that one for you." She removes another one from the bag. "I had an idea while I was in the store. You're doing the wedding-themed subscription boxes. I thought you might consider doing a subscription box for mothers-to-be. It still relates to your theme of love. Who doesn't love babies?"

And just like that, the ground gives way under my feet. I'm underwater, struggling to breathe, her words both clear and garbled to my ears.

I stare at the bunny, trembling fingers stroking its soft fur.

Don't let her see me fall apart. Not this way.

"Simone? Are you okay?"

I glance up. Emily's blurry features come into focus. "I'm fine. Good idea, but I'll have to think about it." I command my hand to pass the rabbit to her, but my body and mouth disobey. "Can I hold on to the bunny a little longer?"

"Of course." Her phone pings from inside her purse. She pulls it out and checks the screen. "Kim texted to see if we want to join her for coffee at Treats."

I pull the mask of a smile back on my face. "I'll pass, thanks. I want to finish cleaning before Lucas returns."

"You sure?"

I nod. "Say hi to the girls for me."

"Will do." Her gaze wanders over my face again. "Are you sure you're okay? Your eyes are watery."

"Must be allergies." Clutching the floppy bunny, I walk Emily to the front door. My legs threaten to buckle with each step. A vise clamps around my heart.

The door clicks shut behind her, and my legs succumb to gravity. I slump against the hallway wall and slide to the floor. My ass hits the hardwood. The held back tears release in a sob.

I cradle the bunny to my chest and let the sobbing take over, drowning out my thoughts. The tap of emotions is broken, and nothing can fix it. I don't even have energy to return to the kitchen to call Avery.

She was right. I should have stayed with her in Portland. I thought I could handle the soul-tearing grief, but I was wrong.

I've never...never felt so alone in my life.

I pull my knees to my chest and rest my forehead on my bent arm. The other arm clutches the bunny to my body. The vise keeps on tightening, squeezing my ribs. I can barely breathe.

Jasper's footfalls approach. His soft wet tongue licks my hand. I don't look up. He whimpers and licks my hand again. Then he sits next to me, body pressed to mine, and he waits. For what, I don't know.

I have no clue how long I've been crying when the click of the front door registers somewhere in the back of my mind. It's followed by the slight squeak of the hinges. *It needs oiling. I should oil that before Lucas returns.*

"Simone?" Kellan's quiet, self-assured voice breaks through the numbness I've wrapped myself in. "What's wrong?" He crouches in front of me.

I lift my head. Kellan's handsome features distort into those of a man squeamish at being around crying women. Any other time, I would burst out laughing at his expression.

"Have you heard from Lucas?" he asks.

I shake my head, unable to find my voice. Tears continue to dampen my cheeks, soak into my tank top.

"Is that why you're crying?" He pets Jasper.

I shake my head again.

"Is there something I can do?"

I inspect the bunny, running my fingertips over its loosely stuffed torso. My throat is bone dry, and my voice comes out sandpaper rough when I whisper, "I can't have children. I'm broken."

"Broken? I have no idea what that means?"

"It means I can't get pregnant. Ever. It's not physically possible." I sniff and wipe the back of my hand across my snotty nose and wet cheeks.

"Your doctor told you that today?" He shifts from his crouched position and sits next to me.

"No. I've known it for a while."

"Does Lucas know?" Kellan's voice is low and steady, a slow beating pulse that grounds me.

"No. And please don't tell him." I don't look at Kellan. I focus on the black stitching that forms the bunny's nose and mouth.

"I won't tell anyone, and that includes Lucas. But you should tell him."

I scoff, which sounds awful, thanks to my stuffy nose. At Kellan's puzzled frown, I elaborate. "My ex-boyfriend dumped me when he found out I can't have kids."

"And you really believe you not being able to have kids will make a difference to Lucas?" Kellan's words are soft, but the disbelief in his tone is a bitch-slap to the face.

I shrug because I have no idea what will happen once I tell Lucas the truth.

"Your ex-boyfriend was an asswipe. Lucas isn't going to divorce you 'cause you can't have babies. If you guys want kids, you can adopt. Like you did Jasper."

At his name, Jasper glances up from where he plonked himself next to Kellan. Kellan pets him once more.

I study my brother-in-law's deep blue eyes, so different from the brown eyes belonging to the rest of his family. "Are you glad Joanne and Ian adopted you?"

"I can't complain. But I probably did when I was a kid. Having a biological mother who abandoned me so many times and not knowing anything about my father messed me up. I fucked up after I left the Marines, got into trouble, and had to serve jail time." He cringes, guilt and regret shifting down the corners of his mouth. "I'm probably not a good example, am I?"

I rest the back of my head against the wall. "Probably not. But I'm sorry, Kellan, for how your mother treated you. She was the one who messed up. Not you."

We fall silent, and I bury myself in my thoughts. I can't tell if he's waiting for the chance to bail or wants to sit with me a little longer. I don't feel so alone with Kellan here. But for him, this visit must feel like a hockey puck to the nuts. If he had his way, the silence would stretch until his brother walked through the door. Or until Kellan found a good reason to escape.

"I'm guessing you came here to talk to Lucas?" I ask.

"Em, actually. She said something about swinging by here on the way home."

"You just missed her. She dropped this off and headed to Treats to meet up with Zara and Kim." I show him the bunny. "It's a baby shower gift for Kim."

"And that's what made you upset?"

"Yeah. Pretty much." Needing an excuse to talk about anything that doesn't deal with babies and adoptions, I ask, "This is going to sound random, but does the word catfish mean anything to you?" It's been ping-ponging in my brain since I found the word three days ago in the Greek mythology encyclopedia.

"It's a type of fish and slang for someone who uses a false online identity to lure a person into a relationship. Why?"

Both of them I know. Neither explains why Aiden wrote the word in the book and on the scrap paper I found in my room.

"No reason in particular. I just figured it was something neutral to talk about that has nothing to do with our previous topic."

Jasper's head perks up, and he stands, peering at the front door.

His tail wags so fast, it causes a shift in Australia's weather. The wagging can mean only one thing.

Before I can scramble to my feet, the door opens, and a weary, dirty, unshaven Lucas enters the house.

His gaze drops to Kellan and me on the floor, and his expression shifts into a questioning frown.

Kellan unfolds from the floor. "Shit, man. You look like crap."

An unspoken conversation passes between them. A conversation I can't translate. Kellan nods at his brother, an emotion on their faces I can't read.

"I should go and track down Emily," Kellan says to no one in particular. He flashes me a you-need-to-tell-him look. A look that is supportive and tender. An unguarded expression you don't often see on Kellan.

The front door clicks shut behind him.

"Why are you on the floor?" Lucas's frown hasn't softened. It's even wearier now than it was when he walked through the door.

Avery's words from the other day sneak in. She's right. I need to tell Lucas the truth. All of it. Not just the abbreviated version I told Kellan.

And if I'm hoping to survive the rest of the day, I can't delay any longer. I'm a decrepit high-rise. One strong gust of wind, and I'll turn into a pile of rubble. "It's nothing. Go take a shower, and I'll make you something to eat."

Usually if I tell him to go take a shower, he tries to get me to join him. Not this time. He plods upstairs without another word to me.

I push myself to my feet.

I can do this. One step at a time.

My legs are no less shaky than before, and even though the vise around my chest loosened a bit from talking to Kellan, seeing Lucas has retightened the screw.

While I wait for Lucas, I put away the cleaning supplies and start making some food for him. It's early for dinner, but he's probably hungry. He usually is after returning from a search and rescue mission.

I've just finished making him a sandwich when he walks into the kitchen. He grabs a beer from the fridge and takes his food and drink to the dining room table.

I haven't eaten all day, but I'm not hungry. I don't even bother getting myself a drink. I just want to get this over with.

Clutching the floppy bunny for emotional support, I sit at the head of the table. My stomach feels like I'm on a roller coaster, and the ride's operator is leaning on the acceleration button. I want to grip onto the edge of the table, squeeze my eyes shut, and pray this nightmare ends soon. Pray the nonexistent contents of my stomach stay put.

My gaze lands briefly on the floral arrangement in front of me, and I take the second to pull myself haphazardly back together again.

Lucas takes a long swig of his beer. "Are you going to tell me why I found you and Kellan on the floor, and you'd obviously been crying?"

"It...it can wait." The words come out barely louder than a whisper. Something about his worn-out expression warns me this isn't a good time to spill my secrets.

"Tell me now. Before I start thinking the worst."

"It can wait."

"Just tell me, Simone," he says on a weary sigh.

I glance toward the front door. And will my legs to carry me down the hallway, out the front door, and keep on going so I can avoid this conversation.

"Simone?" My name might be said with a questioning lilt, but the commanding tone in his voice is clear. I don't have a choice. The longer I delay, the more painful this will be.

For both of us.

I nod and attempt to inhale a deep breath. The tightness in my chest prevents me from filling my lungs. Prevents me from calming the panic thundering inside me.

I focus on the floral arrangement again. Several flowers that were fresh when Lucas gave them to me four days ago are wilted. Brown spots mar the red rose petals. "I told you about the accident that resulted in the scar across my stomach."

He nods and takes a bite of his sandwich.

"I didn't tell you everything." I tighten my hold on the bunny. The fur does nothing to ease the storm raging in my stomach, in my mind. "It happened ten years ago today. I was twenty-one weeks pregnant at the time." I close my eyes against the forming tears, but it's too late.

I thought there were no more tears left to cry after I broke down in front of Kellan. I was wrong. So very wrong.

I open my eyes and let my gaze drop to the bunny just so I don't have to look at Lucas. "I lost the baby." I bite on my trembling lower lip, desperate to keep it together for just a few more minutes. *That's all I need. Just a few more minutes.* "I was rushed to surgery, but I started to bleed out. The damage was severe. The surgeon did what he could to save me, but because of that, I can't have any more babies."

I go quiet. Even the appliances behind Lucas seem to hold their collective breaths. We're all waiting...waiting to see how he'll respond.

Wetness drops onto the bunny's fur. I tenderly wipe it away. "I lost my daughter that day." I look up, eyes locking on to his. "I lost *our* daughter."

I glance away, vaguely aware that I'm cradling the bunny—something I never got to do with my daughter.

My gaze returns to Lucas.

In time to catch Lucas's expression shift from shock to sorrow to grief to hurt.

But it's the dark expression that finally lands on Lucas's face that shatters my world.

44

LUCAS

Ever since I got the call Monday morning about the boy lost in the mountains, I'd prayed he would be found quickly and alive.

With each passing hour, the odds of that grew steadily worse. And then the flashback hit me while Sheldon and I were retrieving the boy's body.

Simone's words feel like that moment when I was barely holding on to the cliff, trying to get purchase.

Only now, I'm not wearing the safety harness.

The accident happened ten years ago, and not once did Simone mention she'd been pregnant. Not once did she mention the baby was mine. I've opened up to her about my flashbacks, and she's been keeping this from me? Every time I told her I wanted to have kids, she'd known that we couldn't and effectively lied by withholding the truth? I've been honest with her, but she's betrayed me with nothing but lies.

I feel cold, empty. Emptier than knowing I could be spending life in prison. I want to rewind time to when she told me the reason she was upset could wait. Snatch my words before I can say them, delay this moment of truth.

I...I can't deal with her confession right now—not after every-thing that has happened over the past three days.

I shove away from the table and stand. I can't look at Simone. I'm scared I'll say something I'll regret later.

So I don't.

I stalk out of the living room, phone in hand, grab my keys from the hallway table, and bail out the front door.

Simone doesn't make a sound. She doesn't try to stop me.

She does what she did when she found out she was pregnant —nothing.

She hadn't even bothered to tell me I was going to be a father. She was five months pregnant when she lost our baby, and not once —not once did she inform me I was going to be a father.

Not once did she contact me.

I'm not in the mood to push myself on my usual running trail, so I drive toward the lake, to a place where no one will be around to bother me.

"*Fuck.*" I might have muttered it, but the word screams in my head, ricocheting against the inside of my skull. I want to throw something. Kick it. Whatever it takes.

I might be mad at Simone, but I'm also angry at myself.

I failed her brother and I failed Simone. I fucked up when I returned from my final deployment and never contacted her. Never bothered to check how she was doing. She had stopped writing to me while I was away without giving me a reason or explanation. As far as I was concerned, she was no longer part of my life.

It was the same mistake I made with Aiden. Because of the PTSD and my fucked-up shoulder, I hadn't made sure he was getting help. I was drowning. Drowning and unable to see he was struggling. And then I stayed away while pursuing my physical therapy degree. I never bothered to reach out to Simone.

When her brother died and I knew she would be devastated, I still didn't reach out to her.

I'd fucked up in so many ways.

I park my SUV to the side of a dirt road that usually doesn't see much traffic, and hike through the trees and undergrowth to the narrow path that skirts a portion of the lake.

Christ, how many people knew about the baby when I didn't?

I think back to the last time we were together while I was in the Marines. I grab a stone from the path and hurl it into the lake. My stream of curses carries in the wind.

Why didn't anyone tell me Simone was pregnant? Her friends and Rose never so much as hinted there was a baby. My daughter died while I was deployed, but why not say anything when I returned? Not once in all these years had they said or given anything away about a baby.

Zara, Kim, and Emily are good at keeping secrets, but they aren't that good. Nor are they great actors.

The same goes for Rose.

She would have told my parents I was going to be a father. Had they known, I can guarantee they would've relayed the info to me.

I grab another stone from the path and hurl it.

Which means none of them had known Simone was pregnant. Even if she had begged them to not say anything to me, someone would have accidentally slipped and given it away once I returned.

Another rock splashes into the lake.

No one in Maple Ridge knew she was pregnant. No one was there for her when she had the accident and lost the baby.

No one has been there for her all these years.

No one—except for maybe one person.

Avery. She's the one person Simone is close to who might have known about the baby and who was there for her after the accident. The one person Simone could have possibly turned to for the past ten years on the anniversary of our daughter's death. The one person she didn't have on her side today.

Knowing that kicks the wind out of me.

Once again, I've let Simone down and hurt her.

This time I don't throw a rock into the lake. I hurl it against a thick tree trunk. It doesn't even make a dent in the bark.

My phone rings in my shorts pocket.

Thinking it's Simone, I grab the phone, an apology on my lips.

But it's not Simone. It's Blake.

"What's up?" I answer.

"I've just heard that Sebastian Dryson's body has been found."

"Body? As in he's dead?"

"From what my contact at the Eugene Police Department told me, Sebastian is believed to have double-crossed an associate. And this associate is known to be involved in some shady dealings. The police are investigating Sebastian's involvement with them as one possible cause of his death."

"I don't suppose any of this has to do with the narcotics found in my house?"

"Sorry, as far as I can tell, neither individual is linked to any type of drugs. But who knows what they might be capable of? This could be the tip of the iceberg.

"Sebastian was recently spotted with a man who works for Kincaid Timber Corporation. He was also spotted leaving the alley behind Picnic and Treats just after the truck almost plowed you and Simone down. One of my handwriting experts looked at a copy of the note you sent me, and he's ninety-eight percent positive Sebastian wrote it."

"Why the hell would he do that?"

"Good question. Too bad he can't tell us. But I don't think it was a trap after all. If he had arranged for the truck to hit you or Simone, Sebastian wouldn't have been there."

"Not unless he wanted to witness the truck hit us. Isn't that what some arsonists do? Stick around and watch the show? We might not be talking fires here, but the principle's the same."

"There were better places than the alley where he could've gone for a front-row seat."

The wind picks up, turning the water choppy. New storm clouds lurk in the distance, their ETA another hour or two.

"So, what now?" I ask.

"We wait to see if Sebastian can be linked to the narcotics in your house. But if they were planted to discredit you with the Wakefields, his death doesn't make sense. And whoever he was talking to in the bar will lose out, too. Or maybe not. With Sebastian dead, will his parents still want to build the lodge?"

I select a stone from the dirt path, this time taking care with my choice. "Unless they decide to go ahead with the lodge in memory of their son, his death might put an end to their plan."

"Which is good news for you and your brothers." Blake doesn't sound too thrilled with that possibility. It doesn't take much to figure out why.

"Do the police know who killed Sebastian?"

"No. They have several working theories…"

"And one of them is I have the motive for wanting him out of the picture," I fill in for him.

"The autopsy is tomorrow, then they'll have a rough time frame for time of death. It helps that you, Troy, and Garrett were involved in the search and rescue this week. If the coroner lists the time of death for then, the three of you have alibis."

"But Kellan might not." I finish his unspoken thought, not giving him a chance to point out the obvious.

Fuck. Since when did buying a plot of land get so complicated?

With all the force I can muster, I skip the stone across the water. It jumps ten times before sinking to the bottom. "What do you know about the man from Kincaid Timber who Sebastian was seen talking to?"

"I'm looking into that now. I just wanted to give you an update on everything that's been happening for the past few days."

"Thanks. I appreciate it."

We end the call, and I jog back to my SUV. I text my brothers and ask them to come over a little later. I need to talk to them about

Blake's news, but first I need to go home and fix things with Simone.

"I lost my daughter that day. I lost our daughter."

The memory of Simone's words almost brings me to my knees again.

45

———

SIMONE

The front door slams behind Lucas, and all I'm capable of is staring numbly at his half-eaten sandwich on the dining-room table. A chill takes my body hostage, steals my breath, slows my heart. I feel like I've fallen into the frozen lake, and all I can do is sink, sink, sink to the silty bottom.

I've lost Lucas.

Why? Why did I tell him now? Couldn't I have made something up? Something minor. Like I stubbed my toe.

Why? Because I was tired of keeping the truth from him. That's why. Because Avery was right—I can't face this day alone.

But that's exactly where I am—like I was ten years ago.

Alone.

Jasper jumps his paws onto my lap and licks my hand. He knows he's not supposed to do that, but neither of us cares about the rule right now.

"I guess I misjudged him," I say to no one in particular. "I never should have told him."

God, I miss Aiden. If he'd been alive, he would've kicked Lucas's ass for what happened. My brother would've loved me no matter

274

what. He would never have turned his back on me the way Lucas has.

The need to be near my brother coils around me, sticks my broken pieces together.

I drag my gaze away from the food and smile at Jasper. "How would you like to spend a few days in the mountains?"

He barks, which I translate to mean yes.

I head upstairs to the master bedroom, pack a duffle bag, and grab Jasper's supplies from the kitchen.

I scribble a note for Lucas, telling him I've gone away for a few days and Jasper's with me.

I load Jasper into my car and drive to Picnic & Treats. I park my car in a shady spot in front of the café where I can keep an eye on him and roll down the window partway.

It's midafternoon so the place isn't as busy as it would've been an hour ago. I order a sandwich and fruit salad to go.

Zara comes out of the kitchen and spots me. "Hey, I wasn't expecting to see you here." She walks over to me. "Em said you couldn't make it for coffee. She and Kim just left." Her eyes drag over me, and she frowns.

I changed into jeans and a T-shirt after Lucas stormed out of the house, but the rest of me resembles the hot mess Kellan found when he came over.

"What's wrong?" I attempt a smile, but my lips can't remember how to curve into one.

"Excuse me," a woman our age says. She's tall and gorgeous with flawless ebony skin and black textured curls that brush her shoulders. She must be a tourist. I've never seen her before. "Do you by any chance know where I can find Aiden Hensley?"

Zara and I exchange a puzzled glance.

I bite my lip, struggling to keep everything I've temporarily locked away—the anniversary, Lucas's reaction to the news, how much I miss my brother—from bleeding out like a ruptured spleen.

"He's dead. He died almost three years ago." There's a brittle edge to my voice, a fine-grit roughness to my tone.

The woman's eyes widen and her lips part in surprise. "I didn't realize. What happened?"

"How did you know him?" I'm not ready to admit the cause of death yet.

"Um, well, he and I hooked up three years ago next week. I was moving to London for my job, but we agreed if we were both single when I returned to the U.S, we would hook up again. I wasn't sure if he was joking or not, so I went to his old place but no one answered. Guess I should have waited for him to email back." She huffs out a soft breath, the corners of her gloss-slicked lips dipping down. "He was such a fun and sweet guy. I can't believe he's dead."

Fun and sweet?

I mean, sure, until he changed during his last tour with the Marines, he had been a fun and sweet guy. But, if her dates are correct, he committed suicide two weeks after they hooked up. I'm not an expert on suicide, but unless something happened between when she last saw him and when he ended his life, she's not describing someone struggling with depression.

Not unless he was faking being happy.

Was that even possible? I'm not suicidal, but I had a nearly impossible time dragging myself out of bed this morning. I don't have the energy to fake being happy. Not in the way she just described my brother.

"He committed suicide," I tell her, watching her reaction.

Surprise returns to her face, and she takes a step as if forced back by the blast of my news. "He did? Are we talking about the same Aiden? The man I met was stressed about something—he wouldn't tell me what it was. But he told me things would be better in a few days. Justice would finally prevail."

"Do you have any idea what he was talking about?" Zara asks her.

The woman shakes her head. "We were too busy making the

most of what little time we had left before I had to leave for the airport."

We ask her a few more questions. Kya answers them as best as she can. They had agreed not to keep in contact while she was away. No strings attached. No expectations. But even then, she's visibly shaken at the news of my brother's death.

She leaves Treats looking crushed and heartbroken.

"Did Kya's description of Aiden match how you remember him before he...?" I can't get my mouth to form the words left unspoken.

"I don't really remember. I didn't see him much after he retired from the military. At first when I saw him, he had the same vacant expression as Lucas. Both were zombies in those early days. After Lucas left for Seattle, I didn't see Aiden as much. He hung out at the Veterans Center more than he did here or anywhere else."

I didn't know any of that. Lucas hasn't mentioned it.

And Grams also failed to mention it.

I'd seen Aiden off and on when I knew Lucas wasn't around, but I'd been dealing with my own grief. I'd missed the signs Aiden was struggling. We had talked on the phone fairly regularly, but even then I'd missed the signs. Just like he had missed the ones that said I was also dealing with my own pain.

We had both managed to hide secrets from each other.

"After a while, he looked less like a zombie," Zara says. "It was as if he had found a reason to return to the land of the living. When he died, I assumed something had happened since the last time I'd seen him. It had been a few months."

Maybe that's why Grams was so surprised when he died. She hadn't known he was struggling with depression, even though she saw him once a week. It's possible he was great at hiding it. But I have a hard time believing that.

"I'm going away to my grandfather's cabin for a few days," I tell Zara, doing my best to sound upbeat despite everything we've just learned.

If Zara's expression is anything to go by, I'm as close to sounding upbeat as the Arctic is to Antarctica. Her gaze leaves me naked and vulnerable and wondering if she can peer deep into my soul. "What's going on with you, Simone?"

"What do you mean?"

"You come in here looking like a Ninki Nanka is hot on your tail and you can't escape fast enough. I know you. Something's going on. Is it Lucas?"

I wince, unable to keep the pain from my heart. She grabs my arm and practically drags me down the hallway to the staff room.

"Jasper's waiting for me in the car," I protest.

"Give me your keys."

I consider yanking my arm loose and running, but I'll never hear the end of it from her, Kim, and Emily once I return to Maple Ridge. I hand the keys to her, gripping them for a fraction of a second before letting go.

"Stay here." She returns a few minutes later carrying two mugs with a tall swirl of whipped cream. "Here, drink this. Tracy will take Jasper for a short walk while you and I talk."

Jasper likes Tracy. He'll be in good hands. But that doesn't mean I want to relive what happened less than an hour ago. The memory stings like a festering wound doused with lemon juice. The only cure is spending time at my grandfather's cabin, washing away the bad memory with my childhood memories from there.

"All right, tell me what the dumbass did to make you look like you're having an allergy attack." Zara points to the couch and sits on the armchair opposite it.

I stand motionless for a beat, then sink to the middle of the couch. The sooner I tell her what happened, the sooner Jasper and I can leave for the mountains. I just need time to think. Time to figure out my options.

I sip the drink. Hot-chocolatey goodness fills my veins. A small part of me wants to say screw it to hiding out in the mountain and regrouping my thoughts. Drowning my sorrows in creamy hot chocolate sounds like a better plan.

But visiting my grandfather's cabin will do me some good. I avoided the place after Aiden's death. It's time I go back to face my final memories of him there.

I tell Zara everything. About the pregnancy. The unsent letter. The accident. The grief and depression. How Lucas and I hadn't seen or talked to each other in over ten years until my recent return to Maple Ridge. And how we only got married for business reasons, not for love like we'd told everyone.

And like a tap turned on all the way, I pour out how I failed everyone including my brother.

Especially my brother.

"I wasn't the mother my baby deserved. And I wasn't the sister my brother deserved either." My chest tightens once more, the vise from earlier returning with full vengeance. "I lost them. Just like— just like I've lost Lucas." The words come out in a tearless, weary whisper. "He hates me because I didn't tell him when I was pregnant with his child, and then I lost his baby. He thought he was marrying a whole woman, a woman who could give him kids. But instead...instead he married one without a uterus."

Zara's sorrow meets my gaze. Not a single drop of pity stares back at me. Just understanding and compassion. She pushes herself off the armchair and joins me on the couch. Her arms hug me in a fierce embrace. I stiffen for a fraction of a second, then sink into her hug, needing it more than oxygen.

"I'm sorry you went through that, Simone. I wish I had known so I could've been there for you."

I return her hug, feeling her strength seep into me. "I know. I...I didn't want anyone here to know about the baby until I had spoken to Lucas first. By the time I realized I was pregnant and accepted that I was going to be a mommy, I was already sixteen weeks. So I decided to wait a little longer so I could send him the baby's ultrasound when I told him. And then—and then I couldn't bring myself to tell anyone what happened.

"After the accident, I hadn't been interested in dating. It was easier being a workaholic than dealing with my new reality. I took a chance with Mark, my last boyfriend. But he dumped me when he discovered I couldn't have babies."

"God, that's so effed up," Zara says, her expression a cross between pissed and heartbroken.

I flop back on the couch cushion. "It is. I sank into depression. Felt defective. After his reaction, I swore off dating permanently, not wanting to go through that again. I couldn't deal with another man thinking I wasn't worth it. It's taken me years to cope with the loss of my daughter. Usually I'm okay, but today's the anniversary of her death." I wipe at the fresh batch of tears. "The anniversary always hits me hard. Avery comes to Lily's grave with me and helps me survive the day…"

"But you didn't have that today," Zara finishes what I can't say. I nod. "Instead, your husband let you down."

"I wouldn't say that he let me down as much as it was me letting *him* down. I should've told him the truth from the beginning, but at first, I didn't think it would matter. We weren't marrying for love. But then he told me he could see us one day having kids, assuming he didn't end up in prison. I knew I needed to tell him, but my ex-boyfriend's words kept echoing in my brain, convincing me I was damaged goods."

My gaze drops to my lap. "I couldn't bear the thought of Lucas looking at me the same way Mark had when he found out about the hysterectomy."

Zara hugs me once more, her touch powerful enough to dull some of the pain pumping through my veins. "Your ex-boyfriend was a dick. You're not broken, Simone. Not even close. You love him, don't you? Lucas, I mean. You two might've married for convenience, but you really do love him."

"Yes. I've been in love with him since I was eighteen years old, when he and I were first hooking up behind Aiden's back. Only I didn't realize it at the time. I finally admitted the truth to myself the last time I saw him before he and Aiden left for what ended up being their final deployment."

"Did you tell him how you felt about him back then?"

I lift my shoulders in a shrug. "I'd planned to, but then everything got messed up with the accident. And once he returned to Maple Ridge after getting his degree, I avoided the town. I knew it would hurt too much seeing him again."

"Does he know you love him?"

"You mean, have I told him?"

She nods.

"No. Even though he told me he wanted us to have a normal marriage, I guess I half expected him to change his mind at some point. I lost my parents, my baby, my brother. There's a part of me that's sitting on the edge, waiting to lose him, too."

Which is pretty much what happened when I finally told him the truth.

"I don't think you have to worry about losing Lucas, Simone. The man loves you. He probably needs time to digest everything. He's not callous like your last boyfriend."

"You didn't see him. He was beyond pissed."

Zara looks as though she wants to argue, but then changes her mind. "What are you going to do now?"

"Spend a few days at my grandfather's cabin. I need to figure out what to do next."

I did the right thing telling Lucas about Lily. I should have told him sooner. Before we got married. Then he could've walked away and saved me from my current heartache.

"Did you ever see anyone after your baby died? Like a therapist?" Zara asks.

"I joined a support group. But I was the only single woman in it. I listened to couples share their stories and women wonder what they had done wrong. Wonder if history would be a bitch and repeat itself. But that won't be the case for me."

There are no second chances. No getting pregnant and fearing the baby might be premature, might be stillborn, might die at any point. Fate dealt me the one card, and it's game over.

"I quit the group soon after and buried myself in my work."

"Did that help?" It's a rhetorical question. Zara already knows the answer.

"Once I get back from the cabin, I'll talk to someone. A professional. Until I fully deal with the loss of my baby, with my inability to have kids, and with Aiden's death, I'll never be fully healed...or as close to fully healed as humanly possible. I realize that now."

"I think that's a good idea. And I'll be there for you in whatever way you need, Simone. But are you sure you want to drive to the cabin today? Maybe wait a few days. Talk things through with Lucas first."

I shake my head. "I'd rather go now. I just need to get away and process everything. Jasper and I will hang out. Have some alone time."

Doubt clouds her expression. She's not buying it. But that doesn't matter. I've made up my mind.

A smile stretches across my face, not completely genuine, but not completely fake either. "I promise. I'll be fine."

46

LUCAS

I arrive home to an empty house.

My first thought is Simone has taken Jasper for a walk. His harness and leash aren't where we normally keep them.

I walk into the kitchen only to realize Jasper's bowls are also missing.

My second thought is Simone has finally figured out she deserves better than me. I'm not worth the effort. My reaction earlier was the final straw that cracked the camel's back.

She left a note on the kitchen counter. It just says she's going away for a few days and Jasper is with her. There's no hint of where she went.

Shit.

I flip the paper over. Nothing—other than a blank page staring accusingly at me. I swallow, guilt clawing my throat. I did this. My stupidity, my rashness pushed her away.

I remove my phone from my pocket and call her. After several rings, I'm sent to voice mail.

I don't leave a message.

I text her.

Me: Call me!

Christ, where the hell is she?

The doorbell rings. Zara is on the front porch, along with my brothers and Emily. Emily appears beyond distraught, her face pale.

It's Thursday. They're a day early for game night. Jerome and Kim aren't with them, which is a good thing judging from everyone's expressions.

"Where's Simone?" My grit-rough voice doesn't sound pained to my ears. It sounds destroyed. "Has something happened to her?"

The exhaustion, frustration, failure from the last four days builds to a crescendo, and all kinds of horrifying fates flash in my brain. I snatch up my keys from the hallway table.

Zara places her hand on my chest, not giving me a chance to push past her. "Slow down, Marine boy. We need to talk. As for your question? You know better than anyone what happened."

"Do you know where she is?"

Zara nods.

"Where?" The word fires with the force of an M240.

Garrett glares at me. "Hey. Don't shoot the messenger."

"You're all here because of what happened this afternoon?" I ask.

"No," Troy says. "Garrett, Kellan, and I are here because you texted that you needed to talk to us. These two"—he gestures to Zara and Emily with a jerk of his head—"are probably here to knee you in the package. And frankly, you're on your own there."

I vaguely remember texting my brothers from the lake. I'd forgotten about it after discovering Simone was gone.

"How long have you been out there catching up on everything that's been going on in my life for the past decade?" My tone is no longer pained or abrupt. It's weary and wary and wane.

"Long enough," Troy replies.

I open the door to let them into the house.

Zara walks past me. "God, you look like dog shit."

"Love you, too," I grumble.

They remove their shoes and relocate to the living room. Everyone takes a seat. Everyone except for Zara and me. Like a pack of meerkats, their heads turn to her.

She fists her hands on her hips. She might be eight inches shorter than me, but she still manages to look me down. "Simone tells you what happened to her baby, and you act like a toddler and throw a tantrum. For the past ten years, she's carried the weight of losing her baby and has had to do it alone."

I let each word strike me without daring to open my mouth. I know everything that she's telling me.

And now, I want to find Simone and spend an eternity making everything up to her.

Doing whatever I can to absorb or end her pain.

"I know. I fucked up—"

"And not only that. She's dealing with the physical and psychological ramifications of having a hysterectomy."

At the last part, my body turns cold and brittle and ready to crack. Simone's words—about the damage being severe—rush in with the power to drown.

That's what Simone had meant. She'd had a hysterectomy.

Shit. Shit. Shit. Shit. Goddamn. Shit.

People have been speculating that she's pregnant. I've been talking about us having kids one day. She never said anything. She always became quiet. Like she wanted to be invisible, to disappear into the wall.

And I didn't clue in that something was wrong. Me. Her husband.

I let her down. Again.

My voice is rusty and raw when I say, "As soon as you tell me where she is, I'll fix it."

Or fix as much as I can.

"I'm thinking about it. But it might not be a bad idea to give her some space for a few days to digest everything first."

"That's the last thing she needs, and you know it." Anger, desperation, regret, grief simmer in my veins. Some of the anger is directed at Zara for making things difficult.

Mostly it's aimed at me.

"I don't know what she needs...beyond time to think. And that's exactly why she went away. You two got married for the wrong reasons, Lucas." Zara has the same look on her face that Mom had when I was ten years old and broke her favorite vase. "Yes, I know the real reason for the wedding and short engagement."

Emily sits up straighter. Shock and confusion flicker on her face before she settles on disappointment. "What do you mean?"

Zara is kind enough to give her a quick summary of the reasons we got married. The business arrangement between two former lovers.

"What? You two don't even love each other?"

Emily is wrong. I do love Simone. I've been in love with her since college. But until recently, I'd been too much of an idiot to admit it to myself that what I felt for her back then has never changed.

"Tell your brothers what you wanted to talk to them about, and I'll decide if I should tell you today or wait until tomorrow to tell you where she went." Zara has the stubborn expression I know only too well. The protective lioness in her—all impatience and claws—is getting ready to strike.

"You might as well tell us," Garrett says from the armchair next to where she's standing, his knee bouncing. "You know you won't get anywhere with her until you do." That lands him a smack in the arm from Zara. "Hey, what was that for?"

She lifts her chin. "You know very well why."

He gives a small nod, even though it's clear he has no idea what she's talking about.

"All right, if it means you'll tell me where Simone went..." I explain about the phone call from Blake a few hours ago.

"Sebastian really is dead?" Troy's gaze is locked on mine, his brow creasing.

"Would seem so."

"His poor parents." Em's distress for them bleeds into her tone. "Simone told me he had a twin sister who died when they were teens. And now he's gone, too."

Troy leans forward on the couch. "Do you think his death has anything to do with the Wakefields' property?"

"I have no idea. Blake didn't have any more details."

"You said Sebastian was recently seen with a Kincaid Timber employee." Kellan's lack of surprise at how fucked things have gotten is clear on his scowling face.

"It would help if we knew who it was and how far up the chain of command he is. Blake didn't know, but he was going to see if he could get more information from the Eugene police on the grounds it might be linked to my case."

Zara releases a weighted sigh. "And we're back to square one. Waiting for them to figure out what's going on. Does Simone know any of this?"

"Blake called me after I left the house. I never had a chance to tell her."

Zara throws a look my way. A look that says so many things, I'm an idiot being first on the list. She sits on the armrest of Garrett's chair. "I don't get why you had to be an asshole after she told you about the baby."

"I screwed up. Big-time." The air in my lungs rushes out in a hard breath, leaving shame and guilt and dread to torment me. "Not to justify what I did, but she picked the worst possible time to tell me. I just spent the last four days searching for a lost boy, only for it to turn into a recovery mission."

The fucked-up timing was my fault. She wanted to delay telling me. I hadn't let her. If I had known she'd planned to drop a nuclear bomb, I wouldn't have pushed her.

"What were you and Simone talking about when I found you both sitting on the hallway floor?" My question is directed at Kellan. "Did she tell you about the baby?"

"No. She told me she couldn't have babies, but she never mentioned she'd been pregnant or what happened. But she did ask if I knew what catfish meant."

"Catfish?" Emily echoes. "You mean the type of fish or online predator?"

Kellan shrugs. "No idea. Lucas came home before I could find out why she was asking. Does it mean anything to you?" The question is volleyed back to me.

Garrett rocks from the seat to his feet and paces, muttering "Catfish" to himself on repeat.

I shake my head even though something about the word causes a feeling of *déjà vu*. I have no idea why. "Maybe she knows someone who might be a victim of catfishing."

I mentally repeat the word several times. Garrett does the same out loud but saying it to himself. There's something about *catfish* that isn't sitting easy with me.

"What is it?" Troy asks me. "You look like you've been told to defuse a land mine and don't remember how to do it."

I open my mouth to tell him I've never known how to defuse a land mine, but the reason the word feels like a ten-ton explosive in my stomach comes to me in a flash. "One of the missions I was on in Afghanistan was Codename Catfish."

"Did you ever tell Simone that?"

"No."

"Maybe you said the word in your sleep?" Zara suggests. "I dated a guy in college who mumbled a lot in his sleep. Let's just say you didn't want him working for you if he had access to company secrets."

"Sounds like something for your next thriller," Kellan tells

Garrett. His tone holds the smirk that isn't on his face. "The female agent learns the villain's dark secrets because he talks in his sleep, and she wore him out with lots of sex."

"God, that's so sexist." Zara grabs a cushion from the seat Garrett vacated and hurls it at Kellan.

The man with sharp reflexes doesn't bother to catch it. It smacks him in the chest. Emily laughs.

"Are you going to tell me where Simone went?" Since growling and glaring at Zara aren't working, I go with a different approach. I try for a smile. A remorseful, groveling smile. "Look, I know I screwed up. I should've handled the news about my daughter a helluva lot better than I did. But do you really think it's a good idea for her to be alone?"

My phone rings on the coffee table. I snatch it up in case it's Simone.

It's not.

"It's Samuel." Zara's brother. I answer the phone. "Hey, what's up?"

"Is Simone there?"

"No, I don't know where she is." I throw his sister a dark look, even though she's not privy to the conversation.

"I've been trying to call her, but she's not answering her phone. It's her grandmother." At his urgent tone, the muscles in my body tense. And I'm already on my feet when he says, "Someone broke into her house and beat her up. She's still unconscious."

Adrenaline surges through me, jump-starting my fight mode, but it's not enough to drown out my fears when it comes to Simone.

"I'll tell Simone as soon as I locate her." I end the call. My next words are leveled at Zara. "Rose was beaten up in her home. Now will you tell me where the fuck my wife is?"

47

SIMONE

My car pulls up to my grandfather's cabin, a small building surrounded by forest. A building I haven't seen in more than ten years.

I'm not sure what I expected to find. Maybe a cabin that had fallen into disrepair. A building that looked abandoned. Forgotten.

That doesn't describe the cabin in front of me. The place has been renovated, repainted, the roof retiled. Yes, the paint has faded over the past few years, but it's obvious Aiden had been working on the cabin. This...this doesn't make me think of someone struggling with depression. Not to the point where they're suicidal.

The thought of my brother has my insides clenching. This is the place, just beyond the trees, where he died.

I put the car into park and rest my forehead on the steering wheel, talking myself down from the sob-fest that's preparing to suffocate me.

Once I've pulled myself together, I climb out of the car and let the happy memories of the cabin and surrounding area seep into me.

"Why did you have to give up on life?" I call out since this seems like the perfect place to talk to my brother. "It sounds like things

290

were getting better for you. And Kya—I met her today. She's really nice. She's sad you're not here. I mean, not here-here. In Maple Ridge."

I turn on the spot, taking in the forest that my brother and I used to love playing in. "I miss you, big brother." My voice cracks like a piece of dry wood tossed in the fire. "I miss you so, so, so much." A small sob escapes, and I close my eyes for a second, pulling myself together. "If you're in heaven with my daughter, can you give her a hug and tell her how much I love her?" Another hiccupped sob.

A bark comes from my car. I wipe the tears with my hands and open the back door. "Sorry, Jasper. Didn't mean to make you wait."

I attach his leash. The last thing I want is for him to go chasing after a squirrel and get lost.

He jumps down and sniffs the ground. And I gather up my steely resolve to get through the next few days without falling apart quite so much.

The ghost of a wind tugs at me, hinting at another approaching storm. I hadn't paid attention to the weather before leaving the house. It was only when we were almost here that I realized what we'll be facing—beyond the phantoms of my past.

"You wanna explore first, or should we unpack?"

Jasper lurches forward, tugging me along. He's getting stronger and more muscular with each passing day.

"All right, let me show you around." I take him past the side of the house to the firepit where Grandpa told Aiden and me stories while we toasted marshmallows. No one could spin a tale quite like our grandfather. It was Grandpa who got Aiden hooked on the various mythologies.

I sit on one of the logs skirting the firepit.

Memories of Aiden, my parents, and Grandpa aren't the only ones surrounding me. Lucas, his family, Jerome, Emily, Kim, and Zara also stayed at the cabin from time to time with us. It was here when I first noticed Lucas as something more than my brother's best friend.

We were sitting around the fire, opposite each other. I looked up and caught him watching me. It was in that moment, with the flames dancing between us, my heart became his.

I blink away the memory. Once Lucas and I have a real conversation—not one with him storming out of the house during it—I'll file for divorce. I deserve to be with a man who loves me no matter what. A man who is there for me during my darkest hours. Like today. On the day that causes me so much pain.

I didn't ask for the drunk driver to hit me. I didn't ask for a hysterectomy, but that's exactly the future the Fates saw for me. I might've married Lucas for business reasons, but now I want more than that.

Maybe it's time I share my own personal journey online. Not because I'm hoping it will bring in new clients. I want other women who've lost a child or had a hysterectomy at a young age to know they aren't alone. I want to let women get to know the real me, not the perfectly made up, professionally photographed version of me with Lucas and Jasper.

And I want other women to know that they don't need to be married to understand what true love looks like—and that we're worth more than the front we put on for the benefit of the world.

After Jasper and I explore the area for a few minutes, we return to my car to grab my duffle bag and the box of supplies. I sling the bag's strap across my shoulder, hoist the box into my arms, and shut the trunk. Eager to keep exploring, Jasper strains on his leash, which is hooked on my elbow. It's a miracle I don't drop the box.

I climb the porch steps and lower the bag onto the Welcome mat. Balancing the box on one hip, I unlock the cabin door with the key that has never left my key ring all these years and step inside. The place smells like I remember, of chopped wood and marshmallows and adventures. And dust.

A thick layer of dust blankets every surface, and cobwebs crowd the corners of the room. Guess I know what I'll be doing tonight for entertainment. Hopefully Grams's old broom is still in the storage closet.

I lower the box onto the coffee table and unhook the leash from Jasper's harness.

Aiden hadn't just renovated the outside of the cabin. The inside also looks better than I remember. He'd mentioned he wanted to update it. I had no idea this is what he meant. The wood interior has been stained a warm honey color, contrasting against dark wooden beams that weren't here before.

The boring fireplace, now covered in stone, has been turned into the focal point of the room. And built-in bookshelves fill one wall where old storage shelves once stood. Even the old, worn-out sofa and chairs have been replaced.

The kitchen is as small as I remember, but it's been updated with several new appliances. And the cabinets have been stained hunter green.

The place looks incredible. So much better than the old hunting cabin I remember.

I head into the tiny bedroom Aiden and I used to share and dump my bag on the floor. The bunk bed is still here, the bedding rumpled from when Aiden last stayed in the cabin. The room is the same as the last time I was here, with no sign of any renovations.

I peek into the master bedroom. My brother's magic touch has been in here, too. The furniture hasn't changed, but the walls have been stained.

Why? Why go to all this trouble with renovating the cabin if he didn't plan to stick around to enjoy it?

I return to the living room and walk to the bookshelf, hoping to find an explanation for why Aiden wrote CATFISH on the paper and in the book he sent me. I can't for the life of me figure out what it means. For all I know, he wanted to catch a catfish in the lake. But I don't think that was the reason.

Aiden loved mythology, but that doesn't mean he believed writing down his wishes would make them magically happen.

I pull out a thick book on Greek mythology from the shelf and thumb through the pages. The illustrations and paper are old. None contain handwritten words. I remove the Norse encyclopedia from the shelf and leaf through it.

Like with the first two books, the pages are free of handwritten notes...until I get to Forseti, the god of justice.

CATFISH is scrawled on the page, along with *Aiden4justice*.

I glance up at the ceiling. "What are you trying to tell me?"

Jasper barks.

"Really?" I say to the ceiling. "You're answering me through my dog?"

Jasper keeps barking, and it's only then I notice he's barking at the door.

"What's wrong? You wanna go chase a squirrel?" I return the book to the shelf, grab his leash from the coffee table, and clip it on to his harness. I open the cabin door.

And the source of Jasper's barking is immediately apparent.

A familiar dark-haired man with a scraggly beard and wearing camo pants and jacket is standing there, tall and solid like a hundred-year-old oak. But it's the gun in his hand leveled at me that has my heart scrambling into my throat.

Always excited to make a new friend, Jasper jumps his paws on the man's leg. He's grown quite a bit in the past two months, but not enough to budge the mountain.

The man nudges him aside with his foot. The gun doesn't sway so much as an inch. "Put him outside." The man's tone is lethal, uncompromising.

"He's just a puppy. He'll get lost."

The man doesn't say anything, which I translate to mean he doesn't give a damn if I lose my dog.

"I said, put the fucking dog outside!" He steps aside, but not far enough for me to get past him.

Not that I'm deluding myself into believing I can escape. He's not planning to let me go anywhere. Fear grips me in its evil clutches. I can taste its foul breath on my tongue.

I don't speak or move. My body is frozen, turned to concrete. Incapable of even flinching.

"Put him outside or I'll shoot him."

That's all I need to kick-start my body into action. I unclip the leash. "Okay, boy. Go chase squirrels." *And find someone to save me.*

Jasper doesn't need to be told twice. He barrels out the door, spotting his target as a cluster of fall leaves tumbles across the dirt in the strong wind.

The sky is darker now, the air heavy with the smell of the approaching storm.

The door shuts, barricading me from the rest of the world. My limbs are no longer frozen. An uncontrollable tremor travels through them, threatening to tumble me like a tower of cards. "Wh-what do you want? I-I don't have anything valuable here?"

"Where is it?" The boom of his voice penetrates the tension-thick space.

"Where's what?" I can barely get my vocal cords to form the words, and they come out like the rough squeak of a rusty hinge.

"Don't play dumb! You know what I'm talking about."

A flash of lightning momentarily brightens the room. With it comes the loud crack of someone ripping the sky in two. A bark comes from outside, the sound of a puppy who isn't fond of thunder.

I step toward the door. The man scowls at me, murder frigid in his dark eyes, the gun still aimed at my chest. I freeze once more. "I have no idea what you're talking about. I just came here to get away for a few days. I haven't been here in more than ten years."

The man studies me for a second, possibly gauging how much of what I said is true. "In there." He points to the master bedroom.

I walk to the open doorway, conscious my phone is in my purse, which is in the box on the coffee table. But unless things have changed since I was last here, there are no cellular towers nearby, no Wi-Fi or phone lines.

I'm completely alone with no chance of calling for help.

He grabs my arm and shoves me so hard into the bedroom, I stumble. "Lie on the bed."

My mouth goes dry, my legs weak. My chest is tight and my heart rate picks up, loud enough to drown out the noise of the rain hitting the window. I shake my head, desperate and pleading.

God, not that. Please, no.

Tears overflow and the sound of screams reach my ears.

My screams.

A loud slap. My cheek burns. My ear rings. And my head feels slightly woozy. It's enough to cut off my screams.

"I'm not going to rape you." His tone bites as if the very idea of violating me offends him.

Right, but you will kill me. I have no doubt about that.

"On the bed!" he snaps.

I crawl onto the squeaky bed, praying he has nothing to tie me to the frame with. Praying he'll leave me alone in the room, giving me my only chance to escape.

He looms over me, his face contorted into pure anger, and I shudder. "Stay here."

He leaves the room. Relief ebbs and flows in me, but the emotion is only temporary.

Careful not to set off the bed's squeaky springs, I slowly slide to the side opposite the door and climb off the mattress.

The soft *thud* of items hitting the wooden floor comes from the living room, the storm outside almost masking the noise.

What the hell's he looking for?

Since I don't want to stick around to find out, I walk to the window, conscious the floor squeaks in places. I don't know if the man has hawklike senses. And I'm not interested in finding out if he does.

I glance over my shoulder for a heartbeat, making sure he isn't about to burst into the room, then turn back to my only hope of escape.

The bars on the window aren't designed to keep people locked in the room. They're designed to keep people out. Grandpa updated them after a group of students died in a house fire almost two decades ago. They were in a basement suite and couldn't escape through the windows because the bars didn't have a quick-release mechanism. They died of asphyxiation.

Their deaths might possibly save my life as long as the mechanism isn't rusty.

It takes me a few seconds to figure out how to remove the bars. I place them on the floor, careful not to make a sound that will alert the asshole of my escape plan.

I return to the window and try to slide it open. It doesn't budge. I try again. Still nothing.

No, no, no, no...

I didn't get this far only for something so stupid to prevent my escape.

My fingers fumble around the window and stumble on another lock. I quickly unlock it and slide the window open. It doesn't glide as easily as I would like, thanks to the years of disuse, but at least it's relatively soundless.

I scan the forest outside the window for anyone guarding my escape route.

No one seems to be lurking in the shadows. God, I hope I'm right about that.

I hoist myself up and squeeze through the small frame. There isn't enough room for me to leapfrog my feet onto the windowsill. I can only awkwardly wiggle my way to freedom.

I half lower myself, half fall onto the wet ground. Cold rain immediately soaks through my jeans and long-sleeved T-shirt as I deliberate which way to go. I almost expect Jasper to barrel toward me, desperate to get out of the rain. But there is no puppy, no anything except for the punishing storm.

And the man inside the cabin who will likely kill me if he finds me.

An angry curse comes from the other side of the open window, propelling me into action.

I push myself to my feet...and run.

48

LUCAS

Rain pelts my SUV as I drive the winding mountain road toward the cabin belonging to Simone's family. The windshield wipers are working overtime on double speed. Even then it's difficult to see the slick road through the deluge.

"You'll keep us posted?" Troy asks the person on the other end of the phone line. He's sitting in the front passenger seat. Kellan is in the back seat. Garrett stayed with Emily and Zara in case Simone changed her mind about the cabin and is headed home. We have no reason to believe Simone is in danger, but we also don't plan to assume she's safe.

Troy ends the call. "Rose is conscious. The cops have no idea yet who broke into her house and why. They couldn't even tell me if anything was taken, but whoever broke in ransacked the place."

"Which means they also have no idea if the attack was linked to the hit-and-run." I tighten my grip on the steering wheel, my blood turning to lava, thirsty to burn anything in its path.

A heavy dose of anger is also directed at myself. I'm the one who drove Simone away this afternoon.

Not Zara.

Me.

"You think the two are related?" Kellan's eyes make contact with mine in the rearview mirror.

"I find it hard to believe Rose is involved in a hit-and-run and a home break and entry, all within two and half months of each other," I say. "Rose isn't a magnet for those kinds of things."

"So whoever did this wants her dead? And if so, why?"

I glance at Kellan in the rearview mirror. "I'm not sure if they do want her dead. If they did, she wouldn't still be alive. They would've made sure she wasn't just unconscious."

"I don't know about that," Troy says. "If they were planning to kill her, they might have been scared off when her neighbor went over to check on her. Rose told the cops the man who attacked her wore a mask."

Forty minutes later, I steer down the single-lane road to the cabin. Simone's car is parked in front of the cabin. As is a black SUV that I don't recognize.

My muscles tense and anger flares inside me like a gasoline-doused campfire. "Who the fuck does that SUV belong to?"

It could be Avery's vehicle, but that lead feeling in my gut tells me it's not. The owner could be anyone, but after what happened to Rose, I only imagine one person.

Jasper's frantically scratching the cabin door to be let in. There's no way Simone would've left him outside, especially during a storm. "Fuck. Something's wrong here."

Memories from a lifetime ago resurface, of all the times I was here, but I don't have a moment to appreciate them.

I reverse my SUV and park it behind a thick grove of trees. The narrow stretch of road isn't visible from the cabin. If Simone is in danger, we need the upper hand, the element of surprise. If we were spotted, the SUV's owner might assume we'd turned down the wrong road and then realized our mistake.

I turn off the engine. "I'll check the cabin and see what I can find. You two want to search the SUV to see who it belongs to?"

My brothers nod, and we climb out of the vehicle, taking care not to make a sound or movement that will betray our location.

We're wearing dark jeans and dark T-shirts. Not the best clothing for camouflage, but with the storm nailing the area, we're less noticeable than if we'd been wearing light colors. I retired from the military over six years ago, but my Marine training pumps through my body as though I never left. Pumps through my body with a heavy dose of adrenaline.

Keeping to the cover of the trees, I approach the cabin, stealth my best friend. Jasper continues scratching the door, his whimpers breaking through the wind.

I get into position near the house. The sky lights up with a flash, giving me a brief view of the living room. No one is inside the room as far as I can tell.

Shit, where is she?

I creep up the porch steps, the loud crack of thunder masking my footfalls.

Jasper turns to me and barks. His small body shortens the distance between us. I crouch and press my finger to my lips. "*Shhh. You need to be quiet.*" My voice is low, the command not enough to silence the excited puppy.

In the Marines, I wouldn't have gone on patrol without a weapon. I feel naked now. Helpless. I have nothing to protect Simone and myself with other than my bare hands. Bare hands that have been trained to kill.

Especially if the element of surprise is on my side.

I listen for signs of life inside the cabin. Nothing. Fuck, where is she? And who the fuck does the vehicle belong to?

An irrational spark of jealousy ignites. My gut quickly extinguishes it. It's not a secret rendezvous between lovers. Simone is in danger.

"Lie down," I tell Jasper. He does what he's told, but I don't know how long that will last. His training is a work-in-progress. "Stay!"

I stand, press my body against the wall, and cautiously turn the doorknob.

Slowly, I push the door open...

49

———

SIMONE

I disappear farther into the forest, trying to orientate myself as I step on decomposing leaves and slippery mud. My sneakers sink and slide, but I keep on running.

I dart between the trees, their trunks too narrow to provide much cover. My breathing is fast and ragged, and my heartbeat isn't any quieter.

I'm not as unfamiliar with the area as the man is, but that doesn't mean much. All I know is that I'm heading in the opposite direction to where I need to be—the road.

Growing up, I rarely wandered off the trails. Unlike Aiden. I didn't want to risk getting lost.

Now, I don't have that luxury. Sticking to the trails makes it easier to find me.

On the other hand, running on the trail might make less noise than me traipsing through the underbrush.

Using the cover of the storm to drown out the noise, I continue running, taking care not to trip or fall. Cursing that Lucas is the one who runs mountainous trails while I stick to the familiar streets in Maple Ridge. My lungs burn from the challenge of the steep incline.

A loud bang echoes through the forest. Small pieces of bark from a tree to my left splinter the air, pushing my pulse skyward.

I release a startled gasp, and my feet stumble under me.

Shit, shit, shittedy. Shit.

The snapping of stepped on undergrowth warns me my assailant is rapidly approaching. I cut to the right, not bothering to be quiet.

I risk a glance over my shoulder at the forest behind me, and the world vanishes from under my feet. A shriek alerts him where to find me.

I tumble down a steep incline, protruding rocks and sharp undergrowth doing nothing to slow my descent. If I survive this, I'll be one big bruise and scrape tomorrow.

I land on my side, the impact knocking a pained grunt from me.

There's no time to inventory the damage. I stagger to my feet and scan the area for a place to hide. My only chance of survival is circling back to the cabin, grabbing my car keys, and getting the hell away from here.

A ledge protrudes not far from where I fell, tree roots forming a shelter. I stumble toward it, doing my best to ignore a dull ache in my ankle. Fear pushes me forward.

The slope to the hiding spot isn't as steep as the one I fell down. I scramble up it, my sneakers slipping on the wet leaves. A loud crack splits the air, followed by a resounding boom. The noise vibrates through the forest, mocking me. Reminding me life is short.

I push the thought aside.

I'm going to survive this.

I've got to survive.

The hiding spot is filled with spider webs. The image of their owners and other insects crawling over me and biting me scuttles into my brain. Without giving it another thought, I jam my body into the small space and squeeze my eyes shut. My heavy breath and rapid heartbeat seem to echo off the dirt wall behind me.

I strain to make out any signs that the man is closing in on me. The only noise I hear is the storm pelting down. Maybe he returned to the cabin. Or better yet, maybe he's driving away.

I'm about to crawl out of my hiding space, but then change my mind. For all I know, he's standing on the ledge where I fell, waiting to fire a round of bullets into me.

I scan the mud for something to throw to try to distract him. A rock protrudes from the ground in front of me, partially visible to anyone overlooking the ledge—if they happened to be looking in the right direction.

I stretch as far as I can, the movement slow so as not to attract attention, and start digging the rock out. The mud makes it easier to press my fingertips into the soft dirt. But it also makes it more difficult as mud slides back into the hole as I'm digging.

It takes several minutes before I pry the rock free. I swing my arm toward my head, flinging the rock into a bush. The leaves jostle from the impact, but it's barely noticeable with the storm and the wind.

Rivulets form in the dirt where I'm hiding, the soil becoming more saturated with each passing second. I can't stay in this hiding spot much longer.

I inch my way out of the space. No one attempts to shoot at me. For that, I'm grateful.

Free of the roots, I clamber to my feet. The cold wind and rain assault me.

I shiver uncontrollably. My muddy jeans and long-sleeved T-shirt are plastered to my body, doing nothing to keep me warm. My teeth are hit with the overwhelming need to chatter, accompanying the fast, staccato rhythm of my heartbeat.

I half climb, half pull myself up the slope, my sneakers failing to gain traction on the wet grass and leaves. I'm practically crawling by the time I make it to the top of the ridge.

I scan the area, searching for signs of where the man went.

Nothing. Not even a tiny hint that he's given up the pursuit, gone home to whatever pit he slithered from.

I move forward as I figure out which way to go, but then pause to reorient myself. I have no idea which direction I need to go to find the cabin.

A hand, large and rough, covers my mouth. Panic spears me, spreading its poison through my body. I freeze for a nanosecond; then a rush of adrenaline spurs me on.

I squirm and elbow my captor in the gut. His rock-hard gut. At his muffled grunt, a pinch of satisfaction eases in.

"*Shh*. It's me," Lucas's voice grits out, his lips brushing the shell of my ear. He removes his hand from my mouth and turns me to face him.

Then his lips are on mine.

The kiss isn't filled with passion or heat. It's not enough to warm me up or stop my trembling. The kiss...God, the kiss...is filled with so many unspoken words.

Words of love and sorrow and hope and despair.

It's enough to create a spark. A spark that will keep me going a little longer. Keep me going until we get home.

Lucas pulls away. He's holding a gun I've never seen. He doesn't own any.

"Where did you get the gun from?" I drop the volume of my voice. The last thing we need is for me to broadcast our location.

"From whoever the asshole is who parked their SUV outside your cabin. Troy and Kellan found a stash of weapons in the back. Do you know who it belongs to?"

"I didn't think to ask him while he had his gun pointed at me. We have to find Jasper. The man kicked him out of the cabin before I managed to escape."

"Jasper's safe. He's in my SUV. You injured?"

"I hurt my ankle, but it's fine. Just a little stiff. Not bad enough to keep us from getting the hell out of here."

"Any idea what the asshole chasing you wants?"

"I have no idea. He kept asking 'where is it,' but he didn't specify what he was talking about. He shot at me when I escaped, so I'm guessing he's willing to kill to get whatever he's searching for."

Lucas curses under his breath. "Okay, we're getting out of here. I don't need him coming back for us."

He leads me through the forest, gun at the ready, his attention focused on the wet terrain and our surroundings. Our progress is slow due to my sore ankle and because we're trying not to make a sound. The rain and wind have died down, making us faster, but now any noise we make is only that much more noticeable.

Lucas tugs me behind him. He aims his gun at the foliage. Then he's shoving me to the ground. We hit the dirt as a shot rings out, Lucas landing on top of me. The impact knocks the air from my lungs.

"Are you gonna tell me where you're hiding the files or are we doing this the hard way?" The man's tone is the snarl of a rabid dog.

The snap of twigs underfoot warns me of his slow approach. I look up. He gestures with his gun for us to stand. We obey.

"What files?" I attempt to say, my teeth chattering from the cold or fear or both.

"Don't you work for Kincaid Timber?" Lucas's icy voice is smooth and unbending and dangerous, the frozen surface of a deep, deep lake.

I frown. "Timber? Why would I have files from a logging company?"

"Does this have something to do with Sebastian's untimely death?" Lucas asks.

I gasp. Sebastian's dead? When?

The muscle in the man's jaw twitches, and I almost feel sorry for his teeth. Almost.

"Put the gun down." His weapon is directed at Lucas.

Lucas doesn't move. His gun remains pointed at the man. "I don't think so."

The man shifts his weapon so I'm now the one who'll be on the receiving end of a bullet. The move would've caused my heart rate to skyrocket if it wasn't already beating at supersonic speed.

Lucas positions his body between the man and me. "Drop to the ground," he whispers. "And stay down."

I want to ask him what he's planning on doing. But I don't. I drop onto my stomach, making myself as flat as possible on the wet ground, my arms covering my head.

A loud bang punctures the air, and every muscle in my body clenches. *Oh, God, no.* Please don't be Lucas. Fear pummels me, unrelenting and swift. I'm too scared to look and see what happened. Too scared to see who's still standing.

I'm not ready to be a widow. Not yet. Not ever.

Muffled sounds yank me from my fear-riddled thoughts, and I turn my head to the side, bits of leaves sticking to my face. Lucas is no longer standing in front of me. He and the man are facing off in hand-to-hand combat. Neither man is holding a gun.

I push myself to shaky knees as Lucas shoves the man into the thick tree trunk behind him. Lucas fists the man's shirt and pins him against the rough bark.

The man side-chops his arm across his body, his forearm breaking Lucas's hold on him. The man kicks Lucas's feet out from under him.

Lucas goes down. Before he can recover, the man strikes out with his booted foot. The blow barely skims Lucas's side as he rolls away from him, anticipating the man's next move.

The guns. Where did they go?

I stand and survey the nearby ground. Nothing. The gun Lucas was holding has to be here somewhere.

I frantically pat at a pile of wet, dead leaves in case the gun ended up there. Grunts and heavy breathing from Lucas and the man as they continue to battle prod me to keep searching. They won't last much longer at this rate.

Lucas takes a swing at him, his fist glancing against the man's jaw.

Where is that damn gun?

I crawl forward, desperately shoving the dead leaves aside from another pile. My fingers brush across cool metal. I clear the leaves away, revealing Lucas's gun.

I wrap my shaking fingers around the handgrip and stand. I don't know the first thing about guns. I hate them. Which means I have no idea what to do with the one I'm holding.

The man makes a move to punch Lucas. Lucas deflects the blow.

I raise the gun and point it at the man. "Stop or I'll shoot." The command might have been a little more convincing if my voice wasn't as shaky as my body.

Both men pause long enough to see that I'm now holding the gun.

The man takes a step toward me, but Lucas is quicker. He backs up to where I'm standing. His eyes still on the man, he gently removes the gun from my hand and aims it at him.

50

LUCAS

"**P**olice! Put your weapons down."

A quick glance toward the voice confirms the man in body armor is who he claims to be. He's not alone. Several other state troopers descend on the area, their guns trained on us.

I slowly lower the Glock to the muddy ground, avoiding any sudden moves. My lungs are working overtime, recovering from the fight.

The man who attacked Simone and me appears to be weighing the odds of escaping. But he's also breathing hard, so it's unlikely he'll get far.

The state troopers can shoot him for all I care. Relief coils around me. It's over.

Simone is safe, and it's over.

I tell the state troopers that the man tried to kidnap my wife and shot at her. When I found the cabin ransacked, I knew Simone was in danger. When I heard the gunshot, I thought I'd never see her alive again.

I also inform the troopers that the man had a gun, but he

dropped it when I tried to get it away from him. My plan could have gone wrong in so many ways, but thank Christ it didn't.

I hug Simone, keeping her close. Confirming to myself that she's alive.

Kellan and Troy approach the group. And never have I been happier to see my brothers than I am now.

"How—? Where—?" Simone starts to ask but seems to give up forming the rest of the questions.

"Zara told me where to find you," I explain. "Someone attacked your grandmother—"

A half gasp, half whimper falls from Simone's lips, and she sags into me. I tighten my hold on her. Her shivering is more pronounced than it was earlier.

"She's gonna be okay," Troy quickly tells her. "The hospital is observing her for twenty-four hours, but she should be fine."

I kiss Simone's temple. "Sorry, I should have started with that."

One of the state troopers approaches us.

"I'm taking my wife to the cabin to warm up," I inform him. "You can question us there." What I really want is to show her how sorry I am for how I reacted earlier. To do whatever it takes to make things up to her. And to tell her I love her.

Especially to tell her I love her.

But that will all have to wait.

"All right." He lets the other troopers know where we're headed and joins us.

Once we're in the cabin, Troy locates some blankets and hands one to me. I wrap it around Simone's shoulders, and my arm circles her waist. I don't give a damn if the troopers want to interview us separately. I'm not leaving her side for the foreseeable future.

I'm not failing her again.

The paramedics arrive, and one of them checks out Simone's ankle and makes sure she doesn't have any other injuries that require medical attention.

"The man you arrested might be associated with Kincaid Timber Corporation," I explain to the trooper. "You might want to contact the Eugene police about a murder investigation they're now involved in with the death of Sebastian Dryson. He could be linked to that."

If he's linked to Sebastian's death, why come after Simone? It doesn't make sense. Did Kincaid think that by threatening Simone's life, we would drop the bid? We would have, but we wouldn't let things slide that easily. They have to know that.

It can't be that. There's something else we're missing. Does the file he was looking for have something to do with Sebastian's murder?

Knowing that doesn't settle well in the pit of my stomach. Who else's life is at risk while the cops try to figure it out?

While my brothers and I try to figure it out?

An hour later, the troopers are gone and we're getting ready to leave. In a burst of nervous energy after the troopers left, Simone straightened the mess the man made while he searched for the mysterious files. She didn't want to leave the cabin until she'd finished tidying up.

"You asked Kellan earlier what catfish means?" I pick up the box of food and dog supplies from the coffee table.

"That's right."

"Why? Does the word mean something to you?"

"No, but I think it meant something to Aiden. Two months ago, I found a piece of paper in my bedroom at Grams's. The only thing on it was the word catfish. The paper fell out when I opened the desk drawer. I'd forgotten about it until this weekend when I went to Portland. I found the same word written in the Greek mythology encyclopedia Aiden sent me a few weeks before his death. It was on the description for Themis, the Greek Titaness who is the symbol for justice. In both cases, it was Aiden's handwriting."

She walks over to the bookshelf and removes a book. I return the box to the coffee table and join her.

She leafs through the book and shows me a page. "And here it is again, under Forseti, the Norse god of justice. But this time he also wrote 'Aiden4justice.' I was about to check the other mythology books, but Jasper started barking at the door...and well, you know the rest. With everything that happened, I forgot about it."

She hands me the book and pulls out another one. Roman mythology. She flips through the pages and lands on Justitia, the goddess of justice. This time the only thing on the page is the name of an email provider.

"Why would he write the email provider in a book?" I ask. "Aiden wasn't the type of person who wrote notes in his books. He didn't even do that in college when it came to his textbooks."

Troy points at the handwritten word. "Could this have anything to do with the mission you and Aiden were on?"

"I don't know." I catch Simone up on the conversation from earlier, my mind spinning back to what happened with Aiden and me eight years ago.

Simone shivers again. She's visibly exhausted, and her wariness is directed at me. Before I can even think about Aiden's messages and what they all mean, she and I need to talk.

"I need to get Simone and Jasper home, warmed up, and fed," I tell my brothers. "Why don't you come over in two hours, and we'll see if we can figure this out? And tell Garrett while you're at it."

Simone and I don't talk on the drive home about the past four days. There are conversations we need to have, but they're better had when my concentration isn't on the wet roads.

So we listen to music and make small talk. None of it defuses the tension lingering in the air. Neither of us says what's on our minds, but I know Simone's wondering the same thing I am: did the break-in at Rose's home have anything to do with the sequence of events at the cabin? Given both places were ransacked, it seems likely.

But does that mean the asshole who attacked Rose then

followed Simone to the cabin? Or was Simone simply in the wrong place at the wrong time?

I park the SUV and unfasten my seat belt. "How's your ankle?"

"Better. I got lucky." She doesn't give me a second glance. She's out of the vehicle faster than I can say sniper.

I let Jasper out of the back seat, and we follow Simone into the house. The blanket from the cabin is still wrapped around her shoulders. Inside, she begins to climb the staircase.

"Where're you going?"

She turns to me. "To take a shower."

"Sounds like a plan. We're going to talk. In the shower." At the mocking tilt of her eyebrow, I walk up the steps so I'm level with her and clarify, "We both need a long hot shower. This way we conserve water and can have that talk sooner." I brush a featherlight kiss on her lips.

Her smile is uncertain, the corners of her mouth fluttering, then they commit to a soft smile. "All right."

On my way to the SUV to get her stuff, I text my brothers and tell them to show up in two hours from *now* instead of when I originally told them to come. Simone and I need that time to start fixing the bridge between us that I tore down.

I put Jasper in his crate and head upstairs to the bathroom. Simone is in there waiting for me. Our clothes are still damp, even though I had the heat blasting on the drive home to warm her up. I have a feeling it'll take a lot more than a heater to do that.

I caress her cheek with my thumb. The ache I experienced earlier when she told me about being pregnant and losing our baby returns, spreads through my chest. "I'm sorry for how I reacted when you told me about our daughter. Things hadn't gone the way we'd hoped with the search and rescue, and then finding out I'd failed you Sind our baby..." My voice comes out scraping-my-throat rough. I attempt to swallow back the pain. "I was shocked and didn't handle the news very well."

I kiss Simone's lips once more and lift the hem of her long-sleeved T-shirt, slowly stripping the muddy fabric off her body. Bruises are starting to form on her skin, but it could have been so much worse. "I'm sorry you had to go through all of that alone, not only the night of the accident but afterward. I should've been there for you. I wish I'd been there for you."

"I wasn't alone." Simone's voice is whispery soft. "Avery was with me."

A wry smile slips onto my lips. "I wondered why she obviously wasn't a fan of mine when we got married, even though she and I had never met. This does explain things."

"She wanted me to marry for love and not to settle for less. The fact that you were only interested in me for business reasons didn't make her very happy."

"I can understand why. You deserve to be with someone who loves you, Simone." I stroke her cheek, absorbing the feel of her soft skin. "The way I love you. I've been in love with you ever since college. I didn't want to risk having a girlfriend while in the military. You deserved better than waiting for a man who might not have come home alive or returned the same way as he left." The latter being exactly what happened.

"The night we were together during my leave, I came close to telling you how I felt. But I chickened out. I'd planned to tell you when I returned, but you stopped sending me letters and never replied to the ones I sent you." And then things went to hell during Operation CATFISH, and nothing was the same after that. "Once I returned, I was too scared to tell you how I felt. I let Aiden down and wasn't there for him when he needed me the most. I was scared of letting you down, too."

But I had let her down by not being here when she needed me the most after his death.

"What are you talking about? You never let him down, Lucas. I was the one who was too afraid to return to Maple Ridge because it hurt too much to see you. I put my own needs above those of my brother's. I just—I just didn't realize how broken he was after returning from Afghanistan. How broken you both were. I thought he was getting better. That things had improved for him."

Simone's beautiful hazel eyes are filled with love and understanding and compassion. None of which I deserve after how I reacted earlier. Don't deserve, but I still take them in with long thirsty gulps.

"I love you, too, Lucas. I've been in love with you for forever. I might not have realized I was in love with you when I agreed to marry you, but the love has always been there."

This time when our lips meet, peace, hope, love, desire flicker hotly in my chest. My tongue glides against hers, doing what it can to heal her pain.

Her fingers duck under the hem of my T-shirt, and she strokes the skin just above the snap on my jeans. In one easy move, I strip off the damp top and dump it on the floor.

That's about as long as I let my mouth leave hers.

She makes quick work of the snap and zipper on my jeans. I yank the damp fabric down my legs, taking my boxer briefs with them. My cock springs free, already missing being inside her.

Simone wraps her hand around the thick length. The gleam in her eyes shifts to mischief. "Maybe we should do something about this before we shower?"

"I think, Mrs. Carson, that's a brilliant idea." I unzip her jeans and remove them, my fingertips tracing the length of her body, worshiping the strong and beautiful woman beneath the soft skin.

My gaze lands on her right hip. On the lily tattoo with the single white wing.

An angel wing.

My heart tightens and my breath stalls and my stomach freefalls onto a land mine. The force is enough to cause my knees to crumble under me. Not a gentle, controlled crumble.

One that crushes dreams.

Christ, all this time I thought it was a bird wing.

How could I have been such an idiot?

Kneeling, I graze my thumb across the tattoo. "You didn't get this because you loved the picture on Pinterest, did you?"

"That's right." Her voice is the soft brush of a feather, and it pulls at my heart. "I named our daughter Lily." She traces the petals and swallows. "I did this so she's always with me."

I press my lips to the symbol for our daughter. An image of what she might've looked like—a reflection of Simone—flickers in my mind. Dark hair that shines like a flame in the sun. Large brown eyes full of questions and kindness and a heavy dose of stubbornness.

A breath-stealing smile.

A beautiful soul.

I rest my forehead on Simone's hip, and an overwhelming emotion crashes into me, a giant wave against jagged rocks. Guilt, pain, grief, bitterness drag me beneath the surface. Threaten to drown me.

I can't breathe.

I can't breathe.

I can't breathe.

I drag in a great gasping lungful of air.

A distant sob assaults my ears. A raw, soul-shattering sob.

I realize then that the sound isn't coming from Simone. My body shakes from the force of my grief.

Being weak isn't in my bones. I have faced down the enemy and I have faced down the demons that tried to destroy me. I've lost people who meant a lot to me.

But this...this is worse.

Simone doesn't say anything. She just gently strokes her fingers through my hair, soothing me. Telling me it's okay. We'll be okay.

I stay like that for a minute, then straighten to my feet. The love shining back at me from Simone's tear-damp face gives me a strength I didn't realize I was missing.

She wipes the tears from my cheeks and rests her head on my

chest. Her arms go around my waist. "I love you," she murmurs. "I love you so very much."

The words are a life preserver for my heart. I only hope they're enough to get me through what still lies ahead for me.

What still lies ahead for us.

51

SIMONE

Lucas's heart beats strong and steady against my ear.

I loved him before, but seeing him react the way he did when he realized the meaning behind the angel wing elevated the love I feel for him to a new level.

I never expected him to respond that way. Never expected him to feel the grief as strongly as I do.

I was wrong. So heartbreakingly wrong.

I move my head from his chest and peer up at him. "I want to make love to you, Cannon. Here. Now."

The smile that grows on his face yanks my breath away. "I think that can be arranged."

He slips his thumbs under the lace of my panties and drags them down my legs. Then he lifts me onto the edge of the bathroom counter and spreads my knees apart. The surface is cool against my butt.

He steps between my legs, and his fingers find the soft wet heat that's waiting for his touch. I gaze into his eyes as he teases me, strokes me, brings me closer to the stars. My lips part, releasing needy pants.

"Christ, you're gorgeous, Trouble. So fucking gorgeous."

Our mouths meld together and our tongues taste, tangle, caress. This…this is heaven. My heaven. I wouldn't have it any other way.

"You don't have to wear a condom if you don't want to," I murmur against his lips. Now that he knows the truth, there's no need to use protection. The condom was nothing more than protection for my heart, a way to keep him from learning the truth.

I thought his smile was breathtaking before. How naïve of me. His new smile, this smile, lights up his face, warms me to my bones.

He positions his tip at my entrance and slowly enters me. Our gazes remain locked, and the intensity of the moment almost consumes me.

Makes me crave for him to be inside me in a whole other way.

Once he's fully seated, he continues to watch my face as he circles his hips, the movement controlled, unhurried. The love reflected on his face is unmistakable. Beautiful. Pure.

I hook my legs behind him. He maintains the pace until I'm an inch away from begging him to go faster, harder.

I last a few more thrusts of his hips, and my control shatters with a moan. He picks up the speed until we reach the point of no return. There's no going back. Not that I want to.

"OhGodOhGod. Oh, Goooooood." I come apart around him, disintegrating into a million satisfied pieces.

He chuckles at my enthusiasm, then releases inside me with a grunt and my name on his lips.

His head rests on my shoulder. "Wow, that was good."

I laugh, the sound echoing off the bathroom walls. "Yes, it was. Better than good."

He lifts his head and grins at me with his panty-dropping smile —or would be panty-dropping if I had panties on. "You're right. It was so much better than just good."

His mouth explores mine for another moment, the movement slow. Exquisite. The kiss is the glue to bind us back together after everything we've endured.

He pulls away from me, his breath teasing my lips. "Are you ready for a shower now?"

"Definitely."

Lucas might've warmed me up, but I'm more than happy to wash off the rest of day.

He helps me off the counter and turns on the hot water in the shower.

Then the two of us spend the next while washing each other, confessing our love, and making love once more.

LUCAS TOLD HIS BROTHERS NOT TO SHOW UP FOR TWO HOURS. HE knew he and I would have a lot to talk about first. It's a good thing he had that foresight. We're just clearing away our dinner plates when the doorbell rings. Three times. In rapid succession.

"That would be Garrett." Lucas puts the last plate in the dishwasher.

I head for the front door to let Garrett in. Kellan, Troy, Emily, and Zara are with him on the porch.

"Have you checked yet if any of those messages in the mythology books were an email account login?" Kellan asks as soon as he walks through the front door.

"We've been slightly busy." Lucas's words are for Kellan, but his eyes—full of love and amusement—are directed at me.

Lucas's laptop is on the coffee table. We all take a seat, with me sitting next to Lucas on the couch. He turns the laptop on and tries to log into what we figure is the correct email account. After a few attempts, we're in. Aiden4justice is the login name. CATFISH is the password.

I don't know what I was expecting to find, but it wasn't the dozen or so emails that we discover were sent from this account back to this account. Each email has a file attached. They are the only emails in the inbox.

Lucas clicks on the first email received. He reads the contents. "Fuck!" He mutters the word, but the seismic boom can be felt around the room.

My insides knot, and I can barely breathe, waiting for him to tell us what he's found.

"What is it?" Zara asks.

He scrubs his hand down his face. "What do you know about how I injured my shoulder?"

Zara and Emily exchange puzzled glances. "You injured it while you were in the Marines, and it led to you being honorably discharged from the military. You were later diagnosed with PTSD, but other than that..." Zara lifts her shoulders in a that's-all-I've-got shrug.

"The day it happened, Aiden and I had been assigned to do security surveillance." He threads his fingers with mine, and I have a feeling whatever he's about to tell me has far-reaching consequences. "We had done this numerous times and had gotten to know a few of the town's civilians. One in particular was a seven-year-old boy. He didn't speak English, but he always had a smile for us. The candy bars Aiden sometimes sneaked him probably didn't hurt either."

A not-quite-there smile curves on Lucas's face. Even though he's sitting next to me on the couch, his expression hints he's back in Afghanistan. With the little boy.

The smile vanishes, replaced by a storm cloud of emotion. Pain? Disbelief? Confusion? It's impossible to get a grasp on what he's feeling. And if not for the slight tremor in his hands, I would think he'd been turned into a stone statue.

My heart aches for him. Aches for everything he's had to deal with in the past twenty-four hours. His memories of what happened in Afghanistan won't make things any easier for him tonight when he sleeps.

If he sleeps.

I squeeze his fingers, letting him know he's not alone. I'm here for him.

"We had just been talking to the boy and were walking away when a series of gunshots went off behind us." Lucas stares at the coffee table without seeming to see it. "We dove for cover and tried to figure who was doing the shooting: allied soldiers or the Taliban.

"That's when we saw the boy was on the ground, bleeding. Without thinking what we were doing, Aiden and I ran toward him. I have no idea what we planned to do. Save him? Maybe. A bullet hit me in the shoulder. I don't remember much after that. Aiden and I were discharged due to injuries sustained that day, but neither of us were the same after that. That mission's codename was Catfish."

My chest feels as though the air has been knocked from my lungs, and it's taking several seconds to draw the oxygen back in. This is the first he has shared with me about his time in the military. Now I understand why. It also explains so much about the past twelve hours, including his reaction to not being able to save the boy who went missing in the mountains.

"The email account Aiden set up," Kellan says, "it has to do with the mission?"

Lucas nods. "It basically details the truth about what went down that day. Only it wasn't the enemy who was responsible for the boy's death and possibly the bullet that found its way into my shoulder. It was Captain Andrew Tanner." Lucas looks at me, his expression tortured, bleeding. "You know him as Drew. Ashley's father."

"Oh, God." I barely hear the whispered words over my thundering heartbeat, my brain piecing together what this could mean for Ashley, for her family.

"From what Aiden's email states, one of the men in our unit was killed the day before by one of our own. I knew the man had died. I didn't know how. Drew went to cover it up, and in the process, accidentally killed the boy. There's a list of individuals also involved in the cover-up—all five of them."

Silence shrouds the room in a heavy veil as we try to digest everything Lucas told us. A dizzying silence that sucks my thoughts from the room—that leaves me unable to put words to the truth. A silence that leaves my words too broken to piece back together.

"When are the emails dated?" Troy asks after a few stunned moments.

Lucas studies the screen. "Five days before Aiden died."

"Did he send any emails from that account to anyone else?"

"As far as I can tell, no. Unless he deleted them from his send box. That's always a possibility."

"But why not tell anyone about it?" Emily looks to the four brothers in turn for answers. "Why end his life before he could send the evidence to someone who could open an investigation?"

Good question.

One I wish we had answers for.

"Is it possible he didn't commit suicide?" All eyes swing to Zara. "Kya, the woman Simone and I spoke to this afternoon, was surprised when Simone told her Aiden was dead and how he died. From what she said, it sounded like the last thing on his mind was ending his life. He told her that in a few days things would be better. Justice would finally prevail. Maybe this is what he was referring to." She points at the laptop.

I nod, the pieces of the puzzle slowly sliding into place. "It would explain why I kept finding the clues in the mythology books under the individuals who symbolized justice."

Kellan leans forward in his armchair. "If he didn't kill himself, how did he end up at the bottom of the cliff?" He grimaces apologetically at me. "Sorry."

"It's okay." I have the same question.

Garrett pushes himself out of his chair and begins pacing. "It could have been an accident. He misjudged the stability of the edge and it gave way. But there were no signs of that from what the police report said."

Shock widens Lucas's eyes, as well as my own. "How did you get the report?" he asks.

"I knew someone on the force at the time, and he might have spoken in hypotheticals. Purely for research purposes, of course."

"And there were no signs of foul play?" Lucas strokes his thumb along the side of my hand, knowing how painful this conversation is for me. It's painful for both of us.

But painful or not, they are questions I want answered. For Aiden. For Grams. He wanted justice served for the boy's death. If someone was responsible for what happened to my brother, I want justice, too. I don't want him to be remembered as the man who killed himself. He deserves so much more than that.

"If there were signs of foul play, they were missed. Aiden had a history of PTSD. It probably made more sense to the cops that it was suicide instead of an accident."

"Or murder." The strangled word squeezes past the pain and tears clogging my throat. An image flickers in my thoughts of someone shoving my brother off the cliff. Ending his life. I push the thought away. "If anyone on the list was aware of the evidence he'd compiled against them, it would be a motive for wanting him out of the picture. Why take the risk he might expose the individuals involved in the cover-up or threaten to blackmail them?"

Lucas shifts his arm to curve around me, and I lean into him, needing his strength to get through this conversation. Needing to share my strength with him. None of this is easy, for either of us. But this time we'll be there for each other. We'll be stronger. Together.

Garrett continues pacing. "It's possible the man who tried to hurt you today was looking for the evidence. You said he kept demanding that you hand over the files, but you had no idea what he was talking about." He points at the laptop. "This could be what he was talking about."

"But why now?" I ask. "Aiden died three years ago. Why wait this long to get his hands on the evidence?"

"We can speculate all night, but in the end it's the military and civilian police who will need to find the answers." Lucas picks up his phone from the coffee table and taps on the screen. "Hey, Mathews, I need your help…"

52

SIMONE

Two weeks after the incident at the cabin, Grams and I walk along the trail to the half-dozen picnic tables in the meadow belonging to Tuuli and Robert. The stream where Lucas and I made love while in college is just beyond the maple trees.

Joy and nervousness have hijacked my body. Not because there are so many memories of Aiden and Lucas tied to this land. Not because Grams and I are here to celebrate Tuuli and Robert's fortieth wedding anniversary. Their ruby anniversary.

It's because I haven't heard from Lucas since he left for Eugene this morning. He was meeting with Blake.

The late-afternoon sun shines on the partygoers, glinting off their sparkly red hats. John walks over, a wide grin on his weathered face. I hug Grams's boyfriend and leave her in his capable hands while I go see if Zara needs my help. She's catering the event.

On my way over to the table where she's standing, I check my phone for the two hundredth time since Lucas left this morning. He still hasn't texted or called. *God, what's taking so long?*

Tuuli and Robert step away from a couple they were just talking to. I stop and hug them. "Happy anniversary. I hope you're planning to share with Lucas and me all your wisdom for a happy marriage."

Tuuli laughs. "From what I've heard, you two don't need our help." She glances around the area. "Speaking of which, where is your husband?"

"He'll be here soon."

My phone rings. I check if it's Lucas. Avery. "Hey," I say, walking away so I can hear her better.

"I got your message that you wanted to talk to me."

A group of little kids go racing past, chasing after a soccer ball that one of the adults kicked.

"How's the job hunting going?" I ask her.

"I'm still looking. Why? Have you heard of any positions?"

"As a matter of fact, yes. I need to hire someone to help me out with the subscription boxes. Things were busy before Clementine Hollis posted about the boxes on Instagram. But after she shared the video on social media, things have been going crazy with the subscriptions. A good crazy. Except now I'm having a hard time keeping up with everything. And I could use your help and skill sets...if you're interested. And if you're okay with moving to Maple Ridge."

Avery has always been underappreciated at the ad agency, and I know she has the potential to do so much more. I'm hoping that what I'm offering her will be a start while she figures out where exactly her future is headed.

There's a squeal from the other end of the phone. "Yes! I would love that."

We talk for a few minutes about the job and her move to Maple Ridge, then we end the call, and I join Kim, Jerome, and Em standing near Zara.

"How are you holding up?" Kim asks.

"Nervous. Have you heard from him yet?"

Jerome shakes his head. "Not yet. But I'm sure it's going to be okay."

I'm glad one of us is confident. I've been an emotional mess ever since Lucas contacted his connection in the military and informed him of the evidence we'd found. The evidence resulted in a number of police departments also being brought in. The linked crimes involve several jurisdictions.

Garrett, Kellan, and Troy walk toward us from where everyone parked their vehicles.

God, where the hell is he?

I bounce my fingers against my legs and bite my lower lip.

"Lucas texted that he's on his way," Troy tells me.

I attempt to read their faces, to find out if Lucas told his brothers how things went this morning. Their expressions tell me as much as if I'd tried to read the information in Grams's tea leaves.

Damn their military training.

Laughter comes from Grams and her friends over by another table.

I smile at the group. I swear the next person who tries to hurt her will find himself minus a dick by the time I'm finished with him. While the cops still have no suspect for the hit-and-run, they do have the man who assaulted her—the same man who followed me to the cabin. Bail denied.

A pair of strong arms hugs me from behind and pulls me into a hard body. My favorite smell of mountains and sunshine and Lucas folds around me, and I smile.

"Miss me?" a deep voice murmurs in my ear and my panties go up in smoke.

I turn in his arms. Lucas winces. "What's wrong?" I ask. He wasn't injured when he left the house this morning.

I glance down. On the inside of his forearm is a single angel wing that wasn't there earlier. Under it is the scripted date of when our daughter died.

"It's beautiful," I whisper, the choked words squeezing past the lump in my throat. "I had no idea you were going to do this."

"I wanted Lily to be a part of me like she is for you." He brushes his fingers over my tattoo. "And I wanted it to be a surprise."

This man...this sweet and amazing man. Tears blur my eyes and I can't put words to my thoughts. So I kiss him. Deeply. Showing him that what he did, the tattoo...how much it means to me. How much *he* means to me.

Hoots and cheers break out from Grams's table. For us? I don't know. And I don't care. I just want to keep kissing Lucas.

Lucas and I have talked about our options when it comes to having a family. For now, we're leaving things open, enjoying being newlyweds. We've also started seeing someone to help us manage the grief. While the accident might have occurred ten years ago, the grief Lucas is experiencing over the loss of his daughter is very real and very fresh. So we're taking things step-by-step for now.

And that includes going to Portland this weekend and visiting Lily's grave.

I finally admitted the truth to Grams. It was hard at first, but she hugged me a lot, cried, and hugged me some more. I know deep down she still hurts that I waited so long to tell her the truth, but she also understands.

Lucas has also been talking to someone about the flashbacks and the occasional nightmares he's had over the past few months, to make sure they're kept under control like they were until recently.

"So?" Garrett says once we come up for air, reminding me that everyone is here, waiting to hear how Lucas's meeting went. "Are you going to tell us what happened?"

Lucas releases me, but his hand remains on the small of my back. "The drug charges have been dropped," he tells us. "Drew confessed to arranging for the narcotics to be found in my house."

"Why would he do that?" I ask. "I thought he was your friend."

"I thought so, too. When my flashbacks started up again a few months ago, I emailed him. He got scared I was coming close to figuring out what really happened that day in Afghanistan. He thought that if I was locked away, maybe it would prevent the truth from surfacing. He also said that Aiden never tried to kill himself. It was an accident."

Surprise hitches my heart and my voice, and I'm not sure how I feel about the news. "An accident? Why did he think it was an accident?"

The muscle in Lucas's jaw jumps, the pain and sorrow and heartbreak on his face real. Real for the man he once considered a friend. "A few weeks before it happened, Ashley was diagnosed with leukemia. Drew couldn't afford to have the evidence revealed and end up losing everything. His medical coverage. His time with his daughter. He'd been thinking about Ashley and nothing else when the argument broke out with Aiden.

"He hadn't planned for Aiden to die. He swears it was an accident, but he didn't think anyone else would see it that way. So he left Aiden at the base of the cliff, and did everything he could to cover up that they had been together that day. He knew about Aiden's previous struggle with PTSD and hoped his death would be ruled a suicide."

A frigid numbness seeps into my body, pumps through my veins. How could he...how could he have killed my brother and left him like that? For Aiden's body to be found by a hiker.

How could he steal...?

I swallow, knowing exactly how he could do any of those things.

Love.

I saw how much Drew loves his daughter. She's his world, his everything.

My mind spins at what Lucas is telling me. "But how did he manage to do any of that if he's in a wheelchair?"

"Drew wasn't a paraplegic back then. That happened eleven months later when Ashley was in remission. His car lost control on an icy patch. The accident was bad, and he sank into depression. That's when I started spending time with Ashley, making sure she didn't get forgotten with everything going on."

That explains a lot. Explains why she thinks of Lucas as an uncle.

"What will happen to Ashley?" Despite everything that has happened, my heart aches for what she and her family are going through. And it will only get worse now that the truth is out.

The little girl who I watched play hopscotch with Lucas will never be the same.

"I don't know, but I still want to be there for her."

His words don't surprise me.

"Me, too." I hug him, doing what I can to absorb his pain.

"If Drew is in a wheelchair," Kellan says, "how did he manage to plant the drugs in your house?"

"That's where the man who attacked Simone comes in," Lucas explains. "Drew hired him. Turns out the man makes a career out of fixing people's mistakes. His link to Kincaid Timber is currently under investigation. The police will have their hands full for a while with multiple investigations, including Sebastian's death. I don't know if they have a suspect yet for his murder."

"Wow," Emily says. "That's a lot to take in."

I lean into Lucas. "Poor Crystal and Walter. I hope it doesn't take too long before the police lay charges. So they have some closure. They've already lost so much."

"They have." Lucas's eyes gleam, hinting I'll like what's coming next. "The good news is now that the charges have been dropped, I have my job back at the Veterans Center."

"Oh, thank God." I hug him and kiss him and congratulate him and kiss him some more. "I'm so happy for you."

"Hi, everyone," Robert announces, loud enough for us to hear him. He's standing on the bench of one of the picnic tables. Tuuli is standing next to him, beaming and holding his hand. "Thank you for coming to celebrate Tuuli's and my fortieth wedding anniversary. I know some of you didn't think my marriage would last long." He flashes a mocking grin at a group of men his age, and they hoot a laugh. "It's been a wonderful forty years, and I'm looking forward to many more with my gorgeous wife."

We all cheer and whistle for the pair. Lucas kisses me on the temple, and I beam at him, my cheeks tugging my mouth into a wide smile.

"Now, before we get back to the party, I wanted to make one more announcement. As many of you know, Tuuli and I have decided to sell some of our land. After much consideration, we've decided to sell it to someone who has been dear to Tuuli and me for many years. He and his best friend used to play on this land when they were kids."

My heart nearly trips over itself at Robert's words. Lucas's arm tightens around me. Neither of us speaks. Or dares to glance at each other.

"It's the same land that he and his beautiful wife used to make out on, just beyond those trees, when they thought Tuuli and I didn't know." Robert looks at us, a massive grin teasing at the corner of his lips. "Oh, we knew. We knew a lot more than you realized." He winks at us.

Lucas bursts out laughing, his body shaking because he's laughing so hard. I cover my burning face with my hands.

"Tuuli and I are delighted to announce that we're selling the land to Lucas, Troy, Garrett, and Kellan Carson for their outdoor program for military vets."

The cheer from the crowd is as loud as it was for the first part of Robert's speech. Zara, Kim, Em, and I hug the brothers as they celebrate the great news.

Everything they've been fighting for—that we've been fighting for—will finally come true.

Lucas's vision for the program and his career goals will finally come true.

"I HAVE SOME NEWS TO TELL YOU." KIM SMEARS GOLD PAINT ACROSS my stomach, just above my scar. The gold bikini I'm wearing and the paint glimmer softly in the glow of the setting sun.

Zara and Emily are with us near the edge of the lake. Lucas, his brothers, and Jerome are farther up the sand, deep in their own conversation.

"You're having twins!" Emily grins, her mind no doubt spinning with all kinds of twin-related baby shower possibilities.

"No, this little one is definitely on their own in there." Smiling, Kim cradles her small baby bump, leaving a gold handprint on her light blue long-sleeved T-shirt. "Jerome and I are moving to Portland in two months. He's been offered a job with a civil rights law firm. It's an incredible opportunity for him."

Kim smiles, the love and pride and adoration on her face sparklier than the gold paint on my stomach. The smile flickers away, replaced by a slight grimace. "But it means I won't be able to do the wedding photography anymore. I'm sorry, Em."

Emily waves it off. "Don't worry about it. I'll find some other photographers who can fill in. They won't be as amazing as you." She points at the paint smeared on my belly. "But since most brides and grooms aren't looking for award-winning photographers to shoot their wedding day, it will be fine. I'll just miss having little Kim or little Jerome running around."

"Me too," I say. "We'll be the best aunties they've ever had... along with Evie, of course."

"You'll still get to be the best aunties the baby could ever ask for. We'll still visit. Our parents wouldn't be thrilled if we didn't come back to Maple Ridge at least once a month."

Zara laugh-snorts. "Yep, Momma will never let Jerome hear the end of it if she doesn't get to see her grandbaby at least twice a month. She'll be dragging Dad up to Portland to visit you guys as often as you'll let them."

Kim smears another streak of paint on my stomach. "I hope so. I love your parents."

Satisfied with how the paint looks, she has me step into the lake. Cold water gently laps my ankles.

It's easy to see why her photos are so stunning. Even when she's photographing people who aren't professional models. She has a way of getting the best out of her subjects while making the session fun. I don't feel awkward and exposed.

Just the opposite.

After she shoots a bunch of photos, she waves for a shirtless Lucas to join me. I'm not the only one with gold paint on their body. Kim directs us as to how she wants us to pose. To honor our daughter. To recognize those women who've had a hysterectomy during their child-bearing years. To recognize what it cost them.

To remind them they're still strong and beautiful.

And as Lucas's mouth descends on mine, a breathtaking smile on his face, I'm reminded that I am strong and beautiful and loved.

For now and forever more.

EPILOGUE
LUCAS

One month later

A month after the drug charges are dropped, Simone, Jasper, and I are on the deck of a rustic honeymoon cabin, overlooking the shimmering surface of the Northwest Washington State lake.

Simone snuggles into me on the love seat and takes a sip of her wine. "It's so beautiful and romantic out here."

I smile at her. "It is." But as beautiful as the scenery is, it's nothing compared to the breathtaking woman in my arms.

"Now I understand why you went to Seattle for your degree."

I chuckle, the sound a low rumble in my chest. "I went there for lots of reasons, but the romantic scenery wasn't one of them."

She laughs, and I gently kiss her. "I love you, Trouble."

She returns my kiss. "I love you right back, Cannon."

I remove the wineglass from her hand and place it on the coffee table. And kiss her more thoroughly.

My hand sneaks under the hem of her long-sleeved T-shirt and down vest. There's a definite disadvantage to honeymooning in a location with cool fall temperatures when you're watching the sunset. But I wouldn't change where we are for anything.

My hand cups Simone's breast, and I brush my thumb across the peaked nipple. Simone moans, and I deepen the kiss.

Jasper barks.

I groan, but not because of the kiss. The cute little cockblocker has plans to prevent our make-out session from going any further.

I pull away from Simone, only to notice Jasper isn't paying attention to us. He's standing at the gate to the deck, barking at whatever is out in the woods. "No barking, Jasper."

He stops and jumps his front paws onto the closed gate, his tail wagging.

I stand, pull Simone to her feet, and we go to the railing to investigate what has him so excited. It has to be a wild animal. This isn't the first time he has reacted this way since we arrived five days ago.

But the last time he did that it wasn't a wild animal that had him excited.

I peer down, searching for the reason he was barking. Searching to see if it was the same one as yesterday.

"There she is." Simone points at the ground covered with a colorful array of fall leaves.

And a small white kitten who can't be more than two months old.

"Hold Jasper back," Simone tells me. "I'm going to make sure she's okay."

I grab hold of Jasper's collar and fuss over him, distracting him from the kitten. Simone opens the gate and walks down the steps. She returns a minute later with the mewing kitten in her arms and sits on the love seat.

She strokes the kitten, who seems content to remain where she is. "Where did you come from, little girl?"

We spotted her yesterday and asked the owners of the cabins

about her. The kitten doesn't belong to them, and they have no idea where she could've come from.

"You must be hungry," Simone coos. "You want something to eat?"

The kitten continues to mew. Jasper's curiosity can't be contained any longer, and he tries to drag me over to the love seat. Fortunately for the kitten, I'm a lot stronger than Jasper.

Simone places the fluffy kitten on the deck and goes inside the cabin. She returns less than a minute later with a small plate with what I'm guessing is a tiny amount of Jasper's food on it. She also puts a bowl of water on the deck. "I'm sorry. We don't have any cat food," she tells the kitten. "Jasper, I hope you don't mind sharing yours."

The kitten lunges at the plate, hesitantly sniffs the food, and starts eating it.

Jasper whimpers.

Once the kitten has had enough to eat, she meows and walks over to Jasper. Jasper plonks himself down on the deck and watches the kitten with interest.

The kitten lets out a tiny hiss. Jasper doesn't react. He doesn't even jump to his feet like I expected him to or try to play with the kitten. He does want to play with her, that much I can tell.

The kitten shortens the distance between them and sniffs Jasper's face. Then she cuddles up against him and proceeds to go to sleep. Jasper seems to decide to do the same.

Simone is smiling at the pair, her eyes shining. And I know what my wife is thinking.

"She's not the British shorthair cat you were planning for," I point out.

"Doesn't matter. She needs a family. We're her family."

"Are you sure that's what you want?" I grin because I know that's exactly what Simone wants.

"I'm positive. You and Jasper and Snowball are what I want." She loops her arms behind my neck and kisses me.

And just like that, our little family has grown.
And I can't think of a more perfect way to end our honeymoon.

Get your free copy of the bonus holiday short story at
https://BookHip.com/RZVSGXT

Read on for a special sneak peek at One More Secret, the next exciting story from the Carson Brothers series.

ONE MORE SECRET

TROY

I pull into the small parking lot near the lake, frustration simmering due to the news I learned a short while ago. News that I might've missed the chance to buy the house I'd planned to renovate and flip. Flip and donate the proceeds to my best friend's widow and toddler daughter.

I kill the truck's engine, climb out, and open the rear door. Butterscotch hops down and bounds over to the grassy bank separating the parking lot from the beach. It's early evening, and my truck is the only vehicle here.

He disappears into the long wild grass that's dry and bent over from the winter snow that once weighed it down.

I survey the area, something that's second nature after serving with the Marines. The sloped embankment leading to the beach. A potential hiding spot for a sniper. The tangled undergrowth, bare and a challenge to vanish behind. Unless you're skilled at camouflage.

I fill my lungs with the cool, pine-scented mountain air and slowly release it. The crisp pine scent is one of my daily reminders that I'm here in Oregon and not back in Afghanistan.

The enemy isn't waiting to ambush me.

I walk along the path that cuts through the grass to the beach. Butterscotch is near the lake, grabbing at a stick half-buried in the sand.

It's only when I'm on the sand that I notice the woman sitting farther ahead on the beach, her gaze on the water.

She's wearing jeans and a navy sweater, and she's burying her toes in the sand. Her long blond hair blows in the breeze. She attempts to tuck it behind her ears, only for the wind to tug it free again.

I don't need to see her face to know I've never seen her before. I would remember her hair and the way the sunlight catches it. She's probably a tourist passing through town.

I head toward her, curiosity driving me forward. Usually when tourists come to the beach, they aren't alone. I glance around, but there's no sign anyone's with her. "Hey, there."

She startles and scrambles to her feet, turning to face me. Her eyes are wide, and something about her expression makes me think she's on the verge of bolting.

I raise my hands. "Sorry. Didn't mean to scare you."

She stares at me with anxious eyes. Even from where I'm standing, I can see the dark shadows under them.

Butterscotch walks over to her, moving slowly enough so she can retreat if she feels threatened. There's a reason Butterscotch makes a great emotional support dog. He reads people's emotions. He knows when someone is nervous. He also knows when someone needs his type of loving.

The woman's gaze remains on me, her muscles tense. Shit, what has her so scared?

Butterscotch drops his ass near her feet and gives her a friendly bark.

The woman flicks her gaze to him and then looks back at me. The corner of her mouth is pulled down by a scar that cuts from the corner of her mouth to her jaw. Possibly a knife wound.

It's not an old laceration. The redness suggests the scar is less than a year old.

The scar isn't the only one on her face. There's also a smaller scar on her right cheek. What has this woman been through? It's no wonder she's scared—especially if they are the result of her being attacked at some point.

I take a cautious step forward. "His name is Butterscotch. He volunteers as an emotional support dog at Maple Ridge Veterans Center."

She crouches and slowly reaches out to him, offering her hand for him to sniff. Butterscotch closes the distance, and she strokes his small body. The tension in her shoulders lessens.

I take another step. When she doesn't balk, I walk closer. But I don't push my luck. She doesn't know me. I could be a psychopath in her mind.

Her clothes swamp her body, as if they're two sizes too big, but they appear new. There's something familiar about her that I can't identify. I don't mean I recognize her. It's just something about her, her reactions, that stokes the unease in my gut at just how deep her scars run.

"You're sweet." Her voice comes out stiff and rough as if she hasn't used it in a while. She continues stroking Butterscotch. She doesn't acknowledge me.

"Are you staying in Maple Ridge or just visiting?" I don't advance any closer, giving her a chance to soak up Butterscotch's therapy.

"Yes," she says, her message clear. It's none of my business.

I glance farther down the beach and spot an old-fashioned bike perched in the metal stand. It's not a mountain bike, nor is it a regular street bike. So she's probably not a tourist here to make the most of our mountain bike trails.

"Do you like ice cream?" I ask, mostly to see if she'll respond.

She doesn't look at me. Her focus is strictly on Butterscotch, but

I have a feeling she's very aware of every move I make, no matter how small. "It's too cold for ice cream."

A low laugh rumbles in my chest. "You're definitely not from around here. For locals like me, it's never too cold for ice cream." I can't imagine her thin sweater is doing much to keep her warm. I shrug off my jacket and hold it out to her. "You look cold. Put this on."

Her gaze flicks up for a fraction of a second, and that's all it takes for me to become mesmerized by the honey brown of her eyes. Her attention returns to my super content, tail-wagging dog. She keeps petting him, not missing a beat. "I don't need your coat. And yes, I like ice cream."

I let my arm fall to my side, wanting her to look at me again. "Do you have a favorite flavor?"

"Does it matter if I do or not?" she asks, her words soft, almost thoughtful.

"I guess not."

She straightens, her back stiff, her eyes never leaving me as if she's worried I might attack. "It's mango."

A smile ghosts my mouth. "Good choice." There's something about her that sets off a warning in my gut and makes it hard to walk away. "Are you okay?"

"I'm fine." She hugs herself as if she's trying to keep her pieces together, to shield herself.

The unease in my gut flares. She's so distant, she's acting like my best friend Colton and my brother when they were battling PTSD.

That doesn't mean she's got the same thing, though.

Shit, what the hell happened to her? What's her story?

"You do realize that when a woman says she's fine, it usually means she isn't?" I say.

"And sometimes it means exactly that. She's fine. Good. Happy." She smiles as if to make a point, but the scar prevents the smile from fully forming.

The smile falls away. She grabs her shoes and socks and walks toward her bike. Her bare feet sink into the loose sand, making her movements awkward, as if she's limping.

Or in pain.

"See you!" I call after her.

She doesn't reply or look back. Once she reaches the bike rack, she pulls on her shoes and pedals away.

I walk along the beach, my mind unable to let go of what might have happened to the woman and who'd possibly hurt her. Her eyes linger in my thoughts. Eyes that have seen too much. Who the hell is she? And what is she doing in Maple Ridge?

Shit. And what are those honey-brown eyes like when she's happy? Are they as spectacular as I think they'll be?

My mind flicks to the earlier conversation at the Veterans Center. About organizing a fundraiser to help the veterans and first responders with PTSD and their families. People like that woman.

I don't know the first thing about organizing a fundraiser, and I'm not going to kid myself into believing it will be easy. But what if it were a success? It could mean the difference between someone giving up on life the way Colton did—the difference between a wife losing a husband, a child losing their father—and a family remaining together and healing.

I grab my phone from my pocket and hit the speed dial for Zara. Butterscotch trots alongside me.

My brother's best friend picks up on the second ring. "Hey, Troy."

"Hey. I need your help with something..."

ACKNOWLEDGMENTS

When I set out to write *One More Chance*, I knew the storyline about Lily would be challenging. My oldest child was thirteen weeks premature and spent ten weeks in the NICU in two different hospitals. It was one of the most difficult times of my life. During that time, I met several mothers in the NICU who would go on to lose their babies. Some lost their babies shortly after birth, the babies born too little to survive. Or the baby had a rare genetic disorder and didn't survive to their first birthday.

One of the mothers became pregnant again before she and her husband made the heartbreaking decision to take their son off life support. He had already spent many months in the hospital and would spend the rest of his life on life support, unable to move, eat without assistance, or even open his eyes. The mother went on to have a healthy son, who ended up being in my son's elementary class, and they became best friends. The mother and I are still friends.

I wrote *One More Chance* in memory of those brave mothers, the fathers, their little angels, and the NICU nurses who helped us during our darkest days.

This book would not have been possible if not for several people. My brilliant new editor, Lauren Clarke, helped to make this story shine brighter than I ever dreamed possible. I couldn't imagine writing this new series without you, Lauren.

I would also like to thank Margie Lawson and my immersion sisters (Monica Corwin, Jenny Hansen, Lainey Cameron, Linda

Dindzans, and Cassandra Shaw). Thank you for challenging me and making me laugh during our Zoom meetings.

And thanks also go out to Shauna from Wildfire PR for helping to spread the word about *One More Chance*. I couldn't have done it without you and the bloggers and bookstagrammers.

During the 2020 Covid lockdown, one of the families on my street adopted a puppy. A golden Labradoodle. And the family named him Jasper. I can see their front lawn from my office, and I'd watch them take their adorably energetic puppy outside every day. He's so sweet, and I had to make him a character in the book. So thank you, Jasper, for being the inspiration for Lucas and Simone's dog.

Troy's dog Butterscotch got his name from my Facebook group, Stina's Sweethearts. I posted a photo there that I'd found on Pinterest and asked for name suggestions. The group was also responsible for suggesting the Carson brothers' last name. Thank you, Sweethearts, for your help when it comes to naming the characters and the pets in my stories.

And finally, I would like to thank my husband and our three adult kids for their love and support. I would especially like to thank my daughter for being my greatest cheerleader. xox

ABOUT THE AUTHOR

Born in Brighton England, Stina Lindenblatt has lived in a number of countries, including England, the U.S, Finland, and Canada. This would explain her mixed up accent. She has a kinesiology degree and a MSc in sports biological sciences.

In addition to writing fiction, she loves photography, and currently lives in Calgary, Canada, with her husband and three kids.

For news about her books, social media sites, and to sign up for her newsletter, check out her website at stinalindenblattauthor.com.